JUST THE THOUGHT OF YOU

"I'm going to the store. You want me to get you anything?" Norah asked.

"Nah. I'm good." Kai returned her smile and the tension between them dissipated.

"I'll be a while since I have to go get books for your mom too. Do you know what kind of books she reads?" She didn't know why she said it, but her mouth got away from her.

He shook his head.

"She reads romance. And not the longing looks from across a ballroom and maybe some hand-holding kind either." Norah leaned a little closer and lowered her voice. "She made me read a sex scene to her last night."

The look on Kai's face was priceless. Even under the golden hue of his cheeks, a blush rose. "Christ, I'm sorry."

Norah bent over on a peal of laughter. "If you could see your face . . ." Those were the only words she could handle because laughter stole her breath. She laughed until tears streaked down her cheeks. "Sorry. I just had this image of her asking you to read to her before bed."

In truth, the deep, rumbly sound of his voice would be enough of a turn-on regardless of the words he read. Suddenly, she wanted the audiobook of that.

"Sorry," she said again and they both knew it was an empty apology.

"It looks good on you."

"Huh?"

"The uncontrolled laughter. It looks good. Even if I'm the butt of your joke. And for the record, I will not be reading porn to my mom."

A giggle bubbled up in Norah's throat, so she swallowed. She couldn't afford to think of him and porn in the same sentence.

Books by Shannyn Schroeder

The O'Learys

More Than This

A Good Time

Something to Prove

Catch Your Breath

Just a Taste

Hold Me Close

Hot & Nerdy

Her Best Shot

Her Perfect Game

Her Winning Formula

His Work of Art

His New Jam

His Dream Role

For Your Love

Under Your Skin

In Your Arms
(coming in January 2017)

Through Your Eyes
(coming in Summer, 2017)

under *your* skin

SHANNYN
SCHROEDER

ZEBRA BOOKS
KENSINGTON PUBLISHING CORP.
http://www.kensingtonbooks.com

ACKNOWLEDGMENTS

With every new book I tackle, I find myself reaching out to people for more information and research for my characters and plot. In *Under Your Skin*, I spend a lot of time on Norah's decision to create an adoption plan for her daughter. I knew almost nothing about adoption when I started. Lucky for me, a good friend, Ryann, adopted her son and she put me in touch with her adoption counselor, Katie Gattone at The Cradle. Katie and her boss, Dana Mullhall, were fabulous in answering many, many questions about the adoption process. I also want to give a shout-out to fellow romance writer, Averil Reisman, who answered my questions about knee replacement surgery because she had gone through the surgery and rehab. As always, thanks to my wonderful Chicago-North RWA chaptermates who critiqued the first twenty pages and let me know how big an ass Kai was being. And finally, a huge thanks to my beta readers: Pamala Knight, Melanie Bruce, and Molly Strzelecki—your help is greatly appreciated.

Chapter One

Norah O'Malley woke like she had every day for the past two weeks: lying in her brother's bed, in her father's house, rubbing her pregnant belly like it was a Magic 8 Ball that held some mystical answers for her fucked up life. Her bladder was full to bursting, another perpetual condition these days. Struggling to sit up, she shifted to get to the bathroom. This was not how she expected her life to look at twenty-two.

After taking care of business, she studied herself in the mirror. Did she look different? Of course from the chest down her body was no longer hers and hadn't been for some time. Her face looked the same though. Right? She pressed closer to the mirror, propping her belly on the sink. What would Avery see if they met today?

Her older brother Jimmy had been pressuring her since she came home weeks ago to call Avery and tell him she was pregnant. She knew she had to and it had been crappy of her to keep this from him, but she knew Avery. He'd want to take care of her. He was that kind of guy. She could definitely appreciate such nobility in the hero of a book or movie, but in real life, choices like this sucked.

She wasn't sure she was ready to be a mom. Old stirrings

of Catholic guilt hit her—years of parochial school had that effect—but she couldn't imagine trapping them when they weren't ready. She shuffled back to bed and sat on the edge. Every time she thought about Avery, her stomach fluttered. Her short time with him had been magical. She'd never felt so loved by any other boyfriend she'd had. Part of her wanted him to be with her through this. A huge part.

Another part was afraid of disrupting his life. She'd dodged his calls all summer, not knowing what to say. He was looking for summer fun, but fun ended for her at the sight of two pink lines.

And now she was afraid of her brothers' reactions. They didn't handle news of her pregnancy well. They would threaten to go after Avery again. If nothing else, she needed to protect him until she figured out what she wanted.

The baby kicked her now-empty bladder and elbowed her ribs. Must be breakfast time. She crept downstairs hoping to avoid running into her brothers, especially Tommy. Tommy was nearest in age to her and they'd always been close growing up, even after Jimmy had shipped her off to live with Aunt Bridget in Boston. Tommy had come to visit her often and called her a few times each week. They had always been more friends than siblings.

She'd expected Jimmy, Kevin, and Sean to blow up when they found out she was pregnant. Telling them over the phone probably would've been better than just showing up on their doorstep six months pregnant. But Tommy was supposed to be on her side. He'd raged the night she came home and the anger had been at a slow burn since.

He barely spoke to her. His first and only question was always: Who is he?

Avery didn't deserve to be on the receiving end of that wrath. The guy had done nothing wrong.

In the kitchen, she poured herself a bowl of cereal and

grabbed the last yogurt. As she sat to eat, the basement door opened and Tommy strode in.

"Good morning." She tried for a cheerful tone.

"You offering a name yet?"

"Are you promising not to go after him?"

Tommy snorted.

"Then you have your answer."

He turned from the refrigerator and slammed the orange juice carton on the table in front of her. "Why are you protecting him?"

"Because he did nothing wrong. We did this together, and he doesn't even know I'm pregnant." Maybe an explanation would help. She owed him that, and Jimmy had handled it pretty well. She kicked a chair out next to her.

He gripped the back of the chair but didn't sit.

"He wasn't a one-night stand, Tommy. We met over Christmas break and had a great couple of weeks. Then he went back to school. We tried the long-distance thing. He visited a few weekends, but it didn't work. When I found out I was pregnant, I didn't know what to do. He came back to Boston for spring break, and I planned to tell him then. But it felt so good to have him back. I felt good with him and I didn't want to lose that."

Tommy shoved off the chair and rubbed his head. "He's not even a real boyfriend."

She shrugged. "It felt real."

Pushing away from the table, she stood close to Tommy. "When I came home, all I wanted from you was to have you in my corner. I know I fucked up. In so many ways. I miss you."

Tommy's shoulders sagged. Finally she saw the opening she'd been looking for for weeks. He stared at her with worry in his eyes. A welcome change from the anger she'd been seeing.

"I've missed you too, squirt."

She laughed and the motion caused the baby to kick and jump again. "I'm far from being a squirt now."

The corner of his mouth lifted but he didn't fully smile. "See you later."

Then he walked out the back door without even drinking the juice he'd taken from the fridge. Norah sighed. At least she'd made some progress with one of her siblings.

She knew if she could win Tommy over, he'd help with the others. As she finished her breakfast, she developed a plan. Tommy shouldn't be too difficult to crack now that she'd slipped past his defenses.

Norah spent her morning cleaning the house and making sure her dad took his medication. The stubborn old man never wanted to do what he was supposed to. It was no wonder Jimmy had felt the need to move back home to take care of their dad. Someone had to keep an eye on him or his diabetes would get out of control. Sean and Tommy were pretty useless in that area. They couldn't even remember to put away their hockey gear. How would they remember to make sure Dad regulated his insulin?

Once that was done, she went online to look for a job. She couldn't possibly sit around the house all day with nothing to do. She couldn't enroll in school because she'd have to take time off after having the baby. There had to be someone who'd be willing to hire her at least temporarily. The outlook was pretty dismal, so she closed the laptop and moved on to the next phase in her plan to make Tommy happy. Rice Krispies Treats had always been his favorite, but for whatever reason, he had a mental block when it came to making them himself.

She ran to the store for ingredients and whipped up a batch to take to him at work. Since he was a tattoo artist, he worked strange hours. Sometimes he'd work in the afternoon, other times, he'd be there half the night. She'd overheard him telling Sean he had some touch-ups to do on a tattoo this morning and then he had a long session this afternoon.

She hoped the dessert would be a peace offering.

On the way to the tattoo parlor, she stopped at a drive-through and grabbed some burgers for them. She rubbed her belly and wondered how bad it was to feed the baby fries. The baby *really* wanted fries. She hadn't craved fries this much since she was fifteen. The only thing she wanted more than fries was lime yogurt. Luckily, the baby didn't require them together. That would just be gross.

She was out of breath from the short walk from the car to the shop because the baby decided to tumble around pressing on who knew what. She walked through the door of Ink Envy gripping the bag of food and plate of treats. On the wall hung frames showing various drawings and photos of tattoos. Looking around, she saw stations, like in a beauty salon, separated by short partitions. Different styles of chairs, none appeared too comfortable.

"Hi, can I help you?" a short, pudgy guy with sleeve tats asked.

"I'm here to see Tommy."

Just then, Tommy came from a back room and caught her eye. "What are you doing here?"

"I came bearing gifts." She set the food on the glass-topped counter.

"What do you want?"

She sighed. Maybe it was too soon. "I want you to not be mad at me anymore. I brought Rice Krispies Treats."

"A bribe? Really?"

She lifted a shoulder. "And burgers. Whatever works."

He dragged a couple of stools to the counter and pointed for her to sit down. The counter was tall enough that when she sat, her stomach was mostly concealed. Knowing

Tommy would start with dessert, she slid the plate of treats over.

He peeled back the foil and pulled a square from the pile. "This doesn't change things."

"It changes them a little. You're at least talking to me."

He chewed and swallowed before asking, "What are you gonna do?"

"I don't know. I think about it all the time. I know I need to tell the father. And I will. Soon. Until then, I want to settle in and restart my life. I spent the morning looking for a job. I don't suppose you know of anything?" She munched on her fries while they talked.

"No one's gonna hire you. You're a liability."

Norah rolled her eyes. Tommy wasn't saying anything she didn't already know.

"Maybe you should take it easy for a while."

"That'll make me crazy. I can't sit at home with Dad all day."

"Come on, you know you like pricking him with a needle."

She laughed louder than she'd intended, but he was right. She did enjoy it a little. But laughing with Tommy was the best feeling she'd had in a long time.

Kai Ellis came from the back room to the musical sound of female laughter. The girl sitting across from Tommy at the front counter had an awesome rack spilling out of her tank top and her tits jiggled as she laughed.

"Hey," he called, "I told you no girls while you're on the clock. Get busy on your own time."

Tommy dropped the food in his hand. "Gross, man. This is my sister."

She wiggled her fingers. Then she pointed. To Tommy,

she said, "Let's ask your friend here, I'm sure he's made mistakes in his life."

"Boss." Kai crossed his arms. He had no intention of answering questions about his mistakes, but it annoyed him that she jumped to the conclusion that he'd made them. Part of the reason for opening his own business was so he would never have to answer to anyone about his past again.

"Huh?"

"I'm his boss."

She continued on as if he hadn't spoken. "It's normal for people to make mistakes, right? Even if they're huge mistakes, you still learn from them. Life lessons and shit."

He knew all about making life-altering mistakes, but he still wasn't about to discuss them. Addressing Tommy, he said, "Girlfriend or not, she needs to go."

Her eyes popped wide and she slid from the stool. Tommy laid a hand on her arm. "It's fine." He twisted on the stool. "Kai, this is my sister, Norah. She just moved back to town."

Norah stepped around Tommy with her hand extended. Her belly stuck out full with a baby. He'd forgotten about Tommy bitching about his pregnant sister.

When he didn't move, she dropped her hand. "Sorry. I thought I'd catch Tommy before his client came in. I brought him lunch and dessert." She turned and picked up a plate from the counter. "Want a Rice Krispies Treat?"

Her smile was friendly as she spoke, but her light blue eyes filled with mischief. Like she was offering up more than marshmallows and cereal. It was a good thing that belly was between them. He stayed rooted to his spot. Then his phone rang. *Again*. He'd ignored Jaleesa all morning, but if he planned to get any work done, he'd have to deal with her.

With his phone in hand, he spun and walked back out the way he came. "Yeah."

"It's about time. I've been calling you all morning."

"I'm aware."

"Mom's surgery went fine. She came through with flying colors."

He'd figured as much. It was just her knee. "Good to know."

"Are you coming to the hospital today?"

He walked until he hit the back door of the shop and stood in the alley. "I don't know. Depends on how busy I get."

"Kai, it's not like this was some surprise. We scheduled it. You could make sure you're free. You're choosing not to."

"And?"

His sister's sigh whistled in his ear. "We need to talk about where Mom will go when she's released from the hospital. She'll only be here a few days."

"I thought you were looking into a rehab facility."

"I tried, but it made her upset. She thinks we're going to dump her off and leave her for good."

"So explain to her that's not the case. She knows she won't be able to get around your house. It's not like she lost her mind."

"She's feeling vulnerable and she's worried about being alone."

"I don't know what you want from me, Jaleesa."

"Maybe she could stay with you."

"I have stairs in my house."

"Five, Kai. Five measly steps to get up to your door. Everything else is on one floor. You have the space."

What she really meant was that he could make the space for his mom to move in. He didn't want to. His house was set up exactly as he wanted. He would have to move all of his workout equipment somewhere, probably to the base-ment or the garage. He had no furniture for her. No bed or anything. He didn't have guests and he liked it that way.

"I can't take care of Mom. I don't know what to do with her."

"And I do? You figure it out, Kai. That's what you do for family."

"I have a business to run and I keep long hours."

"At least think about it. We can probably hire someone to fill in when you're not around so she's not alone, but she'll feel secure in your house."

"Why can't we hire someone to help at your house?"

"Stairs."

"Maybe we can convert some space to make it work."

"My whole family isn't losing our living room so you don't have to man up."

He shook his head, not wanting to lose this argument. "We'll talk about this later. I have to go."

"Try to stop by the hospital. It'll make her happy."

"Yeah." He clicked off and stared at the brick building across from him. He was tempted to throw his phone to hear the satisfying crack of plastic against the wall. Instead, he inhaled deeply and closed his eyes. The air he sucked in was rank with the smell of rotting garbage. Tomorrow was pickup day and the heat did no favors for the Chinese restaurant on the corner.

The sun beat against his skin, searing it. Five minutes of quiet without thinking about his mom at the hospital. Anything was better than the damn hospital. Leaning against the back door, with his eyes closed, he allowed the sun to sink into him.

The door thumped against him and he stepped away. So much for his five minutes. Tommy stuck his head out. "Your appointment's here."

"Okay."

Tommy eyed him up and down, but said nothing.

"What?"

"You're wound a little tight today. Everything okay?"

"Fucking peachy."

"Alrighty then."

Kai grabbed the door and swung it wide to go back in the shop. "Your sister gone?"

"Yeah, but she left the Rice Krispies Treats if you want one."

"I'm not six, so no thanks."

"You don't know what you're missing."

As he walked to the front, an image of Norah's jiggling tits gave him some idea what he was missing. She was cute, but knocked up. He definitely didn't need to think about her tits. His client, Marcus, waited on the battered leather couch having a conversation with Puck, another of Kai's artists. Puck was chewing a Rice Krispies Treat.

Kai raised his hand in greeting and then ducked into his office to grab the artwork. Marcus stood at the counter waiting.

"Here's the art." Kai slid the sheet in front of him.

"Looks great," Marcus said, nodding.

"Good. Pay Tommy here and I'll go set up." He handed Tommy the invoice and returned to his station. He made the thermal of the design—an eagle flying with the American flag—and set up his ink.

In here, with the buzz of the machine and the color of the art, he didn't have to think about anything else. He didn't have to worry about his mom or fighting with his sister. The art was everything.

Norah stared at her laundry basket full of clothes. She had no space to call her own. When she'd come home, she more or less commandeered Jimmy's room, which was almost a full apartment in the attic. Growing up, it had been the boys' bedrooms, but Jimmy remodeled so he could have a living room, bedroom, and bath. Little had he known that Tommy and Sean would both move back home. They lived in the basement. Kevin was the only one who left and stayed gone.

She'd been here for weeks, but it was still Jimmy's room and it wasn't fair for her to take it over.

Two quick knocks sounded at the door before Jimmy stuck his head in. "Hey."

"Hi. I was just thinking about you."

"Yeah?" He came into the room.

"I have no idea what Dad filled my old bedroom with downstairs. I tried looking through it, but he yelled that I need to keep my hands off his stuff."

Jimmy rubbed a hand over his head. "I don't really know what's in there either. I forget that room exists."

"I told you before that I'd move in there so you can have your room back. But you gotta do something about Dad."

"You can stay here. I don't think I'll be needing the space much longer."

Norah's eyes widened. "What do you mean?"

Where the hell was Jimmy going? She'd just come home. She wasn't ready for him to leave her life again. She'd been counting on him being there.

He sat on the edge of the bed. "I was planning on talking to all of you guys at once, but since you're the only one home, I'll start with you." He patted the spot beside him.

She sat and a sinking feeling gripped her. The last time Jimmy spoke with her like this, he'd told her he was joining the army and she was being shipped off to Aunt Bridget's.

"Moira and I are serious. I've asked her to buy a house with me and move in together."

"What? You like *just* started dating. Isn't that rushing it a bit?" He was leaving, just like she feared. The one guy she needed in her life to lean on and he was leaving.

"I love her." Jimmy put his arm around her shoulder.

"We're going to look for something in the neighborhood so I'm close to Dad and you. I'll be around, but it's time for me to start living my life."

She shot up. "Start? You've been living your life for years. That's why you got rid of me when I was twelve. So you could go be a soldier. Then a cop."

"I always made sure you were taken care of."

"It's not the same. And now . . ." She rubbed her tight belly where the baby did a flip. Her breaths shortened and she stepped farther away from Jimmy.

"You're not alone, Norah."

Right now, she felt completely alone.

"We're all here for you. We've tried to help, but you're not letting any of us in. I'm not going anywhere."

"Yeah, you are. You're already gone." She focused on slowing her breathing and calming her system. Being upset wasn't good for the baby.

"I'd like to take everyone out to dinner tomorrow so you guys can all get to know Moira."

"Doesn't everyone already know Moira? She grew up across the street. You're best friends with her brother. I haven't lived here in ten years, but I know that." She didn't know why she was feeling ornery. Part of her wanted to lash out at his happiness, even though she knew it wasn't fair.

"Yeah, they know who she is, but they don't know her. You'll like her if you give her a chance."

Norah had nothing to say. She suspected she would like Moira, given how much grief Moira had given Jimmy. And that was only the little bit Norah had gleaned from hiding out for the past few weeks while Jimmy fell in love.

"Whatever." She couldn't give him the satisfaction of knowing she liked the woman who kept him on his toes.

She looked over the room. "If I'm going to stay in here, you think I could have a few drawers or something?"

"I'll do better than that. I'll clear it all out except for the furniture. Make it yours." He stood and stepped closer to her. "You are staying, right? Not going back to Boston?"

"There's nothing in Boston for me." Avery wasn't even there because he still had one more year of college. More than anything she wanted to be at home. For all the years she'd lived in Boston, it had never felt like home. The few short visits she'd made to Chicago each year had felt like a homecoming.

"Have you decided what you're going to do?"

She shook her head.

"Have you called the father?"

"Not yet." She raised a hand to cut him off from yelling at her again. "I said I would and I will as soon as I know what I want to do. There's a lot to weigh. What if he wants me to come back to Boston? I don't know if I want that."

"I guess what I'm really asking is if you want to keep the baby."

She pressed her lips together for a moment before answering. "It's not about what I want anymore. It's about what's best for the baby. I'm not sure what that is."

"We can make it work." He nodded and left, closing the door behind him.

She wasn't sure what she was supposed to take away from that. Knowing Jimmy, he meant she should keep the baby, that he'd help out. She knew he would, but it wasn't his responsibility. He was getting ready to start his own family.

Norah sat with her laptop and began her search. She'd ignored thinking and making a decision for almost seven months now. Complete denial was the basis for the beginning of her pregnancy. She'd worn baggy shirts and told no one. Then when she had to face the pregnancy as well as her aunt's fury, she'd switched to survival mode. She'd focused on passing her classes while couch-surfing to have a place to live.

It was time to get real.

What would it take for her to keep the baby? What were her options for adoption? The questions alone made her heart hurt. Although she'd done a bang-up job of keeping emotionally distant from the baby growing inside her, she still cared. More than she wanted to.

And now she only had weeks to figure it out. She'd wasted too much time already.

She searched for adoption agencies and began clicking away. The Open Door sounded promising. She spent more than an hour on the site. She took a quiz to determine if she was ready to be a parent. Her answers split right down the middle. Half said she was ready, the other half not. Looked like there were no easy answers to be found.

The Web site offered a wealth of information. She gleaned a basic understanding of open and closed adoptions. She could click or call or text and be connected with a counselor who would answer questions and talk with her. Voicing those options and questions were scary though. She wasn't ready for that step.

Instead, she clicked back to job Web sites to find a way to make money. She feared she wouldn't have any more luck there.

Kai strode into the hospital carrying a bouquet of roses for his mom. Horrible memories of visiting injured friends hit him. Hospitals reminded him of bad times. His adolescence spent running the streets of Chicago with a gang meant he was used to seeing friends hurt. Fistfights, knife fights, gun fights—he'd witnessed it all. Walking in here was never a happy thing.

Jaleesa had already texted him the floor and room information. From inside his mom's room, he heard Jaleesa's melodic voice reading. Their mom had always been a bookworm so he wasn't surprised.

He pushed through the door. When she looked up from her bed, Lani smiled at him. She looked small and weak and so unlike how he was used to seeing her.

"Come here, boy."

He walked to the bed and bent over to hug and kiss her as best he could without disturbing her leg.

Jaleesa stood and took the flowers from him. "I'll find something to put these in." She patted his arm in acknowledgment. She probably thought he wouldn't come.

He almost didn't. He didn't like to see Lani this way. Although a small woman, she always seemed big, mostly because she had a way of yelling at him that could make him feel tiny. Dragging Jaleesa's vacated chair closer, he sat beside his mom. He took her hand. "How are you?"

"I'm fine. Doctor says I'll be dancing again in no time."

He wanted to believe her, but behind the smile, he saw the pinched expression of pain in her eyes. "That's good."

"They say I should be out of here in three days or so."

"About that. Jaleesa and I have been talking. We think you should go to a rehabilitation facility. Jaleesa's house would be too hard for you to maneuver until you're back to full strength."

She narrowed her eyes at him. "I'm not going to an old folks' home."

"That's not what this is. People of all ages go there to recover. The staff knows what to do and you'll have someone around to make sure you're okay."

She folded her hands on her lap and pressed her lips

together, but not before he saw the tremble. "You both just want to get rid of me. I see how it is."

"No, Mom. Listen."

She shot him a mean look. "You listen, Kai. I'm not weak or stupid. If you don't want me around, say so. You wouldn't be the first man to do that."

And she lobbed the jab he'd learned to expect. His father had left them when Kai was young, and Lani held it against all men, even her son. Of course it hadn't helped that he'd been in so much trouble as a teenager. He'd been no help to her.

He sighed and stood. "I'll be back to see you tomorrow. You want me to bring you anything?"

She sniffed and turned her head. For an old woman, she sure did know how to act like a child. Kai pushed through the door and almost ran into Jaleesa in the hall. She held the flowers in a plastic pitcher.

"Leaving already?"

"It's time. Where are the kids?"

"At home with Matt." She hitched her chin toward the door behind him. "What happened?"

"She got mad when I brought up the rehab facility."

Jaleesa shook her head. Hugging the flowers to her chest, she leaned against the wall. "You should've waited for me."

"What would that have accomplished? Then she'd be mad at both of us. What are we gonna do?"

"She'd feel better and probably recover faster if she feels safe. Your house is a safe place for her."

"We've been over this."

"And you said you would consider it."

"I can't take her, Lees. I have a job and hockey. I can't stop doing everything to have her live with me."

Jaleesa stood to her full height, nearing his own six feet, and leaned close. Her long, black hair swished like a wave down her front. "I have three kids underfoot all day and I manage to care for *our* mother."

"It's not the same. When she's healthy, she helps with your kids. You love having her around. I wouldn't. It won't work."

"No man is an island, Kai. You remember that. You do your best to keep everything in your life from intersecting and it's not normal. Take Mom to work with you. You can take her for a walk in between clients."

He snorted. "She'd love being around tattoo artists all day. The language alone might give her a heart attack. Should I bring her to hockey practice too? I'm sure sitting on the bleachers will be great for her knee."

"Don't be an ass, Kai."

"Don't expect what I can't give."

"Won't. Not can't. Again, you choose this life."

He inhaled deeply and closed his eyes. He and his sister could do this all day, and he didn't want to.

The touch of Jaleesa's hand on his arm made him open his eyes and stare at her.

"You're not a child anymore. You've moved past all your mistakes. When we helped you get the studio, I really thought you were moving on."

"I have."

"No you haven't. Get a life." She smirked. "A real one. You can't keep everything compartmentalized. It's not normal."

"You don't make any sense. And don't try to shrink me. You're not my caseworker." He knew exactly what she was talking about, though. Separating the sections of his life was the only way he had to dig out. He worked successfully on each area and then moved on. Without overlap, everything worked. And if he screwed up, he wouldn't lose it all again.

She shook her head. "I'm going back to read to Mom."

He eased away from the wall.

As she opened the door, she asked, "Will you be back tomorrow?"

"Probably."

He left the hospital and thought about what Jaleesa had said. His little sister always pushed advice on him in one form or another, but this felt different. This wasn't her usual nagging about getting a girlfriend when she meant wife. This wasn't about being more involved with his nieces and nephew. Or even about how to run his business like a real job. Today's attack felt personal.

Which wasn't like Jaleesa at all. She was one person who had always been in his corner no matter what stupid shit he'd done. She was the only one to visit him in jail when all of his "friends" abandoned him. She'd convinced her husband to lend him the money to open Ink Envy. He couldn't understand why she pushed at him now.

He drove back to Ink Envy in a foul mood. Coming in the back door, he tossed his keys on the desk in the office and noticed the plate with a single Rice Krispies Treat. His stomach grumbled so he took a bite. The damn thing was so sticky he was afraid he'd lose a filling. Before he got a chance to sit down, Tommy knocked on the door frame.

"Got a minute?"

"What?" He didn't feel like talking to anyone right now, but he had a business to run.

"My sister's looking for a job."

"And?"

Tommy shrugged. "I thought maybe you'd hire her?"

"Can she ink?"

"No. I meant like office shit. Making appointments and stuff."

"Do I look like a babysitter?"

Tommy crossed his arms on his chest. His lanky frame

would never look threatening. "She's pregnant. No one's going to hire her. I thought maybe you'd do something nice."

"I'm not in business to be nice." Plus, with his luck, she'd go into labor on his watch and there was no way he wanted to deal with that.

"Couldn't hurt to ask." Tommy spun on his heel and left.

Kai had managed to go years without anyone asking him for anything. Suddenly everyone had expectations. What the fuck was that about?

Chapter Two

Norah tugged at the T-shirt she wore. It stretched so tightly over her belly, she looked like the Hulk busting out of her clothes. Maybe she had to buy maternity clothes. Until now, she'd gotten by wearing old, worn-out shirts and unbuttoned shorts. The baby and, in turn, her belly, weren't done growing and she didn't think her clothes would last.

But then she'd have to ask Jimmy for more money and she hated that. Especially for something she'd only need for a month or so. And if she kept the baby that would be even more money, at least until she could get a job. Where did that leave school? She couldn't imagine having a baby, working full-time, and going to school. She enjoyed sleep too much.

"Norah!" Jimmy's bellow came from downstairs.

"Coming!" she called back. She forced a smile. Tonight she'd officially meet Moira, Jimmy's girlfriend. She walked down the stairs. All of her brothers sat around the living room waiting for her.

Dad sat on the couch, flipping through channels on the TV.

"Did you test your blood?" she asked him.

He answered with a grunt.

She sighed and went to his bedroom to grab the kit. He'd been battling diabetes for years and whenever Jimmy turned his back the old man didn't bother to do anything he was supposed to. Tommy and Sean didn't try to get him to do anything. She didn't think they even knew what the steps were. Jimmy came in from the kitchen.

"Seriously? We're supposed to be out the door already and he didn't test?"

"Did you tell him to test?"

"He knows." Jimmy reached for the kit.

"I got it." She took the kit and stood in front of her dad. Without prompting, he held up his index finger. A quick prick and Norah saw that he was fine. She packed a dose of insulin just in case. Then she turned back to Jimmy. "Why are you here? Shouldn't you be driving with your girlfriend?"

Kevin snickered from his perch on the chair. "He doesn't trust us to show up on time."

Jimmy pointed to the small clock on the mantel. "And I was right. Moira's meeting us at the restaurant. Let's go. Who's driving?"

Sean shrugged. He never drove a car when it was warm enough for his motorcycle.

Kevin stood. "I'll take Dad and the boys. You can have Norah."

He was still pissed she wouldn't tell him who the baby's father was because he wanted to go to Boston and beat someone up. It was a point of contention between him and Jimmy. Jimmy sided with her and protected her from all of them.

"Don't you already know Moira? You were in the same grade together in school."

Kevin tucked his hands in his pockets and rocked back

on his heels. "Yeah, I know Moira. But Jimmy's buying dinner."

Jimmy pointed a finger at him. "You need to be nice. No causing trouble with Moira."

Kevin just smiled.

That's when Norah remembered the times Kevin would come racing into the house because he'd teased Moira so badly her brothers had chased him home. Norah had been too young to understand, but there was a story there. Jimmy puffed his chest like he was gearing up for a fight with Kevin. Norah grabbed his arm. "Let's not keep your lady waiting." She led him out the front door.

Behind her, she heard her brothers and Dad moving out as well.

Once Norah was settled in the car, she asked, "So what's the story with Moira and Kevin? Did they used to date or something?"

Jimmy grunted, which she interpreted as a no.

"That doesn't explain much."

"Kevin was always an ass to her. In school and out. He tries to torment her."

"Then why bring him to dinner?"

He blew out a deep breath. "Because she's part of the family now. They need to be around each other without fighting." He smiled. "And Moira knows how to fight."

With each new piece of information, Norah decided she liked Moira a little more. She had to admire anyone who'd give Kevin a run for his money. Jimmy pulled up to a casual chain restaurant.

"What? No fancy food for us?" she joked.

"Hell no. Moira suggested we go to the restaurant Liam works at, but our brothers are animals. I'm not taking them someplace with cloth napkins. I don't even know if any of them own a tie."

Norah laughed. The truth was, the only time she'd ever

seen her dad in a tie was when he attended a funeral. "It's good though because I don't have anything nice to wear either. At least until I get back to my normal size."

Jimmy got out of the car and came around to her side to meet her. "If you need something, let me know."

"I'm okay. I've been looking for a job, something to make some money, but I'm not having any luck. I have no experience for the jobs I'm finding online and one look at me for an in-person application and I don't have a shot."

"You don't need to work. We'll take care of you."

She leaned close to him as they walked into the restaurant. "I know. You've always taken care of me. But I need to do something for me, to keep busy, keep my mind off things. Most important, I need a break from Dad."

Jimmy smiled. He knew better than anyone how difficult their dad could be. As soon as they entered the building, Norah saw Moira. She was hard to miss. Her red hair was like a flame and her bust led the way. Norah thought her boobs were big since getting pregnant, but she had nothing on Moira.

Moira went on tiptoe and kissed Jimmy. Then she turned to Norah. "You must be Norah. It's nice to meet you."

They shook hands and Moira looked behind them. "Where's everyone else?"

"They drove themselves. They should be here soon."

Just then their brothers barreled through the door.

"Moira, baby, good to see you." Kevin pushed past them all and wrapped his arms around Moira. She immediately leaned back and shoved at Kevin's shoulders.

"Would you grow up?"

He tried to pull her tighter, but Jimmy's hand slapped on his shoulder.

"I'm just welcoming her to the family." Kevin snickered.

Moira placed a gentle hand on Jimmy's arm. The anger in Jimmy's eyes melted when he looked at Moira. Norah wanted to sigh. She never thought about her big brother being in love, but he was. He was like a new and improved Jimmy.

She had a feeling Moira had quite a bit to do with that.

The hostess showed them to a table and passed around menus. The guys all ordered a beer and Norah's mouth watered. She hadn't had a drop of alcohol in a long time. She missed going to clubs and parties with her friends.

"Just a water for me," she said, and went back to perusing the menu. Since she wasn't going to rack up a bar tab, she could splurge on dinner. Maybe dessert.

Moira, who sat next to her, leaned close. "Whatever you do, save room for the brownie sundae. It's awesome. Not as good as Super Cup, but still delicious."

"Can you read minds? I was just thinking about dessert."

Jimmy eyed her over Moira's head. "Dessert's a given with Moira, especially if there's chocolate involved."

After they'd placed their orders and had drinks in front of them, Jimmy cleared his throat. "I wanted you all to come out tonight because I have something to tell you."

He reached over and held Moira's hand. "I know you all know Moira since we grew up across the street from each other, and you know we've been dating. But I asked Moira to move in with me."

"Dude, the house is a little crowded, don't you think?" Sean said.

"We plan to buy our own house, not move in there." He looked to their dad and waited for a comment.

Seamus O'Malley was usually a man of few words, unless you counted cursing, so Norah didn't expect much. But he raised his bottle of beer. "I guess a congratulations is in order then. To Jimmy and Moira."

Everyone raised their drinks and said congrats. After the announcement, Jimmy seemed to relax. He talked with Dad about cases he was working on and Tommy, Sean, and

Kevin discussed some car thing that Norah had no interest in. She managed to feel completely out of place with her own family.

Old resentments bubbled up. She wouldn't feel like this if they hadn't sent her away.

Moira turned to her, stopping her train of thought. "So tell me about yourself."

"What do you want to know?" She rubbed her belly. "I'm obviously pregnant. Not married. Haven't finished college. I don't have a job." She sighed. "My life is pitiful. Tell me about you and how the hell you manage to put up with my big brother."

Moira laughed loudly. "He's not easy, that's for sure. It's like he's missing the gene that gets people to talk. He grunts and sometimes yells, but getting information out of him is exasperating."

"Noticed that, did you?"

"But I love him. He's a pretty amazing guy."

"Yeah, he is," Norah conceded. For all of his shortcomings, Jimmy had always taken care of her, even from a thousand miles away.

"I'm a journalist. I do freelance work."

Jimmy leaned back to catch Norah's attention. "She goes to parties every day and then writes about it. Tough life."

Moira smacked his arm.

"Just kidding. She writes some amazing things about the charity work being done in the city to improve people's lives. She'll make you want to pull out your wallet."

Norah liked seeing Jimmy being playful. Over the years, he'd always been too serious.

"Yeah, Mouthy Moira always did have a way with words."

Moira shot Kevin a dirty look. Then she leaned closer and lowered her voice. "I do go to a lot of parties. It's a pretty kick-ass job."

The waitress delivered their food and Moira continued to talk. "What was your major before you left school?"

"Nursing."

"Do you plan to go back?"

"I'd love to, but I need to at least take a semester and figure out where I can transfer and not lose credits."

"It's a lot to handle all at once." She waved at Norah's plate. "Eat up. We'll order dessert and talk some more. Maybe we'll send the guys home and make it a girls' night."

"You don't have to be my friend. I'm happy for Jimmy. Even if I hated you, as long as you made him happy, I'd suck it up."

"That's good to know. I want to be your friend. You're all important to him and that makes you important to me. Maybe not Kevin, but the rest of you. Plus, you just moved back to town, so I'm guessing you don't have many girlfriends. Jimmy's great, but he's not a woman."

Norah stared into Moira's wide bright blue eyes. She was serious. "I think that would be great. I miss being around another girl. Thank you."

As Kai rounded the corner to his mom's hospital room, he heard, "Come on, Mrs. Ellis. You can handle this. Step off the edge of the bed."

Kai entered the room and saw a woman leaning over his mom trying to pull her to standing.

"Should she be doing that yet?"

The woman looked over her shoulder at Kai. He recognized her as the nurse who'd been caring for his mom. "She needs to exercise often. She has to get used to the knee. It's a process, but it won't work unless she cooperates."

"What's the problem, Mom?"

Lani jabbed a finger at the walker near the bed. "That

thing. I'm not old and crippled. I don't need that. I know how to walk."

He rubbed a hand over his face. "Can I have a minute with my mom?"

The nurse nodded. "I'll be back in five."

When she was gone, Kai didn't get a chance to say anything. "Don't start with me, Kai. That thing is the beginning. I use that and all of a sudden I'm too feeble to take care of myself."

His mother's stubbornness might kill him. "Walking will be hard at first. This is just to help."

Her eyes filled. "If I need the walker, then you'll have reason to get rid of me. Leave me in that old folks' home."

"I told you, it's not an old folks' home."

She sniffed, fighting back the tears. He realized it wasn't stubbornness, but fear that drove his mom. She'd never been afraid of anything. It was a stab to the heart to see this. He sat on the edge of the bed. "You'll be back at Jaleesa's in no time."

"No. Old people like me, they never get to leave those places. They suck the life out of you." She spoke like she was spilling a secret, something she was sure of, but wasn't supposed to know.

He knew then he couldn't send her to the rehab facility. He sighed and swallowed hard. "If you do what you're supposed to do here, I'll bring you to my house until you're back to normal."

Her mouth eased into a shaky smile.

He pointed at her. "That means you do everything the doctors and nurses say, even if you have to use a walker. If they tell me you're being uncooperative, off to the facility."

She touched his arm and her wrinkly hand looked older than it should. When he leaned close to kiss her good-bye, she rubbed his jaw. "You need a shave."

"Be good. I'm going to check with Jaleesa."

He left the hospital and went home to move his stuff. On the way, he called Jaleesa and told her the plan. Jaleesa said she'd organize getting the equipment, like a rented hospital bed, delivered. He hadn't even thought about that.

At home, he spent his entire morning moving his weights and benches down to the basement, which meant he also had to move his poker table over and rearrange the space for his biweekly game. Fuck. He couldn't let his mom anywhere near the guys. If she knew he was still friends with them, it would be an epic battle.

How did his mom have a way of making him feel like a kid when he was a grown man?

Didn't matter how she did it. He knew that he'd have the guys come in through the basement door around back to keep them from her. She wouldn't be able to manage the basement steps for weeks. And if she could handle them, it would be time for her to go back to Jaleesa's.

After organizing his workout equipment, he went back upstairs to make sure the house was clean. The doctor had said his mom should be discharged within a day or two. He didn't want to hear complaints about dust.

By the time he made it to the shop, he was cranky and tired. The last thing he needed was Tommy and his sister standing at the counter laughing. Karla, his piercer, was laughing with them.

He looked at Tommy. "Don't you have work to do?"

"Client just left. I was giving Norah a tour."

"And explaining some of the more creative slang you guys use around here. Pussyball is something that I know should offend me, but it's so ridiculous, I can't stop laughing every time I think about it." Then she tossed a tennis ball at him. They handed the ball to anyone who couldn't handle the pain of a tattoo. Hence the name *pussyball*.

The sound of her laughter shot straight to his dick and that was all kinds of wrong. But it was like she knew the effect she had. She eyed him from behind lowered lashes, the same mischievous look he'd gotten from her on her last visit.

"See you for dinner tonight?" she asked Tommy.

"I think so."

She stepped around Tommy and wiggled her fingers. "Nice to see you again, Kai."

What made her think they were familiar enough that she should use his name like that? Wiggling her fingers and flirting.

"This isn't a social club," he said to her.

"I know. I didn't come to socialize. I came in as a potential client."

Kai scanned her body, the bare skin he could see, and saw nothing but stretches of smooth tan canvas.

"You're not getting a tattoo," Tommy said.

"I'm an adult. I can do whatever I want with my body." As she spoke that last part, she intentionally looked at Kai.

This girl was trying to stir up trouble.

"Isn't that right, Kai?"

He liked the way she spoke his name, like a tease.

Tommy spun around. "You can't ink my sister."

Kai blinked to focus and pull away from Norah's hypnotic eyes. "She's right. If she's got the cash, she can do whatever she wants."

"Told you." Then she turned and pushed the door open to leave. "See you later."

"She's my baby sister. You can't do it."

That was no baby that just walked out. "Look at it this way—if she decides she wants a tat, she'll get it somewhere. Better here, by you or someone you trust instead of some dive."

Tommy sank onto the stool behind him, looking devastated with the realization that Kai was right.

"I have art to work on. I'll be in the back." As he walked

to his office, an image of Norah splayed in his chair ready
for ink flashed in his mind.

Shaking his head, he closed his office door. He had to
stop thinking about her. She was off-limits. He didn't need
to imagine her unmarked skin waiting for his touch.

Norah walked down the block away from Ink Envy feeling a little bit naughty. She had no idea what was wrong
with her. The pregnancy hormones were getting out of
hand. Instead of going straight to her car, she went for a
walk in the sun.

She'd never admit it to Tommy, but she'd gone to Ink
Envy today in hopes of seeing Kai. It was sick and she
could admit that. She had no business thinking about sex,
especially given her current condition, but she couldn't
help herself. When she was there last time, something
about the way he looked at her made her a little tingly.

Today was a test to make sure she hadn't imagined it.

Nope.

He might've been gruff and cranky, but a girl knew when
she was being checked out. A simple thrill ran through her.
She was aware it wouldn't go anywhere. That it couldn't go
anywhere. But she enjoyed feeling like a woman. Plus, the
hormones. God, the hormones.

She hadn't totally misled Tommy about her reason for
showing up. She'd often thought about a tattoo. When she'd
visited in the past, she'd tried to convince Tommy to draw
something special for her, but he'd refused. She never had
the guts to go somewhere else for one.

The fact that Kai didn't back down to Tommy was cool.
Of course, he towered over Tommy so she didn't imagine
Kai backed down to too many people. Something made
him look almost menacing. He had longish hair that he kept

tied back. His dark eyes revealed little. Maybe menacing was the wrong word. Gruff. That fit.

After a brief walk around the block, she went back to her car and drove home. At this point, she was just procrastinating, but she needed to call Avery. She still hadn't decided what to do about the baby, but breaking the news to him needed to happen. Preferably before she went into labor.

As she parked, she noticed Moira hobbling up the front steps with a plastic bin. From the sidewalk, Norah called, "Hey, what are you doing here? Moving in to make Sean crazy?"

Moira set the bin on the porch and turned around. With her hand over her eyes to shade them, she said, "Jimmy told me you didn't have any clothes that fit. My sister-in-law just had a baby so I borrowed her maternity clothes for you."

Norah walked closer as Moira spoke. "You didn't have to do that, but thank you. I figured I'd make do." She tugged her shirt and stretched it away from her belly.

"Don't thank me yet. Although I'm sure it'll fit, Quinn's a teacher and she delivered in early June, so she might not have a bunch of casual stuff. All she asked is that you return it in good condition. She's planning on more kids."

"Let me get the door. If you kick it inside, I'll have one of the guys carry it upstairs for me later."

She held the door open for Moira who hefted the bin and set it in the living room.

"So what do you have going on today?" Moira asked.

Norah looked around to make sure none of her brothers were lurking. "I'm going to call the baby's father and tell him."

Saying it out loud felt like a real commitment.

"Wow."

"You want a drink or something?" Norah asked as she pointed to the kitchen.

"I'm good." She angled her head and studied Norah. "Would you like me to stay while you call him?"

The thought hadn't occurred to Norah, but the offer from Moira appealed to her. She didn't want to be alone, but she couldn't ask one of her brothers to be with her. They'd be too focused on gathering information about Avery instead of being supportive. "Would you?"

"Of course."

Norah pulled out her phone. "I think maybe upstairs would be best. You know, in case someone else comes in."

"You want me to come up or wait here?"

"I might need you in the room to make sure I don't chicken out again."

Moira followed her upstairs and when they were closed in the room, Norah sat on her bed. Moira took a chair on the other side of the room, offering some privacy.

Norah stared at the phone. Her thumb hovered over the contact for Avery. He might not even answer. She could be getting worked up and nervous over something that might not happen right now. Taking a deep breath, she hit call.

The ringing in her ear fought against the blood-rushing.

"Hey, Norah. Where the hell have you been? I've called you all summer."

Well, damn. So much for hoping for no answer.

"Uh, I came back to Chicago."

"Classes start soon. Will I be able to see you before I leave again?"

"No. I'm, uh, living here now. That's why I'm calling." She took a deep breath and glanced at Moira. She was studying her cuticles, but Norah knew she could hear. "I moved back because I'm pregnant."

There. It was out. Silence met her. "Avery?"

"Oh. Well, I know we didn't talk about exclusivity or anything, but I didn't expect . . ."

He thought it was someone else's. Damn. This was

harder than she'd expected. "I'm seven and a half months. It's yours."

"What?"

"Remember when you came home to Boston for a long weekend? By my estimation, that's when it happened."

"You said you were on the pill."

She hated the accusation in his voice. This wasn't going how she pictured. "I was. But I was getting over bronchitis and the antibiotics must've ruined the effectiveness."

"Are you sure it's mine?"

Never had she thought he'd say that to her. What did he think of her that he believed she'd make this up? "Fuck you," she whispered.

"Are you sure?"

"There hasn't been anyone else since we met."

"I don't know what to say."

"I know the feeling. That's why I haven't called."

"What are you going to do?"

"I don't know."

More silence. Then, "Let me know when you figure it out."

He hung up. Norah stared at her phone. She was as alone as she thought.

Moira was at her side. "Should I even ask?"

"He questioned if it was his. Like I would lie about something like that." Tears leaked from the corners of her eyes. Tears of hurt and frustration and disappointment. Avery was better than that and she knew it.

"Not that I'm defending him, but this was kind of a big deal to dump on a guy you haven't seen since what? March?" Moira pulled her into a hug.

"I know." She also knew she had this coming. She'd always done everything on her own. This was no different.

Norah had never wondered what it would've been like to have a sister until now. She held on to Moira and let the tears fall. After a few minutes, she pulled away. "I'm not even sure why I'm crying. Hormones, I guess. They're running rampant these days."

Moira nodded and didn't call her a liar. "I'm around if you need to talk." She went to the desk and scribbled on a piece of paper. "That's my number. I work from home mostly, so I'm free for lunch or coffee or talking."

"Thanks." Norah wiped at her face. "I'm okay. I have more thinking to do, but it feels good having that weight off me. Do me a favor, though, and don't tell Jimmy I called Avery. I'll tell him."

"I'll keep my mouth shut. For now. But you need to let your family in and let them know what's going on with you."

"I know. It's just . . . I've been on my own for a long time. My aunt took care of me, but we were never close or anything. She policed me. Although Jimmy would help with anything I asked, I didn't want to run to him all the time. So I got used to figuring things out on my own."

Moira swooped in for another hug and whispered, "You're not alone anymore."

Norah bit her lip to stop the flood of more tears. This was why she came home. She knew she wouldn't be alone. Now she just needed to figure out how to deal with having a family again.

Kai watched as the delivery of rented hospital equipment was brought into his house. How could one woman with a bum knee need so much crap? His spare room was filled, but the most disturbing thing he saw in the room was a bedpan. Jaleesa said nothing about him playing nurse. *Take her for a walk. Help her do her exercises.* At no point did Jaleesa say *empty her bedpan.* He'd never been violent toward his sister, but this might push him over the edge.

His head thumped with a headache. He'd kept his schedule for the afternoon clear to get his mom settled in, but there was no way he'd miss hockey practice tonight. He needed to take the edge off. After he flipped off the light in the bedroom, he turned to the bathroom to get something for his head. There he saw grab bars installed by a toilet with an extra seat to raise the height and more bars and a bench in his bathtub. It was as if it wasn't even his house anymore.

He swallowed a couple of aspirin. If he was this stressed before his mom even got there, how would he last weeks of living with her?

Jaleesa honked from outside to let him know they were there. Kai went out to meet them and help get his mom in. At the car, she leaned pretty heavily on him to get out, but then she waved him off as she switched to a four-footed cane.

Her progress to the front door was approximately that of a sloth. Kai grabbed her suitcase and followed behind. By the time she got to his stairs, he wanted to scoop her up and carry her in, but knew she wouldn't have it, and she needed the practice. She gripped the cane and the rail so hard her hands shook with effort.

Over his shoulder, Kai asked Jaleesa, "Didn't they give her anything for the pain?"

"Don't speak like I'm not standing right here."

Jaleesa shook her head. "She's on over-the-counter painkillers now. And she mostly refuses that."

Kai bit down his response. He knew his mother. She'd raised them to suck it up and she expected no less from herself.

When she finally made it to the porch, he jumped up and

opened the screen door for her. She hobbled through and paused in the living room. Kai waited for her to comment. Although she'd been in his house before, she would have something to say. He eased past her and pointed down the hall with her suitcase. "I have your room set up over here, Mom."

Halfway to the bedroom, she paused for another break. Kai looked at Jaleesa who nodded to let him know this was normal. He waited in the doorway for his mom to catch up. She still hadn't said much of anything.

Jaleesa took the suitcase from him. "I'll get you set up here." She opened the suitcase on the bed and then turned to the small dresser Kai had picked up at the thrift store.

Lani shuffled into the room and eased onto the bed. "My underwear and socks go in the top drawer."

The thought of handling his mom's underwear made him grateful Jaleesa was there. He left them and went to the kitchen.

A little while later, he heard the TV go on and Jaleesa joined him in the kitchen. She pointed to the living room. "She's settled in front of some talk show."

"What the hell is with the bedpan? You said she could handle her bathroom issues."

"She can. She's been making the trip to the bathroom for the last couple of days. I had them bring one just in case she had problems in the middle of the night. It would be more embarrassing for her to wet the bed than to use a bedpan. She probably won't need it." Jaleesa moved around his kitchen as if it were her own and made a pot of coffee.

"If she uses it, you're coming over to empty it."

Lees rolled her eyes. "Can we talk about a schedule?"

"What schedule?"

"Mom. She's okay being alone for short periods, but if someone's not here to make her do her exercises, she won't.

She's already complaining about the CPM and how she doesn't want to use it."

"The what?"

"CPM—continuous passive motion machine. It basically makes her move her leg. She doesn't like it, but her therapist suggested we get one to make sure she's moving."

It was all too much to grasp. Right now, all he wanted was the buzzing of the tattoo machine and a client who wanted some ink.

"I have hockey practice tonight. Is that going to be a problem?"

"What time?"

"I leave here at seven thirty and I'm not back until eleven, later if I go out with the team."

"I can stop by to check on her before she goes to bed and then she should be fine. Since it's her first night here, try to make it an early night in case she needs something?"

"What is she going to do when I'm at work all day? I can come home sometimes to check on her, but I can't babysit."

"I know. We'll figure it out." She closed her eyes and rubbed her forehead. "I need a break. This has been so draining."

Kai looked at his sister and for the first time saw how exhausted she was. She always handled everything and held them together as a family. Now he saw the toll it was taking. He was a bigger asshole than he thought. "I'll figure it out. I'll hire someone to come in and be with her."

She opened her eyes and stared up at him. "You sure?"

He pulled her into a hug. "It's the least I can do. You've done everything and I've taken it for granted."

"Does that mean Mom can stay here for good?"

"Hell no. I'll get her back on her feet, then she's all yours."

Jaleesa slipped away from him, laughing. "Just kidding."

"Kai," Lani called from the other room. "What do you have to drink?"

"I have coffee on, Mom," Jaleesa answered.

"How much waiting on her am I supposed to do?"

Jaleesa lifted a shoulder. "For the first week or so, maybe quite a bit. She can't stand for long periods to cook, and she's still getting used to the cane. Walking and juggling food might be hard. But then, she'll get better, use the cane a little less for short distances, doing more for herself."

Kai sighed. These next few weeks were going to be miserable.

Chapter Three

"Please, Tommy? I have to get out of here." Norah folded her hands and batted her eyes at her brother.

"Why are you asking me and not Sean?"

"Because you're my favorite brother?" She added a wide smile for effect.

"Hockey practice isn't a good place for you to hang out."

"Why not? I'm sure it won't be too crowded. And I like to watch you play."

"You don't know anything about hockey."

She shrugged. "I'm willing to learn." She moved across the room to where he was packing his gym bag. "I've been cooped up here for days. I'm going crazy. Please."

"If you drive with me, you have to take my car to drive yourself home because we go out for drinks after."

"I could come with you."

He pointed at her belly.

She rolled her eyes at him. "I didn't say I'd drink alcohol, just that I'd come with you. You know, be social, talk to people who *aren't* my family." She watched him weigh what she'd said. "I'll even be your wingman."

He chuckled. "Like I need help."

"So is that a yes?"

"We leave in five."

"Thank you." She kissed his cheek and went to grab her purse.

Two hours later, her butt was numb and her back ached from sitting in the hard chair watching her brothers practice. Tommy was right. She knew nothing about hockey other than they needed to get the puck into the goal. She even had a hard time figuring out which players were her brothers. With all the gear on, they were almost indistinguishable. Some were taller or bigger, but they moved so fast across the ice, she couldn't focus on any of them.

A woman sat beside her. "Hi, I'm Caitlyn. Who are you watching?"

"Hi. I'm Norah O'Malley, Tommy and Sean's sister." She thrust out her hand to shake.

"I'm Chris's girlfriend. If you want, you can move over to the section where we all usually sit." She pointed to a section near the center of the rink.

"We?"

"Wives, girlfriends, family." She lifted a shoulder. "We hang out during games mostly, but sometimes we tag along for practice and then go out after."

Norah's entire body buzzed. "I'd love to join you. I just moved back to town and I don't know anyone."

"Come on then." Caitlyn stood and held out her hand to help Norah up.

She followed Caitlyn up and over, walking carefully so as to not lose her balance, which was getting more difficult by the day. When they reached the group, Caitlyn pointed to everyone and mentioned names, but Norah knew she wouldn't be able to keep them all straight. She was just grateful to be among other people.

They settled in and watched practice. Caitlyn pointed.

"That's Chris. He's right wing. Your brother Sean is left wing."

"Where's Tommy?" She watched all the players on the ice and still couldn't pick out her brothers.

"He's on offense right now, playing right wing. Sometimes during a game, your brothers will play at the same time and it's a thing of beauty to watch. They get into this rhythm like they have their own language. I think that's why the coach has them on different teams for practice."

Nothing Caitlyn said about her brothers surprised Norah. Tommy and Sean had always been close.

Just then one guy rammed into another and smashed him against the glass.

"Ouch! Who was that? I thought they were all on the same team."

"They are. That's Kai. He's playing defense and his job is to make sure the puck doesn't come his way."

Norah shuddered. "He seemed kind of mean about it. No wonder there are always so many fights in hockey." She watched for another minute, thinking about the name. What was the likelihood someone else was named Kai? "Is that Tommy's boss?"

Caitlyn shrugged. "Tommy knows him outside of hockey, but he's a quiet guy. He doesn't talk much so it never occurred to me to ask."

Norah absorbed the information. Kai appeared to be a man of few words and not just around her. She glanced over her shoulder to try to figure out who was there to watch Kai. It shouldn't have mattered, but she wanted to know.

As if sensing what Norah was doing, Caitlyn added, "He doesn't bring anyone. Ever. Not to games or practice or to the bar after. I don't think he's ever brought anyone to the end-of-the-season party either. He's kind of a loner."

Norah said nothing but returned her attention to the

game. Now she was doubly glad she'd talked Tommy into bringing her with them. She liked her strange flirtation with Kai. Tommy and Sean would throw a fit if they caught wind of it, but she didn't care.

She needed something to feel normal and interesting and attractive now more than ever. Especially since her conversation with Avery. All she'd been able to think about since the call was her time with him. It wasn't a fling; they'd had real feelings for each other. The fact that he thought she'd lie about the baby being his really stung. Worse was his distance, offering no input.

Moira had been right. He needed time to think about it. It had to have been a blow to a guy who thought she was calling to make plans for the end of summer. Guilt poked at her for ignoring him for months. He'd deserved better. And if she'd invited him into this whole process earlier, he might've been willing to help her decide what to do. She owed him an apology.

A buzzer sounded and guys moved around on the ice. Her gaze tracked Kai. He wasn't as fast or graceful as some of the other guys, but he was no less interesting to watch. He suddenly spun around, skates skidding to a stop, and looked directly at her. At least that was how it felt. Her skin prickled and a wave of heat washed over her, making her light-headed. She swallowed hard.

Caitlyn's attention was back on her. "Are you okay? You're looking a little pale."

"Yeah. I just got hot all of a sudden."

Caitlyn nodded. "Hot flash. My sister had them all through her last trimester." She dug around in her bag and pulled out a bottle of water. "Here. This might help."

Norah took the bottle and chugged half.

"First one?"

Norah didn't know if she was asking if it was her first

pregnancy or her first hot flash, but it didn't matter since the answer was the same. She nodded and sipped more water.

"Sit tight for a few minutes and it'll pass."

Norah forced a smile and prayed Caitlyn was right. A hot flash would disappear, but she wasn't as sure about the feeling she got when Kai looked at her.

Kai was miserable. Practice had barely taken the edge off his irritation. He wished his mom would just yell and bitch like other women. Instead, she made small comments he was supposed to read something into. And that didn't even touch on him trying to understand her pain or what he could do to make her feel better.

Jaleesa had tried to reassure him that he'd be fine, but he had doubts. A lot of them. He changed after practice and checked his phone. Jaleesa texted to let him know Mom was in bed asleep. He looked at his teammates who were all getting ready to go to McGinty's. One beer wouldn't make him too late.

He walked into the bar and sought out the rest of his team. The guys with wives and girlfriends had pushed together a few tables. The single guys held back, some sitting at the bar, others at tables, mostly waiting to see if they'd pick up company for the night. Unfortunately, that wasn't an option for him.

Sitting on a stool, he set his phone on the bar in case his mom called. He ordered a beer and when the bartender turned, he added a shot. If he was only staying for one, he wanted it to count. As he waited for his drink, something shifted, drawing his attention. Norah. No way would he acknowledge her. He didn't understand why she kept showing up in his life.

The girl, however, couldn't take a hint and sat on the stool beside him. The bartender set down his drinks and Kai downed the shot.

"Hi. Buy me a drink?"

His gaze slid to her belly.

She rolled her eyes. "A Sprite. Why does everyone feel the need to do that? Look at my stomach. As if there's some chance I might forget I'm pregnant."

Kai waved the bartender over so she could order. Then he slid money on the bar to pay for the drinks.

"Thanks. Interesting game."

He sipped his beer and looked at her. He had no idea what game she was playing. If she were his woman, there'd be no way she'd be sitting in a bar chatting up some other dude. Pregnant or not, but definitely if she were carrying his child.

His woman. His child. The alcohol hadn't even hit his system yet, but he was thinking like a drunk.

"Shouldn't you be with your brothers?"

"They're hitting on some girls at the other end of the bar."

"Maybe it's time for you to go home."

She twisted on the stool and swirled her straw in her drink. "Did I do something to piss you off?"

"No." Another drink of beer.

Norah stared at him as if she were waiting for more information. Caitlyn stepped up to the bar and ordered a pitcher. "Hey, Kai, Norah. Tommy was saying something about you going back to school. How much more do you have left?"

"About a year, maybe a year and a half depending what credits will transfer, but then I'll have my nursing degree."

The bartender slid a pitcher over to Caitlyn. She paid him and turned back to Norah. "Better not let the guys know. It's hard enough getting them to go to the doctor when they get hurt. If they know you're a nurse, they'll use it as an excuse to never get checked out."

Caitlyn left with the pitcher, but her conversation stayed with Kai. This girl was going to be a nurse. If she weren't pregnant, she'd be the answer to his problems. She needed a job and he could pay her to take care of Lani. But she was pregnant, and if that wasn't bad enough, every time she saw him she flirted. He didn't need any part of that.

He chugged the rest of his beer and stood.

"Leaving so soon?" Norah asked.

"Yeah." As he walked through the bar, he felt her eyes on him. He needed to get as far from her as possible, especially when he started thinking about giving her access to his life.

He'd had a hard enough time reconciling playing hockey with Tommy and then hiring him at the studio. In his world, things were separate, distinct. It was how he'd been able to function for years. People from the studio—clients, employees—never saw him outside the shop. He never brought his childhood friends anywhere, only the poker game in his basement. Hockey was team time.

If all the parts bled together and he fucked something up, his entire world would implode. Having Norah tag along at hockey was more than enough when he'd already seen her at the studio and she talked about getting a tattoo. He didn't need her in his home as well.

He drove home and crawled into bed. Even though his mom was sound asleep, not making any noise, the presence of another person in his house set him on edge. It was like he could hear her dreaming and breathing and taking up his space. He punched his pillow and rolled over. He knew he was being ridiculous.

"Kai."

He rolled over and pulled his pillow over his ear before he heard it again.

"Kai!"

Then it registered that his mom was calling. He shot out of bed and ran to her room. Fuck. It was still dark outside. "What is it, Mom? Are you okay?"

"I need the bathroom and the stupid cane fell out of my reach. I can't get up."

Even though he didn't want to, he flipped on the light, momentarily blinding them both. He blinked and looked around for the cane. Bringing the cane to her, he offered his arm to get her out of bed.

"I can do it," she said, but they both knew it was a lie.

He helped her from the bed. She hobbled from the room and he sank onto the edge of the mattress to wait for her to come back. He'd wanted to follow her to the bathroom to make sure she didn't fall, but he knew it would piss her off.

Sleep tugged at him while he sat and it took all of his control to not lie back. Finally, Lani came shuffling back into the room.

"Go to bed. I'm fine."

"Lees got you a bedpan if you need it for the middle of the night. You know, in case I'm not here."

She sniffed. "Like you have somewhere better to be at three in the morning. I'm not an invalid. I've no use for a bedpan."

He nearly sighed because he hated the idea of a bedpan almost as much as she did. "Do you need more pain meds?"

"I'm fine. Just tired. Now get out of my bed."

He stood and held her elbow to help get her in. She didn't try to shake him off this time and he wondered how much pain she was in.

Once she was settled, he stumbled back to his room and tried not to think about how many more nights like this he had in store.

* * *

Norah sat at the table tapping her fingers and then her toes and then played with the napkin dispenser. She'd spoken to Teagan, but had no idea what she looked like. Glancing around the small coffee shop, Norah took note that she was the only pregnant woman, so at least she was easy for the adoption counselor to spot.

A small tap on her shoulder and she turned.

"Norah?"

Norah moved to stand, but Teagan waved her off and took the seat across from her.

"Hi," Norah said, and clasped her hands in her lap beneath her belly. "I'm really nervous."

"There's nothing to be nervous about. I'm here to offer information. You don't have to decide anything today. We're just two girls talking."

Teagan's response calmed Norah's racing heart. The waitress came over and Teagan ordered a cup of coffee. Norah stuck with water.

"Tell me about yourself."

Words came flooding out. "I've been living in Boston for almost ten years. My mom was killed when I was a baby and when my oldest brother, Jimmy, joined the army, everyone thought it would be best for me to live with my aunt. This past year, I was in college. I met a boy and fell for him and got knocked up. I thought I was being careful. I'd been on the pill. After months of pretending it wasn't real, I came home." Her rambling caused a surge of embarrassment. She drank a gulp of water. "I didn't know what to do."

"You have options, and that's what I'm here for."

"I don't think I'm ready to be a mother, so maybe adoption is right for me."

"I can help you with whatever you choose. If it's lack of readiness, we can get you into parenting classes. We can find you a mentor."

"It's not just the parenting. I haven't finished college. I don't have a job. I don't really have support." She immediately thought of Jimmy, but it wasn't his job to support her child. "I don't feel ready because I haven't lived my life yet. I don't think I can give what a baby needs."

"I can help with finding a job, getting financial support. Help you find a lawyer to get child support. However, if you want to talk about an adoption plan, we can go over that too."

"My family is better than I make them sound. My brother Jimmy would take care of me and the baby, but I don't want him to have to. It's more than money and jobs. I don't feel like a mom." Because of this, she felt like there was something fundamentally wrong with her. Most women would be cooing over little pajamas and baby strollers. She hadn't even looked at one.

"Right now, I think the only thing holding me back from jumping at adoption is guilt. I spent a lot of time on your Web site. I like the idea of an open adoption. I don't want my baby to feel abandoned." Tears filled her eyes with the thought. She knew that feeling too well.

Teagan reached across the table and held her hand. "We'll work toward whatever makes you comfortable. This is about you making the best choice for you and the baby, not assigning guilt or blame."

Norah didn't know what she had been expecting. Maybe someone berating her for stupidly getting pregnant without a plan. Maybe someone telling her she should give her baby away. But she hadn't expected someone to hold her hand and tell her it would be okay. Surprisingly, it made a hell of a difference.

"Tell me how open adoption works. I read about some of it online, but if I decide on adoption, what happens?"

"We talk, like we are now, about what you want and what you expect, both in adoptive parents and life after adoption. Then we try to find a match." She sipped her coffee, but still held Norah's hand.

"What if I change my mind?"

"After you have the baby, by law you have to wait three days to make the adoption official. It gives you time and space to reconsider. You can take all the time you need."

"What about the baby's father?"

"Do you know who he is and how to reach him?"

Norah nodded.

"We'll contact him and ask for a waiver. If he refuses, adoption is still possible. It will take longer and there's more paperwork to make it legal. It's easiest if he's on board."

"I get to choose where the baby goes? Like someone here in Chicago?"

"You would go through profiles we have on adoptive parents, and then you can choose to meet some. The choice is completely up to you."

Norah drained her water glass. There was so much to this.

"There's no hurry. You have time to think about what you want for you and the baby as well as what your expectations are. I'm only a phone call away at any time."

Norah stared into Teagan's dark brown eyes. Her wildly curly hair bounced around her shoulders as she talked and offered reassurance. She was pretty and confident and knew what she was talking about. Norah vaguely remembered feeling that way herself.

Over these past few months, she lost herself somewhere. She was starting to come back, though. After a few weeks in her family's house, surrounded by her brothers and helping with their dad, she had started to feel normal again.

"You'll probably think of more questions, so feel free to give me a call. Is there anything else I can do for you?"

"Unless you can make this decision for me, no."

Teagan smiled. "You'll be okay."

Norah wanted to believe that. Teagan paid for her coffee and left a tip on the table. Norah walked outside into the glaring sun. Teagan had given her plenty to think about. Could she give her baby to someone else and not be consumed with guilt? She wasn't sure she had the strength to walk away, but in her gut, she felt like it was the right decision.

Norah sat on the front steps waiting for Jimmy. He didn't spend many nights at home these days, but he said he'd be here when she called. He was like that. She regretted not calling him in the spring or even the beginning of summer when she left Aunt Bridget's.

Although she hadn't made a definitive decision, after talking with Teagan, she felt like adoption would be a good choice. She couldn't say she'd bonded with this baby because she'd spent most of the pregnancy in denial and fear, but she loved it on a gut level. It was something she would never be able to explain.

She wanted what was best for the baby and she didn't think she was it, especially as a single mother. Yeah, Jimmy would help, but it wasn't fair to him. Tommy and Sean would mean to help, but they wouldn't really. It wasn't in their nature.

A huge part of her felt like a total shit for even considering it. She'd spent years feeling abandoned by her family. They'd sent her off to live with Aunt Bridget when she was just starting puberty at a time she needed her family most. She blamed Jimmy for that. They fought about it often over the years and while she understood why Jimmy had done it, old resentments still bubbled up from time to time.

Now she realized that Jimmy was only a couple of years younger than she was now and he'd been responsible for all of them for a long time. Who could blame him for sending her away?

The sun was sinking off to the left, still hot enough to warm her legs and make her wonder if she'd end up with a weird burn pattern. Her ass numbed on the concrete, so she shifted her position and leaned back on her elbows. Closing her eyes, she listened to her neighborhood. Kids down the block were running through a sprinkler. Some houses had windows open and she heard the noises of dinner being made and TVs blaring. Rush hour traffic hummed in the distance.

The sounds of Chicago weren't that much different than those of Boston, yet it felt different here. A shadow shifted in front of her and she opened her eyes.

"Hey, squirt."

She laughed at Kevin's use of the nickname. "Not so little these days," she said, rubbing her belly.

He dropped a laundry bag at her feet.

"I know you don't think I'm washing your smelly clothes."

He shook his head. "Machines are still busted at my building. This is better than a Laundromat. There's free beer."

He sat beside her. She waited for whatever he planned to lob at her.

"I want this guy's name, Norah. We've given you time and space, but the games have to end. This guy has a responsibility here."

"I know, but it's not your problem to handle. I'm taking care of it." She saw the barely controlled anger in his eyes. "I appreciate your concern. I know you're worried about me, but I'm okay."

At least she told herself that daily, willing it to be true.

Kevin jumped up. "This is bullshit. I'm going to call

Aunt Bridget. I don't know why Jimmy hasn't already done that."

Norah shaded her eyes from the sun as she looked up at her brother. "She can't give you what you're looking for. She doesn't know him. And I'm not going to have you running off to hunt him down. We did this together."

"I sure as fuck can blame him for not being here now."

"Nope. That blame is on me."

"But you didn't tell him because you knew, didn't you? Knew he'd be a useless piece of shit who wouldn't man up. What kind of losers did Aunt Bridget let you date?"

Norah leveraged herself off the step. "Really? I'm an O'Malley and in case you haven't noticed, we tend to do whatever the hell we want. You guys might've shipped me off to Boston but you didn't remove my DNA. Aunt Bridget couldn't control who I dated any more than you can control what I do now."

"This is bullshit." He grabbed his laundry, gave her a dirty look, and stomped up the stairs and into the house.

She inhaled deeply, filling her lungs as much as she could with a baby pressing on all of her vital organs. She wasn't upset. Kevin irritated her, but she wasn't stressed out and torn up like she'd been her first night at home when she felt like all of her brothers were ganging up on her. She handled it.

Holding on to the rail, she lowered herself back to the step. A few minutes later, Jimmy pulled up. Part of her had been wishing he'd have Moira with him. His girlfriend was someone Norah considered an ally. She was kind of short on those these days.

Jimmy walked up to her and held out a hand to help her up. Instead she flipped her thumb to the spot next to her. He sat, extending his legs out in front of him, the crease in his pants still visible after a day of work.

"I think talking out here would be better. Kevin's inside doing laundry and I pissed him off again."

"He'll get over it." Jimmy looked at her clothes.

She tugged at the maternity top. "Moira borrowed stuff from her sister-in-law. At least now I don't feel like an over-stuffed burrito."

"You look good. Happier."

She wrinkled her nose. "Not happy, but better."

"What do you want to talk about?"

Her hand automatically went to her belly again. She'd always thought it weird when pregnant women did that, but now she understood. You couldn't really control it. "I've done a lot of thinking. And I called Avery—" She stopped with the realization that she let his name slip. But not even Jimmy was good enough to track him down with only a first name.

Another deep breath in and released. Jimmy had stiffened beside her. He was better at covering his anger than Kevin, or any of the O'Malley boys for that matter.

"I think I want to give the baby up for adoption."

Jimmy ran a hand over his face and then stared out at the street. He said nothing for so long that Norah couldn't predict his response.

"Are you sure?"

"No." She almost laughed. "But I talked with a counselor and discussed my options."

"You want to give up your baby?"

Both hands now rested on her bulging torso. "It's not about what I want or don't want. I have to think about the baby and what's best for him or her. Let's face it. I'm a mess. I'm not ready to be a mom, definitely not a single mother. I don't have a job. Crap. I don't even have a mother to teach me how to be a mom." The last words caught in her throat.

Jimmy reached out and put his hand on top of hers. "Sweetheart, I told you, you're not alone. I meant it."

"I know you did. But this baby isn't your responsibility any more than I am."

"You are mine. Mom would've expected it."

"It's not fair to you."

"Life isn't about fair. It's not fair that we have a whole family full of siblings to look out for each other and some people have no one. We can't control fairness."

"I want my baby to have a shot at a good life, one with parents who love and want him or her." She swallowed hard. She hadn't voiced these ideas to anyone and they hurt. Feeling incompetent stung.

"It's up to you and I'll support whatever you want."

She blinked away unshed tears. "Who are you? Jimmy O'Malley would never just offer blanket support without telling me what to do."

"We've all done some growing up."

"Mmm-hmm. I think Moira has a whole lot to do with that."

He smirked. "Maybe."

They sat in silence for a few minutes. Then Jimmy stood. "I'm going in to see Dad and say hi to Kevin. Don't rush your decision. You have time. You have to be completely sure."

She nodded. "I know. I haven't done anything but think and talk about it, but I like what the adoption counselor had to say and I'm leaning in that direction."

With his hand on the rail to go up the steps, Jimmy asked, "Do I want to know what the guy's reaction was to the pregnancy?"

"Probably not." She couldn't look him in the eye when she admitted that.

Jimmy bent over and kissed the top of her head. "Say the word."

He said nothing more, but his intention was there. All she had to do was open the door and he'd go after Avery. He meant for it to be protective and sweet, but it was kind of scary. It made Norah glad that she'd been living in Boston when she started dating.

Knowing that Kevin was still in the house and Jimmy might tell him about her thoughts, she decided a walk was in order. The weather was beautiful, and for a change, she was breathing easy.

Kai clamped his jaw shut as a tiny wisp of a woman barked orders at his mom, putting her through motions that were clearly too painful. Jaleesa had arranged for the physical therapist to come to his house for the first few weeks until Lani was able to travel. The session only lasted an hour with a bunch of breaks throughout, but his mom needed a nap by the time Tanya was finished.

As they left the bedroom, Tanya gave him more instructions to help Lani with her exercises, which she was supposed to do for fifteen minutes at a time throughout the day. Why the hell had Jaleesa thought he'd be able to live his life? He couldn't leave his mom alone.

He'd told Jaleesa he'd hire someone and that's what he needed to do. When Lani woke from her nap, he sat by her bed. "We need to talk about getting some more help for you, Mom."

"I don't need help. That little Tanya just wore me out is all."

"And she'll do it every time she comes here. But you need to do your exercises throughout the day so you can get better. I can't be here all day every day. I have a business to run. I'm thinking about hiring a home healthcare worker."

"I don't need a nursemaid."

"If you don't do your exercises, we'll have to send you to a rehab facility. We won't have any other option."

"I'll do them. Do you think I like being all cooped up

like this? Not able to see my friends and do what I like?" She humphed at him.

"We'll see how today goes, okay? I have to go to work. Do you need me to get you anything before I go?"

"Help me up out of this bed and I'll be fine. I might move slow, but I'm still moving."

Kai helped her get to her feet and watched as she shuffled to the living room. Once she was settled on the reclining couch, he handed her the remote.

She lowered her brows and pressed her lips together.

"What is it? You need more meds?"

"No. My book from the table in the bedroom."

He should've guessed. He grabbed the book and her phone and set them both on the couch beside her.

As he walked out the door, he called, "Don't forget your exercises."

She mumbled something back at him, but he tasted freedom and didn't wait. Instead of turning on the air conditioner in the car to combat the heat, he rolled his windows down and turned the music up. He hadn't realized how much he needed to escape.

His freedom was short-lived, however, because his phone started ringing before he even reached the shop. He turned the music down and answered. "What's up, Mom? I just left you."

"I know. I'm not senile. You need to go grocery shopping. Get some food in this house."

He sighed. His grocery shopping tended to consist of buying frozen meals and some fruit. "I'll call Jaleesa and have her bring stuff when she comes later."

Lani huffed out a breath and then hung up. Kai cranked the music and drove the last few blocks in peace.

When he strode into the studio, Tommy was working on a woman's ankle. A thorny rose twisting around. Kai stopped to check his work. It looked good. The kid had talent.

After making sure his station was prepped for his client that afternoon, Kai sat at his desk in the office and focused on drawing a scene from Hell. With every line, he felt like he was filling in the illustration of his current life. He worked for more than an hour, doing a simple line drawing in pencil to make sure he had it right. He'd send a copy to the client and then talk about colors and fill. The guy wanted the complicated picture on his back. He would need at least three sessions, maybe more.

His phone buzzed in his pocket. A text from Jaleesa.

You were supposed to tell me to bring groceries?

Fuck. He'd totally forgotten to call Jaleesa. Sorry. Forgot.

I brought her lunch, but I don't have time to go shopping. Kids will be getting out of school.

I'll handle it. He slid the phone back in his pocket and stowed the drawing for later. His client should be here soon. It was a touch-up and fill job on a tattoo he'd finished a couple of weeks ago.

At his station, he checked his tools again as his client pushed through the door. Joe called, "Hey, Kai. Ready for me?"

Kai nodded. "Have a seat. Let me take a look."

Joe pushed up the sleeve of his shirt. The tattoo had healed well.

"You're good," Kai told him. "Take the shirt off and we'll get started."

Just as he snapped on his gloves, his phone rang again. He was tempted to ignore it as he usually would in front of a client, but knowing his mom was home alone made him check. It was her. He tapped Joe's shoulder. "Sorry. I have to take this."

Joe shrugged and relaxed in the chair.

Pulling off his glove, Kai answered. "What's wrong?"

"Your sister didn't bring food and I need more books."

Kai pinched the bridge of his nose. Of course it wasn't a real emergency. "I forgot to call Jaleesa. I'll handle it. What about books?"

"I'm on the last chapter of the book I'm reading and I only have one more. It won't last the night. I need more."

He couldn't believe she was bothering him at work over some fucking books. "I'll see what I can do," he bit out, and hung up. How was he supposed to focus on work? Kai looked up at Tommy, who was staring at him. "What?"

Tommy shrugged. "I don't think I've ever seen you take a personal call at work. It's weird."

A sudden thought hit him. It might not be the best idea, but it would solve his immediate problem. He pointed at Tommy. "Your sister still looking for a job?"

"Yeah."

"Is she trustworthy?"

"Of course. She doesn't have a record and she's clean."

"Tell her to get her ass over here now. She's hired." As soon as the words left his mouth, his muscles relaxed.

"For what?"

"I'll tell her when she gets here." He sat down beside Joe and got to work. If things went as he planned, he wouldn't have to worry about stupid calls again.

Chapter Four

Norah dug through the pile of maternity clothes at a frantic speed. She had no idea what to wear. What does one wear to work at a tattoo parlor? Tommy didn't know what Kai wanted her to do so he'd been no help. She didn't want to wear a pretty dress only to find she'd be scrubbing toilets.

Then again, she didn't know if she'd take the job if she had to scrub toilets.

Yeah, she would. She was desperate enough to do just about anything. And the thought of *just about anything* sent a surge of lust through her again. She remembered the way Kai had looked at her. She shook her head. That was wrong. Hormones were interfering with her thought process again. Between the hormones and her ongoing loneliness, her body didn't have a chance.

She grabbed the sundress and slipped it over her head. The sneakers on her feet would stay because once she removed them, her ankles started to swell. Then nothing would fit. After brushing her hair, she twisted it into a braid and grabbed her keys.

From the couch, her dad looked at her. "Where you going?"

"Job interview."

He hadn't spoken to her much since she'd come home. He tolerated her nagging at him about his meds, but he didn't mention her pregnancy once. She didn't know what to think of it. He was like this extra body in the house that she cared for but didn't know.

"Good luck," he said.

"Thanks." That was about as real as any interaction with Seamus O'Malley went for her. She didn't have time to diagnose her relationship with her dad. Far too many things already crowded her brain.

She walked out the door into the oppressive August heat and humidity. The air was so thick she almost had to swallow it to fill her lungs. At least the AC still worked in her car. She started the engine, but stood outside until the air in the car circulated.

Once she was on the road to Ink Envy, her nerves attacked. She knew nothing about working for a tattoo artist. Maybe he had some office busy work for her. But Tommy said he'd asked and Kai shot him down. She wondered what had changed.

It was early enough in the day that rush hour traffic hadn't started yet, so she made good time getting there. Her luck held as she found a parking spot two doors down. It was about time something went in her favor.

She pushed through the door of Ink Envy and saw Kai working on a client. For a moment, he froze, looking at her. He didn't say anything so she sat on the old leather couch at the front. She wondered where Tommy was.

"You ready for a break?" Kai's low, rumbly voice danced over to her, even though he spoke to the guy less than a foot from him. "You want a drink or something?"

"Sounds good."

"Hey, Tommy."

Tommy came from the back somewhere. "Yeah."

"Get Joe something to drink. I'll be right back."

Norah stood and that's when Tommy noticed her. His face brightened with a smile. That was something she worried she wouldn't see again. Tommy's easy smile directed at her. Kai peeled off gloves, tossed them in the trash, and walked toward her. Then he kept walking to the front door.

Weird.

She followed him outside. She squinted in the sun, but Kai moved and blocked the glare. Her own personal eclipse.

"Tommy says you're trustworthy."

"Okay. Is there a reason we're out here?"

"Yeah. I don't take care of personal matters at my business."

"So hiring me is personal?" She was so confused.

"I need someone I can trust. I assume with the exception of your condition," he said as he pointed at her belly, "that you're able-bodied and can do things like run errands."

"Yeah." This was sounding fishier by the minute.

"My mom just had knee replacement surgery. She's staying at my house until she's back to normal. I need help. She's fucking driving me crazy with phone calls for stupid shit like groceries and books."

Norah bit the inside of her cheek to stop from laughing. His face filled with frustration but she found it amusing he thought food was frivolous. "What are you hiring me to do?"

"Whatever my mom needs. Groceries, books, remind her to do her exercises."

"I can't lift her. You know, given my *condition*." Her hand waved in a circle over the baby.

"I can get her out of bed in the morning and she's been okay from the couch to the bathroom. My sister stops by to check on her. I need you to get her what she needs."

Norah thought about it. She could handle this as long as she didn't have to lift the woman. Running errands for an hour or so would get her out of the house and keep her moving. "How much are you paying and how often would you need me?"

"Shit. I hadn't thought about that. Ten bucks an hour?"

More than she was expecting, but she didn't let it show.

"The hours might be weird because I don't work regular hours. But it's not like it would be full-time. Maybe a few hours a day?"

"Sure. It's not like I have people knocking down my door to hire me."

He reached in his pocket and pulled out keys. "For future reference, don't tell a prospective boss no one is looking at you. They'll think you're tainted."

He worked a key from the ring.

Watching his hands, she said, "Right now, I pretty much am tainted. I'm a single pregnant woman without a college degree and little work experience." She left out the fact that she didn't look at him like a prospective boss. More like a delectable piece of meat.

Kai took her hand and placed a key on her palm. "You're not tainted. You're pregnant. It's temporary."

Warmth spread through her as he spoke. Was he still holding her hand?

"Key for my front door. My mom won't answer if you knock." He pulled out his wallet and handed her a hundred dollars and a business card. "Have her make a list of whatever she wants and then go get it. The address is on the back of the card."

"Anything else?"

"Keep her happy and away from calling me. If you could get her to do her exercises, that would be great."

"Okay." She fished her keys out of her purse and tucked his key and cash in the side pocket. "Is she expecting me?"

"I'll call her."

Then he walked back into the studio without another word. Talking to him was like talking to Jimmy. He only offered the minimum number of words.

As she got back into her car, she was grateful she wouldn't be scrubbing toilets after all. Ten bucks an hour wouldn't make her rich, but it would be enough that she wouldn't feel like a total sponge living off her family.

It didn't take long to get to Kai's house. She didn't know what she'd expected, but this wasn't it. A cute little brick ranch house with green shutters on the sides of the windows. As she walked up the sidewalk, she glanced around back. Fenced backyard. She hadn't thought to ask if he had pets. A small dog would be cute, but Kai struck her more of a beast of a dog kind of guy. She knocked on the front door before using the key. No dog answered, so she figured she was safe.

"Hello, Ms. . . ." Crap. She didn't know Kai's last name. What was she supposed to call the woman? She should've looked more closely at the card he'd given her. The one she'd left in the cupholder in her car. She shut the door behind her and called again, "Hello?"

"In here."

Norah turned the corner and saw an old woman sitting in a reclining couch. She stared at Norah for a moment and then said, "You're Kai's *friend*?" The way she'd said the word made Norah think she didn't believe Kai. Even Norah had to admit that calling her a friend was pushing it. She didn't think he even liked talking to her.

"Yes. I'm Norah." She walked forward and held out her hand. The woman gripped it tight.

"Lani Ellis."

"Nice to meet you, Ms. Ellis."

"You have good manners. Kai said you're not a home nurse."

"Nope. I'm just doing him a favor. He said you need some groceries and something about books." She reached into her purse and pulled out a small notepad and pen. "If you make a list for me, I can run to the store and get what you want."

Ms. Ellis rattled off a list of groceries and then a list of authors whose books she wanted. Norah hadn't heard any of them before but she'd mostly been reading textbooks for the past few years, so it wasn't unusual. As the lists grew, Norah imagined the hundred bucks dwindling. Quickly.

"Kai also asked me to remind you to do your exercises. Do you need help?"

Ms. Ellis's eyes got squinty and then she pointed at a machine beside her on the couch. "I hate this thing."

"If your doctor wants you to use it . . ."

She folded her hands in her lap. "I can't get my leg up into it."

Norah set her purse on the floor. "I'll help. Turn your body and I'll lift."

It was slow-going, but Norah got her strapped into the machine. "Can you handle it from here?"

"Yes."

Norah retrieved her bag.

"Thank you."

It was more than she'd gotten from Kai. "No problem. I'll go to the grocery store and get everything there and bring it back. Then I'll go to the bookstore." The added trip, while not efficient, would allow her to check on Ms. Ellis. Kai hadn't told her to check up, but if her job was to keep his mom off the phone, Norah would have to make sure everything was taken care of.

The grocery store at the end of most people's workday was not the place Norah wanted to be. Over the past few weeks, she'd only gone to the store midday when there were no crowds. This sucked. Halfway through her trip, she had to find the bathroom to empty her bladder. Again. Besides not being able to see her feet, having to pee approximately every ten minutes had to be the worst part of pregnancy.

She pushed her cart through the store and checked things off her list. She grabbed some more yogurt for herself as long as she was there. Her back ached as she stood in line to pay. Usually the self-checkout moved faster, but today her luck had run out. People moved slowly, the scanner bleeped more often than necessary. Norah began to question if she was ever going to get out of the store.

By the time she returned to Kai's house and unloaded the groceries, she was ready for a nap. She sat at the kitchen table for a minute to rest her feet and ease the ache in her back.

"Hey, girl."

Norah's head snapped up. Had she dozed off? How embarrassing. She pushed to her feet and went to the living room.

"I need my leg out of this thing."

Norah moved toward the couch. "I'm more than happy to help you, but my name isn't girl. It's Norah, Ms. Ellis."

"I just met you the one time. I didn't catch your name."

More like she couldn't be bothered to remember it. Her father was the same way. Snapped at people to prove he had some kind of authority. Norah undid the straps, lifted the woman's leg, and set it back on the floor.

"Get me my cane." She pointed toward the floor near the edge of the couch. Sure enough, a cane lay on the floor.

Norah raised her eyebrows at her. "You commented on

my good manners. I assumed that was because you had them too."

"Please."

Norah half bent, half squatted to get the cane. Once it was in front of Ms. Ellis, the woman gripped it and tried to stand.

"Do you need help?"

Pressing hard onto the cane and using the arm of the couch, she rose a few inches off the cushion. Then sank back.

Norah let out a slow breath. "Come on, then." She held out her arm and helped hoist Ms. Ellis to her feet. Norah had told Kai she couldn't lift anyone, but his mom was far from heavy and she'd pulled enough of her own weight to make it possible for Norah to help.

"You shouldn't be lifting me or anything else in your condition. You look ready to burst." She inched forward and step-shuffled toward the kitchen.

"I have weeks left. Almost a month. Can I get you something from the kitchen?"

"I need to walk. Part of my exercises."

Norah sat on the chair near the couch and waited for her to come back in case she needed help sitting down, which was exactly what happened. "I'll go to the bookstore now. I don't know if they'll have all of these books. Do you want me to get as many as they have or would three be enough for now?"

"It's getting late. It'll keep until tomorrow. You can come back then and I'll let you know how many to get. It's almost dinnertime. Did you buy food to cook?"

"I just bought what you gave me on the list. Kai didn't tell me to plan meals for you."

Ms. Ellis sighed. "That boy. Jaleesa, that's my girl, Kai's sister, she brought lunch earlier. There might be leftovers. Could you warm them up?"

Norah nodded. She went back to the kitchen to figure out dinner. Norah saw what was happening. Ms. Ellis was lonely. If Norah did all of the shopping today, she probably wouldn't have a reason to come back tomorrow. It wasn't quite the deal she'd made with Kai, but Norah couldn't just leave.

She knew the pain of that kind of loneliness and she wouldn't wish it on anyone.

Kai finished giving aftercare instructions to his client and yelled to Tommy that he'd be back in an hour or so. He rushed out the door and drove as quickly as possible to his house. He'd tried calling his mom and she didn't answer, so he got worried. He shouldn't have left her alone.

He burst through the front door to find her sitting on the couch, already in her nightgown, a book on her lap.

Norah came in from the kitchen.

"What are you doing here?" they asked each other simultaneously.

His mom looked annoyed by them.

Norah pointed over her shoulder. "Can I talk to you a minute?"

"You okay, Mom?"

"Yes." She acted as if it were a stupid question. He went to the kitchen. Norah leaned against the counter. He had no idea how she managed to make that look sexy and inviting, but she did.

She held her hands up as if to stop an argument. "I'm not trying to milk hours. In fact, you probably don't need me. I mean, you can order groceries online and have them delivered and you can get your mom an e-reader and she can one-click to download all the books she wants."

"She scared you off already?"

Norah snorted at him. "Hell, no. You've never met my

dad. Google 'cantankerous old man' and an entire wiki is set up in his honor. She doesn't need a whole lot of care. I helped her off the couch and into and out of her machine, but mostly, I think she's lonely."

He hadn't thought of that. His mom was used to being around Jaleesa and the kids all the time.

"Anyway, I bought the groceries she asked for, but she neglected to say that you have like no food in your house, so you still need to buy groceries for dinner and lunch and stuff. I was going to go to the bookstore but she said it would keep until tomorrow. Instead, I made her dinner and hung out a while."

"Thank you."

Her eyes widened. Was he that much of a dick that she thought he wouldn't thank her for taking care of his mom?

"Kai," his mom called. "I'm ready for bed."

"Be there in a minute," he yelled over his shoulder. Turning back to Norah, he asked, "You willing to stay on?"

"For what?"

"Whatever my mom wants. If she hasn't scared you off, she must like you. And she probably is lonely. The schedule will be weird because I work at all hours. You'll still have to run errands because I'm not going online to order groceries." He waited.

"You're going to pay me ten bucks an hour to sit around here with your mom?"

"And run errands. And make sure she does her exercises."

"Deal." She grabbed her purse and rummaged around. "Here's the receipt for the food and the change. I can use that for her books tomorrow if you want."

He looked at the crumpled bills and loose change. He pulled a credit card out of his wallet. "Use this for whatever she wants."

Norah smiled and winked. "Ooo . . . Aren't you afraid I might run off on vacation with all your money?"

"If you steal from me, I'll break your brother's hands, so no, I'm not worried."

She sobered quickly. "It was a joke. You need to lighten up."

"Kai."

He looked over his shoulder and back to Norah. "She's going to bed, so you can leave now."

"Okay. I'll finish the dishes before I go."

He went back to the living room where his mom was trying to push herself off the couch. He quickly bent and scooped her to standing.

"I can do it myself."

"So I've heard. She's not supposed to lift anything. She's pregnant."

"Think I don't know that? I might know a thing or two about being pregnant. I used her for balance. We did fine. Help me get into bed." She shuffled toward her room. She added, "Grab my book there."

He picked up the paperback and followed her to the bedroom.

When they got there, she stood beside the bed and said, "I like her. She nags a little, but she's good." Lani lowered her voice. "But don't tell her I said so."

"Wouldn't dream of it."

She sat and he helped get her legs up. "Did you have your meds?"

"Yes. Your *friend* made sure I took the right ones."

"Why do you say it like that?"

"What?"

"Friend." He refused to use the same inflection she had. It would just encourage her.

"Because you can call it what you want. She's not a

friend. Your souls know each other. She's like you—troubled."

"You're talking like a crazy woman. She's pregnant with another man's child."

"Is that man around? I think not or she wouldn't have spent her day with me."

"She was doing me a favor. She'll be back tomorrow, so be nice."

She sniffed. "Take your own advice. I'm fine."

He bent over her and kissed her cheek. "Good night, Mom. I have one more client coming in tonight, so I have to go back to work."

He got as far as the door before she called, "Send your girl in."

"Her name is Norah and I told her she could go home."

"But she hasn't left yet."

He sighed and went back to the kitchen. Norah was in the refrigerator pulling out containers of yogurt. "Stealing food?"

Her shoulders drooped. "I bought these when I was at the store. Check your receipt. I paid separately."

Damn. *He* needed to lighten up? Maybe he needed to forgo trying to joke. "I was kidding." He grabbed a carton. "Lime?" Sounded disgusting. His face must've shown his thoughts.

She snatched it back. "The baby likes it. Never in my life have I liked lime anything. But I can't seem to get enough of this."

"You can leave it here if you want. It doesn't make sense to carry it back tomorrow."

She bit her lip as if she needed to think about it. Taking three containers, she turned back and put them on the top shelf. Then she shoved the other three in a plastic bag.

"My mom asked you to come to her bedroom before you leave."

"Why?"

He shrugged. He watched her move, carrying her yogurt and purse, careful to give him a wide berth as she walked by. His mom wasn't far off the mark when she'd said Norah was troubled. He knew the baby's father wasn't in the picture. He didn't have to ask and didn't care when Tommy came into work weeks ago bitching about his sister.

The rest of the crap about his soul knowing hers was crazy. He'd never believed in that kind of bullshit. He only believed in what he saw, what he knew, what he understood. He'd admit there was chemistry between him and Norah. He felt it every time their eyes met or she tossed out a flirtatious smile. He also knew it wouldn't go anywhere because she was pregnant.

On his way out, he stopped in his mom's room and found Norah sitting in a chair beside the bed with a book in her hand. When he walked in, she looked up.

"Thought you were going home."

"Your mom asked me to read to her."

"The light is too dim in here," Lani said.

"What time you want me back tomorrow?"

Kai thought about his schedule, but he couldn't remember when his first appointment was. "Probably not until noon, but I'll call you and let you know."

"You have my number?"

"No, I have your brother's."

She laughed and shook her head. "I'll leave my number on the kitchen table."

He turned to leave and heard Norah's voice as a quiet murmur as she returned to reading. He stood in the middle of the living room as the sound of her voice coasted over him. The words she spoke were unnecessary because the rhythm and melody tugged at him. He didn't know how long he stood there not really listening but wanting to. His phone vibrated in his pocket, jolting him back to reality. Puck texted him to let him know his client was at the shop.

Something about this arrangement with Norah made him believe he'd made a mistake. But knowing his mother was safe and content was worth whatever the error in judgment would cost him.

It was near midnight by the time Kai parked in front of his house. The light was off in his mom's room, but a small lamp glowed in the living room. He unlocked the front door and was met with silence. His day felt like it had lasted the length of four. In the living room, he stopped in his tracks. Norah lay sleeping on his couch.

He stepped closer and thought about touching her, but she looked peaceful. Not at all the troubled girl his mom saw. Her hair brushed her cheek and his finger twitched wanting to slide it back behind her ear. He shook his head and pulled out his phone. She was obviously tired so he didn't know if it was better to wake her up and send her home or just let her sleep.

He texted Tommy. Norah fell asleep on my couch. Should I wake her?

A moment later Tommy responded. Up to you.

Kai stared at the shadows playing across her sleeping face. It wouldn't be safe for her to drive this tired. I'll let her sleep.

Thanks for letting me know.

Kai stood there for a few more minutes debating carrying her to his bed. His dick responded with a *hell yes*. His mind had control over the rest of his body, however. He wouldn't touch her. If for no other reason than that she carried a baby inside her. If he picked her up she would wake and he didn't think she'd stay so he left her on the couch.

He crept to the bathroom and took a quick shower and

did his best to forget Norah was in his house in the middle of the night. He was fucked up to be thinking about getting in bed with her. The complications alone would be enough to strangle him.

His mom was right. She was a girl in trouble who was doing him a favor by helping with his mom. He'd barely have to see her. He'd just treat her like any other employee.

As he left the bathroom he glanced into the living room. Just another employee. Yeah, right.

Norah sighed as a soft touch caressed her cheek. With her lids still closed, she tilted her face to seek more. Her eyes fluttered open and she was staring into a pair of dark, nearly black eyes.

"Hey." His voice was barely above a whisper.

Startled, she bolted upright, but Kai caught her arm. "Slow down. I didn't mean to scare you."

She blinked rapidly and focused. She was in Kai's house. She must've fallen asleep. Her fingers brushed a soft blanket she knew she didn't have when she lay down. Bright sunlight glared through the window. Crap. She'd spent the entire night?

Kai was still staring at her, not saying anything, just watching her figure out what the hell she was doing.

"What time is it?"

"Eight. I was going to let you sleep, but I thought you'd want to go home and change before coming back to be with my mom."

She rubbed her eyes. Her brothers would be worried if they noticed she hadn't come home. She swung her legs off the couch and they bumped into Kai's. "Sorry," she mumbled.

The way he continued to watch her made her wonder if she'd been talking in her sleep. What could she have said?

Something that invited him to caress her cheek and whisper to her? Her heart thumped with worry about the many ways her hormones could've embarrassed her.

"I texted Tommy last night and let him know you'd fallen asleep." His voice was still low and thrummed along her nerves.

"Thanks." At least her brothers wouldn't be looking to hunt anyone down. Her gaze met his and held. Something arced between them and she could no longer tell if her hormones were in overdrive acting autonomously or if he was sending out signals. She shifted to the side and stood, breaking all contact. As she moved, the book she'd been reading fell to the floor. Her face flamed.

Ms. Ellis read some sexy books. Norah wondered if Kai had any idea. When he retrieved the book, he barely glanced at it, so she was sure he had no clue. He tried to hand her the book.

She shook her head. "It's your mom's. I was passing time and fell asleep." In truth, she very much wanted to see what happened between Bret and Carrie, the characters who had sucked her into their world.

He stood, too close for comfort, but not threatening. "You will be back, right?"

"Of course. I'm going to shower and change." Yeah, tell the sexy man how your bloated body will be naked. That's a hell of an image to leave him with.

"Take your time. I'll be here."

She nodded and grabbed her stuff and went to her car. As she drove home, she tried to screw her head on straight. She didn't know what was going on. Kai held a certain appeal, but he was not the kind of guy she normally fell for. Add to that the fact he barely spoke to her and thought she might have an inclination to steal from him, there was no way he could be interested in her. Even if she wasn't pregnant. Which she was. Very.

But then there were moments when he was kind and gentle, like when he handed her his house key and said she wasn't tainted or when he woke her with a sensual caress this morning. She couldn't figure out how much was real and how much she was imagining.

When she unlocked her front door and walked into the living room, her dad looked up from the newspaper.

"Where the hell have you been?"

"Work."

"In the clothes you left in yesterday." It wasn't a question, more like an accusation.

"I fell asleep at work."

"Don't you think you've gotten into enough trouble?" He pointed at her belly.

Her stomach clenched. Her dad hadn't spoken at all about her pregnancy. He acted almost as if it didn't exist. Until now. "It's nice to know what you really think of me. I made a mistake and I'm feeling the repercussions of that. Maybe if I'd had better parents, I wouldn't be here now."

She leveled the blow quickly and left the room. He sputtered as if he planned to respond, but she was already on the steps to her room. The baby kicked and elbowed her, not liking the new tension and stress. Norah would take shit from Jimmy because Jimmy had practically raised her after their mom was killed. Jimmy had always been there for her, taught her everything she needed to survive, supported her every way he knew how.

Her father, on the other hand, provided for her, but never offered anything else. She lived with him for the first twelve years of her life, but she had few memories of him being in her life. Her childhood had been filled by her brothers, and her dad was a fleeting image. She wouldn't listen to him berate her now.

She took a long shower and tried to relax. Although she'd slept well, Kai's couch wasn't quite as comfortable as a bed. The hot water eased her tense muscles. The baby seemed to enjoy the water and quiet, so Norah stood there until the hot water seeped away. After she got dressed in fresh clothes, she sat on her bed. She would have to walk past her dad again in order to leave. There was no getting around it.

She rubbed her belly to soothe the baby. No matter what, everything she did now was about the baby. She had to make things right for the baby. If that meant she had to avoid her dad, that's what she would do. She'd have to enlist Jimmy's help, though. She had a doctor's appointment tomorrow. Since she was so far along, she would have weekly appointments. The realization made everything seem too real, final, inescapable. As long as the baby was inside her, she had choices.

Digging through her purse, she found the business card for the adoption counselor she spoke with. Teagan had said Norah could call at any time to talk, but Norah didn't want to talk. She texted Teagan and asked if they could meet at a coffee shop after her appointment tomorrow morning. She'd tell Kai she couldn't be there until the afternoon.

Teagan quickly responded that she would be there. She wanted to move forward, which meant she needed to make a plan, a decision. Keeping the baby would mean bringing it into this semi-toxic situation with her dad. Her job with Kai wouldn't last forever and she had nothing else. She couldn't expect Jimmy to support her indefinitely. And she really wanted to finish college.

Taking money out of the equation, would she choose to keep the baby? A little fist—or was it an elbow?—stretched her skin. "I love you," she said aloud. She wanted the baby to hear it from her first. Even in this messed-up situation, she felt such an unfathomable love for this little being inside her. And knowing that, she knew she couldn't be a mom. She hadn't lived enough of her own life yet to give it up. She never wanted to resent her helpless baby. More than anything, she wanted this child to be happy and she didn't think she could provide that.

Before she lost her nerve, she called Jimmy.

"Hey, everything okay?" he asked.

"Yeah. I've been thinking. A lot. I'm going to give the baby up for adoption."

"Are you sure? You want to talk about this?"

"Actually, I'm calling to ask if you'll come with me to talk to the adoption counselor after my doctor's appointment tomorrow morning."

"Of course. Anything. You want me to drive you?"

"No. I'll need my car because I'll have to go to work right after."

"Work?"

Jimmy didn't know something? Either he was falling down on his usual nosy role or the family blab system was crumbling. She could only hope. "Kai, Tommy's boss, hired me to help with his mom. She had knee surgery and needs help with errands, and someone to keep her company."

"You don't need to work weeks before having a baby. I can give you money."

"I don't want you to give me money. I want to make my own. Plus, being with Dad all day won't be good for me right now."

"Fuck. What did he do?"

"Don't worry about it. We'll talk tomorrow. I'll text you the information."

"Okay."

She paused, and he didn't say anything for a moment. As much as she loved Jimmy, she wished she had a mom to help her with this. "Hey, Jimmy?"

"Huh?"

"Do you think Moira would come too?" Moira wasn't

exactly a mother figure, but she'd definitely pass for a big sister.

"I'm sure she will if there's any way she can. Want me to ask her or do you want to?"

"Can you? I don't want her to feel pressure from me. I'm sure she won't have a problem telling you no if she can't."

"Yeah, she has no problem telling me no. But I know Moira and you can count on her to be there."

That's what Norah hoped. If she surrounded herself with people who were willing to support her in a positive manner, she'd be able to block out the crap.

Chapter Five

Kai sat at the kitchen table drinking coffee and trying to forget the feel of Norah's skin under his fingers. He shouldn't have touched her this morning. He'd known it was a mistake even as his hand reached out and stroked a silky lock of hair. He couldn't start anything with her. Especially when she was having someone else's kid. He was a crappy uncle to Jaleesa's kids. And if growing up with his mom taught him nothing else, it was that it was unfair to come into a kid's life and then disappear.

However, Norah was going to be in his life, in his house, caring for his mom every day. He could only avoid her so much. He didn't want her to think he disliked her because then she might quit.

"Kai."

The sound of his mom's voice caused a spear of dread to shoot through him. He loved her, but he wasn't a caregiver and she was pretty needy right now. He didn't like seeing her like that. He went to the bedroom to help her out of bed and to the bathroom.

Even though this was only their second day together, he knew this was the hardest part of the day for her, both physically and mentally. He walked behind her en route to the bathroom and waited outside the door. "You want a shower today?" *Please say no, please say no.* Jaleesa or the PT could help with that tomorrow.

"I'll just wash up. Jaleesa said she'd be here tomorrow morning."

Thank God. He heard the water running, so he got comfortable leaning against the wall across from the door.

"You have coffee made?"

"Yeah." He'd already drunk two cups thinking about Norah.

"Is Norah coming back?"

He took note of the fact she'd used Norah's name. Biting back a smile, he said, "She should be here around lunchtime." He left out the part about her sleeping on the couch.

His mom opened the bathroom door. "If she's smart, she'll eat before coming here. You have no food. It's depressing." She shook a finger at him. "You'd think you didn't know how to eat. I taught you better than that."

"I'm not home all that much. Tell Norah what you want and she'll get it from the store today."

"Can she cook?"

How the fuck should he know? He swallowed the words to avoid the slap they'd earn from her. Instead he shrugged. He led her back to the bedroom so she could change and he went to get her a cup of coffee. When he returned, Lani was dressed. Kai set the coffee on the nightstand. "Let's get the first round of exercises done before I go to work."

She grumbled a bit but allowed him to help her get back in bed and start the exercises. They were still slow-going and his mom appeared exhausted afterward, but she pushed up and reached for his hand to get out of bed.

"I'm not going to lie in bed all day like an invalid. I have programs to watch." She moved toward the door. "Bring my coffee."

By the time she was settled on the couch with her coffee,

the remote, and her book, Kai needed to expend some energy. He needed to work off some of his frustration, so he went to the basement to lift weights. With each repetition, his muscles burned in a way that said he was building something. He pushed hard to rid himself of all of his selfish thoughts.

Norah knocked on the door but used the key to let herself into Kai's house. He was probably already at work, and Ms. Ellis couldn't answer the door. Well, she probably could, eventually, but Norah wasn't about to sit there to find out how long it would take.

As soon as she had the door open, she called out so Ms. Ellis would know it was her. "Hello, it's me."

"Hope you fed that baby before coming here. Still no food."

"I did buy food yesterday. Everything you asked for, Ms. Ellis. But I can go back to the store today." She tossed her purse on the chair and sat on the edge. "What kind of food do you want me to buy?"

"Can you cook?"

"A little. I'm no gourmet or anything. Mostly easy meals for college students."

"Well then, you already have my grown son beat. Get some fixings for sandwiches and whatever you can cook for dinner."

Norah began to think about possibilities.

"And get to the bookstore. I'm almost done with this one."

Norah stared at her. The woman must've been some kind of speed reader. "We were barely at the halfway point last night."

"I like my stories. Characters keep me company."

She had a point. It was a hell of an escape to live for a

while in other people's lives to avoid your own problems and situation. "I'll see what I can find."

Norah stood.

"Before you leave, can you start a load of laundry for me? I don't think Kai would feel comfortable touching my unmentionables. There's a small basket in my bedroom."

Norah narrowed her eyes. Although she hadn't gotten a grand tour of the house, she hadn't remembered seeing a washer and dryer either. "Where are the machines?"

"In the basement."

"Okay. I'll start that and then go to the store." Leaving her purse on the chair, she gathered the dirty laundry and found the door leading to the basement. She picked her way down the wooden steps carefully. A bare bulb dangled at the bottom lighting her way. A *clink* caught her attention. This was like a scene out of a bad horror movie.

She pushed on. At the bottom of the stairs, she saw the source of the noise: Kai lying on a bench lifting weights. He was shirtless. His bronze skin glistened with the effort of his workout. He continued to lift the bar and his arms bulged and flexed. A tidal wave of testosterone crashed through the room and into her.

She swallowed hard and moved another step before he caught her staring. Then she saw he had earbuds in, so he couldn't hear her. She moved as silently as she could to the washer. A loud *clunk* made her jump and she dropped the basket. Turning, she saw Kai sitting up.

He yanked the earbuds from his ears. "What are you doing?"

Her heart thundered. "Your mom asked me to do a load of laundry." She pointed at the basket at her feet as if he didn't know what dirty clothes looked like.

He stood and walked toward her. A patch of dark hair rode across his pecs. She stared at his body as he moved. Tattoos decorated his skin. Across his ribs, on his upper arm, his shoulder. Without looking, she knew she'd find more on his back.

Standing in front of her, he was close enough that she could trace a bead of sweat that trailed down into the waistband on his shorts. His breathing was slightly faster than normal. At least he had the excuse of lifting weights. All she'd done was walk down the stairs and ogle him. He bent and she shivered as his body lowered.

He grabbed the basket and held it to the side. She tilted her face up. He stared into her eyes, but then his gaze traveled over her whole face, landing on her mouth. The look was so intense that she could almost feel the phantom pressure on her lips.

He jerked back. "You shouldn't be carrying this. You're pregnant. It's not part of your job."

God damn she hated hormones. She'd almost had herself convinced he was going to kiss her. All he really wanted to do was yell at her. Typical.

She inhaled deeply. Then she snatched the basket from his hands before speaking. "You hired me to take care of your mom. She asked me to do a load of wash. This basket weighs less than the groceries I carried in yesterday. I'm fine."

Turning her back to him, she walked to the washer and started dumping clothes in. She couldn't wait to have this baby so she could have her body back. She'd never had a problem controlling her hormones around guys. If she was attracted to a guy, it was usually mutual. There were *signals*, for crap's sake. This whole pregnancy thing threw everything out of whack.

Even now, as she messed with the dials on the washing machine, she felt like he was staring at her. When she turned, he was.

"I'm not trying to be an asshole. I don't want you to hurt yourself or the baby doing stuff around here."

"I'm fine. I don't overdo it, which should be evidenced by the fact that I fell asleep on your couch last night."

"Okay. You know what you're capable of. Don't do too much on account of us."

His words did all sorts of new things in her. To have a man trust that she was smart enough to take care of herself meant something. He didn't view her as a weak, inferior being as she often felt her brothers did. She smiled. "I'm going to the store. You want me to get you anything?"

"Nah. I'm good." He returned her smile and the tension between them dissipated.

"I'll be a while since I have to go get books for your mom too. Do you know what kind of books she reads?" She didn't know why she said it, but her mouth got away from her.

He shook his head.

"She reads romance. And not the longing looks from across a ballroom and maybe some hand-holding kind either." Norah leaned a little closer and lowered her voice. "She made me read a sex scene to her last night."

The look on Kai's face was priceless. Even under the golden hue of his cheeks, a blush rose. "Christ, I'm sorry."

Norah bent over on a peal of laughter. "If you could see your face . . ." Those were the only words she could handle because laughter stole her breath. She laughed until tears streaked down her cheeks. Her stomach grew tight and a little uncomfortable, so she straightened. Rubbing both hands on her belly, she took slow, deep breaths. "Sorry. I just had this image of her asking you to read to her before bed."

In truth, the deep, rumbly sound of his voice would be enough of a turn-on regardless of the words he read. Suddenly, she wanted the audiobook of that.

"Sorry," she said again and they both knew it was an empty apology.

"It looks good on you."

"Huh?"

"The uncontrolled laughter. It looks good. Even if I'm the butt of your joke. And for the record, I will not be reading porn to my mom."

A giggle bubbled up in Norah's throat, so she swallowed. She couldn't afford to think of him and porn in the same sentence. "Okay, then. I'm going to the store."

He grabbed his earbuds and held them near his ears. Before putting them in, he said, "Be careful."

As if she needed a warning from him. Careful was one thing she sucked at but it was necessary now more than ever.

No matter how loud he turned up the music, the only sound blaring through Kai's head was Norah's laughter. Although he didn't want to consider the topic that made her laugh—his mom and sex—he enjoyed the sound more than a man should. He added more weight and lifted until his muscles burned.

He finished his workout and went upstairs to shower and get ready for work. To his surprise, his mom was on the couch actually using the motion machine she'd sworn she wouldn't. Wiping the sweat from his forehead, he pointed to the machine. "I thought you hated that thing. Told Tanya you wouldn't use it."

"Norah nags. She locked me into it. Reminded me that the faster I get moving, the faster I get back to my friends and my grandbabies."

Looked like his mom was as anxious to get back to their real lives as he was. "I'm going to take a shower and then to work. You need anything?"

"I'm fine." She picked up the book in her lap and all Kai could think about was Norah's comments about sex.

He clenched his jaw and left the room. He yanked on the rubber band holding his hair back and turned on the water. Once under the spray, he considered his options for getting laid. With his mom living with him, bringing someone here was out of the question. He had a few women he could call, but as he tried to bring their faces to his mind, all that popped up was Norah's bright blue eyes, smiling with laughter.

Fuck. He needed to get those images gone. He wrapped his hand around his dick and stroked himself hard. He gripped and stroked, thinking of sinking into warm, wet pussy, the shower not quite doing him justice. Since he couldn't imagine Norah not pregnant, he envisioned her on her knees taking him in her mouth. Lips tight around his cock as a glint of laughter sparked in her eyes. She'd like to watch him while she sucked him off. Fuck, yeah.

It didn't take long for his balls to tighten and his already-strained muscles to tense with his release. As he leaned against the wall recovering, he told himself it was better to fantasize about taking Norah than to actually make a move. She'd never know what happened in his mind when he was alone. As he washed, he refocused his brain around his workday.

He stepped from the shower and used a towel to wipe the steam from the mirror. He studied the beard he had growing before trimming it. With a towel wrapped around his hips, he stepped from the room. Normally, he'd walk out naked, but he didn't want to risk running into his mom.

Running into Norah was almost worse. As he turned the corner to get to his bedroom, she yelped. Instinctively, he grabbed the knot of the towel.

"You need to wear a bell or something."

"Me?" she asked with her hand over her heart. "You're the one springing out at me when I thought you left for work."

"I'm heading out now. I shouldn't be too late, so after

my mom goes to bed, feel free to leave." He didn't want to find her sleeping on his couch again.

"I have an appointment tomorrow morning, so I won't be able to be here until the afternoon. Will that be okay?"

Kai nodded. "The physical therapist comes tomorrow and Mom will need a nap after, so whenever you get here is fine."

"Is it safe to venture back into the basement? I don't want to interrupt you again."

Her interruptions were only a small part of his problem. "You're safe."

She smiled and that small glint of flirtation appeared in her eye again.

Knowing there wasn't much safe about her, he added, "I'm leaving as soon as I get dressed." He had no idea what was going on between them, but it needed to cool off.

Once again, Norah sat at a table in the restaurant alone. This time, however, the table was bigger since both Moira and Jimmy would be joining her and Teagan. In her hand, she held her baby's first picture. Sure, it was a little creepy and alien-looking, but Norah knew she would be beautiful. *She.* Norah smiled. The baby was a girl so now she knew which pronoun to use. Not only had she found out the sex of the baby, but the doctor also said everything looked healthy and right on track for her October delivery. Less than a month to go.

Jimmy and Moira came in together, looking happy and in love. Norah was envious of that. She missed having a boyfriend for the little things, like holding hands the way Moira and Jimmy were. Who was she kidding? She missed the big things too.

She waved them over. Moira gave her a hug. Jimmy sat beside her while Moira took the seat across from them.

"How was the doctor?" Jimmy asked. He always asked. How he managed to keep track of everything she had going on amazed her.

"Good. The baby is healthy." She slid the small picture on the table. "She's a girl."

"Wow." Jimmy took the paper and studied it.

"Let me see," Moira said as she reached for the picture. When Jimmy handed it over, she added, "How cute."

Norah laughed. "Not really, but the potential for cuteness is there."

Teagan strode up to the table. "Hi, Norah."

"Teagan. This is my brother Jimmy and his girlfriend, Moira." They all shook hands and Teagan sat beside Moira.

"I've decided to make an adoption plan." Norah blurted the words out as soon as everyone appeared settled after their greeting.

Jimmy turned and stared at her as if he hadn't expected that.

The waitress came and poured coffee for everyone, except her. Norah placed her hands on the table in front of her. "I'm not ready to be a mother. In fact, I don't know that I'll ever be ready. I want a better life for my daughter than I can offer her." She reached over and touched Jimmy's arm. "I want her to have something better than we had."

Her eyes stung, but she got through it.

Teagan watched the conversation for a minute before interjecting. "It's a tough decision. It will be hard and you'll grieve. After carrying the baby for nine months, you say good-bye. But if it's the right decision for you, you'll know."

Norah nodded. The more Teagan talked, the easier it became to envision adoption as a reality for her.

Teagan pulled out a small notebook. "What do you want? What are you looking for in an adoptive family?"

"I want someone who wants my little girl. I want them to be from this area so I can see her. I want two parents.

Definitely." Her hand tightened on Jimmy's arm and she looked into his eyes. "You did a great job, but you were a kid taking care of a bunch of kids. I'm not much more than a kid now. I want my daughter to have a mom and dad who will give her everything we didn't have."

Jimmy nodded. She knew he understood.

"Anything else that's important? Like religion or race? Do you care if the couple is gay?"

Norah hadn't considered it. She thought for a moment. Her dad would flip if she gave her baby to a black or Hispanic family, but it didn't matter to her. She shook her head. "As long as they're not part of some weird cult and calling it a religion, it doesn't matter. I'm not religious. But I think I want her to have a mom and a dad, something traditional?" God, she probably sounded like a bigot right now, but after growing up without a mom, she wanted that for her daughter.

Teagan didn't react to anything, so Norah continued. "It might be nice if my baby had a stay-at-home mom, but it's not a deal breaker." Norah had always fantasized about having a mom at home. Someone who made her lunch and baked cookies after a bad day. Instead, she usually came home from school and found her brothers brawling in the living room while Jimmy cooked dinner and their dad slept.

"We can meet in a day or two and I'll give you the complete profiles of a few families who meet your criteria. In the meantime, if you want, you can look through the profiles we have online." She pulled a business card out of her bag and slid it between Norah and Jimmy. "Feel free to call with any questions or concerns."

Since she already had Teagan's card, Norah wondered if she was leaving it for Jimmy, but she didn't ask.

Teagan left and Jimmy leaned back in his chair. "You sure about this?"

"Yeah." Continuing to say it out loud made it feel right.

"But like Teagan said, I have time. The baby's not due for weeks yet. I'm going to e-mail Avery and let him know I've decided on adoption. I think that should come from me before he gets official paperwork."

Moira reached out and held her hand. "We're here for you."

"Thanks."

Jimmy put his arm around her and pulled her close. "I wish there was something else I could do to help."

Norah laid her head on his shoulder like she had many times as a child. "Knowing you're here is enough. That you support my decision. Now if you could deal with Dad and our brothers, you'd be my hero."

"Don't worry about them. I'll handle it."

Maybe she was a chicken because she not only asked him to do it, but she would actually let him.

Norah left Jimmy and Moira and drove to Kai's house. Before going in, she sat in her car for a few minutes and e-mailed Avery. It took a few tries, especially since she was typing on her phone, but she wanted him to know what her plans were and she asked where they should send the paperwork. He'd probably already started classes, so sending things to his parents' house wouldn't be a good move.

After she hit send, she sat and just breathed. It felt like a weight had been lifted. Movement at Kai's house caught her attention. A tall woman swung out the door. Her cascade of black hair hung down her back. Kai held the door open for her as they spoke. The woman laughed and Norah almost rolled down her window so she could hear it. The woman stood nearly as tall as Kai and she leaned over and kissed his cheek. When she turned to walk down the stairs, Norah stared. The woman was stunning. Like goddess-level amazing. If that was what Kai normally liked, it was no wonder he had no interest in her.

Besides the whole big-belly pregnancy thing.

She needed to get her head on straight and focus on the future. She was moving forward, making plans. She'd get her life together and then find someone. Maybe even someone better than Avery.

She left her car and went to the door. Rather than let herself in, she knocked since she knew Kai was still home. She didn't want to walk in on him in an inopportune moment again. Like fresh from a shower. She'd almost needed to hose herself down after yesterday. She'd thought seeing him lifting weights was bad, with all the glistening skin. Wearing nothing more than a towel was unbelievable. His damp hair was down and had a little wave to it. And all that inked skin . . .

Ugh. She was supposed to be getting her head on straight. Not thinking about a mostly naked Kai.

Speaking of . . . he answered the door just as she tried to shove those images from her head.

"I gave you a key."

"Yeah, but I knew you were home because I saw you walk your guest out. I figured you didn't need me walking in on you taking a shower again." Double crap. She hadn't wanted to say that last part out loud.

His lips twitched as if he might smile. He said nothing as he stepped away from the door. He stood in the entryway and waited for her to step over the threshold. He spoke in a near whisper. "My mom finished her therapy and fell asleep on the couch. We thought it would be easier for her to get up from there."

"Okay. Any errands today?"

"Ask her when she wakes up." He walked through the living room, grabbed his keys, and nodded a good-bye before he walked out the door.

Norah stood in the living room where Ms. Ellis snored quietly on the couch. She had nothing to do, so she picked up Ms. Ellis's book to find out what Bret and Carrie had been up to. She easily got lost in the characters' love story.

The following morning, Norah checked her e-mail while she ate her yogurt. Avery had responded. She clicked and tried to ignore the flutter in her stomach.

Norah, We need to talk. Don't sign anything or do anything permanent until we do. Classes just started and I'm swamped, but I'll call you late tonight, maybe around 10.

Avery's words warmed her. Maybe he had just needed time to think about it and process it. He didn't want her to make a decision yet. Maybe he wanted them to raise this baby together.

She tossed her spoon in the sink and let that thought gather speed in her brain. She wasn't ready to be a mom. Would Avery's presence and willingness to help change that?

As scared as she was about everything, she knew it might change things. While she wasn't madly in love with him, she cared about him and could see herself falling in love with him. But they didn't need to be in love to raise their child.

Norah got ready to go to Kai's house. She packed her laptop so she could check into her options for school during Ms. Ellis's nap. As she drove to work, she tried to tamp down the anticipation and excitement brewing. Avery wanted to talk about their baby. That was huge because she'd already written him off.

When she arrived at Kai's house, Ms. Ellis was awake

and barking orders at Kai. This day just got better and better. He looked up at Norah and she was pretty sure he was relieved to see her. Ms. Ellis was fighting about using the motion machine on the couch.

"Hi, Ms. Ellis."

The old woman grunted at her.

"You know, it's a beautiful day out. Instead of sitting on the couch with the machine, maybe we should try a walk down the block."

"She can't do stairs."

Ms. Ellis crossed her arms and Norah rolled her eyes.

"You have what? Five stairs out there? She needs the practice. It'll be good for her to get out in the fresh air."

Ms. Ellis smiled. "Help me up," she said to Kai.

He helped her to her feet and then followed her to the front door. Norah pocketed the house key. On the porch, she pushed past Kai. "We got this."

He leaned close and whispered in her ear, "What if she falls?"

"She won't."

"I can hear you, Kai."

"We'll take it slow. Take breaks as needed." Norah tilted her face up. "Everyone needs to feel the sun sometimes."

Her own words hit her hard. She needed this almost as much as Ms. Ellis. To breathe fresh air and bask in the sun without worry.

Kai threw his hands up. "I'm going to work. I have a late client tonight, is that a problem?"

"Nope," Norah answered. Then she remembered her conversation with Avery. Ms. Ellis would be asleep by then, so Norah could talk to Avery in private. Taking the conversation here would be even better than at home where nosy brothers might try to listen.

Kai disappeared without another word and Norah helped Ms. Ellis down the front walk. It was slow but steady and the pace allowed Norah's mind to wander over thoughts of Avery and what life with him might look like.

Her imagination had decided to rule the day. She couldn't stop thinking about Avery and finally talking to him after all these months. Her day sped by with thoughts of him interrupting every task, but she kept busy helping Ms. Ellis with exercises and making her lunch and reading to her.

Kai came home to help get his mom into bed. He said nothing other than good night to his mom and left again. As Norah closed the novel she'd been reading to Ms. Ellis, anticipation surged through her. She kept checking the time, wondering exactly when Avery would call.

When ten o'clock neared, she grabbed a glass of water and sat at the kitchen table willing her phone to ring. It finally vibrated in her hand and she almost jumped out of her skin. "Hello?"

"Hey, Norah."

His voice was smooth and friendly and she realized how much she'd missed him.

"How are you?"

"I'm good. I'm doing okay." She twirled her glass of water. This was stupid. She didn't know what to say. "The baby is healthy. A girl."

"A baby girl," he whispered. "I'm sorry I was an asshole when you called. Why did you wait so long?"

She shrugged and then sighed. "I was scared and confused. I didn't want to be pregnant so I acted like I wasn't. Until I couldn't. Then my aunt threw me out and I was a mess. It took coming home to Chicago to get my act together. I'm sorry. I should've called you a long time ago."

"It's a lot to take in, you know? I don't have answers. I still have this year of school to finish and then I have to find a job. That's where all my focus has been. Except for thoughts of you. I couldn't figure out why you were blowing me off this summer. I thought we had a good thing."

"We did. And like you said, it's a lot to take in."

"Don't give our baby away." His words came out in a rush.

Norah's heart jumped into her throat and lodged there, beating rapidly, cutting off her air supply.

"You know my parents have money. That I have money. I can provide for my child."

Norah smiled. She knew Avery was a good guy. "I know. I never implied you couldn't. I just don't think we're ready. Do you?"

Silence met her.

"Avery?"

"I'm still here. I don't know what you expect."

The sudden edge to his tone cut her. She swallowed hard before continuing. "A baby needs more than money. How would we raise her? Where? As a couple or two independent parents?"

"I'm offering you financial support."

Those five words hanging between them were enough to make her cry. Financial support. That's all her own father had ever been. Her eyes filled and her throat burned, but she pushed on. "Money isn't enough. I can't be a parent by myself."

"So you're going to abandon our baby?"

The tears started to fall and her breath caught. Of all the things he could've accused her of, it was like he knew this would hurt the most.

"You're going to leave her just like your family pushed you away."

"It's not the same," she choked out.

"Yeah, it is."

Her anger rose above the hurt. "You're not stepping up to be a father. You think it's okay to abandon her as long as you throw some cash her way. She needs to be loved and cared for. I am *not* abandoning my daughter. I'm finding a place for her where she has a chance at a real life with people who not only want her and are ready for her but will also love her."

"Well, I guess you're going to do whatever you want. Send the papers to my school. I'll text you the address." He disconnected without another word.

Norah sat staring at her phone until a text buzzed through with Avery's address. Huge sobs jerked her body. Why the hell had she thought he'd want to be with her? That they would make some kind of family? She was in this alone and she needed to accept that.

Chapter Six

Kai parked in front of the house and saw Norah's car still there. He'd figured she'd be gone since his mother was always in bed before ten. With his luck, he'd find Norah sleeping peacefully on his couch and then he'd have to rein in the desire to touch her.

For the past couple of days, they'd fallen into a routine where he'd been successful at having very little contact with her and it was working for him. She'd given him a hard time about his mom this morning, but their interaction had still been minimal. Which was fine by him.

He let himself into the house determined to wake her and send her on her way so he could enjoy the remainder of his night in peace. Except she wasn't on the couch or in the living room at all. He peeked into his mom's room where a small night-light illuminated the space. Mom was sound asleep. Where the hell was Norah? No sound came from anywhere in the house.

He moved to the kitchen and flipped on the light. She bolted from her seat, swiping at her face.

"Sorry. I didn't realize you were home." She stared at the floor as she moved around the table.

"What's wrong?" Even as the words left his mouth, he knew he shouldn't ask. That he shouldn't care.

"Nothing. I'm fine." Her voice wobbled as she spoke and he thought she might not be done yet.

He stood in her path and touched her shoulder. "What happened?"

"It's nothing. You know, hormones." She waved a hand but still didn't look up.

He knew all about the hormones she'd been throwing around, but this wasn't the same. Even he wasn't clueless enough to buy that. Then he did the unthinkable. With his fingers, he touched her jaw, tipping her face up. "Tell me."

Her throat worked and she licked her lips. The movement had him wanting to shift closer to taste her. He locked his legs to prevent movement.

"I had a conversation with the baby's father. I told him I planned on adoption."

"And the problem?"

She pulled from the slight grasp he had on her face. "It's stupid. It's me and my dumb imagination. When I e-mailed him that I planned on adoption—"

Kai cut her off. "You did that in an e-mail?"

"Our last conversation didn't go well. He accused me of lying about the baby being his." She licked her lips again. "Anyway, he e-mailed back he didn't want me to make any decision yet." She shook her head. "In my twisted mind, I interpreted that to mean he wanted the baby."

"What does he want?"

"Basically to hand me money to raise our child. He doesn't want any further involvement."

Kai thought of his own deadbeat dad. "It's more than a lot of guys would do."

"Really? So I should be grateful?" She looked up. Fresh tears welled in her eyes.

Fuck. "I didn't say that."

"Forget it. I'm sorry I stayed so long. I lost track of time." She moved to step around him, but he didn't budge.

He couldn't let her leave like this. Her hands shook. "You're too upset to drive."

"I'm fine." Yet she was back to staring at the floor.

He shifted closer and held her face again. A surge of lust shot through him and he squashed it. "You're not fine," he said quietly.

Tears fell and he wanted to run but couldn't. Her pale blue eyes were crystal clear and drew him in. "What did you want from him?"

A tear tracked down her cheek and hit his hand.

"It's not even what I want. It's what I thought. Part of me—okay, a lot of me—thought he was going to want to be together. That he'd want us to be a family to raise our child."

More tears fell and Kai brushed them away with his thumb.

"It's stupid." Her lips trembled.

She looked defeated, which didn't match any other image he had of her. It made him angry. "Do you love him?"

Kai didn't really want the answer. It was torture to even ask.

Her laugh came out as a half choke, half sob. "That's the sick part. I don't think I do. I think I could've if we gave it a shot, but I haven't seen him in months." She closed her eyes. When she spoke again, her voice was barely above a whisper. "When we were together though, it was good."

He didn't want to try to explain why he felt relieved by her answer. He didn't want her to love a guy who didn't want to be with her. No wonder his mom saw Norah as being like him. She was searching for a safety net. It was why she'd come back to her family.

Kai didn't have any words to comfort her, so he continued down the path of doing what he shouldn't. He pulled her close and held her. At first she stiffened in his arms, but when she realized it was nothing more than a hug, she relaxed. A breath shuddered through her and she hiccupped. Another moment passed and her arms wrapped around him and she held tight.

He'd wanted to comfort her the way he'd comfort Jaleesa, but no matter what he thought, his body had a different reaction. She smelled delicious and inviting as the scent of her perfume or shampoo wafted up to his nose. He caught a breath full of her and he wondered what it would be like to bury his face in her neck and inhale.

When her crying stopped and his shirt was damp, she pulled away. Her face was blotchy and her eyes red-rimmed. Heartbreaking sadness filled her face.

She wiped her cheeks. "I'm sorry. I shouldn't have pulled you into my drama."

"It's okay." But it wasn't. He'd spent years carefully crafting his life to be drama-free. He didn't want to care. It didn't stop him from wanting to pull her close again.

In the quiet of the kitchen, the only sounds were the hum of the refrigerator and their breathing. She stared at him and he couldn't help but look at her mouth again.

She let loose a nervous laugh. "I'm a mess." She pushed at her hair and patted her cheeks.

"You're gorgeous." Even with her blotchy cheeks and tearful eyes, her smile was beautiful.

She snorted and averted her eyes again.

Hand on her jaw, he brought her face up as he lowered himself to be eye to eye. "Don't."

"What?"

"Don't put yourself down." She stood so close, her eyes pleading for proof of what he said, and he lost the bit of control he'd been clinging to. The hand cradling her jaw slid back to her neck and brought her mouth to his.

She sucked in a quick breath but didn't protest. Her

eyes fluttered closed. Her lips parted immediately, inviting him in to taste her. Her hand fisted in his shirt as their tongues met.

The rush he felt told him it was a mistake. He could get drunk on her like this. Anything more would be explosive. And he couldn't afford that.

With a hand on her hip, he pushed her gently as he pulled away. The small distance was like a cold breeze blowing over his skin. She blinked, eyes wide.

His fingers flinched. "Sorry." He released her and took a full step back. "I shouldn't have done that."

She took a step toward him, but he held up a hand. Regardless of how much he wanted her right now, he said, "You should go home now."

She froze, looking more stunned than she had when he'd first walked in the room. He waited for her to tell him off, call him an asshole, something. Instead, she nodded and left the room. He leaned against the wall and tried to figure out how many ways he'd just fucked himself when she came back into the kitchen with her purse on her shoulder and keys in hand.

"What time do you need me tomorrow?"

Such an innocent and unassuming question. He needed her now, wanted her more than he'd ever let on. Yet he strove to answer her question as normally as possible. "Weekends are really busy. I usually go in by ten and I could be there until midnight, but I can have Jaleesa come by for a while if you can't be here all day."

"I have another appointment but it shouldn't take too long. I can be here by noon if that's okay."

"It's fine." Better than fine because then he'd already be gone before she arrived and he could go back to keeping a safe distance.

She walked silently through the house and all he heard was the quiet *click* of the front door as she left.

* * *

Norah left her meeting with Teagan with five folders containing the profiles of couples Teagan thought Norah might like. Norah had told Teagan about her conversation with Avery, leaving out the ridiculousness of her imagination. She gave Teagan his address to send him the information.

Now on her way to Kai's house, she realized how much she loved the regularity of having a job. Sure, the hours were a bit wonky, but so was her sleep schedule these days. The baby kicked and punched every time Norah crawled into bed. And being at Kai's house gave her a chance to be alone to think. Ms. Ellis didn't need much and she always went to bed early.

Since Kai had said he'd be working until midnight, Norah had told her brothers she'd be late. She planned to use the late-night quiet to look over the profiles from Teagan. She hadn't mentioned anything else to Jimmy, not her conversation with Avery or her meeting with Teagan. Although she liked knowing Jimmy was there for her, she felt the need to do this on her own.

Norah knocked on the door before using her key. Kai had said his sister would be here this morning, so Norah didn't want to assume she'd have gone already. She'd learned her lesson every time she'd thought Kai was gone. Just as she was about to pull out her key, the door swung open and the beautiful goddess from the other day stood before her.

"You must be Norah."

"Uh, yeah."

The woman stepped back from the door. "I'm Jaleesa, Kai's sister."

His sister? Now she felt dumb for jumping to conclusions. She forced her feet forward. "Nice to meet you."

"I can't thank you enough for taking this job. I'm sure it's not easy."

"I like it. Your mom isn't hard to work with."

Jaleesa let out a laugh that seemed too big to come from her thin frame. "You must be playing nice then because difficult is something she's perfected."

Norah smiled. "Like I told Kai, my dad owns the real estate on the corner of crotchety and cranky. Difficult is nothing new to me."

Jaleesa laughed again, which put Norah at ease. Now that she got a close look at the woman, she could see the resemblance between the siblings, height not being the only thing they shared. Her eyes were as dark as his and the wave to her hair reminded Norah of when Kai had just gotten out of the shower. Hearing Jaleesa laugh made Norah wonder what Kai's laugh sounded like.

As she walked ahead of Norah, Jaleesa spoke over her shoulder. "I already made lunch for my mom and we've done her exercises for now. Kai told me you got her out of the house the other day. It would be great if you could make that happen again."

Norah followed her through the house to the kitchen where Ms. Ellis sat at the table finishing a sandwich. She looked up from her food. "'Bout time you got here. These children of mine treat me like I can't do anything."

Norah smiled. "I guess we know better, don't we, Ms. Ellis?"

"I think you can start calling me Lani."

Norah wasn't sure she could do that. "We'll see."

The woman laughed and waved her hands. "You've washed my underwear and read about sex with me. I think we're friends."

Norah froze and her cheeks flamed. Jaleesa ran a hand down Norah's arm. "Mom, you're embarrassing her." She leaned over and said, "I'm aware of the smut my mom reads. Don't even pay attention."

Norah wanted to defend Ms. Ellis and then realized there was no need because the woman spoke up just fine for herself.

"It's not smut. They're good stories. Better than most of the junk on TV. It keeps my brain working too so I won't have to worry about Alzheimer's and being put in a home."

Jaleesa rolled her eyes. "The woman's greatest fear is being put in a home."

Norah helped Ms. Ellis—Lani—back to the living room while Jaleesa cleaned up the dishes. Jaleesa seemed to be the opposite of Kai. She was friendly and talkative and made jokes. She was as beautiful as he was hot, so they had that in common, but their personalities were so different.

She thought about her own brothers. They weren't that different. Sure, Kevin was always starting trouble and making jokes, but none of them would qualify as talkers. She supposed it was a guy thing. Jaleesa thanked her again on the way out, and Norah and Lani spent the afternoon reading and taking a couple of small walks.

By nine o'clock, Lani was tucked into bed and Norah curled on the couch to read the profiles that had been tugging her attention all day. She didn't know what to expect. How would she know who would be the right parents for her baby girl?

She did a cursory look at all of them and found that all five were structured in a similar manner. They contained a letter to expectant parents and tons of photos of family and friends and their homes. Norah immediately put two of the files aside because the couples lived in an apartment or condo. They were nice places and more than Norah could hope to afford, but she wanted her daughter to have a backyard and neighbors to play with. She wanted her to have a neighborhood like she had grown up in.

Then she read the remaining three. They all seemed like decent, caring people. She studied the pictures, waiting for something to jump out at her like a beacon saying "This one!"

Unfortunately, that didn't happen. Lila and James, Kim and Trevor, and Brittany and Robert all appeared to be competent adults who wanted a child. She returned to the files again and read the letters the couples wrote. Kim and Trevor made her laugh with their dorkiness. She liked that. The other couples were very serious in their letters, and there was nothing wrong with that. Her heart went out to them. But she liked that someone could be silly and joke.

She sat for hours in the dim light of the living room. At some point, she must've dozed off because suddenly she felt someone staring at her. Her eyes popped open to find Kai standing in front of her, keys in hand.

"Didn't mean to scare you."

"It's okay." She fumbled with the folders on her lap, gathering them like they were a secret.

"You could've left after my mom went to sleep."

"I know. But in all honesty, I like the quiet here. I had some stuff to go through." She sighed as she stared at the folders.

Kai shifted awkwardly. He always seemed to be out of his element with her. It didn't help that he'd kissed her yesterday and then immediately regretted it. She needed to get out of here and give the man the space he obviously wanted.

She stood and two of the three folders slid from her grasp. Kai bent at the same time she squatted to retrieve them. There on the floor, they were eye to eye and their hands brushed on top of the folders. The touch was nothing, yet every time he was this close her pulse spiked like it was the first time a boy looked at her.

Stupid hormones.

Kai grabbed the folders and stood, holding out a hand to help her up. She knew better, knew she should use the couch for leverage, but she couldn't help herself. Palm against his, she allowed him to haul her up. The baby chose that moment to pummel her. "Oh." Her free hand went to her belly.

"You okay?"

"Yeah. I guess she doesn't like sudden movement."

"Shit. Sorry. I shouldn't have jerked you up."

"It's fine." Their hands were still connected and she liked the warmth she found there, but she let go to reach for the folders.

Before handing them over, he read the cover. With only a raised eyebrow, he returned them to her.

"Prospective adoptive parents."

"You get to pick?"

Norah nodded.

"That's cool."

She shook her head. "Not really. It's a shitload of pressure. What if I choose wrong? How do you know who's good enough? Is anyone really?" She was rambling and couldn't stop. And she *knew* he didn't care. "On paper they all look fabulous but that's the plan, you know? Even I can make myself look awesome on paper. That doesn't tell me the real stuff, the deep down who-you-are stuff."

To his credit, Kai stood and listened. He didn't say anything. He just let her rant. She hadn't even realized how frustrated she was by the process.

"We all carry baggage. How do I know if their baggage is greater or less than mine? What if they turn out to be assholes?" Then she voiced her greatest fear, the words barely making it out. "What if they don't love her as much as they say they will?"

Tears clawed at her. She was so tired of crying. She was

not a crier. Not when kids teased her for her lack of style as an eight-year-old. Not when she'd broken her arm wrestling with Tommy when she was ten. Not even when Jimmy sent her away at twelve. She pressed her lips together to stop the embarrassing tremble.

"Ah, shit," Kai whispered.

Suddenly she was enveloped in his arms again. She breathed deeply and enjoyed the sensation of being held, but she didn't let the tears fall.

"Haven't they been vetted?" Kai asked.

"Of course the agency does that. But some assholes are good at covering up how bad they are." She spoke into his chest because she wasn't ready to be alone again.

A low laugh rumbled under her ear. It wasn't a full laugh like she'd heard from Jaleesa, but it was pretty damn good.

"You have a point. Some of us are good at hiding our true asshole nature."

She laughed, the tears creeping at the corners of her eyes. "I wasn't making any reference to you. Besides, I'm not sure you qualify as someone who hides it."

He took a half step back and put a hand over his heart. "And I thought you bought my act."

"Yeah, well you don't fool me." She touched his arm to convey she knew better. Under the tough guy act, he was nice. "Thank you."

He pointed to the folders. "So what are you going to do?"

"Hell if I know."

"I think you go with your gut. Like when you go to the dog pound to get a puppy. They all look cute and they're vying for your attention. You choose the one you immediately have a connection with."

She snorted on a laugh. "Did you seriously just compare the adoption of my baby to choosing a puppy?"

"I guess I did. I'm not saying it's the same. Follow your

gut. All things being equal, who's the one couple you felt connected to?"

That was easy—Kim and Trevor because their profile made her laugh.

Kai pointed at her. "Right there. Whoever came into your mind right now." He bent and grabbed her bag for her, sliding it carefully onto her shoulder.

It definitely gave her something to think about. She shoved the folders in her bag. "Thanks. I don't mean to keep dumping my problems on you."

He lifted a shoulder causing the muscles of his chest to ripple. "I dumped my mom on you."

She smiled. "True, but you pay me for that."

"Jaleesa said great things about you. She bent my ear for my entire dinner break. She said my mom really likes you."

"I like her too." She pulled her keys from her bag. "Do you need me tomorrow? I know Tommy doesn't usually work Sundays, but I didn't know if you're closed."

"Sometimes I'll make an exception, but I'm mostly closed on Sundays. Take the day off."

"Monday?"

"Monday's light for me, too, so take the extra day."

"Good night." She left Kai's house with too many emotions fighting for attention, much like the puppies Kai mentioned. She thought about Kim and Trevor, though, and decided she should meet them before making a decision to look further. That small resolution helped with her battered emotions. Who'd've thought Kai, man of few words, would manage to say just the right ones to help her?

Norah stayed in bed late on Sunday morning. Well, at least as late as her bladder would allow. The sun brightened her room. After going to the bathroom and brushing her hair and teeth, she lay back in bed debating getting dressed. She had absolutely nothing to do today.

The thought should've bothered her as much as it had last week, but since she was among the land of the employed she was content to have a day off. Her bedroom window was open allowing a breeze to flutter the curtains.

She heard Tommy and Sean working on Tommy's car at the curb.

"When the hell was the last time you changed the oil?" Sean was practically yelling.

The lack of response from Tommy made her smile. He was kind of forgetful. Norah pushed off the bed and looked outside.

Sean was bent and the top half of his body was under the hood. Tommy stood back with his hands in his pockets.

A cab pulled up at the curb drawing Norah's attention. Cabs didn't ride through this neighborhood. Even when people needed to get to the airport they asked a neighbor for a lift.

A man climbed from the cab and Norah's heart stopped. Avery. She pulled back from the window as he approached the house. As she turned toward the stairs, she heard Tommy ask, "Can I help you?"

Oh, shit. She waddled down the stairs and to the front door as quickly as her swollen feet would carry her.

Pushing out the screen door, she found both Tommy and Avery on the porch. Sean stood at the curb, leaning against the car as he watched.

Tommy pointed at Avery. "He says he knows you. From Boston."

Norah's mouth dried as she moved forward to get between them. Tommy would never hit her.

"Yes, I know Avery." She placed her hands on her belly. Tommy's eyes narrowed. "This is him?"

She inhaled deeply. "Avery is the baby's father."

Tommy's hands clenched. She patted his arm. "It's okay."

He nodded and looked at Avery over her shoulder. "I'll be at the curb watching."

Tommy walked down the stairs and spoke quietly to Sean. Norah turned to Avery. "What are you doing here?"

"I wanted to see you. I don't like the way we left things."

Norah looked at her brothers and then at the house. Her dad was in the living room as usual. Which would be worse?

She opted for remaining in view of Sean and Tommy. "Want to sit?" she asked, pointing to the steps.

He nodded and held her arm as she lowered herself to the concrete. When he sat beside her, Tommy stared. She tried to ignore him. At least he'd handled Avery's appearance better than she'd thought.

"How are you?" he asked.

"Okay. I feel huge and can't see my feet, but the baby is healthy."

"I'm sorry for what I said on the phone about abandoning our baby." He reached over and took her hand. "It was a horrible thing to say."

Tears pricked the backs of her eyes. "I've thought a lot about this, Avery. It wasn't a decision I made lightly."

"I know, but it's huge."

"Yeah." She huffed a small laugh and rubbed her belly. "I considered keeping her. My brother Jimmy said he'd help and I know he meant it. But I want more for my kid than what I can offer. I want her to have a better life than I did growing up."

"I can support our kid."

"But it's more than money. I had financial support

growing up. It's not enough. Neither of us is ready to be a parent."

He nodded, his eyes never leaving her face. "You're right."

Avery still held her hand, but she felt nothing. None of the old stirrings cropped up. Sure, now her hormones fled.

"I'm sorry for the way I handled this. I should've told you right away."

"Why didn't you?" he asked.

She smiled and bit her lip. "Truth?"

He nodded.

"I was afraid you'd want to stay together and raise it."

"Oh." He slid his hand away as if she expected a proposal.

"I just . . . I know you're a stand-up guy. Even without getting married, I thought you might pressure me to keep her." She wiped her palms on her thighs, suddenly nervous and feeling like a fool.

"Well, you got it half right. I shouldn't have tried to pressure you. But I'm not ready for marriage. We've known each other for less than a year and most of that we were apart."

"I know." She shook her head and stared at the street where her brothers went back under the hood. After all the hoopla when she came home, they were leaving her to handle this. They trusted her. Go figure.

"So what do we do now?"

"I'm working with an adoption counselor. Teagan. She'll be sending you the paperwork. Right now, I'm looking at couples who want to adopt."

"You get to choose?"

"Yep. I have a couple I really like. We're meeting tomorrow if you want to join us." She turned to face him.

He sank against the step. "I can't. I'm flying back out tonight. I have class tomorrow."

"You flew all the way to Chicago for a day? To see me?"

He smiled. It was open and friendly. The kind of smile that drew her to him in the first place. "I needed to know we were okay. I want to know about how the adoption works. I want to hear it from you."

"Come inside and I'll show you the profiles of the couples I have, especially the one I think is a good fit." She angled and reached for the rail, but Avery jumped up and held out his hands for her. He hauled her to her feet. "I'm glad you came."

"So am I."

She waved to Tommy who had turned his attention back to them. "We're going in." As Avery walked up the steps, she mouthed to Tommy, *Thank you.*

She led Avery through the living room and to the kitchen where they might get a little privacy. Pulling the files from her bag, she said, "These are the first five I got. I immediately cut two because they don't live in houses. I want our baby to have a house with a yard and a neighborhood with friends and a mom and dad."

"It's a good way to grow up."

She knew he understood. He'd grown up that way. She put Kim and Trevor's file on top. "This is the couple I like. The couple I'm meeting tomorrow."

He opened the folder and she let him read in peace. He chuckled just as she'd done when she read the letter. When he moved on to the other profiles, she tried to fill him in on the process.

"So the baby will grow up knowing she's adopted and who you are?"

"And you if you want. You can visit and be part of her life." She swallowed. "That's how I know I'm not abandoning our baby. I'll be there, but I won't be the person responsible. I can love her and not worry about screwing her up."

"You'd make a great mom."

"I don't know. Maybe one day."

"When do you think you'll decide about who gets the baby?"

"Do you want to be part of that? I mean, we can make more appointments to meet with couples or maybe we can Skype the meeting. I don't know."

"I trust you to pick someone good. That's part of why I wanted to be here. To make sure you were sure. But it seems like you have this handled. If you want to call me and give me updates, that would be good, but I don't think I want to choose parents for my child."

"Okay. But you'll sign all the papers, right?"

"Yeah."

Avery stayed for an hour and her family left them alone. They didn't try to bully Avery, but they were there if she needed them. Turned out, she didn't. Avery had accepted her decision. He'd even talked to his parents about it. It had been at their urging that he came to Chicago.

When a cab showed to take Avery back to his hotel, Norah walked him out. She promised to keep him updated about her plans. He waved as he climbed into the car and Tommy jogged up the steps to her.

"You okay?"

"Yeah. I'm glad you didn't beat him up."

"I really only wanted to do that the first night you came home."

She shot him an incredulous look.

"Okay. Maybe a little longer. But you were right. You made your decisions. He didn't do this to you and he was man enough to show up here. I'm assuming he wanted to discuss plans?"

"Yeah. We're good." She threw her arms around him and hugged him as tightly as she could. "Thanks."

"For what?"

"Being here."

"Anytime, squirt."

Chapter Seven

Kai had no idea his mom could be so exhausting. How the hell had Norah done this all week? Every time he turned around, Mom was calling him for something else. He only hoped that by eight she'd be as tired as he was so he could have his biweekly poker game without interruption.

Right now, she sat on the couch reading a book with some news channel droning in the background. This might be his only chance to escape to buy the beer he needed for tonight. He grabbed his keys. "I'm running to the store, Mom. I have some friends coming over."

"Friends? Like a party?"

"No. We play poker. Don't worry. We'll be in the basement so no one will bother you."

"Do I get to meet these friends?"

His muscles flinched at the thought. "No." He didn't offer any other explanation, including the fact that she already knew—and hated—most of the guys that were coming.

Before she could bitch or ask anything else, he rushed out the door. He couldn't wait for her knee to return to normal so he could have his house and his life back. At the store, he grabbed a case of beer and as he cut through the next aisle, he noticed the yogurt display. He knew Norah had finished the few containers she'd left at his house. He tried to remember what she liked. Something gross. Then he remembered the green label. Lime. He scanned the shelf and stacked cups on top of the case of beer before moving carefully to the checkout.

The cashier glanced at his purchase and smiled. "Interesting blend. Lime yogurt and beer."

He handed her cash and grabbed the bag with the yogurt and his beer and left. Back in his car, he had no desire to go back home. How long could he sit parked before his mom started calling him?

He was being selfish and he knew it. On the way home, he stopped to pick up dinner. Although he handled most of the same things Norah had done for his mom all week, including a slow-as-hell walk a few houses down, he wasn't going to cook dinner. Chicken in a bucket would be fine.

Juggling the bag, the bucket of chicken, and his beer, he nudged the car door closed and stomped up the stairs. "Hey, Mom. I brought dinner," he called as soon as he cleared the door.

He turned the corner and saw his mom standing, leaning against the chair, gripping tight to the back. Dumping everything on the table, he rushed to her. "What's wrong?"

"I got up to go to the bathroom. I did okay. But then I couldn't get back onto the couch. My leg didn't want to cooperate."

"How long have you been standing here?" He grabbed her elbow and felt the tremble.

"Not too long. I knew you'd be back soon. The store is like a repellent for you."

He didn't believe her for a minute, but let her have the lie. He eased her back to the couch. "You okay now?"

She released a deep breath. "I'm fine." Then her gaze landed on the table. "What'd you buy?"

"I brought chicken for dinner. Beer for poker."

"In the bag." She eyed him like she knew.

"Yogurt for Norah."

"Hmmm."

"Don't hmmm me. I was at the store. I remembered there wasn't any in the fridge. If the only perk she gets for spending her entire day with you is disgusting lime yogurt, it's the least I could provide."

"Of course. I think it's nice you think of her on her day off is all."

For Christ's sake. He grabbed the bag of yogurt and pointed at her. "Do not try any of your matchmaking bullshit. Norah has enough going on in her life without you meddling."

In that moment he realized what his mother had done. He told her not to interfere in order to protect Norah, not himself. Unlike his normal self-centered response. His mom had routinely pushed herself into his life to *fix* it, and he'd always told her to butt out. These women were going to make him crazy. He took the yogurt to the kitchen and shoved the whole bag into the fridge.

It had only been a week. How the fuck had they wheedled their way into his life? His mom, he'd expected. He liked her living with Jaleesa for that reason. The physical separation meant less interference. But he hadn't seen Norah coming. He shouldn't give a fuck. He knew better. But it had only gotten worse since he kissed her. She so openly let him into her life in a way he didn't understand.

And he didn't want to.

Maybe some extra space would be good. He was glad he'd given her the extra day off. She deserved it and if it gave him some distance from her, even better.

He grabbed plates and silverware for dinner and pushed

Norah from his mind. Poker night was exactly what he needed to forget about women.

Hours later, his mom was in bed, cell phone beside her in case she needed to reach him, and he was in the basement setting up for poker. Beer cold in the mini-fridge, ashtrays out for cigars or whatever else the guys might smoke, chairs in place, cards ready. He'd already texted the guys and told them to come around back to the basement door, which he'd left propped open.

Rooster was the first to show, bottle of whiskey in hand. "Afraid to let your neighbors see us now? Were they complaining about the thugs you brought to the neighborhood?"

"Yeah, asshole, you're an embarrassment." They shook hands and Rooster thumped his back.

"Sorry about your mom. She okay?"

"We both know you two can't stand each other, which is why you had to use the back door. She's upstairs."

"I ain't got no gripe with your mom. She hates me. I get it. History, you know? But I wouldn't wish her any harm."

Just then, Eric and Carlos came in. "What's with the secret entrance bullshit?"

"My mom is upstairs recovering from surgery." He didn't say anything else. These were his childhood friends, the guys his mom had done everything she could to keep him from because they were a bad influence. She hadn't been totally wrong, but they were still his friends.

The guys each popped the tops on their beer and opened the chips Eric had brought. Rooster took a swig directly from the whiskey bottle and passed it to Carlos. They settled in to their usual catching up while they waited for Dean. He showed up a few minutes later and the game was ready to begin.

Carlos opened the deck of cards and shuffled as everyone pulled out money. They didn't bother with using chips.

Their pot was all cash. With an unlit cigar in his mouth, Carlos asked, "Your mom doing okay?"

"She's getting better, for the most part. It's a long road though."

"What do you do with her all day? Why not put her in rehab?" Dean asked.

"She refused. I got a girl who comes in and stays with her while I'm at work."

Rooster laid his cards on the table and leaned forward. "A girl? You holding out on us?"

"I pay her to take care of my mom."

"What else does the pay cover?"

"Shut the fuck up and play cards."

Rooster picked up his cards and arranged them in his hand. "When do we get to meet her?"

"Never. Your ugly ass'll scare her away." He tossed a buck into the center of the table.

"She must be hot if you're trying to keep her all to yourself."

He knew Rooster was fucking with him and he shouldn't let it bother him, but it did.

"Come on, man. We always used to share."

Kai ground his teeth together. Shit like that reminded him why he only saw Rooster at the poker game. They ran together for years, but Rooster never moved past teenage stupidity.

"Ante up," Carlos called, breaking the tension.

Kai's phone buzzed on the table. He glanced at it. Mom. "Fuck." He slammed his cards down. "I'll be right back."

He went up to help his mom get to the bathroom. Hopefully it would be the last trip for the night. He tucked her back in, made sure her phone was close, and turned off the light. He hadn't even gotten to the stairs when she called him.

"Yeah?"

"Can you get me a glass of water?"

He sighed, but got the water and delivered it to her. "Anything else?"

"I'm good."

Back in the basement, Dean looked at him when he took his seat. "Problem?"

Kai shook his head. He wouldn't give any of them, especially Rooster, the ammunition to give him shit over taking his mom to the bathroom. Over the next hour, she managed to interrupt two more times before he called her on it.

"No more, Mom. I know you don't do this to Norah."

"I don't know what you're talking about."

He sighed. "Good night."

Back at the poker table, where he'd lost every hand and was easily down fifty bucks, he barked at Dean, "Deal."

"Yes, sir," Dean mumbled.

Kai stared at the crap hand he'd been dealt. Like his life. He folded quickly, not wanting to lose more money.

Rooster followed and while the rest of the guys played out their hands, Rooster sat at the weight bench and did some curls. "Hey, man. I want to talk about getting some new ink."

Kai didn't even turn around. "Talk somewhere else. You know I don't do that."

One rule he'd made for himself after getting out of jail was no more gang affiliation. No jobs, no tattoos, nothing. Rooster was his only connection to the life he left behind. Even the other guys had grown up and left it all.

The weights clunked back into place. "Come on, man. You know I don't roll like that anymore. I want this one for my kids."

Rooster had three kids with three different baby mamas.

"I want them here." He tapped his chest right over his heart.

"So go to whoever gave you the rest of your ink."

"That's bullshit. My money's as good as anyone else's."

"Anyone who comes to me looking for gang tats is told to hit the road."

"This is personal. I've always preferred your work. You know that." He stood and went back to his seat to get ready for the next hand.

Kai wasn't sure how deep Rooster was still into the gang. Kai hadn't been with them long. Not compared to most guys. Long enough to get busted. He and Rooster broke into a house. They had a job to steal the drugs that were there and anything else they could grab was theirs. Kai had been stupid enough to think it would be easy. In and out. The gang had their back. They were going to look out and keep them safe.

It was a lesson learned. Kai did his time and steered clear of the gang after that.

Rooster had stayed on and for a couple of years tried to convince Kai to return. Kai might not have been the smartest kid in the neighborhood, but he knew enough to learn from his fuckups.

"Will you at least draw it for me? I'll have someone else do the work."

"Maybe." He drank a gulp of beer and swiped the whiskey from Rooster's side of the table. If he couldn't win at poker, at least he could get a buzz on to salvage his night.

Norah sat in the not terribly comfortable chair across from Teagan's desk, gripping Jimmy's hand. The baby punched and kicked against the stress Norah felt.

"You okay?"

"No." She shook her head. What if this went wrong? What if they weren't the right couple?

"Say the word and we'll leave." With his free hand, he rubbed her arm.

She appreciated the sentiment, but she needed to do this. "I had a good feeling about them when I read their profile. I'm just nervous. What if they don't like me? What if I chose the wrong people?"

"First, I don't know how much it matters whether they like you. Second, this isn't anything binding. It's a meet and greet. You can leave here and never see them again. On the other hand, they might be the parents for your baby."

Norah leaned her head against Jimmy's shoulder. He always made her feel better. A knock sounded at the door a second before Teagan stuck her head into the room. "Ready for us?"

Norah nodded and released Jimmy's hand. She smoothed her T-shirt over her belly. Teagan swept the door wide and Kim and Trevor entered behind her. Teagan moved behind her desk and sat.

The couple stood awkwardly waiting for Norah to make a move. She stood and shook Trevor's hand. "I'm Norah." She pointed at Jimmy who now stood beside her. "This is my brother Jimmy."

Kim moved forward and hugged Norah. In her ear, she whispered, "No matter what happens, thank you for meeting with us."

Immediately, Norah's nerves settled. They took seats across from Norah and Jimmy. Teagan folded her hands on her desk. "Now that introductions are out of the way, this is your chance to get to know one another. Norah, anything you'd like to say?"

"I don't know where to start."

Kim leaned forward and patted Norah's knee. "How about

anything you want to know about us? Ask anything. I'm an open book."

Norah laughed. She knew Kim was being serious, but she couldn't help it. "Sorry. I come from a family of guys who aren't open about much and hardly talk. So this is a foreign concept."

"Funny," Jimmy mumbled.

"Well, then, I'll start. I'm a teacher. Trevor is a lawyer. We tried having a baby for a few years and then found we're unable. We want an open adoption because we want our child to have as many people care about him or her as possible. I can't imagine how hard this is for you. It takes a lot of courage to do this."

Norah ignored the remark about bravery because she didn't feel brave. "Lawyers work a lot of crazy hours, don't they?"

Trevor nodded. "Sometimes. But I am home every night and on the weekends. I'm established in my firm so I don't have to take on cases I don't want to. And Kim will take time off to be with the baby."

"It's important to me that my daughter have two parents. My mom died when I was little, so I never knew her. I want my baby to have what I didn't." Proud that she made the statement without tears, Norah waited for a response from Trevor.

"I plan to be more than a provider, Norah. I have to work, especially if Kim decides she wants to stay at home full-time. However, I will be there. I can't make promises about what that will look like because I've never been a dad. But I want to be one more than anything." He reached for Kim's hand without looking away from Norah.

It was a seamless movement that made Norah smile.

"Do you have space for her in your home?"

Kim raised her hand. "That's the second time you mentioned a girl. You know for sure it's a girl?"

Norah lifted a shoulder. "That's what they tell me."

"We have a room set aside for a nursery, but it's empty. I don't want to decorate or fill it until we know we have a baby coming home. We also live in an excellent school district and there are at least three parks within walking distance."

"Is there anything you want to know about me?" Norah asked.

Kim and Trevor looked at each other and then shifted. They were nervous. Norah couldn't imagine being in their shoes, afraid to say the wrong thing to turn a mom off and blow their chances at a baby. To ease the pressure, Norah gave them something. "The baby is healthy. I've never done drugs or smoked. I might've had a drink or two before I knew I was pregnant, but the doctor has said she looks healthy."

They nodded but said nothing.

"I cared about her father," she blurted. For some reason, she didn't want them to think she was someone who slept around and got pregnant by someone who didn't matter. "But we're going in different directions and neither of us is ready to be a parent."

"Okay," Kim said. "Does he know we're meeting?"

Norah nodded. "I saw him yesterday but he had to go back to school. Teagan will send him the paperwork, but he doesn't want to have to do this."

Jimmy put an arm around her shoulder. For once, she was glad he didn't feel the need to talk. After that, things lightened up and they spent almost an hour talking about all kinds of things from the trivial to the serious. Both Kim and Norah shed a few tears. At least Norah could blame the hormones. Trevor and Kim left with an open invitation to contact them at any time if she had questions or wanted to talk.

Teagan walked them out and when she returned, she asked, "So what do you think?"

"I like them."

"Shouldn't you meet with some other people before you decide?" Jimmy asked.

Teagan answered. "It's up to you. You can. We have plenty of couples to choose from. If you want me to give you some more profiles, let me know."

Norah's nerves returned. "Should I?"

"I've never bought the first car I looked at and this is way more important than a car," Jimmy said.

"I guess you have a point."

"Like I said before, I don't want you to rush into anything."

"Okay. Do you want to change any of your parameters?" Teagan walked behind her desk as she spoke.

"No. I think you gave me a good group the first time."

She reached into her desk drawer and pulled out four more folders.

"You have some ready for me?"

"I had a feeling you might want to keep looking."

"Well, don't tell Kim and Trevor. I still like them and I think they'll be a good fit. I just want to take my time."

"And that's fine." She handed Norah the new profiles. "No worries. Do you have any questions?"

"No." She stood and so did Jimmy. They said good-bye and left the office.

In the parking lot, Jimmy asked, "How are you really doing?"

She climbed into his car. "I'm okay. Today was hard, mostly because I didn't know what to expect. I'm going to look at these new profiles, but I think Kim and Trevor might be the best. Didn't you like them?"

"They were fine. I didn't get a bad feeling about them or

anything. I just want you to be sure. This isn't something you can take back once it's done."

"I know." There was no turning back anything now, so she had to forge ahead and do the best she could.

Although Norah mostly enjoyed the extra day off Kai had given her, she had too much time to stew. She'd pored over the profiles and found herself comparing each new couple to Kim and Trevor. She didn't know if it was fair to the couples, but she'd spoken with Kim and Trevor, felt a small connection to them. She tried not to read too much into it.

She dressed and gathered her things to go to Kai's. She was almost ready when she heard voices downstairs, which was weird because the house was normally quiet. Sean and Tommy came and went, but since they slept in the basement, she usually couldn't hear them. And her dad was only loud when he yelled at the TV.

When she got to the dining room, the sight before her made her stomach jump. Three of her brothers and her dad were all sitting in the living room, eyes on her. The last time she'd come into this scene, they'd gathered to tell her they were sending her to Boston. Jimmy had done all the talking and Tommy wasn't there. He'd been too angry.

This time, Jimmy was the one missing and unease crawled up her neck. "What's going on?"

"We want to talk to you," Kevin said.

She bristled. It might've just been her reaction to Kevin given their last conversation, but she was gearing for a fight. She eyed Tommy. "Everything is settled with Avery. No need for you to track him down."

Kevin's voice softened. "It's not about that. Sit down." He scooted over on the couch to make room for her.

"I have to leave for work soon."

"This won't take long."

Gripping her bag on her shoulder, she sat on the edge of the couch, ready to bolt. Her brothers shouldn't make her feel like this. She looked back at Tommy. "What's going on?"

"Jimmy told us you're giving the baby up."

She wished Jimmy would've told her he'd done that. Yeah, she'd wanted him to, but a little warning would've been nice. "I am."

"Why, squirt?" Kevin asked.

She turned away from Tommy. "Because I'm not ready to be a mom. I want my child to have something better than I can offer."

"We're its family," her dad said. It was the first time he spoke of the baby.

"I know. And this wasn't an easy decision."

"So you're just going to give away my grandchild?"

"I'm not in a position to raise her. What do I have to offer?"

"We'd all love her, Norah." Tommy sounded pained to speak.

"I know, but it's not enough." She stood and turned to face all of them. "It's my decision. I want her to have more than this." She waved across the room.

"What's wrong with my house? It's a good place to raise a family." Dad was getting worked up.

"I suppose it might be, but it wasn't good enough for me, was it, Dad?"

"It's not the same."

She couldn't have this fight with him. It was over. Her childhood was long gone and it made no sense to argue about it now. "I'm not going to fight with you. I have to do what's best for my baby."

She turned and walked out the door, her heart racing.

The door creaked and slammed shut behind her. Tommy had followed. "Norah, wait."

Pausing by her car, she shaded her eyes from the glaring sun. "What?"

"I told them we shouldn't all come at you." He shook his head. "It wasn't supposed to be like that."

"Really? What was it supposed to be like? Were you all just going to tell me to keep the baby and that would be it?" Crossing her arms over her belly, she waited for an answer.

"No. Well, maybe. We want to help you. You don't have to do this."

"I know I don't *have* to do anything. I've thought about it for a long time. I'm thinking of her now, not me." She dropped her arms and stepped closer to Tommy. She didn't want to lose the closeness they'd rediscovered lately. "I met a couple yesterday. Did Jimmy tell you that?"

Tommy nodded.

"They were really nice. They have steady jobs and a great house. They desperately *want* a baby. They can give her what I can't." She touched Tommy's arm and stared into his eyes. "Two parents, Tommy. A family I never had."

"Ah, shit." He pulled Norah into a hug. "We're your family."

"I know, and I love you guys, but I want her to have it all. And I can't do that." Tears pricked her eyes. She pushed away. "I need to get to work."

"So how's it going? With Kai."

"Really good." She didn't mention the peace she felt hanging out at Kai's house or the lustful thoughts he always brought to mind. "I like his mom, and it's a relatively easy job."

"Make sure he treats you right. He can be an asshole."

She knew Kai had that asshole exterior, but she'd seen another side to him. The side that hugged her, held her, let her cry. The gentle way he touched her face awake or the way he'd kissed her. She knew he was not the asshole he wanted the world to believe he was. "He's nice to me."

Tommy laughed. "I think we need to work on your definition of nice."

She rolled her eyes and got into her car. Once she was alone, she let the tears fall that she'd held back while with Tommy. He hadn't tried to make her cry. She knew that. Tommy loved her. All of her brothers did. She believed even her dad did, but they didn't know how to handle her or even talk to her, for that matter.

They were really good at screwing up with the best of intentions.

Kai was up and drinking coffee as soon as the sun rose. He'd found it was his only chance for peace. He'd spent half of yesterday at home in order to give Norah the extra day off. He realized quickly what a stupid idea it had been. The thought of spending the whole day with his mom made his stomach turn.

Jaleesa had come over for the other half of the day. She took note of his thoughtfulness in giving Norah a day off and she also commented on the yogurt—after his mom pointed out he'd gotten it for Norah. Why couldn't he have had a brother?

He relished the quiet of the morning, but it ended all too quickly when his mom woke. Then he was counting down the minutes until Norah arrived so he could leave.

He absolutely wasn't thinking about seeing her at all. He simply wanted to go to work. And more importantly, get away from his mom. On his third trip of pacing through the living room, his mom said, "Just go already. I'm sure Norah is on her way. I'm fine."

But he remembered his trip to the store the other day and what had happened with her. He was afraid to leave her.

Norah had to be aware of that too in case she needed to run errands. But Mom wouldn't want her to know.

"I'm going to wait outside until she gets here."

"Mmm-hmm."

He pointed at her again. "Don't. I already warned you about that."

"What? I'm not the one trying to be alone with Norah."

He clamped his jaw shut. He wouldn't rise to her bait. Sitting on the front steps, he took a deep breath of fresh air. There was a hint of fall swirling around even though the leaves hadn't started to drop. The temperature would shift soon enough and winter would barrel in. But for now, he could enjoy the warm sun and cool breeze.

"Must be nice to have a life of leisure where you can just sit on your ass."

He straightened in his spot to look at Norah. "It is."

She laughed, but the sound was empty. He studied her face and noticed the streaks and blotches. He stood. "What's wrong?"

"Nothing. You can go to work." She stepped to the side as if he'd let her go without more.

"You've been crying."

"Yeah, well, I seem to do that a lot lately."

"What was it this time?"

"My brothers. They all gathered and treated me like I needed an intervention."

"Huh?"

"They don't think I should be considering adoption, so they wanted me to know."

"And how'd that go?"

"I told them it was my decision."

Somehow, he didn't think it was all that calm. "You want me to beat up Tommy for you?"

"Nah, but thanks for the offer. And thanks for the extra day off."

"It doesn't sound like you were able to enjoy it."

"I did. They did this right before I left the house this morning. On my day off, I sat on my ass with nothing to do. It was nice." This time, when she smiled, it appeared a little more genuine. "But I'm ready to get back to work."

"About my mom."

Norah froze. "Is she okay?"

"Yeah. I went to the store the other day and when I came back she was standing in the living room, stuck. She'd gotten up by herself to go to the bathroom, but then couldn't get back on the couch. Her knee locked up on her or something. I don't know. She said she'd only been standing there a few minutes, but I think if I'd taken any longer, she would've fallen."

"Wow. But she's okay?"

"Yeah. I wanted you to know in case you go out anywhere. Don't stay gone too long."

"Of course. Anything else?"

"I don't know how late I'll be."

"Don't worry. I don't have anyplace to be and I like your house. It's quiet and I can think."

He snickered. He used to think that about his house too. Not so much anymore. "See you tonight then."

"Yeah."

Something about the exchange made him want to lean in and kiss her, as if that should be part of their routine. He shook the thought loose. He'd had two Norah-free days and it was supposed to set him straight.

He watched her walk into the house. Before she closed the door, he heard her greet his mom warmly.

Maybe he should think about hiring someone else. Someone old and ugly. Someone who wasn't pregnant. Norah would have to stop working soon anyway, right? She was supposed to be a temporary solution until they figured out something more permanent. Then somehow, everyone assumed she'd be here for good.

He got in his car and drove to the studio. He didn't have a client coming in for hours, but at least there, he wouldn't have to see any women until Karla showed up. And she didn't count as a woman. He didn't have a problem seeing her as nothing more than an employee. Too bad he hadn't been able to do that with Norah.

Chapter Eight

Norah dropped her bag on the chair in the living room. "Ready for a walk, Lani?" She needed to practice saying the woman's first name so she wouldn't have to hear the constant corrections anymore.

"I guess so." She set her novel to the side. "Story's in a slow part anyway."

Norah held out her arm to help her up, but Lani waved her away. "I've been practicing." Leaning heavily on her cane, she forced herself up.

"Did your therapist say this was okay? You're ready for it?"

"Shoot. She's been nagging me from the beginning. Said I wasn't pushing myself hard enough. She'd be thrilled." With her free hand, she waved ahead. "Let's go. I think we'll make it all the way to the end of the block today. I'm feeling good."

Norah sure hoped so because if Lani wasn't able to make the entire trip, Norah had no idea how she'd get her back home.

"Come on, then."

Norah helped Lani down the stairs, which she seemed better able to handle. "You're really motivated today. What's changed?"

They headed down the block, Lani moving slowly, leaning on the cane. "I miss my friends. My book club meets tonight and I have to miss it. I need to start driving again. The sooner I can walk, the sooner I can drive."

Norah understood. Lani must be lonely sitting in Kai's house all day alone. It wasn't like Norah was her friend. "You were living with Jaleesa before your surgery?"

"Yes. Her house has too many stairs for me. Another reason for me to get back to normal. I miss my grandbabies. They're always underfoot and in the way." She looked at Norah. "You'll know all about that soon, won't you?"

Norah sighed. "No, actually I won't. I plan to give her up for adoption."

"Really?" Lani said it as if it were an interesting fact.

Norah waited for another comment, but none came. "No opinion?"

"It's your business what you do. If I had to do it all over, I would've waited longer for children. I wasn't as young as you, but it took me time to find a man. Then I rushed the babies. I should've taken time to better know the man. I love my kids, but I wish I'd had more time for myself. I suppose I'm getting that time now, but look at me." She paused her walk and touched Norah's arm. "You do what's right for you as long as it's also right for the baby."

"Thank you." She didn't need anyone's permission, but having Lani express the same desires Norah felt helped.

"Besides, being a single mama ain't no joke."

"Kai's father wasn't in the picture?"

"When they were young, he was. But then he decided it wasn't the life for him. Some men are like that. They like the idea of a family but aren't up to the responsibility of having one."

Norah thought about it for a moment. Sounded like Avery. And her dad. Her dad had been there. Although he'd never acted much like a father, he always made sure they were cared for and had what they needed.

"You look more troubled today than usual. Talk while we walk." Lani turned and started down the sidewalk again.

"It's nothing. Men are stupid."

Lani chuckled. "Tell me something I don't know. What did Kai do?"

Norah stiffened. "It wasn't Kai."

"Who then?"

"My brothers and my dad. They want me to keep the baby."

Lani sniffed. "Are they going to care for it? Wake up in the middle of the night for feedings and diapers? There's more to child-rearing than providing money."

"That's what I said." Norah laughed. She wondered if she would've had this type of conversation with her mom.

"And the child's father?" The question was quiet as if she wasn't sure if she should ask, which went against everything Norah knew about Lani. "You don't need to tell me if you don't want to."

"He offered money. Said he could provide for his child." The thought still had her swallowing back tears.

"Like you said, men are stupid."

They reached the end of the block. "Do you need a break?"

Lani turned slowly, looked back at the house, and said, "No. I got this."

On their way back, Norah decided she wanted to do something nice for Lani. They talked about unimportant stuff like the weather and then Lani spoke about her grandchildren. When they arrived at the house, Lani paused before trying to climb the stairs. "I need to work up to that."

"Take your time. It's a beautiful day." Norah turned her face to the sun.

"You're a beautiful girl."

Norah felt the rush of blood reach her cheeks. "Thanks."

"Kai's lucky to have you."

"It's not—"

Lani raised a hand. "You can say what you want, believe what you want, but I see the way you look at each other. Circumstances are in the way right now." She pointed to Norah's stomach. "Be patient with him."

Norah released a nervous laugh. She wasn't totally convinced Kai even liked her. "I think you misunderstand, Lani."

"No. I know my boy, and I have a feeling about you." Lani's dark brown gaze bore into her.

Norah sighed and took a chance. "It's me who doesn't understand him at all. Sometimes he's sweet and he gives me this look, but then other times he avoids me like I'm contagious. And like the rest of the men in my life, he rarely talks, so I have no idea what he's thinking."

"Kai's like that. Never was much of a talker. When he was a child he had a stutter. I think that's what caused his reticence. He outgrew it, of course. But it's who he is."

"That doesn't really help. I can't guess what's going on. I'm done with that." Norah held out her arm. "Ready to go up?"

Lani nodded. "Remember what I said about patience."

Norah didn't know what to make of that. She knew she and Kai exchanged some heated looks, but never in Lani's presence that she could remember. Not to mention Kai was king of the mixed signal. She'd told Lani the truth—she was done guessing what others thought. If someone couldn't be up front, they weren't worth her time. Now, she just needed to convince her hormones.

Kai's phone bleeped with a text from Norah. **Can you give me Jaleesa's number?**

Instead of texting, he called. "What's wrong?" he asked as soon as Norah answered.

"Nothing. Your mom went for a long walk and she's napping. I want to ask Jaleesa about your mom's book club, that's all."

"Oh."

"If there was some emergency, I would've called. I texted in case you were busy."

"I'll send you her number."

"Thanks."

He hung up and Tommy looked up from the paper he was sketching on. "Problem?"

"No." This was why he preferred to take personal calls outside or in the comfort of his office. He forwarded Jaleesa's number to Norah and wondered what the hell his—what was Norah?—needed to talk to his sister about. That hitch in his thought process was bothersome. He should think of her as an employee. But he wanted more, which was pretty fucked up.

It was almost eleven by the time he closed up the studio and went home. He'd been able to put Norah out of his mind for the remainder of the day until of course he parked and saw her huddled on his front steps. He rushed from the car thinking that something went wrong today and she needed to talk to him without his mom hearing. As he neared, she pushed up from the step, belly first. She wore one of his sweatshirts, which mostly swallowed her, but couldn't hide her baby bump.

"What's wrong?"

She raised her hands as if being held up. "Before you go in, know that I meant well and I thought they'd be gone by now."

Before he had a chance to ask any other questions, noise from in the house—loud laughter—filtered out to them.

What the hell? She was having a party? He shot Norah a dirty look.

"It's not what you think."

He stomped up the stairs, taking them two at a time. "Sounds like a party in my house."

"Okay, well, maybe it is kind of what you're thinking."

He'd trusted her, given her complete access and this was how she repaid him? He burst through the door and froze. This was *not* the party he'd imagined thirty seconds ago. His mom sat on the couch in her usual spot. She was surrounded by an army of old ladies.

At the sight of him, Lani said, "Well, ladies, party's over."

Unlike the breakup of a teenage party, no one lingered. They all stood, gathered their things, and kissed his mom's cheek before leaving. He watched as they filed out. He didn't know any of them.

When the last one closed the door behind her, he turned on Norah, but his mom jumped in. "Don't you yell at that girl, Kai."

Norah's sharp blue eyes widened, waiting for the verbal hit, and he couldn't do it. It wasn't even because of his mom's warning. He couldn't lay into her because she looked scared. He lowered his voice. "Go home."

"I'll clean up before I leave."

"I'll handle it." He turned back to his mom. "Let me get you into bed. It's late."

He moved to help her up. From the corner of his eye, he saw Norah gathering her things in her bag. In the bedroom, he handed his mom her nightgown.

She snatched it from his hand. "You stop being mean to her. She's a nice girl."

"She had no business throwing a party in my house. Not for you or anyone else without my permission."

Hobbling to the bathroom, she mumbled, "Norah was right. Men are stupid."

Kai thunked his head against the wall. What had he done to deserve this?

He went back to the living room to clean up and saw some of the mess was already gone. Norah's bag sat on the chair. Damn girl couldn't follow directions for anything. He picked up the remaining glasses and mostly empty bottle of wine and took them to the kitchen.

There, Norah was filling the sink and loading it with dishes. Her spine straightened as soon as he entered the room. Without turning around, she said, "I'll leave as soon as I clean up. It's my fault there's a mess and it's not your job to fix it."

Her voice was as stiff as her posture and held no emotion. It sounded foreign. He set the glasses on the counter and reached around her to pour the rest of the wine down the drain. The movement brought them much too close. He didn't know what he was thinking.

"Look—"

She spun, putting herself nearly in his arms. She pointed a finger at his chest as she tilted her head up to meet his eyes. "No, you look. I get that you have a certain way you live. I don't understand what it is and I'm not entitled to that. But you told me to take care of your mom. To give her whatever she wanted."

"She asked for a party?"

Her shoulders sagged. "Are you even aware that your mom has a life? She has friends and activities. All of that has been sidelined because of her knee. She's lonely."

The words hit him hard, as hard as the first time she'd said them to him.

"She mentioned her book club was supposed to meet tonight. I called Jaleesa and asked her to call your mom's friends to see if they would meet here." She shrugged.

"How was I supposed to know that 'book club' was code for 'senior citizen drinking party'?"

Amusement lit her eyes now and he much preferred that.

"You don't know my mom that well."

He still stood too close. Norah's belly brushed against him. If he leaned in he could easily taste her lips. Which he'd told himself he wouldn't be doing again. He stepped back and sought to find the anger he had when he'd walked in. "You shouldn't have done it without talking to me."

"Point taken. I thought they'd come and go and you'd never know."

"So you thought lying would be a good way to keep your job?"

Her eyes widened again and fear flickered through them. He wasn't being fair and he knew it, but he needed distance.

"I'm sorry. I'll get this stuff washed and be out of your way." She returned to the sink and began cleaning glasses and dishes. He backed out of the room. "Do you want me here tomorrow?"

He huffed out a breath. As much as part of him would like to say no, he had no one else. "Yeah."

He went back to the bedroom to see if his mom was ready to get into bed. She sat on the edge and narrowed her eyes when he came in. "Did you make her cry?"

"No." He helped her get her leg on the bed and adjusted the blankets. "But I've been thinking about placing an ad for someone new."

She smacked his arm. "You fired her because she invited my friends over?"

"No." He stepped back and ran his hand through his hair. "She was supposed to be temporary and she's pregnant. She's going to have to stop working soon. It makes sense to have someone else in place."

She crossed her arms. "I'll run them off."

"What?"

"You bring someone else in here and I'll run them off. I'll make your life miserable."

She had no idea how close she was to doing that already. "You're being childish."

"So are you. Why do you really want to get rid of her?"

"I told you. Plus, she had a party in my house without asking me."

"If she had asked, what would you have said?"

He sat on the chair beside the bed. "If she'd told me it was for you, I wouldn't have cared."

"Then why do you care now? She was doing something nice for me. I like her and so do you."

"I like that she cares about you. That's all."

"You keep telling yourself that."

He pushed up off the chair, suddenly feeling exhausted. "Fine. She can stay, but when she has the baby, I have to hire someone else. You're not ready to be alone all day or for going back to Jaleesa's."

"You need to apologize to her."

"I did nothing wrong."

"Mmm-hmm."

He flicked off the light and left the room. If she didn't get well soon, he might not survive this. He probably did owe Norah an apology, but he wasn't sure for what. He'd been an ass to her, sure, but she had that coming. He'd almost kissed her again, and in his mind, that was the greater offense.

There was no sign of her in the kitchen and when he checked the living room, her bag was gone.

Norah drove home in silence, dread filling her. She needed this job. Not just because of the money, although that played a huge role. She liked spending time with Lani and having Kai's house as a place of peace. If he fired her, she wouldn't be able to find anything for probably a couple of months. She parked and rested her forehead against the steering wheel.

This day had to qualify as one of the worst ever. Maybe if she asked Kai really nicely tomorrow, he wouldn't fire her. The car was getting colder, so she opened the door and dragged herself to the house. Then she realized she was still wearing Kai's sweatshirt. It was comfy and smelled like him. She wondered if he'd miss it.

She rolled her eyes at herself. Of course he would notice it missing. The guy noticed everything. Truth be told, it was a little unnerving. He was like Jimmy that way.

After changing for bed, she plugged her phone into the charger and at the same time it buzzed with power, a text came through. From Kai.

Sorry I yelled at you.

The simple text made her laugh before she responded. I grew up with 4 brothers. I don't think you know what yelling is.

She lay in bed and waited for him to say something. When nothing came back, she thought that was all she'd get. But she craved more, so she called.

"Hello." His voice was deep and craggy and she imagined him in bed, his hair loose, his long limbs spread everywhere.

"I'm sorry I invited people over without checking with you first. I wanted to do something nice for your mom."

"I know. I was an asshole."

"Why? It couldn't just be that you had a house full of old ladies."

He was silent for so long, she thought he wouldn't answer. "You make me crazy."

"I don't mean to. Tell me what it is and I'll try to stop." She heard rustling on the line and pictured him sitting up, throwing the blankets off.

His quiet chuckle vibrated across the line and through her, doing delicious things to her body. "You can't. It's just you. Who you are."

The words came like a slap. Had she turned into the epitome of the annoying little sister? She had no other role to play? Then she remembered the way he'd kissed her, the look in his eye when he'd stood surrounding her in the kitchen tonight. "What do you want?" she asked softly.

"That's the problem, Norah. You make me want. And I don't like that."

What she'd thought had been one of the worst days of her life had just turned on its head. His words filled her with a surge of emotions, none of which could she name. "I don't know what to say."

"There's nothing to say." He paused. "What about your boyfriend?"

She jerked back from her phone. "You mean Avery? We were a brief thing. It's been over."

"But he came for you."

"For the baby. Not me."

Kai sighed and mumbled something that sounded like "Stupid."

"If it helps, I feel the same," she admitted. If he could put it out there, the least she could do was not make him feel alone.

"That doesn't help a damn bit."

"I'd apologize, but it would be a lie and you've made it clear how you feel about lies."

"You're killing me, you know that, right?"

"It's been a long time since someone made me feel like this."

"I'm sure I'll regret asking, feel like what?"

So many things: sexy, wanted, hot—even in her whale-like state. But she settled for "Special."

"Having this conversation is stupid. It'll cause trouble. You have to know that."

Of course she knew. She was pregnant and the only reason she was in his life was because of his mom. But she wanted to hold on to the fantasy for a little while. In the quiet dark of her bedroom, none of that mattered. "I know. Right now I don't care."

"You need to care, Norah. I'm not the kind of guy you belong with. I'd only end up hurting you."

"You wouldn't be the first and sometimes the hurt is worth it."

"I don't think it is."

"I guess we'll have to see then." She smiled because Kai liked her. Maybe he didn't like the fact he was attracted to her, but it was enough that he admitted it. "Good night, Kai. I'll see you tomorrow."

She disconnected and rolled to her side, putting a pillow between her knees for comfort. She'd always known she came from a messed up family, but she really took the cake. She just spent the night flirting with her boss who was also her brother's boss while pregnant with another man's baby that she wasn't keeping. It had daytime TV written all over it. But like she'd said to Kai, she didn't care. It felt good to be wanted. It made her feel normal and she'd been missing that.

Only a few more weeks and she could start getting back to normal. What was the harm in enjoying time with Kai until he no longer needed her to take care of his mom? It wasn't like it could go too far. She was pregnant, and even after having the baby, it would be weeks before she could have sex and probably even longer until she felt good enough to want to. When it was time to move on, they both would. They could just take it for what it could be: a good time.

Over the course of the next week, Norah met with Teagan and spoke with Kim and Trevor. She'd decided they were the best match for her. Her appointments with the doctor seemed to come faster and faster even though they were only a week apart. Life had become a pleasant routine albeit a bit physically difficult. Where Lani was gaining strength and speed in their walks, Norah was slowing down. Lani hadn't sped by yet, but Norah had no doubt it might happen soon.

On the first of their daily walks, Norah's head was filled with the e-mail she'd received from Avery. He'd gotten the paperwork and said he'd sign and return it.

Overall, the e-mail was friendly. Little more than businesslike. She had a hard time remembering what she liked so much about Avery. The more she thought about it, the more she realized that she'd been in love with the idea of her and Avery, not the man himself. Not too surprising, since she'd been in love more times than she could count since she'd discovered boys at the age of twelve.

"You're awful quiet today," Lani commented.

"Lot on my mind."

"When are you due?"

"Couple more weeks. Although the doctor said since this is my first, don't count on being on time. She said she'll induce after two weeks." She inhaled as deeply as the baby would allow, which wasn't much. "Seems like a long way off."

"It'll happen sooner than you think. You spend those last weeks praying to get that thing out of you and when it's ready, you're not anymore." She chuckled.

Norah didn't like the sound of that any more than she liked the idea of waiting another month.

"What about after?"

"What about it?"

"Do you have plans?"

Norah shrugged. "Not really."

"Then you'll come back here."

"Well, uh . . ." She didn't know what to say. Kai hadn't mentioned how long this job would last, but he'd made it clear he'd hired her because no one else would. "Kai hasn't said—"

"Pssh. We already discussed how little that boy says."

Something about the way she always referred to Kai as a boy made Norah smile.

"My therapist will stop coming here within the next couple of weeks. Then I'm supposed to make it to them. I'll probably be here for at least another month."

"Well, Lani, we'll see." She patted the woman's arm. As much as she liked the job and enjoyed the pay, she couldn't assume Kai didn't have plans to replace her when she had the baby. She didn't know how much recovery time she'd need.

After their walk and lunch, they played a game of gin rummy where Lani stomped her. Norah was grateful they didn't play for cash. The woman had no mercy on the pregnant girl. Then Lani settled on the couch with her latest novel, which meant she'd be napping soon.

Norah checked the time and hoped Kim was done with teaching for the day as she dialed the number.

"Hello?"

"Hi, Kim? It's Norah O'Malley. Teagan gave me your number and said it was okay to call."

"It's definitely okay. I'm glad you called."

"I wanted to let you know that I received an e-mail from

the baby's father and he'll sign off on everything, so we're okay."

"Excellent. How are you?"

"I'm okay. The baby is kicking up a storm and pressing on things that don't feel like they should be squooshed, but my doctor assures me it's all normal."

"And how are you after getting the e-mail?"

It was kind of her to ask, but Norah should've expected it. Kim had been so kind and generous every time they spoke. "I'm okay, really. Thanks for asking." She paused, suddenly unsure if she wanted to continue.

"Was there something else you wanted to talk about?"

"Yeah, actually. You know I'm due in two weeks."

"Mmm-hmm."

Norah heard the restrained excitement in her voice. She wondered how many times Kim and Trevor had been this close to having a baby and had someone change her mind. She wished she could offer some kind of reassurance.

"Well, although I can't sign the papers and make everything official for three days after she's born, Teagan said I can decide who she goes home with. I'd like that to be you."

"Uh. Could you hold on a minute?" Kim sounded near tears. "I'm putting you on speaker. Trevor just walked in."

"Hi, Trevor."

"Hi," he answered. "What's up?"

"I was talking to Kim about naming you guys as the people who would take the baby home. I don't want to take her home with me and I really don't want her in a foster home for three days. That's not fair to her. She belongs with people who love her."

"Are you sure?" Kim asked.

"I get it. I do. You're worried that I'll tell you to take her and you'll fall in love with her and then I'll want her back. I won't. I'm not lying to myself and acting like it's not a big deal, but I'm okay with this decision. I can't bring her home with me."

"Yes," Trevor said, his voice clear as if he'd moved closer to the phone. "Of course we'll take her."

"You can think about it. We have a couple of weeks at least." She took a deep breath. "There's one more thing. In the hospital, they're going to ask me to fill out the birth certificate. It seems stupid for me to name your baby. Then you'd have to file paperwork to change it. If you tell me what name you want, I'll write it in."

Kim came back on the line. "Her name isn't important. If you have something you like, we'd be okay with that."

"So if I named her Butterfly, you'd be okay?"

Silence met her joke.

"I was kidding, guys."

Nervous laughter followed. Norah rolled her eyes. "Really. I don't have any special names." She'd never sat around as a teen picturing her wedding and naming imaginary babies.

"What do you think about Ella?" Kim asked quietly, her words just above a whisper.

"I take it the name is special to you?"

"It was my grandma's name and we were close. I think it's pretty and timeless."

Norah admitted the name was pretty. "Ella it is then."

They said their good-byes. As crummy as her life was, she at least brought happiness to Kim and Trevor over something as simple as a name. It made her feel good.

More days passed and Norah was increasingly frustrated with Kai. He had yet to address their late-night phone call. She hadn't brought it up because she figured he needed time to think things through. He always measured his words carefully, but he was making her crazy. He barely spoke a few measly sentences since his revelation.

She arrived at his house early, hoping to catch him lifting weights in the basement or at least before he ran out the door. As she walked into the living room, he came from around the corner, thankfully dressed, but his hair hung loose at his collar, still damp from the shower. God, how she wanted to touch it.

"You're early."

"Yeah. I was hoping we could talk."

"Shoot."

She glanced around for Lani, but didn't see her. "Alone?"

He stiffened at the word. Was she really that bad?

One sharp nod and then he grabbed his keys and pointed toward the front door. He obviously didn't want Lani to hear anything. She followed him outside.

At the bottom of the steps, he turned to look at her, but said nothing.

"We need to talk about that phone conversation. About us. This." She waved a hand between them.

"You want to talk about a talk?" One eyebrow—the left one with the small scar above it—arched.

"You know what I mean. We said stuff that can't be unsaid."

"So?"

"So what are we going to do about it?"

"Nothing."

The word was sharp and jabbed at her. But really, what did she expect? That he'd been simply waiting for her to say something before sweeping her off her feet?

"Why not?"

"A lot of reasons." He stepped closer and palmed her belly. "She's the biggest one."

The fact that he referred to her child as *she* shouldn't

have been endearing, but Norah melted a little over it. "She'll be out of the picture in a couple of weeks."

Just then, Ella kicked and flipped. "Whoa." It was hard enough to steal Norah's breath.

Kai jerked his hand away. "You okay?"

Norah nodded.

"Just because you have her doesn't mean she'll be gone. You have a lot going on."

"So a little escape would be good."

"I'm not an escape. Go find some little frat boy."

She wrinkled her nose at him. "I don't want a frat boy. Been there, done that. I want something different. I like you."

"You don't even know me."

Well, damn, he had her there. "I like the parts I know. You remembered what kind of yogurt I crave and bought me some, even though it's disgusting. You held me and let me cry on you when my ex was an asshole. You offered to beat up my brother for making me cry. You love your mom even when she makes you crazy." She stepped closer, her belly brushing against him. "And I really, really liked the way you kissed me."

"You choose to see what you want. You wouldn't like the rest. This can't go anywhere."

"You said you want me."

"I'm no stranger to wanting what I can't have."

"But you can have me."

He turned and stepped away. "No, Norah, I can't."

"Why not?"

He didn't answer. He got into his car and pulled away. Norah went back into the house, even more frustrated.

Lani was dressed for their walk. "Ready?"

"Sure. Let's go." Maybe a little exercise would relax her tense muscles and calm the baby.

As they eased down the sidewalk, Lani talked about her

latest book and how she couldn't wait for her next book club. Norah only halfway listened because she had to focus on walking. Her breaths were a little shallow and it felt like she wore a belt that tightened with each step.

"What do you think?" Lani asked.

"I'm sorry, what?"

"I said, do you think Kai would let me host again? The house is so quiet while he's at work and we don't have to censor our language."

"I don't know, but you should ask." Norah knew he wouldn't deny his mom's request, even though he'd hate every minute. She touched Lani's arm. "Do you think we can cut this a little short today? I'm not feeling well."

"Sure. Are you okay?"

"Yeah, it's just stress, maybe some gas." She took a slow, steadying breath. They walked back to the house, which suddenly felt like it was a mile away.

Crap. If it was already this hard to keep moving, how would she ever last beyond her due date? She and Lani held on to each other as they climbed the steps. In the living room, they both sat on the couch.

Norah rubbed her belly in rhythmic circles.

"You're not looking so good."

"I'm fine. Just need a break." She closed her eyes and imagined sitting on the beach, water lapping at her feet. Nothing calmed her though. Her breathing still felt short and she was restless. The need to move forced her back to her feet. Her back ached and the tight feeling around her belly constricted, but at least the baby stopped kicking. She probably fell asleep to the motion of Norah's swaying body.

Norah walked to the kitchen and grabbed a glass of water. She hoped the cool liquid would soothe her. That was when the first sharp pain hit. Her knees almost buckled. She knocked the glass over on the counter and it rolled until it fell and shattered on the floor.

"Norah?"

Norah took a deep breath as the pain subsided. "I'm okay. Just dropped a glass."

She straightened and inhaled to make sure the pain was truly gone. She was okay, so she lowered to the floor with some paper towel to clean up the glass. Great. In addition to feeling like an ox, she had the grace of one as well. After dumping all of the shards in the trash, she wet the paper towel to grab the pieces that were nearly unnoticeable.

The simple task wore her out. She washed her hands to make sure no glass stuck to her and went back to the living room. As she neared the couch, another pain hit.

"Norah, you're pale. And that didn't look like a baby kick. I think you're in labor."

No. *No.* She wasn't due for another week and a half. Maybe more. She shook her head. Lani pushed up from the couch and walked over to where Norah had a death grip on the armchair.

Norah pushed back. "I'm okay. See?"

"That's the way contractions work. They start, stop, start. I think we should call an ambulance."

"No. I can't afford an ambulance. Plus, they'll take me to the closest hospital. I want to be with my doctor. I'll call Jimmy."

She dug her phone out of her purse. She got Jimmy's voice mail, so she left a message and hoped it didn't freak him out too much. Then she called her doctor who started asking questions like how far apart the contractions were. Like Norah paid attention to that? She guessed eight or ten minutes. The doctor said she had time and didn't have to rush to the hospital, but she should get there.

"Lani, you can sit back down. Jimmy will call back. He'll come and get me." Another contraction hit, stopping her from saying more.

"That was no eight minutes."

"It's fine. Jimmy will come." He always did. If she believed in nothing else, she could believe in that.

The restlessness attacked again. She wanted to move, but she didn't. She wanted to sit, curl into a ball, and wait for it all to go away, but then she wanted to stomp her feet. She settled for a short pacing circuit in the living room under Lani's watchful eye.

"It's probably not even the real thing. There's such a thing as false labor, right? That totally sounds like something that would happen to me."

Another contraction hit and Norah began to realize it probably was the real deal. And no way was she ready.

Lani's voice reached her as the pain waned and Norah realized she was talking on the phone. Then she was rubbing Norah's back. "Kai's on his way. He'll take you to the hospital."

"Jimmy will come." Kai wasn't supposed to take her to the hospital. Then she realized Kai would probably send Tommy. Tommy was an acceptable substitute for Jimmy. She took a few more steps and turned again. Lani had disappeared from her side, and Norah appreciated the freedom.

When the pain returned, it didn't seem as bad this time. She didn't even have to bend over. It was like passing a gas bubble—uncomfortable, but not painful. Maybe it was a false alarm. The front door flung open and Kai stomped in.

Chapter Nine

Kai was going to kill his mother for pulling this. She needed to understand he had a business to run. "What the hell is going on?"

"Norah needs to get to the hospital, just like I told you when I called." The look on her face told him she was serious.

"I thought you were playing games." He looked at Norah. "I thought you weren't due yet."

"I'm not. Why didn't you send Tommy?"

"I don't know where Tommy is. He's not working today." Suddenly, his mom was at his side, handing him a towel and a plastic bag. "What's this?"

"Go put the plastic on your seat and cover it with the towel in case her water breaks."

Aw, fuck. That was disgusting. "Call an ambulance."

"No. I want my hospital with my doctor." Norah waved a hand, but he saw she was weak. "Don't worry. I called Jimmy. He'll come."

"I don't know who this Jimmy is, but she called him an hour ago and he hasn't shown or called. She might be delusional."

This was going to fall on him. What the hell? "Come on. Let's get you where you need to be."

His mom slid a purse over Norah's shoulder. "Your phone is in the front pocket."

"Thanks."

"What about you?" Kai asked his mom.

"I'll be fine here. I'll call Jaleesa to stop by." She snapped her fingers. "Take care of that girl."

Norah had made it as far as the front door and then doubled over with a moan. Her face crumpled with pain. Her fingers wrapped on the door frame in a white-knuckled grip. This was ridiculous. With the towel and bag in his fist, he scooped her up in his arms and elbowed the door open.

"Put me down. I can walk in a minute."

"With my luck in a minute that baby will be popping out." He carried her to the car and set her on her feet at the curb. He laid the plastic and the towel on the seat like his mom suggested and then reconsidered. "Would the backseat be better?"

"This is fine." She turned and put her butt first on the seat and then swiveled her legs and feet in.

He closed the door carefully and then got behind the wheel. She quietly told him how to get to the hospital, which by his estimation would take a good thirty minutes. He hoped to God they made it in time. Given that it was still early in the day, he opted to hop on the expressway. Traffic moved smoothly and he coasted at an easy sixty miles an hour across the city.

Another round of pain hit Norah and he had no idea what to do, so he held out his hand. She laced her fingers with his and squeezed through the pain. For such a little thing, her hands were damn strong. When she relaxed her fingers, tears filled the rims of her eyes.

"Thank you."

"For my hand?"

"For everything. For driving me. For letting me hold your hand. For carrying me to the car. Hell, for giving me a job."

"That was purely selfish on my part."

"What?"

"Hiring you. My mom makes me crazy. I'm grateful you took the job."

She laughed quietly. Her free hand rubbed her belly. "You know if I have this baby now, we'll be revisiting our conversation from this morning."

"Why is that?"

"Because Ella will go home with her parents. I'll be ready to move on with my life."

"Kind of soon, isn't it?"

"Do you know how little I've enjoyed over the last six months or so? I deserve a break, some fun."

His thumb stroked her hand where they were still connected. Part of him wished he could take the time to explore with her, to see what they could be. But he knew she was meant for something better than him. "So move on with your life. Put me behind you."

"No."

"No?"

"That's what I said. We're attracted to each other. Why can't we enjoy that?"

"You're about to have another's man's baby. How can you even think about starting something else?"

"At this particular moment, I really need a distraction from the pain. Beyond that, I know life is too short to dwell on your mistakes. I go after what I want."

"Shouldn't be me."

"We'll see."

She seemed to be breathing better now. Like starting an argument with him somehow gave her renewed energy. He got off the expressway and jogged across the side streets to the hospital. "Any idea which lot I pull into?"

"Maybe you should go to the emergency room. I think my water just broke." Her fingers tightened on his again and he maneuvered toward the emergency entrance. He pulled up in front of the door and extricated his hand. "Stay here. I'll get help."

He ran through the doors and told the nurse he had a woman in labor in his car. Within minutes, Norah was in a wheelchair being pushed into the hospital. Kai ran and parked the car and returned to find Norah. They already had her in a room. He knocked on the door and she called for him to come in.

She was waddling out of the bathroom in a hospital gown. A look of shock came over her face. "You're here?"

"Did you think I'd leave you alone?"

She lifted a shoulder. "This isn't your problem."

"I know I said I'm an asshole, and I am, but I wouldn't leave you alone." He reached for her arm to help her climb into bed. She did her best to hold the edges of the gown to retain her modesty. He didn't have the heart to tell her there was nothing she could do.

As soon as she lay back on the mattress, she curled up in pain again. He stood, paralyzed, not knowing what to do for her. A nurse came in and started hooking Norah up to a machine. She talked quietly in a soothing tone that, judging by the scowl on Norah's face, did nothing for her.

"When do I get some drugs here?"

"I can put a call in to your doctor and see what she says."

"She better say you should give me the epidural."

The nurse smiled and patted Norah's leg. Then she took Norah's arm and readied an IV. Norah's free hand flung out toward Kai, reaching. He held it and she squeezed as the needle went in. Then another contraction hit, so she didn't let go.

He didn't want to think about why that didn't bother him.

The nurse left and he sat, holding Norah's hand and staring at her.

"God, don't look at me. I'm probably a mess."

"You look fine. You want the TV on or something?"

She shook her head. "Just talk to me."

Like he was good at that. "What do you want to talk about?"

"Tell me about work."

"What about it?"

"Tell me about the craziest tattoo you've ever done."

He pulled a chair close to the bed and sat. Leaning his elbow on the edge of the mattress, he thought back over the hundreds of tattoos he'd done. There were some that stood out more than others, of course, but crazy? He tried to steer clear of those. Then he thought of one.

"The first month I opened, I was desperate for clients. I handed out business cards and posted flyers everywhere. I spent so much time doodling and praying for someone to come in. Then one day, this guy comes through the door holding my flyer. He says he's got a proposition for me. If I do a tattoo that he wants for free, I can do another of my business card on his body. He'd be a walking billboard."

"No way."

Kai nodded. "I figured the guy wasn't right in the head, so I told him no. But, I really needed the money. The guy swore he could drum up business. The next day, he comes in with like ten friends. They all wanted tattoos. I figured there had to be a catch."

"So what was it?"

Kai shook his head. "I still haven't figured it out. They all paid for tattoos. Needless to say, I did that guy's for free. He's still a client."

"Did you do your business card on him?"

"No. We compromised and I signed him."

Norah laughed. "You mean there's some guy walking around Chicago with your autograph on his body?"

"Yep."

"Why would someone want that? It's not like you're famous or anything."

Kai shrugged again. "Beats me."

The door behind him flung open. "Norah."

Norah shifted to see around him. "Hey, Jimmy."

"Oh God. I'm so sorry. I was in a meeting and didn't pay attention to my phone. I thought we had time." He pulled up short on his way to the bed and looked at Kai.

"Jimmy, this is Kai. Tommy's boss who hired me to help with his mom." She barely got the words out before another contraction hit and she curled into herself without releasing Kai's hand.

By the time he got home, his fingers would probably carry bruises from her grip.

Kai rubbed her hand and up her arm. Jimmy's eyes bore into him. When the pain passed, Norah looked between the two of them.

Jimmy finally stuck his hand out. "It's nice to meet you. Thank you for getting her to the hospital."

Although Kai shook his hand, he took the statement for what it was meant to be: Get out. Kai slid his hand from Norah's. "Good luck. I'll see you."

"Kai," Norah called.

He turned from where he stood with his hand on the door.

"Thank you." She gave him a watery smile.

"No problem." He left the room and the hospital. In the car, he called Jaleesa and his mom. Without Norah, they would need a new game plan. He didn't even know if Norah planned on coming back to work.

Part of him was relieved at the notion. He wouldn't have

to control his urges around her. But more of him didn't like the thought of not seeing her anymore.

He was screwed.

Jimmy sat on the edge of the bed looking down at Ella in Norah's arms. She was the most beautiful baby Norah had ever seen. A shock of dark hair fluffed up on the top of her head and she was tiny and wrinkled. But healthy. The doctor had assured Norah that although she was a little small, Ella was healthy.

"You did good, Norah." His finger stroked the top of Ella's head.

"She's amazing."

"Are you having second thoughts about adoption?"

A tear squeezed out of the corner of her eye. "I'm scared, Jimmy. I love this little girl. I'm so afraid of messing her up."

"We're here for you."

"I know. But I also know she would have a better life with Kim and Trevor. They *want* her. They've been searching for her. They're ready for her. As much as I love her, I'm not. She's going home with Kim and Trevor."

Jimmy wrapped his arms around her shoulders in an awkward hug. "Okay."

His voice was thick and it about crushed her to think she moved her big, bad brother to tears. They stayed like that for a while. She took the strength she could from Jimmy's embrace.

"I've already called Teagan and Kim. They're on their way."

"Already?"

"I don't want to take care of her. I don't want to do anything that will confuse me. I wanted to hold her to tell her

I love her, but she needs to be with Kim." Tears streamed down her face. She knew it was the right decision, but it didn't make it any less difficult.

"The guys want to come meet her."

"Is that a good idea?" She swiped at her face. "I can't handle them telling me I should keep her."

"They won't. I can have them visit her in the nursery. Would that be easier for you?"

Norah nodded. A knock sounded at the door and Teagan poked her head in.

"Can we come in?"

"Yeah."

Teagan came in and Kim and Trevor followed.

Jimmy stood and stepped away from the bed. "You want me to stay or go?"

"You can go."

He nodded and left.

Kim and Trevor hovered by the door.

"Come on in and meet your daughter." She waved to them with her free hand.

They stepped forward together, Trevor's arm on Kim's shoulder. Kim's eyes filled.

"Do you want to hold her?"

Kim nodded and stretched her arms out. Handing Ella over to Kim was easier than Norah thought it would be. Love filled Kim's face and even Trevor looked teary. Her own tears started to fall again. For as right as it was, Norah's arms felt extraordinarily empty.

"After this, they're going to keep her in the nursery until she's ready to go home, so you can visit her there. I just wanted to say good-bye to her."

Kim passed Ella to Trevor and wrapped Norah in a tight hug. "I can never thank you enough for this. She is the most precious gift."

They stayed and talked and Norah told them about her labor, so Kim would have stories to tell Ella as she got older. Their tears stopped and the conversation was a relaxed one between friends, but Norah was exhausted and the baby started to fuss.

"She's probably hungry," Norah said.

"You're sure you don't want to . . ." Kim asked.

"She's all yours." Norah called for the nurse so she could take Trevor and Kim to the nursery to feed and change Ella. Teagan sat on the bed next to Norah.

"Want to talk?"

"Not really. I think I just want a nap."

"Okay. I'll hang out for a while. Is there anything you need?"

"No."

"Don't keep it bottled up, Norah. I'm here for you."

"I know. And I'm really okay. For now." She tugged the blanket up over her freezing arms and shifted on the bed to find a comfortable spot.

She pulled out her phone and called Avery.

"Hi, Norah."

The way he said her name was stiff and so different than the way Kai said it. "I had the baby."

"What? I thought you weren't due yet."

"She had other ideas."

"How are you?"

"I'm okay."

"And the baby?"

"Her name is Ella. She's beautiful. I can send you some pictures I took if you want."

His voice quieted when he spoke. "I'd like that."

"You can meet her too. Kim and Trevor are really cool. I think you'd like them." She thought of the nerdy references on their profile and knew that was part of why she'd chosen them. Avery was like that.

Silence settled between them, but it wasn't uneasy, just sad. "I'll let you know."

She disconnected and wasn't sure how to address the emotions coursing through her. She couldn't help but think how different things might've been if she and Avery had had the chance to be a real couple, build a strong relationship. Would she have wanted to keep Ella then?

She was so wrung out, physically and emotionally. She just wanted this day over.

After two days in the hospital and the rest of the week at home, Norah was going stir-crazy. She'd had a constant flow of visitors with her brothers taking turns dropping in on her, all of them at least feigning support. Ultimately, she wanted to be left alone and now that she'd achieved it, the loneliness threatened to tear her up.

Getting out of bed that morning, she felt blobby and gross. It was one thing to feel like a whale while she was growing a baby inside her, but no one ever mentioned how fat she would stay after giving birth. And she still felt like crying. All. The. Time.

She'd signed the paperwork giving her daughter to Kim and Trevor, and Avery had sent his back. It was officially a done deal. She should feel relieved. In some ways she was, but in others, she just felt empty.

She left her house and drove to Kai's without thinking. They hadn't discussed when or if she'd come back to work for him and she hadn't spoken to him since he left the hospital. Jimmy and Tommy had gotten her car back home so she'd had no contact. She hoped Jaleesa was there instead of Kai. Part of her was afraid to face him, especially after her bold statements in his car while she was in labor.

Maybe she could chalk it all up to pregnancy brain. She

shouldn't be held accountable for things she'd said while in pain.

Instead of using her key, she knocked on the door, not wanting to frighten anyone by barging in. When the door swung open, the shock of seeing Kai in a towel again stole her breath. Didn't this man know the effect he had? He should be required to wear clothing.

"Norah." The single word was filled with surprise but something else as well. She was reminded again of how different he was than Avery.

"Hi."

He stepped back from the door to let her in. His gaze swept over her, making her uncomfortable because she knew she was far from at her best.

"I know we didn't talk about me coming back after having the baby, but . . ." She didn't even know where she was going with that.

"I . . . Shouldn't you be in bed or something?"

She huffed, trying to make it a laugh. "I spent two days in bed. Then I was stuck at my house for days. I needed to get out."

"Are you supposed to work?"

She shrugged. "I didn't ask." Although she knew that technically, if she had a regular job, she would be off for six weeks.

He crossed his arms over his massive bare chest and Norah averted her eyes. He was too easy to stare at.

"Have you hired someone else?"

Kai laughed—well, as much as she'd ever heard him laugh anyway. "My mother made it clear that she would run off anyone we hired. Jaleesa and I have been juggling our schedules."

Norah bit her cheek to stop the smile. She really liked Lani. "So you need me then."

"I guess I do."

This time, she let the full force of her smile hit him. She knew he was referring to his mom, but she wished it was more. "So now's the time to negotiate a raise."

He shook his head. "Nice try. Not gonna happen."

She raised an eyebrow. "Then maybe you should offer some other benefits."

"Also not going to happen." He slid along the wall and turned when he cleared the corner.

She followed with her smile growing again. "Get your mind out of the gutter. I was talking about dental."

There was a brief hitch in his stride and he looked over his shoulder at her. She winked and he shook his head again.

Lani came from the direction of the bathroom. When she saw Norah, she smiled. "You're back."

"How could I stay away from the best friend I have in the city?" As soon as Norah said it, she realized how true it was. She was a woman in her early twenties with no friends. She had Moira, who she could easily see becoming good friends with, but she only had her because of Jimmy. She needed to start getting out and meeting people.

Kai disappeared into his room and a bit of sadness crept into Norah with the thought that he'd return fully dressed.

"How are you feeling?" Lani sat on the couch and patted the cushion beside her.

"Fat."

Lani laughed.

"I'm serious. I don't know why you sat down. We have a walk to get to. You need to build strength and I need to lose weight." She went to the couch and held out her arm to help Lani up.

The woman shook her head at Norah, but yelled, "We're walking, Kai. Have a good day at work."

Kai came from his room, dressed in his usual jeans and T-shirt, but he hadn't gotten around to tying his hair back yet. The dark waves were damn sexy. "Is that a good idea?" he asked, oblivious to her stare.

Norah rolled her eyes. "It's a walk, not a marathon. We'll be fine."

Lani stood. "I'll get my sweater."

When she left the room, Kai stepped closer. "How are you?"

"I'm okay. I was just going stir-crazy. Even if you didn't need me, I think I'd've stayed with your mom for a while. My family was getting on my nerves."

"And the baby and the boyfriend?"

"Ella is with her parents. Avery is still at school." The empty feeling struck again. The one time she counted on Kai being silent, he wanted her to talk. A lump was forming in her throat, so she swallowed hard. She'd come here to escape these feelings.

"As happy as I am that you're back, I don't want you to overdo it. My mom thought you'd be gone for at least two or three weeks."

Three weeks alone with her dad? She'd go crazy. "I feel good. I won't do any heavy lifting. Walking is good for her and me."

He lowered his face so they were eye to eye. "You sure?"

"Yeah." She licked her lips and then whispered the truth. "I need this."

He studied her for a few seconds, then nodded. "Call me if you need anything."

"Ready?" Lani asked from behind Kai.

"Let's go." Norah painted on a friendly smile. She'd take whatever normalcy she could hold on to right now.

Kai fell into his easy routine of having Norah around and he was grateful for it. Fortunately, her flirting was minimal and he'd been able to escape too many thoughts of her naked.

Things were going so well that he'd asked her to work Sunday night so he could have his poker game without interruption.

He still hadn't told his mom because he didn't want to give her any fuel for ruining his night. At the grocery store, he grabbed the beer and detoured down the dairy aisle. His house had been yogurt-free for a while now. Instead of grabbing the lime yogurt, he placed a selection of other flavors in his basket.

Learning from his mistakes, he went in through the back door at home and tossed the yogurt in the fridge to avoid his mom's commentary. He then took the beer straight downstairs. When he came back up, he slid the pizza box on the table in front of her.

"Went all out for dinner tonight, huh?"

"Nothing but the best for you, Mom."

She laughed. "Go get me a plate and a napkin."

He did as he was told. Once she was settled with a few slices, he said, "My friends are coming over to play poker tonight, so I asked Norah to stop by."

"I told you I don't need a babysitter. I'm doing fine."

"It's for me."

Her eyes shot up and a spark of something lit in them. Then he realized how his words sounded. "Not like that. I asked her here so my game wouldn't be interrupted. It's kind of hard to focus when you're calling me every ten minutes."

"I did not call every ten minutes. You're exaggerating."

"It doesn't matter. If you need anything tonight, Norah will be here."

She hmmphed and crossed her arms like a cranky toddler. "I think you should have your game up here so I can play too."

As if he'd *ever* let that happen. "I like to win when I play."

That brought a smile to her face, which was all he'd wanted. "Play a game with Norah. She doesn't know all your tricks." When his mom remained silent, his suspicions grew. "You played cards with her?"

"Just gin. Not poker."

"Forget it then. She won't be dumb enough to fall for that twice."

"What do you know?"

He didn't really. It was just a feeling he had about Norah. She struck him as the kind of person who learned quickly on the fly. She certainly had with his mom.

They sat and ate pizza while his mom commented on some stupid talk show she'd found. He remembered what Norah had said about his mom being lonely. Her physical therapy was going to start in the office this week, so it would be good for her to get out. Maybe Norah could take her to meet with her friends for coffee or something.

Then he thought about how happy she'd been, the laughter he'd heard when he broke up their so-called book club. As long as he didn't have to be there to supervise, what harm could come from letting her host again?

As he cleaned up the mess from dinner, the front door opened and Norah strode in. An unwelcome feeling ripped through him at the sight of her walking through the door like she belonged there. Of course, she belonged. She was his employee. But unlike any other employee, he enjoyed seeing her come in.

"Hey," she called.

Kai held the pizza box up. "Did you eat dinner yet?"

"No. I'd love a slice."

He set the box back down. "Have as much as you want."

"Only one slice for me. I'm trying to lose weight. I packed on pounds for the last nine months."

"Nonsense," his mom said. "It took nine months to grow a baby. The weight will come off when it's ready."

Norah lifted a slice to her mouth, but paused. "Well, I'm just going to help it along." She nudged the box with her knee. "Take this away."

Kai didn't laugh, although he wanted to.

Chapter Ten

As soon as the pizza touched her lips, Norah's phone rang. While she chewed, she pulled it from her pocket. Tommy. What the heck did he want? "Excuse me," she mumbled with a mouthful of pizza as she walked to the kitchen to answer.

"What's up?" she asked.

"Where are you?"

"Kai's. He asked me to work tonight."

"He did? I didn't see any clients scheduled."

"Not for work. He's got friends coming over for a poker game."

Tommy laughed. "That can't be right. Kai doesn't have any friends."

"Whatever."

"I'm serious. I've known the guy for a couple of years now. No one's ever come to the shop to see him other than paying customers. And he's never had anyone show for a hockey game. Not even beers after. I think he's running game."

"For what?" She set her pizza down on a napkin. Was it possible he just wanted to see her and used this as an excuse? She shook her head. Kai wasn't that kind of guy.

"I don't know, but it's fishy."

"Maybe he doesn't want you to meet his friends because you're a dork."

"Ha. Takes one to know one."

Just then Kai came in carrying the pizza box. "Talk to you later," she said to Tommy.

"I want details when you get home."

She disconnected without responding, but Tommy had definitely piqued her interest. Kai shoved the last few slices of pizza into a plastic bag and put it in the fridge.

"Everything okay?" he asked.

"Yeah. Tommy wanted to know where I was since I normally don't work Sundays."

"Is it a problem?"

"Nope. Just my brother being nosy." She reached past him into the fridge for a bottle of water. Then she noticed half a shelfful of yogurt. "Have a hankering for some yogurt?"

His lips twitched and he averted his eyes. "I thought that now . . ." He waved his hands in the general direction of her stomach. "You might be up for trying something new."

She wanted to make some flirtatious, sexy comment about trying something new, but the gesture was too sweet for her to make fun. "Thank you," she said sincerely. "That was thoughtful."

"It's nothing." His eyes met hers. "Besides, lime is really disgusting."

She laughed. "I don't disagree. I don't think I'll be eating any of it again."

"I'll be downstairs. Yell if you need anything. The guys will come through the back so we won't bother you. I'll be up in a while to help get Mom into bed."

"I can handle it."

"I thought no lifting."

"She mostly does it on her own. We make it work."

"Call if you have any problems." Then he went down, closing the door behind him.

Norah wanted to follow, to bug him about why he went out of his way to buy her a variety of yogurt, but she knew it wouldn't get her anywhere with him. He'd do nice things for her, but wouldn't acknowledge the attraction between them. She had to figure out a way to get him to make a move.

For the next hour or so, she and Lani watched TV and Lani filled her in on the latest book club book. As time wore on, the deep murmur of men's voices carried through the floor. Curiosity clawed at her. Borne from her position as the youngest sibling of five, she *had* to know what was going on. It was an inexplicable feeling.

"So, do you know the guys Kai plays poker with?"

Lani waved an annoyed hand. "He tells me nothing. Never brings his friends around me. I have myself to blame. I was critical of his friends when he was young. Had a right to be though. They were losers dragging my son down. Hoodlums."

With each additional detail Norah got, she tried to piece together who Kai Ellis was. She knew him as a talented artist. He'd taught Tommy a lot and for all the jokes Tommy made about Kai, he admitted Kai was a brilliant artist. She'd seen him on the ice as part of the hockey team. They feared and revered him as their muscle.

But she'd yet to see him fully relaxed, just hanging out. As Lani got ready for bed, Norah gathered the dirty laundry. It gave her an excuse to go downstairs to check out Kai's friends. She helped Lani into bed, which was getting easier each day, as Lani needed less and less aid. Norah wondered if Kai understood that, or if Lani played it up for him.

She said good night to Lani and scooped up the laundry from the bathroom. She eyed Kai's bedroom door and briefly considered going in to get his clothes, but decided against it. That would be overstepping and, as curious as she was, she wanted him to invite her in, to tell her things willingly.

After checking that Lani was comfortable and making sure she didn't have anything else to be washed, Norah headed downstairs. She didn't know what she'd expected. She'd grown up with four brothers. But stepping into the basement was heady. If walking in on Kai's workout was a tidal wave of testosterone, this was a veritable tsunami.

Four guys sat with Kai around a table and the air was thick with their manliness. For a moment, she was taken aback. She didn't want to stare, so she turned away from them toward the washer. Conversation dwindled behind her and she felt the stares.

She looked over her shoulder. "Sorry to interrupt. I just want to throw in a load of laundry. It won't bother you, will it?"

Four pairs of eyes locked on her. The only one who didn't look her way was Kai. Big surprise. The only indication of his recognition of her presence was the telltale stiffening of his shoulders.

"Hey, *chica*. Who are you?" A skinny guy stood and smacked Kai's shoulder. "You holding out on us, man?"

Norah set the laundry basket on the machine and took a few steps, arm extended. "I'm Norah. I help take care of Kai's mom."

His hand touched hers in more of a caress than a shake. "I'm Rooster."

She smiled. "Rooster. Interesting name."

Although the other men each looked at her, only Rooster did anything to engage. Norah loaded the clothes into the washer and started the machine. With the task done, she turned toward the stairs.

"Why don't you come have a seat?" Rooster called from the table.

Norah eyed the group. She'd wanted Kai to invite her but it didn't look like that would happen. In fact, it seemed more like he couldn't wait for her to leave. "Doesn't look like there's room. But thanks."

"Hey, there's room right here on my lap."

Yeah, the skeevy feeling she'd had during their handshake? Spot on.

"Stop being an asshole. You'll scare the girl away," another guy said as he shuffled the cards. He tilted his chin toward the corner. "There's a crate there you can sit on. You know how to play?"

She edged around the table toward the crate and waited to check Kai's reaction. As she picked up the crate, he jumped up to take it from her. "It's an empty crate. I can handle it."

"You just had a baby."

"Congratulations," Rooster said. "Where's your man? He shouldn't be letting you hang out in a basement full of hot-blooded men like this."

"I don't have a man." She quickly recognized this as a test. She wasn't sure who was issuing it—Kai or his friends. But she knew she couldn't back down.

Kai scooted his chair over a few inches and set the crate next to him.

Rooster immediately protested. "There's all this space over here. Why she gotta sit with you?"

Kai sent him a chilling look that shut him up. Sitting next to Kai sounded better by the minute. Kai settled on the crate and pointed to the chair.

"I'm only staying for one hand, Kai. I'll take the crate."

The look he shot her wasn't much warmer than the one Rooster received. Well then. She swallowed hard and sat. Being this close to Kai made her tummy tumble in a totally good way. She cleared her throat and looked at the guy shuffling. "I haven't played in a while, but if you keep it simple, I can play." She reached out. "Norah."

"Eric." He shook her hand and then pointed around the table. "Since Kai is feeling antisocial today, that's Carlos and Dean."

She nodded to each man.

"We'll keep it simple for the lady, then. Five-card draw." He glanced at Norah and she nodded. It was basic enough and she was pretty sure she remembered the rules.

"Dollar in."

They each put a dollar in the pot and cards were dealt. While waiting, it was obvious that Rooster had issues sitting still and being quiet. He was about as opposite Kai as one could imagine.

"Why no man, Norah? Baby daddy drama?"

"No. I gave my baby up for adoption."

"Ooo. That's rough."

She gave a small nod. She really didn't want to discuss this, especially with a roomful of strangers.

"Leave it, Rooster." The quiet command came from Kai.

Norah tried not to read too much into it. The cards were dealt and she looked at her hand. She had a pair of kings, a pair of eights, and a three. They each threw another fifty cents in the pot and then exchanged cards. She discarded the three. Surprisingly, her new card was a king. Damn. A full house. This time, as bets went around, she raised a dollar, liking her odds.

Kai dropped his cards. He wouldn't bet against her. Dean and Carlos followed. It was down to her, Eric, and Rooster.

Rooster cackled. "I think you're bluffing." He leaned over the table as if she was unclear he was speaking to her. "Care to make another wager?"

The way he wagged his eyebrows made Norah roll her

eyes. She didn't need to ask what kind of wager he referred to. "No thanks."

"Come on. It'll be fun for both of us. Win-win."

If there had been a thermostat in the room, it would've registered a drop in temperature as Kai said, "Play the game."

"Call."

They each laid their cards on the table. Eric had two pairs. Rooster only had an ace. What the hell had he been thinking in trying to wager more?

Norah smiled and reached forward to scoop up the pot. "Thank you very much, gentlemen. I never thought a single load of laundry could be so profitable." She stacked the bills and took the handful of coins and dropped them all in her pocket.

"Stay," Rooster said.

"Thanks, but I said one hand. I should go check on Lani."

"Lani, huh? You're on a first-name basis. Maybe I should be offended, huh, Kai?"

"Shut up, Rooster."

"Thanks for the game. It was nice meeting you," Norah said.

"I'd like to meet you again, baby."

Norah ignored the comment, but Rooster wasn't about to let up.

"Now's the best time. You just popped one out, no danger of another baking up. It'd be all about the pleasure."

As much as she'd been thinking about sex over the past few weeks, this did nothing but completely extinguish her libido. The guy was a creep. Why did Kai hang out with him?

She didn't say anything, nor did she wait to see if Kai would say something. She turned to the stairs. She'd only gone a few feet, when she felt a presence at her back and a spear of panic shot through her, but she knew Kai wouldn't let anything happen to her. She took a deep breath to rebuff Rooster one last time.

When she turned, it was Kai at her back. She hoped her fear hadn't shown.

He briefly touched her hand but made no other movement. "He's just fucking with you. He's harmless."

While Norah believed he wasn't a threat to her here, in this house, in this basement, she held no illusion that it would remain true in another place.

"Okay." She turned and jogged up the stairs, pretty sure Rooster let out a catcall whistle as she did. In the kitchen she had the urge to wash her hands. Rooster had made her feel gross. Her mission to get insight into who Kai was backfired. That hand of poker had given her nothing, other than the knowledge that his friend was a jerk. The other guys seemed okay though.

As she filled a glass with water, the basement door swung open and she spun to see who followed her.

Kai stood in front of her. "I have a favor to ask."

Those words looked like they caused him pain. "What?"

"Don't mention my friends to my mom."

"Why not? She knows you're having them over."

Then the pieces started to fall into place. Norah linked what Lani had said about Kai's loser friends and how critical she'd been of them to Kai's desire for Lani to not find out who was in the basement. She took the information to file away when she had time to think.

"She doesn't like them and I don't want her getting upset."

"On one condition."

The muscle in his jaw twitched, which made her smile.

"You let your mom host her book club again."

Something flashed in his eye and she knew she should've gone for something bigger.

"As long as it's on a night when I work late and they leave when I get home."

"Agreed." She stuck her hand out to shake on the deal.

Instead of taking her hand, he crossed his arms. "Most people would've bargained for something for themselves."

"Maybe I'm waiting for next time. Lulling you into a sense of security."

"I know better and there won't be a next time." He turned to go downstairs.

Norah called, "How did you know I had a good hand?"

He spun back to face her.

"You didn't bet against me. Why?" she pushed.

He stepped closer—way into her personal space, which gave her no small thrill—and his whisper coasted over her ear. "You can't bluff. You show everything in your eyes."

Her pulse raced, but she said, "Do not."

"Just like you put up a great front with Rooster, but your eyes showed how uncomfortable you were." His hand landed on her hip and he eased a fraction away to look into her eyes. His look dared her to deny it.

"And what do my eyes tell you now?"

"Nothing you should be thinking and nothing I want to hear." His fingers flexed on the fleshy part of her hip, but then he released her and walked away. "If my mom's asleep, you can go."

"Chicken," she mumbled. She didn't know what she was doing. Sticking her nose into his game to meet his friends, bargaining for his mom, wishing he would kiss her. She was a mess. Something about being around Kai set her on edge but made her want more.

Yet he kept pushing her away. Maybe it was time to move on and look for something else.

* * *

Kai was fucked up. He'd been doing good staying away from Norah, but every time he turned around, she pressed into his space, in different parts of his life, demanding attention. When Rooster started hitting on her, Kai had wanted to punch him. But that was just Rooster being Rooster. He wanted to get a rise out of Norah and Kai was proud that she didn't let Rooster know he'd gotten to her.

She'd handled herself well around his friends, which made him like her more. But he wasn't supposed to. She shouldn't have to handle herself around those guys. She deserved better than a poker game in his basement with an ex-gangbanger hitting on her.

He heard her call him a chicken as he left the kitchen. Without a doubt, he was. He shouldn't have crawled up on her like that, but he needed to know the look he saw was real, that he wasn't misreading anything. Not that it should've mattered. It was more like a test of his own sanity, which was barely hanging on.

Rubbing a hand over his face, he went to the fridge and pulled out another beer.

"That was a long conversation you had with Norah," Rooster said.

"I was making sure she knew not to tell my mom you were here."

"Just making an observation that 'keep your mouth shut' takes like thirty seconds to say. You get a quickie up there?"

Kai cringed. "She just had a baby, man, like a week ago. Pretty sure sex is the last thing on her mind." Too bad it hadn't been the last thing on his.

"You talk a good game, but I saw you two looking at each other. Now I know why you didn't want us to meet her."

Eric laughed. "She might be a keeper."

Keeper? What the fuck?

"She didn't run screaming when Rooster hit on her," he added.

Then Carlos jumped in. "Even better, she didn't entertain his ideas."

Rooster threw his hands up. "Hey, now, I was hardly tryin'."

Dean chucked a quarter at Rooster. "Enough. Are we playing cards, or what?"

Since Kai hadn't heard from his mom, she must've been asleep, which meant Norah would leave for the night. The thought allowed him to focus on the game and even win a few hands. Unfortunately, about a half hour later, Norah stomped down the stairs announcing her presence.

"Sorry to interrupt again. I don't want to leave the laundry in the washer to get mildewed."

She said nothing else as she switched the clothes from one machine to the next. He didn't like her ignoring him any more than he liked her stepping in the middle of his business. It wasn't fair and he knew it. He enjoyed their flirtations, but he wanted it to stay just between the two of them. Especially since the flirtation wouldn't become more.

She started the dryer and said, "Your mom's sound asleep, so I'm heading home."

Carlos looked from Kai to Norah before saying, "It's late. You should walk her to her car. Your mama raised you better than that."

Rooster jumped up. "I'll walk you."

"I'm good, thanks. My four older brothers all made sure I had my fill of self-defense classes."

Kai rose. He wouldn't leave Norah alone with Rooster and he *was* raised better than to let any woman walk alone late at night. "Let's go."

He held his hand out for her to lead the way, which turned out to be a bad idea because it gave him the perfect view of her ass as she climbed the stairs.

In the living room, she grabbed her purse. "You don't have to walk me out. I'm right in front."

"Then it won't take long." He walked to the front door and held it open.

"Men," she muttered as she walked past him.

She popped the locks on the doors and, at the car, he reached around and opened the door for her.

"Such a gentleman," she said, leaning against the car.

"You make me want to not act like a gentleman."

Her smile widened. "It's a talent, I guess. Too bad you're too chicken to act on it."

Her goading flipped a switch in him and he no longer thought. He moved in, cupping the back of her head and hauling her into his body. He captured her mouth, tasting her lips and savoring her tongue until she moaned into his mouth. His grip tightened on her hair and he pulled her head to the side so he could taste her neck.

Her pulse jackhammered against his tongue and when he bit down on her sensitive flesh, she gasped. His dick was like iron in his jeans. When he finally dragged himself away from her, they were both breathless.

"I'm not chicken. I'm smart. We're combustible and this would get out of control."

Her eyes fluttered open and met his. "Yeah, well, I've been in control, not enjoying any part of my life for many months. What's the harm in running this until it's extinguished?"

Just as he suspected, this girl would be his death. He leaned his forehead against hers. "Because when it dies down, one of us will be burned. I don't want you to end up in ashes." That was his fear, that he'd somehow destroy her.

"Like I said inside, I can take care of myself. I'm a big girl. I want to escape for a while, no different than your mom reading."

He pushed away from the car before he made another

move toward her. He wanted her too badly. "Find your escape with someone who'll be good for you."

"I bet Rooster would offer one hell of a vacation."

Anger flashed through him. "Don't."

She rolled her eyes. "Obviously, I'm not serious. However, you played your last card and your bluff sucked. You want me, Kai, every bit as much as I want you. I just had a baby, so I have weeks before I can have sex. That should be enough time to wear you down."

He hated that he'd given her confirmation. As if kissing her hadn't been enough.

She winked and slid into the car. "See you tomorrow, Kai."

Her voice was like silk over his skin with just enough tease to make his dick perk up. He slammed the door and stepped back on the curb until she pulled away. He shouldn't have let her get to him. He knew better and he'd been able to keep his distance for weeks. With any luck, by the time she was ready to have sex, his mom would be back at Jaleesa's and they'd part ways.

All he had to do was steer clear and they'd both be okay. Or so he told himself.

His dick, on the other hand, had its own ideas.

Norah was on a new mission—make Kai want to have a fling. She wouldn't go so far as to think they'd have a relationship because that man practically screamed bachelorhood, but between his mom and her pregnancy, they could both use some fun. He made her feel like herself in a way she hadn't in many months. She wanted to reclaim part of herself. And like he'd said, together they were kind of combustible.

So she was going to test the waters.

And if nothing came of it, she'd be ready to move on

anyway. He would be a nice distraction while she got the rest of her life in order. First up, she needed to get her body back to where it should be. She'd read the baby books about what happened to her body and how it would take time to bounce back, but actresses and models did it all the time. She wasn't seeking perfection, just normalcy.

She started her mornings with yoga stretches. After checking her dad's blood and making sure he took his meds, she went for a walk. Alone, she was able to walk a lot faster than she could with Lani, so their walks were reinforcement.

She'd already started to feel better. Her boobs were shrinking back to normal since she wasn't breastfeeding. The excess blood flow had almost stopped. Now, if she could only figure out how to make her hormones and emotions snap back, all would be good.

After her walk, her dad stopped her in the living room.

"What?" she asked, tugging an earbud out.

"I want to talk to you."

She swung her arms out. "So talk."

"Sit down and don't sass me."

She sat on the edge of the chair across from him as he used the remote to turn off the TV. No TV meant serious conversation. It was good to know that some things never changed.

"How are you?"

Kind of a dumb question to start a conversation with. "Fine."

"I mean with the baby and all."

"She's good, Dad. Kim and Trevor will be great parents. And I get to be part of her life. You can too, if you want."

"I wish you would've kept her, but I understand why you didn't."

His acceptance was all she'd wanted from the beginning.

It was a little unsettling to actually get it. "Thanks. I needed to do what was right for her."

"That's why we sent you to Bridget." He sat forward, bracing his meaty arms on his knees. "You were smart and pretty and we were gonna screw you up. With the boys . . . I knew what to do with them. A slap upside the head usually did the trick."

"I wanted to stay," she whispered.

"Jimmy was leaving and you were already acting out. Ditching school and causing trouble. Following in your brothers' footsteps in no good way."

"I was a kid."

"Exactly. At twelve, you were already acting like your teenage brothers. Jimmy and I believed Bridget would know what to do with you. And she was always nagging about how a houseful of men wasn't a place for a young girl. As you grew, you were more and more like your mom. It made it easy to believe she'd do better." His jaw flexed. "We were afraid you'd end up pregnant by some loser."

She almost laughed. Almost. She'd known why Jimmy had wanted to send her away. He didn't trust their dad not to screw her up. They'd fought about it often over the years. Now that she was older, she understood. She didn't like it, but she understood. "You never asked what I wanted. No one did. I felt so alone, Dad. It was like I stopped existing for you."

"That was shitty of me. But watching you grow—hell, even now—you're so much like your mom, my Siobhan. Sometimes, it's hard to look at you."

Her throat tightened. He never talked about her mom. Everything Norah knew about her came from Aunt Bridget and a few stories from Jimmy. She knew she looked like her mom because Jimmy had framed a photo of their mom for her before she'd left for Boston.

Her dad cleared his throat. "So what are your plans now? Back to Boston to finish school?"

One thing she could say for Seamus O'Malley was that he'd never linger over emotional topics. "No. I'm going to find a school here to transfer to. I liked Boston, but it was never home. I want to stay here. Is that okay?"

"Sure. As long as you stop nagging about my blood and my meds." He leaned back on the couch and picked up the remote.

Norah pushed off the chair. "Not likely to happen. In fact, by the time I get my nursing degree, I'll probably get worse." She leaned over him and kissed his cheek. Her dad wasn't much for physical affection, but she needed that little bit to let him know they were good. "I want you around for a long time."

"I'm not going anywhere."

She went upstairs to shower and change before going to Kai's. She pulled out a pair of her old jeans and shimmied into them. Her thighs felt compressed and she had zero chance of buttoning them, but she was getting closer. She peeled them off and resorted to the yoga pants she'd been living in. She flat out refused to continue wearing maternity clothes. She understood why some women did. They were comfy. But since she wasn't raising Ella, she didn't want the questions that would come with the clothes.

Her large T-shirt camouflaged some of her flabbiness and she wore Kai's sweatshirt over the top of everything. She should've returned it, but she decided to wait until he asked for it. It was worn and soft. Unlike Kai who was all hard muscle and attitude.

She caught a glimpse of herself in the mirror as she left. Not quite the tempting outfit she'd need to sway Kai, but she'd figured out that to lure him, she'd need to be subtle and sneaky. Moving forward would have to appear to be his idea, not hers. He liked to be in charge, make the moves.

She could let him have that, but a little maneuvering on her part couldn't hurt.

Walking into Kai's house, Norah called out as she did every day to let everyone know she'd arrived. "Hello. Lani?"

Lani didn't answer because she was sitting on the couch. "Why do you yell like that every day?"

"I want to give you fair warning I'm coming in."

"You want to give *me* fair warning? Or Kai?"

"Whatever." She glanced through the room as if she'd find some evidence to let her know Kai was home, but there was never anything. She knew it was his house because it felt like him, but he moved around almost silently.

Lani sighed. "He's in the kitchen."

"Huh?"

"Don't look at me like that. Kai is in the kitchen. Maybe you should let him know you're here."

"Actually, I might grab a yogurt before our walk. I'm hungry."

"Mmm-hmm" was all Lani said before returning her attention to the book in her hand.

Norah wasn't sure how she felt about Lani making those assumptions about her and Kai. Sure, she wanted to start something with him, but it wasn't something she wanted to declare to his mom. That would be weird.

Kai leaned against the kitchen counter, shirtless again, drinking his coffee. "Enjoying my sweatshirt?"

"Actually, I am. It's very comfortable." She reached into the refrigerator and took out a strawberry yogurt.

Chapter Eleven

Kai didn't want to stay and watch Norah, but he couldn't move. Ever since he'd kissed her by her car, he'd done his best to avoid her because she was some kind of irresistible. Standing there in his battered sweatshirt that had to be three sizes too big, she was cute.

Then she peeled back the foil lid on her yogurt and licked it, managing to make eating yogurt sexy. Without speaking, she said plenty with the way she swirled the spoon over her tongue. She wanted to torment him and she was good at it.

"You shouldn't play games."

With her spoon poised for another dip, she said, "Games can be fun. We're all entitled to a little fun."

"No game is fun when the rules aren't clear."

She jabbed the spoon into the container and set the yogurt on the table beside her. She stepped forward, getting close enough to him that she had to crane her neck to look him in the eye. "So let's lay out the rules."

Standing toe-to-toe with him, she tried to look tough, but he saw her sweet softness. "You don't want to play with me."

"You're wrong. We definitely want to play with each

other. Otherwise you wouldn't have kissed me. Twice. And it was smokin' hot both times. There's no denying it."

He closed his eyes and hoped for strength. Without it, Norah would win whatever battle she was forcing.

A gentle finger stroked down his chest. "Look, we're adults. Our lives had been rough lately. All I'm saying is let's enjoy our time together. Your mom will be moving back to Jaleesa's in a couple of months. I'm not looking for a life partner. I'm looking to have some fun with you until I move on."

"And what does that fun look like?"

She swayed a little as she lifted her shoulders. "We can hang out. Mess around a little, see if the chemistry holds, and when I get the all clear from my doctor, get tangled up in some sheets."

"And you think your brother's going to be okay with us hanging out and . . ."

"Neither Tommy nor any of my brothers get a say in how I live my life and who I see."

He laughed. He might not have been the best brother in the world, but who his sister dated had always mattered. He'd thrown a scare into more than one teenager even though he was only two years older than Jaleesa.

Norah stroked his jaw. "That's a good look and an even better sound."

"What?"

"You smiling and laughing."

He enjoyed the feel of her palm on his cheek. Enough that he wanted to lean down and kiss her again. "So you want to date?"

She shrugged again. "Sounds silly when you say it. I just . . . Don't avoid me. Hang out and drink your coffee while I eat my yogurt and talk for a while." She smiled up at him. "Be friendly."

"Chatting and friendly aren't my thing."

She sighed. "Then what is?"

He pressed a hand to her hip to move her back, checking the urge to squeeze and bring her closer. "My thing? Taking you hard and fast up against the wall until you're screaming." He watched her throat work as she swallowed and her eyes dilated. Damn. He'd hoped to scare her off, but she was getting turned on.

She cleared her throat. "Then let's compromise. A month of my thing, followed by a month of your thing. Then your mom will be better and you won't need me anymore."

"I have to get to work."

"Don't be a chicken. Think about it."

The temptation was great. Two months of Norah being his. Well, a month of her being his and in order to get that, he'd have to what? Be friendly?

"Hey, Kai?"

He turned from the door.

"Do you think I can have Friday night off? I want to go out. Get a break."

Two thoughts immediately hit him: One, he didn't want Norah finding fun with some other guy, and two, he had a hockey game Friday night. But then he remembered his mom's physical therapy appointment was late that afternoon, and Jaleesa had offered to take her. He couldn't do anything about his reaction to the first, but the second could be remedied. "Should be okay. I'll ask Jaleesa to stay with her."

"Thanks."

Kai said good-bye to his mom and drove to work. He parked in front of Ink Envy and saw Tommy leaning against the door. "Where the hell is Puck? He was supposed to open."

Tommy shrugged.

"Damn it. Have any clients come by?"

"I've only been here about fifteen minutes, but haven't seen any."

Kai unlocked the door and pulled out his phone to text Puck. Puck got back to him immediately that his client had canceled so he didn't see the point in opening up. Kai didn't respond. It was a stupid argument to have over the phone. He'd wait until Puck came in.

Tommy plopped on the couch. "You know, if I had a set of keys, I could open for you."

Kai stared at him.

"What? I've been here for over a year. Haven't fucked up yet."

He had a point, but Kai still looked at Tommy like he was a kid. Which, when he considered it, was bad because he didn't look at Norah like a kid and she was younger.

"I'll think about it."

"Hey, how's Norah doing?"

Kai paused in prepping his station and schooled his face. If Norah wanted to include her brothers in their arrangement, it would be up to her. Damn. *Their* arrangement? He hadn't agreed to anything. Yet. "Why ask me?"

"You see her more than I do these days. When I see her, she seems totally normal, like not sad and shit. But then other times, I think I hear her crying." He lifted a shoulder like it was no big deal, but Kai saw the concern on his face.

"She's not as weepy as she was before having the baby." He thought about her toying with him. He'd seen no red flags. Was she that good of an actress? "She seems to be getting back to normal. Not that I know what that looks like."

"I can't figure out if she's faking everything being okay. I just thought she'd be more upset, you know?"

"Maybe she's not upset because she's okay with her decision. Maybe she doesn't have any regrets."

"I guess."

The door jingled and Kai was saved from talk of Norah. He didn't want to worry about her feelings and whether she was faking anything because he knew when they kissed it had been all real. The chemistry between them and her proposition had nothing to do with emotions. And that was the way he liked it.

Norah tugged and pulled the elastic into place. She was going to look good tonight even if it killed her. And it just might because she wasn't sure she'd be able to breathe. With the shapewear in place, she studied her closet to choose an outfit. Jeans and a sweatshirt would be fine for the hockey game, but going to a bar after dictated something sexier. A miniskirt would be too obvious.

But a miniskirt with cute leggings underneath and her heeled boots topped off with a cami—perfection. Enough to draw the eye without actually revealing anything.

She'd missed this so much. Being a girl, hanging out, flirting with guys.

Blowing out a puff of air, she grabbed the clothes. This week, she was determined to make friends, starting with the girls at hockey. With the exception of Moira, they were the only people she'd had any contact with and they'd been nice to her. And right now she was desperate to make friends.

Since it was starting to get cold out, Sean was driving a car and he said she could ride with him. Tommy was going straight from work.

"Norah! Get a move on. I need to leave," Sean yelled from the bottom of the steps.

"Coming." She swiped on some mascara and lip gloss and slipped her feet into her boots. At least they still fit her without help. Scanning herself in the mirror, she decided she was good. On her way out the door, she snagged Kai's sweatshirt to wear. It was warm enough to not need it now, but by the end of the night she might. Plus, she'd have the added benefit of annoying Kai by wearing it.

It had become almost a game at this point. She'd wear the sweatshirt and he'd make a comment about it, but never request she return it.

At the bottom of the stairs, Sean whistled. "Dressed up for an amateur hockey game."

"I haven't been out in ages. I want to relax and have some fun."

Sean chuckled. "Who are you kidding? You want to ogle the sweaty guys."

"Maybe a little." She wasn't about to reveal there was only one sweaty guy she had her eye on.

At the rink, Sean walked her in and pointed to the stands where the players' families sat. She walked down the aisle looking for Caitlyn. Although she might recognize some of the other people, she wouldn't remember names. Just as she was about to give up, someone tapped her on the shoulder. She turned to see Caitlyn behind her.

"Hi."

"Hey, you look great." Caitlyn opened her arms wide and swept them over Norah.

"Thanks." Norah hadn't thought about how to address the whole baby thing. These people had seen her pregnant and at some point they were going to ask about the baby. "Do you think I can sit with you?"

"Absolutely." She pointed to where she already had a seat. "So how'd you get out tonight? We usually don't see girls who've had babies for months at least."

"I gave my baby up for adoption."

"Oh." Caitlyn shimmied down the aisle to her seat.

Norah followed and once they were settled, an uncomfortable silence sat heavily between them. Crap. She managed to ruin the only shot she had at making friends.

"I feel like an ass for asking. I'm sorry," Caitlyn said.

The simple, unnecessary apology let Norah know there was no judgment. "Sorry for what? It was a normal question. You had no way of knowing. I don't mind."

"Thank God. I have a habit of running my mouth. Chris is forever reminding me to think before I say something stupid."

"Nothing stupid. It was a pretty safe assumption for you to make. When we'd met before, I hadn't decided yet, but it was ultimately the best decision for me and Ella. That's her name."

"You got to name her?" As soon as the words left her mouth, Caitlyn's eyes widened. "Shoot, I did it again."

Norah patted her knee. "It's okay. I did an open adoption, so I met with the parents. I chose them. We talked about names and when they suggested Ella, I agreed. I think it's pretty."

"Wow. You're so cool about all this. I think I'd be a mess if I got pregnant right now."

Norah laughed. "Trust me, I spent months being a mess. Now, I'm ready to move on."

"I'm glad you're here. You coming out for drinks after?"

"You bet. I haven't had a drink in forever."

The guys were on the ice warming up and Norah chatted with Caitlyn while watching. She found that now that she knew Kai a little better, he was easier to spot on the ice. Not that a guy his size was ever hard to miss.

She still didn't understand much about the game, but Caitlyn was nice enough to guide her through. The woman was a treasure trove of knowledge. "How do you know all this?"

"Chris and I have been dating since high school. He's been playing since he was five. For him, it would be a deal breaker for a girl not to understand hockey. Plus, when you're exposed to it as much as I am, with him playing and watching every professional game imaginable, it's bound to sink in. You'll see."

"I don't know. My brothers never cared much about whether I watched."

"So you're here for Sean and Tommy?"

"Of course."

One of Caitlyn's eyebrows shot up.

"Well, if you really want to know, I'm here for you. I haven't lived in Chicago for ten years. I don't have any friends."

"Uh-huh. And?"

"And what? My girl crush isn't enough for you?"

"I don't believe you're wearing the cute skirt and cami for me."

"I'm finally starting to get my body back. I want to show it off."

"To who?"

Norah released a long breath. "Am I that obvious?"

"Maybe not to everyone, but I see you checking out Kai. You track *him* on the ice, not your brothers. Not that I blame you."

Norah pressed her lips together and questioned if coming tonight was a good idea. If Caitlyn saw, so might Tommy and Sean. Well, Tommy at least. Tommy knew about her boyfriends in the past and had never been terribly overprotective, but then she got pregnant and it was like it flipped a switch in him.

"So what's the story?" Caitlyn asked as she leaned close.

"We have this chemistry thing and he's hesitant to act on it."

"Why?"

"Not sure."

"Well, if that outfit doesn't work, maybe it's time to set your sights on someone else. Lots of guys on the team are single."

"Thanks. I'll let you know if I need an introduction."

They watched the rest of the game and the guys won, but it had been a tough win. There had been at least three ugly fights and that didn't count the guys slamming against the glass. Norah rode with Caitlyn to the bar since the guys needed to shower and change. She was on her second beer when the team arrived. They crashed through the doors whooping and hollering.

Boyfriends and husbands moved straight to the women waiting for them. Norah couldn't help but look for Kai. When she didn't see him over the heads of his teammates, she thought maybe he went home because Jaleesa had been taking care of his mom. So much for her killer outfit.

Regardless, she was going to stay and have fun. This was a chance to make new friends.

She drained her beer. Sean came over and nudged her elbow. "Better slow down or you'll be puking. You're out of practice."

"Just means I have more to make up for."

He waved the bartender over and ordered a pitcher. While he waited, he scanned the area. "If I meet someone interesting tonight, catch a ride with Tommy."

"And what if Tommy finds someone interesting?"

He smiled. "Call a cab?"

"What kind of big brother are you?"

"One who's looking to get laid. Chicks dig hockey players, especially when we're coming off a win."

She rolled her eyes.

He grabbed his pitcher and said, "Stay out of trouble."

"Like you?"

"Definitely *not* like me."

Even though she was closest with Tommy, Norah genuinely liked Sean. His live-and-let-live attitude was exactly what she needed.

As Sean left to find his conquest for the night, Norah

felt someone watching her. She turned to find Kai making a beeline for her position at the bar. She flashed him a smile that he didn't return.

"I thought you wanted to go out tonight."

"I am out."

"Crashing my party."

She spun on her stool so her knees brushed his thighs. "The thing is, I don't have anyone to go out with. I tagged along with my brothers so I could hang out with Caitlyn. I like her."

He ordered himself a beer and one for her. His gaze traveled all over her body, warming every inch along the way. "You dressed like that for Caitlyn?"

The bartender set two bottles in front of them. Norah laid a hand on Kai's thigh and leaned close. "I wore this for you." She grabbed her beer and hopped off the seat. "Or anyone else who might be interested. Thanks for the beer." She tilted the bottle at him and walked away.

He watched her move. His gaze burned her skin as she walked, so she threw a little extra sway in her hips.

At the table, Caitlyn said, "Well, the outfit did something for him. I'm just not sure what."

Norah smiled and gulped half her beer. The alcohol was hitting her system hard. "I don't care. Let's go dance."

Without a doubt, Norah was doing her best to torment him. Her body was completely covered, yet her skirt accentuated her curves and the boots she wore basically screamed, "Fuck me."

Which wasn't an option.

He drank his beer to cool his throat. He was only supposed to stay for one drink because Jaleesa needed to go home, but damn if he was going to leave Norah in a bar full of guys while she looked like that.

Wasn't his problem. Her brothers were there.

But they were nowhere in sight as she grabbed Caitlyn's hand and pulled her over near the jukebox. Dora followed and the three women put money in the machine and pressed buttons to select songs. As soon as the beat started, Norah's body was moving.

They danced and swayed and she looked happy. Every now and then, she caught him staring and winked or gave him her flirtatious smile to let him know she was aware he was watching.

Then Craig, one of the team's centers, moved in. Caitlyn and Dora shifted over to make room for him, but he obviously was only there for Norah. His hands grabbed her hips and Kai waited for her to shove him off. She didn't. She continued to dance, not shifting away as Craig stepped closer still.

Kai drained his beer and slid from the stool. As he neared her, Norah smiled.

"Here to dance?"

"I don't dance."

"Too bad." And with that, she shimmied a little against Craig.

The look on Craig's face told Kai to get lost because he thought he was getting lucky tonight.

Kai tapped Craig's shoulder. "Can I talk to you a minute?"

Craig's eyes narrowed.

Kai stepped between Craig and Norah, forcing Craig back.

"What's with the cock block?"

"That's Tommy and Sean's sister."

"Oh. Damn. I thought she was a puck bunny."

Kai checked the urge to pound Craig for the assumption. Looking at the way Norah was dressed would easily give a guy the impression she was a hockey groupie, someone looking to be with a hockey player more than wanting to watch the game. "She's not on the market."

Craig raised his hands. "Cool." Then he spun on his heel and left.

Kai moved to a table near where Norah danced. The look she shot at him would've made smaller men shiver.

Tommy stopped on his way past. "Thanks for watching out for Norah. I don't think she's ready yet to pick up a guy."

"Yet?"

"In case you've forgotten, Norah ain't no nun."

"Craig thought she was a puck bunny."

Tommy eyed his sister dancing. "I could see that."

Kai elbowed him. "That's your sister."

"I'm just sayin' I can see where he came to that conclusion. Anyway, if everyone thinks she's here with you, she's totally safe."

As much as Kai didn't want to admit it, he liked the idea of Norah being with him. But she wasn't safe with him either. "Isn't it your job to watch out for her?"

"I guess. But she gets mad at me. She won't take it out on you. You're her boss."

Kai shot him a look. "I wouldn't count on that. I don't think much scares Norah."

Tommy barked out a loud laugh. "You're right. Thanks for the reminder. Now I'm really glad you were the one to get rid of Craig. Those icicles she's shooting this way? Totally for you." He slapped Kai on the back and left.

Kai halfway watched where Tommy went. He was hitting on some girl over by the dartboard. Kai swung back to check on Norah. She was walking straight for him.

"You owe me a beer."

"Why?"

"'Cause you scared off my dance partner and you won't dance with me."

Kai waved a waitress over and ordered a couple more

beers. "Craig didn't want to dance, but you know that, right?"

"I don't know what you're talking about. We were dancing."

"He was trying to ride you fully clothed."

She lifted a shoulder like she thought he was full of shit. The waitress delivered their drinks and Kai squared up with her because after this, he was leaving. Correction, *they* were leaving. Norah obviously already had a hell of a buzz going on and Tommy and Sean didn't seem too worried.

"You had your chance to dance with me."

"If we ever dance, it won't be fully clothed on the dance floor."

Norah smirked. "Sounds almost promising." She reached across the table and stroked a finger on his forearm, tracing the bands of the tribal tattoo. "Does that mean you've been thinking about our situation?"

Hell, yes. "Hard not to think about it when you look like that."

"The first step to being friendly would've been to dance with me instead of scaring off my dance partner."

"I didn't hit anyone, so I think that qualifies as friendly."

She took a pull of her beer with a slight shake of her head.

"Finish your drink and your dance, and I'll take you out for food."

Her eyebrows shot up. "Would that be like a date?"

"It would be a friend making sure you have food in your stomach to counteract the alcohol."

"Semantics." She took another swig and left her bottle behind as she went back to dancing.

Every move that girl made was seductive.

He let her have a dance while he finished his beer. Then he went to where she was dancing. While no one else had approached her, many eyes were staring. He grabbed her elbow. "Time to go."

She didn't jerk away. She pouted. "I don't wanna."

"Don't act like a brat or I might be tempted to give your ass a smack."

"Mmm . . . don't offer what you're not willing to give."

The girl talked more shit than any other woman he'd met. She acted like she'd been around the block and then some, like she could handle whatever came her way, but he saw something different in her. "I've been friendly. You're drunk. Don't push it."

"Sean and Tommy are here. I don't need you to tell me what to do."

"Sean and Tommy are working on getting laid. They have no clue what you're doing."

She allowed him to pull her away from the jukebox. "Where's your jacket?"

"I left your sweatshirt in Sean's car."

He saw Tommy at the end of the bar. He told Norah not to move and he walked over to tell Tommy he was taking Norah. Tommy didn't question any of it.

When he returned to Norah's side, she said, "You're treating me like a kid."

"You're drunk. Every guy in this place can see it. I'm not going to leave you here and hope you'll be okay."

She ran a hand down his chest. "So stay with me."

"Can't. Jaleesa already left my house."

Norah leaned forward and rested her forehead on his chest. "I don't want to go home."

He tilted her chin up. "Why not?"

She looked around his shoulder to where Tommy was sitting. "Let's go outside."

Grabbing his hand and interlocking her fingers with his, she led him out the front door. She kept walking until she turned the corner of the building, out of sight of the windows and door and away from the noise of traffic. But then she didn't say anything. She stood there holding his hand.

"Speak."

"I'm not a dog any more than I'm a kid." Her chin lifted, ready for a fight, but it wasn't in her eyes.

"What's wrong?"

"I don't want to be alone, Kai. Is that so terrible?"

He knew the feeling. Keep busy, keep other people around to stave off the loneliness, but no one was close enough to see it.

"Sometimes, I feel so empty. I have nothing. No school, no job. Shit. I don't even have friends." She offered a weak smile. "Present company excluded, of course." She released a sigh that caused her shoulders to sag. "I only had one thing that was mine and she was perfect and I gave her away."

Kai remembered Tommy asking him how she was doing, whether she'd been faking being okay. Kai wondered if she'd talked to anyone or if she'd kept it all in.

Norah stared across the street, tears pooling in her eyes. Did she regret giving her baby up? Kai didn't know what to say.

She inhaled, her breath hitching. Keeping her gaze on something far away, she continued, "I know it was the right choice, the best thing for Ella, but some days, it's like a crater in the middle of my chest. I'm not ready to be alone tonight, and I'm always alone at home."

Turning to face him, she said, "The loneliness gets to me. Ever since I was twelve and Jimmy sent me to live with my aunt in Boston and I was always alone."

His own chest filled with some awkward emotion because she'd shared this with him. He still didn't have any words for her, so he pulled her close and held her. He waited for the tears to come, but they didn't. She just wrapped her arms around his waist and laid her cheek against him.

"What can I do?" The question was every bit for himself as it was for her. He didn't know how to be in a relationship with someone like her. He liked his women simple, and Norah was everything but.

"Don't leave me."

Fuck. A simple request. He knew she meant for now because she was feeling low and lonely, but part of him couldn't help but feel like it was more.

Chapter Twelve

She shouldn't have said it. She was drunk and like always, alcohol made her talk too much. But Kai made it easy because he never talked. He just listened.

And he held her. God, she loved the way he held her. Like she was an expensive treasure, delicate but not fragile. She tipped her head up and nuzzled his neck. His skin was warm and when she followed with her lips, he growled. She stepped closer, pushing him against the brick behind him.

His fingers flexed on her hips as her tongue trailed up to his ear. His hard-on pressed into her belly, at least as much as she could feel through the layers of cotton and elastic, which was a horrible reminder that she couldn't take this too far. Her body wasn't ready.

Oh, yes I am, it argued.

With his hands firmly at her hips, Kai pushed her away. "Stop."

She tried not to be hurt that he pushed her away. She knew he was attracted to her.

"You don't have to use your body in order to not be alone."

"What?"

His hand came up and cradled her jaw. "Not like this. I won't do this because you're sad and lonely."

She snorted and tried to pull from his grasp. His fingers moved to the back of her head, forcing her to keep her eyes on him. She wanted to laugh him off, like he was so off base, but he saw right through her, which was a bitch.

Staring into his dark eyes, she readied for a lecture. Instead, he lowered his mouth to hers and offered her the sweetest kiss she'd ever received. His fingertips massaged her scalp while his other hand pulled her close again. His tongue caressed hers. It was a slow, patient kiss and she wanted to know what was behind it, what it meant, but her brain filled with fog.

She felt like she was floating and she would've given anything to stay there indefinitely. But it was too good to last. Kai pulled away again, sliding his hand from her hair, down her arm to her hand. Holding it, he said, "I promised you food. Where do you want to go?"

"Everyone knows tacos are the best drunk food."

Kai drove them to a twenty-four-hour Mexican fast-food joint.

"Can I ask another favor?" she asked.

He glanced at her from the corner of his eye and waited.

"Can we get food to go? You need to check on your mom. We can eat at your house."

Now he turned to face her. "What's your game?"

"No game." Damn. Like he couldn't trust her to not throw herself at him. She picked at the hem of her skirt and swallowed hard. Might as well go for it. She'd already embarrassed herself plenty. "I can't eat wearing this."

"Huh?"

"Spanx."

"Are you so drunk you're not speaking English?"

She took a deep breath and let the words rush out. "I

look so good in this outfit because I have spandex holding everything in. I can't eat or I might explode."

He laughed. Like an out-loud, deep rumbly, oh-my-God-strip-me-naked laugh. It vibrated through the car and across every cell of her body. Suddenly being embarrassed wasn't so bad if she got to hear that. She tried to look indignant instead of turned on, so she raised her eyebrows and pointed at the restaurant. When his laugh subsided to a chuckle, he opened the door and stepped out of the car. "You coming?"

She crossed her arms. "I'll wait here."

He smiled and shook his head as he walked toward the restaurant. If she wasn't mistaken, his shoulders were still shaking a little as he stood in line to get food. She wanted to be offended because who liked to be laughed at? But the sound of Kai's laughter did something to her insides that had nothing to do with the alcohol sloshing around. It wasn't even just a lustful thing. Whatever it was, it made her want to smile.

A few minutes later he came back to the car and handed her a bag as he slid behind the wheel. "I shouldn't have laughed. Sorry."

She knew she could use this to her advantage. But the smell of delicious food and the echo of his laugh in her head distracted her. "It's okay. It is pretty ridiculous."

"Why?"

"Why what?" The smell of the tacos called to her and she wondered how rude it would be to steal one and eat before they got to his house.

"Why would you squeeze into something that's so uncomfortable you can't eat?"

"To look good, of course."

"You always look good."

This time her snort was real. "I had a baby a few weeks ago. I'm fat and flabby. No guy wants to see that much jiggle on the dance floor or anywhere else."

Kai shook his head. "Women," he muttered.

"What's that supposed to mean?"

"You call us dumb, but you haven't figured out yet that we don't give a fuck. The sexiest thing a woman can do is own her body and enjoy it."

"Ha! That's like telling a guy a sense of humor is the most important thing. Who are you kidding? Looks matter."

"I'm not saying they don't. But you obviously have a misconception about your body. You were fucking hot when you were nine months pregnant. And you knew it. I don't get where the insecurity comes from now."

He parked in front of his house and they got out. "It's not so much insecurity as wanting to look good. And as long as I'm being totally honest and can deny everything tomorrow because I'm drunk, I wanted to get your attention and maybe make you a little jealous."

"Why would you want to start that kind of shit?"

She thought of how to put it as he opened the front door. "I wanted a reaction. You're always so stoic. Like nothing affects you." He held the door open for her and she looked into his eyes. "I wanted to affect you."

Norah had no idea how much she affected him. She walked by carrying the bag of food and he locked up. Before sitting to eat, he checked on his mom who was sound asleep. It seemed like the only time she was restless was when he needed her to leave him alone, like during his poker game. When he got back to the living room, the food was on the table, but Norah was nowhere in sight.

He went to the kitchen and grabbed some water for them. She was still missing. He knocked on the bathroom door. "Norah?"

"Uh, yeah?"

"You okay?"

"Yeah. Just changing."

He went to the couch and opened the bag of food. A minute later, Norah walked into the room. She was barefoot and wearing her leggings but no skirt. And she wore his T-shirt that he'd left in the bathroom. "Feel better?"

"Lord, yes." After she shoved her extra clothes in her purse, she rubbed her stomach. "I'm starving."

He pointed at what she wore. "Is this stealing-my-clothes thing becoming a habit?"

She smirked, then plopped down next to him, too close for comfort.

"You want a clean shirt instead?"

Glancing down at the one she wore, like she was looking for dirt, she picked up the collar and sniffed. "Nope. This one smells like you."

He decided not to mention that he liked the way she looked in his clothes. Instead, he handed her a couple of foil-wrapped steak tacos. She devoured them in record time.

She tossed her trash in the bag, handed him the TV remote, and settled back on the couch, leaning against him. He needed to drive her home, but then she settled and cuddled into his side.

He gently lifted her back and slid his arm around her, allowing her to snuggle closer. "I have to take you home."

"I know. Let's hang out for a while." She turned her body a little and looked up at him. "We could watch TV or . . ."

"Or?"

Her sexy smirk was back. "Or we could make out."

He thought about laughing, but realized she wasn't joking. Not even a tease. She was serious.

She sat up a little more, pressing her palm on his thigh

to do so, and licked her lips. "It'll be like being fifteen again. Making out on the couch, hoping not to get caught."

"At fifteen, I was sneaking girls into my bedroom and fucking half the night."

"Half the night?"

"It would've been all night if they didn't have to sneak home. Teenage boys have great stamina, but no experience. Such a waste."

"Are you telling me you never made out with someone without expecting to go further?" Her hand still rested on his leg, her fingertips brushing the inside seam of his jeans.

"With my first girlfriend. We made out a few times before I talked her out of her clothes."

"Then you missed out. There's something to be said for the art of making out." She shoved up and swung a leg over his to straddle him. "Getting all hot and bothered and just enjoying the moment makes you look forward to the next time."

He shifted and grabbed her ass, pulling her flush against him. "Getting hard and ignoring it leads to blue balls, which isn't something you look forward to."

"Trust me."

He let her take the lead and they made out on his couch, occasionally coming up for air, shifting positions so he could be on top. They groped and grabbed, licked and sucked, and damn if it didn't feel good. His body screamed for him to tear Norah's clothes off, but he wasn't an impatient teenager anymore.

He didn't know how long they made out, but Kai was stretched out on the couch and Norah lay on top of him. He played with her hair and wondered how he'd gotten to this point. He was nearly thirty years old and he'd just been talked into a make-out session.

Norah shifted and splayed her hand over his heart. "I wish I was still drunk enough to pass out."

"Why?"

"Because if I passed out, you'd be stuck with me. You can't carry me to the car and then into my house. You'd let me spend the night."

"As good as sleeping next to an unconscious woman sounds, you'll need your car tomorrow and I don't want your brothers to kick my ass."

She giggled. "My brothers are pretty tough, but I think you can take them."

"My fighting days are over." He knew she was joking and to a certain extent, so was he, but she needed to understand he was done living like that. He wouldn't fight over a girl. He tapped her ass. "Get up so I can take you home before we both fall asleep."

She rose and lifted the hem of the shirt she wore. "Want your shirt back?"

He grabbed her wrist. "Bring it back tomorrow."

She slipped her feet into her boots. "You're a party pooper."

"Yeah, my partying days are over too. That's what happens when you get old."

"You're not old." She hung her purse on her shoulder and narrowed her eyes. "How old are you?"

"Thirty in December."

"Oh my God. Time to get the walker. Wait, you can borrow your mom's. She'll be done with it by then."

"Funny." He tugged her hair and realized he enjoyed touching her any way he could. This didn't bode well for him keeping things simple.

Norah was so quiet on the drive to her house he thought she'd fallen asleep, but when he parked, she sat straight and unbuckled. She twisted her body and leaned across the console. "Thank you for tonight. I know I wasn't part of your plan."

"You definitely weren't, but I'm glad you pushed."

"Pushy, huh? I can't believe anyone would accuse me of that."

He smiled and hauled her closer for a kiss good night. She was soft and gentle but so fucking hot. She moaned into his mouth and he wanted to spend the night finding all the ways to make her moan. He pulled back. "You need to go in."

Stroking his jaw, she stared into his eyes. "All jokes aside, thank you."

"I like your smiles and laughter a whole lot more than the tears, so it wasn't much of a hardship."

As she slid away from him, Kai realized everything with Norah had been effortless.

When she unlocked the front door, she turned and waved to him. A second realization hit: He was getting in way too deep.

Norah counted the days until her checkup with her doctor that would give her the go-ahead for having sex. She and Kai had been spending a lot of time together after he came home from work at night when they could be alone. During the day, when she came to take care of Lani, they chatted, but it was superficial stuff, as if he didn't want his mom to know they had a thing going on.

That, of course, was part of the problem; they couldn't quite define what they had going on. Because they hadn't had sex, they weren't fuck buddies. Yet they were definitely more than friends.

She got ready for work, finally able to button her pre-pregnancy jeans. All of the extra walks and sit-ups had done their job. Her midsection was still soft and flabby, but she felt good. Downstairs, she grabbed an apple to go. Just as she closed the fridge, the basement door opened.

"Hey," Tommy called.

"Hey."

"Going to work?"

"Yep."

"How long are you going to keep working for Kai?"

She shrugged. "Till his mom is better, I guess."

"What about school?"

She patted the bag hanging on her shoulder. "I have my laptop and I'm talking to counselors this week about what credits will transfer so I can start next semester. What's with all the questions?"

"Seems like you're spending a lot of time over at Kai's."

"It's quiet there. I don't have to worry about running into any of the girls you and Sean bring home. And it's easy money."

"Yeah, but I know Kai left the shop early last night, but you didn't get home until almost midnight."

She crossed her arms. "What do you want to know, Tommy?"

"Are you sleeping with him?"

"Who I sleep with is none of your business, but since it's only been a month since I had a baby, no." So she was hedging the truth a little. She wasn't embarrassed about wanting Kai, but it irritated her that Tommy would ask.

"But you want to."

Not a question. She briefly wondered what kind of vibe she exuded that gave her away. "Does it matter?"

"He's kind of old for you, don't you think?"

She lifted a shoulder. "I never think about his age. I like him."

Tommy sat on one of the kitchen chairs. "I hoped you'd be off guys for a while."

Norah laughed. She couldn't help it. "I was off guys for nine months. Have you ever gone that long without a girl?"

"Well, when you put it that way . . ."

"I thought so."

"I don't think he's good for you, Norah."

"He's a good guy."

"Questionable."

"He's a nice distraction from my life. We're having fun. Neither of us is waltzing down the aisle."

Tommy chuckled. "I'd be willing to pay to see Kai waltz anywhere."

The image was pretty funny.

"You know I'm gonna tell Jimmy."

"Why would you do that?"

"Besides the fact he might kill me if I didn't?"

"I'm an adult. Does he check up on who you're dating?"

"Now you're dating? I thought he was a distraction."

Her arms flailed and she lost her grip on her apple, which went flying and bounced across the table. "I don't know what we are."

Tommy stood and handed her the apple. "You can do better than Kai. That's all I'm saying." He turned and went back down to the basement.

Her stomach churned at the thought of having the same conversation with Jimmy. Sometimes having a crew of older brothers sucked. Kai had never done anything mean to her. He was rough around the edges and he wasn't much of a talker, but he took care of his mom. How bad could he be?

She stopped in the living room to make sure her dad took his medication.

"What are you and Tommy fighting about?"

"Nothing."

"It's never nothing when it's the two of you. Sean and Tommy, they'll scrap over nothing."

"Like the rest of the O'Malley men, he feels the need to question my life choices."

"He's protective. It's his job. All their jobs."

"I can take care of myself."

He raised his finger without argument for her to prick. "Doesn't matter how old you are or how independent you think you are. They'll always look out for you."

"And most of the time, I like it. But sometimes, it's too much. Plus, I'm out of practice." The last thought hit her hard. A flood of childhood memories raced through her mind. All of them had her brothers damn near hovering over her. In her gut, she'd known her brothers all had a protective streak, Jimmy most of all, but until she said it, she'd forgotten how close they'd been.

She checked her dad's blood, which was miraculously fine, and gave him his other medication. "You should go for a walk. The weather is still nice and it'll keep you healthy."

He pointed a finger at her. "Look, I let you poke at me and shove pills down my throat, but I draw the line at nagging over going for a walk."

She smiled because she looked forward to their daily tête-à-tête. As crazy as her family made her, she loved being home with them.

When she got to Kai's house, she let herself in and called out like she did every day. "Lani?"

"I'm coming." Lani turned the corner from where her bedroom was. She was dressed and ready to go. Since her physical therapy appointments were scattered to wherever Jaleesa could schedule them, they juggled who took her. "I'm ready to go."

"Is Kai still here?"

"In the kitchen."

"I'll be right back."

"Getting your morning sugar?"

Norah halted. "What?"

"I'm old, not stupid. I know the two of you are canoodling out here at night."

Norah's face flamed. Lani heard them? "I need to talk to Kai about something."

"Mmm-hmm. Take your time. I don't mind being late."

Norah laughed. "Nice try. We'll be on time for your appointment."

She knew Lani hated the physical therapy because it was hard and painful, but she didn't put up a fight about going. Kind of like her dad no longer fought about testing his blood. Maybe she was the old people whisperer. She could get geriatrics to do what she wanted.

In the kitchen, Kai stood leaning against the counter, drinking his coffee. Shirtless. His hair was down and damp, which meant he'd just come from the shower. He'd probably worked out this morning. Norah damn near sighed. The man looked mouth-wateringly good.

He shifted and she realized she was staring. "Good morning."

When her gaze made its way to his face, she saw his self-satisfied grin. "I think you do this intentionally."

"What?"

"Pose there, waiting for me."

He set his cup on the counter and came to her. She liked that over the past couple of weeks, he'd started doing that. Coming to her.

"Maybe I like the way you look at me."

She leaned in, almost desperate for a kiss, but then she remembered why she came to the room. Placing a hand on his chest—his hard, muscly, sexy chest—she gathered her thoughts. "Stop. For a minute anyway."

"What's wrong?" His hands were immediately on her shoulders and his eyes locked on hers.

"Tommy stopped me as I was leaving. He wanted to know what's going on between us." She filled her lungs and let the air out slowly. "I didn't know what to say. I wasn't going to lie but at the same time, it's none of his business. None of *their* business because now Tommy will be blabbing to all my brothers."

"Okay."

She could tell he had no idea what to say. "I wanted to give you a heads-up in case Tommy says something to you."

"What do you want me to say to him?"

"Mind his own damn business?"

"I could do that."

She shook her head slightly. "It won't work. I don't want to cause problems for you and him at work."

"If he gets too annoying, I'll fire him."

"What? No." She sure as hell didn't want Tommy to lose his job over their temporary thing.

"I'm kidding. It'll be fine." He glanced over her shoulder. "You need to get going or my mom will be late."

"I know." She stepped back to leave, but he yanked her waistband.

"I think you can spare thirty seconds."

It was probably more like two minutes before his mouth released her, but Norah wasn't complaining.

"Have a good day at work," she said as she left the kitchen.

"You too."

As relaxed as the kiss had made her, the thought of Tommy confronting Kai still ate at her. Even if this blew over, what would happen when they stopped whatever they were doing? She'd only thought in terms of her not seeing Kai anymore, but Tommy would have to. She shook the thought away. Her relationship with Kai wouldn't have any lasting impact on Tommy.

Lani stood at the couch, waiting with a huge grin on her face. "Morning sugar is the best, isn't it?"

Norah rolled her eyes, but didn't argue.

* * *

Kai got to work, made a pot of coffee, and braced himself for whatever bullshit Tommy was going to throw. His first client of the day came in and Kai put Tommy out of his thoughts. He enjoyed being the only artist sometimes. With just the music from the radio, he could focus on the art in front of him. No annoying chatter, other than from the client, which only required a grunt here or there to show he was listening.

Unfortunately, his peace was short-lived. Karla strode in, changed the radio station, and started singing. Puck came in a few minutes later, looking hungover, and collapsed on the couch. Karla, of course, took this as an invitation to fuck with him. Sometimes Kai felt like he was in a day care.

Kai was finishing the lettering when Tommy walked in. He felt Tommy's glare, so he paused and looked up. He waited a moment, but Tommy said nothing. At least the kid was smart enough not to start shit in front of a client. Kai went back to tattooing the slogan on his client's arm. He worked in silence, but Tommy kept shooting daggers. It was going to be a long day.

After finishing and explaining aftercare, Kai said goodbye to the client and cleaned up his station. He waited, but Tommy didn't approach. "Hey, Karla, I'll be in back if you need me."

"Okay."

"Leave Puck alone. If he fucks up a tattoo later, he'll blame you."

"How the hell is it my fault he's hungover?"

"Shut up," Puck moaned from his spot on the couch.

"If you're that bad, why'd you come in? Go home and sleep it off," Kai told him.

"My mom wouldn't let me sleep either."

Kai shook his head. Puck was young, but he was no kid. "When are you going to grow up and find your own place to live?"

"It's free to live there. More money for beer."

Kai went to his office and realized that Puck wasn't the anomaly. Sean, Tommy, and Norah all lived at home. He wasn't sure about Karla. He'd never asked. He didn't understand. He couldn't wait to be on his own. And his mom hadn't done too much nagging. It was the idea of being his own person.

He barely got settled behind his desk when his office door opened and Tommy walked in. Kai looked at him. "Problem with knocking?"

"We need to talk."

"About?" As if Kai didn't already know.

"Norah."

"Don't bring personal shit into my place of business."

"Don't fucking dismiss me."

Kai pushed away from his desk and walked past Tommy. Over his shoulder, he said, "You coming, or what?"

Tommy followed him out the back door to the alley. Kai leaned against the brick, crossed his arms, and waited.

"What are you doing with my sister?"

"What business is it of yours?"

"Fuck you. She's my sister."

"You covered that already."

Tommy ran both hands over the top of his head. "I like you, man, but she's trying to get her life together after taking a huge hit."

"I'm not doing anything to disrupt that."

"She's not like us."

That's what Kai had been waiting for. He knew what Tommy was getting at and it was nothing he didn't already know. He wasn't good enough for Norah. He couldn't even believe that Tommy put himself in the same category with Kai. Tommy was better than Kai. He just didn't know how bad Kai was. "Think I don't know that? I tried steering clear of her. She's relentless."

Tommy smiled. "Yeah, she is. So tell her no."

"Easier said than done. I've let her lead on this. She wants to hang out and have some fun. She's sowing some wild oats, working things out of her system before she goes back to school and gets a new job."

"So that's all she is? A piece of ass?" Tommy had gotten close, too close.

Kai straightened, bumping Tommy with his chest. "I didn't say that. I like Norah, but it is what it is. I don't expect anything more than she's willing to give."

"If you hurt her—"

"Shut the fuck up. What are you gonna do?" Kai saw Tommy's fist clench and he knew he needed to diffuse the situation. He raised his hands. He didn't want to fight Tommy. "Look. Your sister is an adult capable of making her own decisions. If she wants to hang out with me, it's her choice. I'm not going to chase her off because you say so."

"She deserves better. Have you even taken her out on a date? Or are you just using her?"

Kai lowered his voice. "I know she's better than me. We haven't gone out. She didn't say she wanted to. As far as using her, I'm not using her any more than she's using me." He stared at Tommy to make sure he heard. "That's the last I'm going to say about it. My personal life is none of your business and if you can't keep it out of here, go home."

He left Tommy standing in the alley. Although he didn't want to lose a good artist, he wasn't going to have his personal life brought out for everyone to see. And like he'd told Norah, his fighting days were over, especially over a girl.

Tommy eventually returned to the studio.

Karla paused before piercing a guy's eyebrow. She looked at Tommy, then at Kai. "Did a cold front just blow through? It's mighty chilly."

"It's nothing," Kai said.

She looked at Tommy for confirmation. He glanced at Kai and then nodded. Good enough.

The rest of the day and evening flew by. They had about six walk-ins, so there was no time for chat. By closing time, he was exhausted. He didn't like the ongoing tension between him and Tommy. They had never been friends, but they got along. Karla and Puck had both taken off. He'd expected Tommy to leave with them, but he hung back.

"You want something?"

"Yeah. Sorry about before. Norah frustrates the shit out of me and we worry about her. It has nothing to do with you personally."

Kai didn't believe that for a second.

"I guess this explains why you were all over Craig after the game last week. Why let me think you were pretending she was with you? Why not just say so?"

Kai looked at him. "Are you serious? You were ready to hit me in the alley."

"Yeah, but then I thought about it. If she was just a piece of ass to you, you wouldn't have cared if Craig pawed her. You wouldn't have made sure she made it home safely."

"Don't make me out to be some kind of saint."

"We all know better." Tommy stuck out his hand. "We good?"

Kai nodded.

As they shook, Tommy added, "I don't think my other brothers will be as cool about this as I am, so be warned."

"I should expect a band of O'Malleys coming to kick my ass?"

Tommy shrugged. "Never know."

Kai drove home not sure what to think. He hadn't been prepared for Tommy to cool off that quickly. What nagged at him most was the reason for Tommy's turn. He obviously thought there was more to Kai's feelings toward Norah than friendship and sex. It was bad enough Kai had been questioning that, but to have Tommy notice spelled out trouble.

He walked in the door, tossed his keys on the table, and kissed Norah's cheek. "Hi."

"Hungry? I have leftovers from dinner."

"No. It's been a long day. I'm going to take a shower."

"You want me to leave?"

Did he? Normally, after a day like this, he would need solitude, but that wasn't the answer that came out. "No. I'll only be a few minutes."

She grabbed his hand as he turned. "Was it bad with Tommy?"

"Ugly for a minute, but he got over it. It's okay." He hated seeing the worry in her eyes. He brushed a lock of her hair behind her ear and kissed her again. "I'll be back."

He took a fast shower and looked forward to sitting on the couch with Norah leaning on him while they watched TV. What he hadn't expected was to find her sitting on his bed when he went to grab some clothes. "Hey."

She smiled and rose to close and lock the door.

"What are you doing?"

She snagged the towel at his waist and yanked, leaving him naked. She licked her lips, which had his dick perking up. "I'd really prefer your mom not catch us with your dick in my mouth in the living room. Privacy, you know?"

She lowered to her knees and he grabbed her shoulders. "Whoa. I thought you had to see the doctor."

Norah sighed. "First, the rule is no penetration until my checkup. Even though I'm done bleeding." It sounded like that part bothered her. "Second, your dick, my mouth, is sex for you, not me. Doesn't get much safer." She leaned forward again and wrapped her cool fingers around his hot skin.

He growled when her lips reached their destination. Her tongue swirled over his head and her hand stroked him. He closed his eyes and his mind went utterly blank. Her nails scraped his thigh and then reached around and squeezed his ass.

Muscles flexing, he thrust his hips forward, wanting to go deeper. She took him.

He opened his eyes and looked down at her. She met his gaze with laughter in her eyes and bobbed her head a little faster, letting him bump the back of her throat. The hand that had been on his ass moved to cradle his balls. She held them and then scraped her nails there, too. Holy fuck, was she hot.

Kai thrust his hands in her hair and held her as he fucked her mouth. "I want to come in you."

He waited for her response. She nodded and slid her hand up his torso to his chest and pinched his nipple. Then she hollowed her cheeks and allowed her teeth to barely graze his skin.

"Fuck, yeah." He thrust until he felt like he was going to explode. His balls tightened and he went deep, half expecting Norah to gag. He came and she swallowed. Then she pulled away, wiping her swollen lips.

"Feel better?" she asked.

"God, yes." When she turned toward the door, he grabbed her wrist. "Where are you going?"

She turned back with a confused look on her face. He didn't wait for an answer. He simply said, "Come here," and guided her to the bed.

"What are you doing?"

"You said no penetration. My mouth on your pussy doesn't get much safer, right?" And man, did he want to taste her right now. The only thing he wanted to do more was bury himself in her and he couldn't do that yet.

She shivered when his fingers undid the button of her jeans. He looked into her eyes. "This is okay, right?"

Chapter Thirteen

Norah nodded because her mouth had become a desert. When she'd impulsively decided to give Kai a blow job, she hadn't expected anything in return. But there was something about going down on a guy that was a total turn-on and she was already wet. Maybe it was the power trip of being in control of his orgasm.

Everything about the experience was awesome. She loved how Kai tried to take control and it gave her a little thrill to let him. Now he undid her jeans and peeled them away. He knelt in front of her to pull them off her feet. His face was at her belly and she became self-conscious about the flab still sitting there. Her hands moved to cover it even though she still wore her shirt. With her pants gone, Kai gently moved her hands away and pushed her shirt up a few inches and kissed her soft belly.

He was almost reverent in his movement and her heart swelled. Letting her shirt fall back into place, he kissed along her panties before sliding them down. He nudged her leg to step out of them and she was bare to him.

"Lie down." His voice was deep and gravelly and it caused a ripple to run through her body.

She did as she was told, lying back on the bed. Kai

yanked her to the edge and spread her legs wide. He kissed her inner thigh and murmured, "Pretty."

Norah squirmed under his intense gaze and his exquisite touch. Featherlight strokes on her inner thighs and the whisper of his breath on her center. She needed to be touched more than anything, but there was no way she would beg for it.

Just as she began to lose her patience, his tongue glided along her slit and over her lips. A slight flick of the tip of his tongue on her clit made her hips jump. Using his hands, he spread her legs wider, holding her in place, and began a slow and gentle assault with his tongue. His rhythm was steady and disarmingly deceptive, almost lulling her into relaxation.

Then without warning he opened his lips and sucked hard on her clit, sending a sharp jolt of pleasure through her. Her hips bucked, but he pressed them back down with his wide palms. He mumbled something against her, or maybe it was just a moan, but the vibrations set off another round of pulsations.

She began to writhe beneath him, at least as much as she could given the hold he had on her. But he didn't let up. He changed the simple rhythm and it became unpredictable. All Norah knew was that she wanted more. Her fingers wove into the silky strands of his hair and she held tight, as if he might try to escape.

The orgasm built and she braced her heels on the bed and rose to meet Kai's mouth. She let go of his head and grabbed a pillow. Placing it on her face, she released a long moan as the orgasm crashed through her. Her muscles quivered and she lost the ability to hold her legs up on the bed.

Kai held her as she spasmed and moaned and slid away. Then he climbed on the bed beside her and tossed the pillow. "Feel better?"

She huffed a weak laugh. He kept throwing her words back at her. "Much." She ran a hand down his chest. "But I'd like it so much more if you could be inside me right now."

He groaned and lowered his face to her neck and kissed her.

"Don't get me wrong, your oral skills, they're phenomenal, but I'm missing the sex part. I want you on top of me, pushing into me, filling me." *Taking me*, she almost added, but that felt going too far, even though she meant it.

"Trying to kill me?" he whispered against her skin, causing a shiver.

"Just being honest."

He pushed up on an elbow to see her. The only light in the room filtered in from the window, an odd mixture of moonlight and streetlight. "So you're saying one orgasm isn't enough."

"It's not that . . ."

But his hand was already stroking her sensitive skin. "You're a greedy girl, aren't you?"

She hadn't been looking for more, well, not like this, but his fingers were like magic against her and before she knew it, her hips were rocking. She pushed hard against his shoulder to make him lie back. "I might be greedy, but I'm not selfish."

Climbing on top of him, she straddled his face and lowered her mouth to his waiting dick. They pleasured each other using only hands and mouths again and all Norah could think was how amazing sex would be once they were finally able to do it.

Round two was more hurried and frantic than the first. It was like a fun race to the finish and by the time they were lying side by side, panting for air, Norah was about as relaxed as she'd ever been. She curled next to Kai and traced the line of a complicated tattoo that covered his side from armpit to hip.

"I want you to do a tattoo for me."

"Huh?" His voice was groggy and she derived quite a bit of satisfaction from that.

She pushed up on an elbow and flipped her hair out of her face as she looked down at him. Man, he was beautiful. Dark hair wild around his head, his dark eyes staring up at her, and golden skin interrupted by ink. "I want a tattoo of Ella's name and something small with it."

"Don't you want Tommy to do it?"

She shook her head. "Tommy will try to talk me out of it."

"Where do you want it?"

"I don't know. What do you think?"

"It hurts less on fleshy parts. Someplace like your ribs will hurt. Your arm or shoulder would be easy."

She smiled. "Right now, I have lots of fleshy parts. But I don't want it where other people can see. It's just for me. Maybe on my hip?" She angled her body and traced a finger along her hip bone.

His hand followed hers. "Not that fleshy. But I can make it work. Ideas for design?"

She bit her lip. "You'll think it's dumb."

His thumb ran down her cheek to her lip, tugging it from between her teeth. "I doubt it'll even make the top fifty dumb things people have had me tattoo on them."

"I'd like a dragonfly."

"Not dumb. I've done dragonflies before."

"So I guess I'm not all that original."

"You don't need to be original. Just have to like it."

She sighed and laid her head on his chest. "I should go. It's getting late."

He didn't say anything, didn't ask her to stay, which while she wasn't expecting it, would've been nice.

"Why'd your family send you to Boston?"

His question caught her by surprise. She listened to the steady thump of his heart before answering. "Jimmy joined the army. Ever since my mom was killed when I was a toddler, Jimmy took care of us."

"What about your dad?"

"He was a cop. Worked a lot of hours. Five kids are expensive. He provided, but Jimmy cared for us." She inhaled deeply. "Anyway, Jimmy was worried about me. I was twelve and hitting puberty and he didn't trust my other brothers to keep me out of trouble. Mostly because they were causing plenty on their own. And I was set to follow them."

His hand stroked lazily up and down her back and she wanted to sleep like that. Murmuring, she added, "They did what they felt was best for me. Like I did for Ella."

She sighed next to him, enjoying the open honesty of the conversation, so she asked, "Why did you become a tattoo artist?"

"I'm good at it."

"You're kind of young to own your own studio though. I would think having to worry about employees would be a lot of pressure." And everything she knew about Kai told her he limited how many people he let into his life.

"I'm an ex-con. Having a felony on your record is one of those things that follows you. I got tired of having to fill out background check forms and having people look at me like I'm less than human because I fucked up." He spoke like it was no big deal, but she felt his muscles beneath her tense.

She said nothing for a minute. She tried to wrap her head around this. He was a felon. That took bad boy to a whole new level for her.

"Feeling like you need to jump out of my bed now?"

She smiled. "No."

"I have a hockey game Friday night. Do I need to ask Jaleesa to come over?"

And the intimate conversation ended as quickly as it

started. His question was too cryptic for her brain. Was he asking her to come to the game or asking her if she wanted another night off? "No. I can work."

"Okay." His fingers stroked up and down her back. "Bring a bag and plan to spend the night."

Her heart did a weird tumble. "Okay," she whispered.

"And I have my poker game Sunday night. Can you come over for a bit to hang with my mom?"

"Why? She doesn't need much help."

"She drives me crazy when she knows I have the guys over. No shit, she texted me like eight times in an hour the first weekend she was here. It was worse than babysitting a toddler who doesn't want to go to sleep."

She chuckled. She could totally see Lani doing that to annoy him. "I'll be here on one condition." She rested her chin on her hand and looked up at him. "Tell me why you don't want your mom to know who you're playing with."

"She doesn't like them."

"There's a story there."

"You asked for a reason, not a story."

"You want me to be here, I want the story."

His sigh could've belonged to any of the O'Malley men, long-suffering and irritated, but resigned. "I've known most of those guys since I was a teenager. We ran in a gang together, got in a lot of trouble."

He tapped her shoulder to get her to move and then he got off the bed. He went into his dresser and pulled out underwear. Must be time for serious conversation, something that clearly couldn't take place naked.

After stepping into his underwear, he leaned against the window and looked out. "We did a lot of shit together, especially Rooster. He introduced me to all of life's darker things. Drugs, booze, women, and eventually crime to pay for those. When I was twenty, I went to jail for burglary. My mom never forgave Rooster."

Norah sat up and reached for her clothes. "But you're not into that stuff anymore, right?"

She hadn't thought to ask him before. He'd offered no indication he was still in a gang, no evidence of drug use.

"No. Jail did what it was intended to do: teach me a lesson. I straightened myself out and I left the life behind. Except for Rooster."

"Is Rooster still into all the darker things?"

Kai nodded. "I let my mom think he's not around because she'd just get upset."

"So you lie to her."

He lifted a shoulder. "By omission. Keeps things simple."

Norah wasn't sure what to do with this information. Her earlier thought of bad boy came back. But Kai wasn't just the ex-con, ex-gangbanger bad boy. He was reformed. In truth it was something that had drawn her to him. A guy who grew and learned from his fuckups, who owned them and moved on, was sexy. Part of her regretted forcing him into sharing his past because he obviously didn't want to. The other part was grateful because if left to himself, he might never tell her anything, and she really wanted to know him.

It shouldn't matter, she reminded herself, because they were temporary. If he chose to keep things from his mom, she had no business judging. Especially since she'd kept her pregnancy from her family for months.

"See you tomorrow." She went up on tiptoe and kissed his cheek.

"I'll walk you out."

She eyed his underwear. "I can handle a walk to the curb."

"Give me a minute." He grabbed his jeans off the floor and jumped into them. "Let's go."

He stood there, shirtless and barefoot with his hair a

mess, and man, did she want to climb all over him. He took her elbow and propelled her from his room. "Stop looking at me like that."

"Like what?" she croaked.

"You just came twice and you're looking at me like I'm an ice-cream cone in August."

She couldn't help it. She licked her lips. He groaned. He pulled her out the front door and straight to her car.

She unlocked the door but turned to find him standing close, close enough that she didn't have enough room to open the door. "Sorry about Tommy."

"Nothing to be sorry for. You managed to completely take my mind off your brother."

She grinned and wrapped her arms around his neck to pull him close for a kiss. His body pressed her against the car and she moaned.

He moved his mouth from hers and kissed her jawline and back to her ear. "Your moans are so fucking hot. I can't wait to hear them when I'm buried inside you."

She shivered. The man was so good at turning her on. He kissed her cheek. "Good night."

"'Night."

"Drive safe and call me when you get home."

Norah rolled her eyes.

He caught her chin and turned her to him. "Call me."

"Fine."

She got in her car and he stood by the curb until she turned at the end of the block. Her heart raced and it wasn't just because he'd gotten her hot and bothered. His words weren't simple. That he wanted her to call when she got home made him sound like a boyfriend. He cared and that was deadly for her.

Any sign of caring would make her fall and she didn't

want to fall for him. He'd break her heart and she knew it. She just didn't know how.

Kai didn't know what was up, but something was. Norah had called and said she needed a few hours off today and that she'd explain when she got to his house. It wasn't like her to spring something on him last minute. When she pulled up outside, he stood on the porch and waited for her.

"What's going on?" he asked as she neared. Her face was filled with emotion, but he couldn't read it.

"I'm sorry to do this to you. Avery called this morning. He's on his way to Chicago." She shook her head. "He wants to talk and go see Ella. I know it's last-minute, but . . ."

Kai watched her speak and heard her words, but didn't know what to make of them. She was torn and he didn't know what he could do for her. "I'll handle my mom. Are you okay?"

"I think so. I just . . . I don't know. I didn't expect to see him again."

Kai didn't want her to see him again. This man had left her alone. "You didn't need to come here to tell me." He would've preferred if she hadn't. Hearing it was bad enough, but to see how conflicted she was made it worse. And there was nothing he could do about it. This was why he'd tried to keep his distance, keep things simple. Her complications tore at him.

"I wanted to let you know why I needed time off and . . ."

"And?"

She reached for his hand. Her fingers slid too easily through his. "I have to do this. You understand, right?"

"Yeah." His rational brain understood. However, the

primal part of him wanted to make her stay. He wasn't sure why. Jealousy? It was an emotion he'd refused to feel.

"That's not too convincing. I can't fight with you about this." Her eyes spoke before the word came. "Please."

He pulled her into his arms. "No fighting, remember?" As he held her, he knew why he didn't want to let her go. Protectiveness. That guy had the ability to hurt her and Kai wouldn't be able to stand by and watch.

She was someone who could get him to fight again. Not with her, or over her, but for her. And that was scarier than anything.

"I get it," he said, trying to reassure her. "I don't like it. I think he's a bigger asshole than I am. But I understand."

"Thank you," she mumbled against his chest. She sighed and held him tight for a full minute before pulling away. "I'll be back later."

"Take the day. Work out whatever you need to."

"Oh. Okay."

Her agreement irked him but he wasn't sure why. He wanted her with him in his house, which was exactly why he needed to let her go.

Norah circled into O'Hare to get Avery from the terminal. She saw him waving from the curb, a backpack slung over his shoulder. Looked like another one-day visit. Her conversation with Kai still nagged at her and she didn't think she was ready to see Ella. The overwhelming emotions pushed at her as Avery climbed into the car.

"Hey," he said with a bright smile.

"Hey."

"You sure it's okay for me to see Ella?"

Norah nodded. "I talked with Kim and she said we can stop by whenever."

"You'll go with me?"

"That's why I'm here."

He touched her cheek, a motion that once would've had her leaning in for a kiss. "Thank you."

She shifted out of his reach and pulled back into traffic.

Avery twisted and bent to dig into his bag. He came up with a fluffy stuffed bunny. "I got her this. Do you think she'll like it?"

Norah smiled. "She's a month old. I think it's too early for her to have preferences. But she'll grow up knowing it came from you. That matters."

He nodded and clutched the animal in his lap.

"Ready?"

"Yeah."

They drove to Kim and Trevor's in silence. She couldn't remember things between them ever being awkward like this. Not even on their first date. They clicked. Maybe there was just too much stuff between them now. And of course, she had Kai.

Kim met them at the door holding Ella bundled in a blanket. "You have excellent timing. She just woke up from a nap."

Kim reached out and gave Norah a one-armed hug. Then she did the same to Avery. "It's nice to finally meet you."

She turned and led them into the living room where she had baby stuff everywhere. A bottle sat on the coffee table. She looked at Norah and Avery. "Would either of you like to feed her?"

Norah shook her head, but Avery stepped forward. Norah hadn't held Ella since the hospital. It was safer that way. Maybe one day she'd be able to do it without feeling the ache in her chest, but for now, she needed to keep her distance. She was afraid if she didn't, she'd long for her daughter and she didn't want that.

Avery sat on the edge of the couch and Kim placed Ella in his arms.

He thrust the bunny at Kim. "I got this for her."

"Thank you." She took the bunny and set it on a bookshelf.

Avery picked up the bottle and began feeding Ella.

Kim said, "Would you like me to take a picture?"

"That'd be great." He looked up at Norah. "Take it with us?"

She wanted to scream no, but she knew she was being irrational. She sat beside Avery who angled Ella in one arm, still keeping the bottle propped in her mouth like a pro.

"Squeeze closer," Kim said. Norah leaned in and smiled as Kim snapped the photo.

As soon as it was done, Norah jumped off the couch. She looked at Avery and Ella and a torrent of emotion ripped through her. Here was this man who she believed she might've loved, holding and caring for their child. She should want this. All she felt, however, was the need to escape.

Kim touched her arm. "I have coffee on in the kitchen. Would you like some?"

Norah nodded because she couldn't speak. In the kitchen, she was able to take a deep breath. She'd come today because she knew Avery needed her to guide the way. She knew Kim and Trevor and theoretically should've been able to ease the awkwardness.

Instead, she felt like she might fall apart.

This was why she hadn't visited. She wasn't ready for all of these emotions. She didn't know how to handle them.

Kim didn't say anything in the kitchen. It was as if she knew Norah might snap. She simply poured a cup of coffee and handed it to Norah. Then she left to check on Avery and Ella. Norah heard the quiet conversation in the other room, but she stayed rooted to her spot.

Believing she'd made the right choice, the best choice, was hard to do when she faced Ella. She didn't know how to hold her and then give her away again. She knew her baby was safe and loved and that's all she ever wanted for Ella.

She dumped the remainder of her coffee down the drain and walked through the house. Looking at Avery, she said, "I'll wait for you outside."

The sun was warm, but a cool breeze blew. She sat on the steps and just breathed until her lungs were full.

The door opened and Avery came out. "Are you okay?"

"Yeah. I'm not ready for this. You don't have to cut your visit short. I'll wait."

"You sure?"

"Absolutely." She didn't want to take this from him.

He went back into the house and Norah walked a few houses down and then back, taking deep breaths of fresh air. Then she went to her car and sat behind the wheel. She didn't know how long it was until Avery came out, but it hadn't been long enough for her to get control of her emotions. He climbed in the passenger side and she lifted her forehead from the steering wheel.

Her throat was nearly closed and she wanted to kick herself for the tears clawing her.

"That was harder than I thought it would be," he said. His voice was husky and she knew he was as messed up as she was.

She turned to face him as a few tears slid past her defenses. He reached out and pulled her into an awkward hug. It didn't offer her comfort. Not really. What she wanted was to be in Kai's arms. For whatever reason, when he held her, she felt safe and secure. She could open up and fall apart and he'd hold her.

Norah pushed back from Avery. "Can I drop you off at a hotel?"

"Yeah. Thanks." He pulled out his phone and gave her the address. "My flight leaves in the morning, but if you want to hang out today or have breakfast tomorrow, we can."

"I have work," she lied. Being around Avery would be a reminder of how awful she felt right now.

She dropped him off at the hotel and then drove around. Dinnertime neared and she went to Kai's house. He'd be working, but Jaleesa would probably be grateful to be able to leave. She knocked and then used her key, calling out to Lani.

"Norah?"

"Yeah, it's me."

"I thought Kai said you needed a few days."

"He was wrong. I only needed a few hours."

Jaleesa came from the kitchen, wiping her hands on a towel. "What are you doing here?"

"I had something to do today, but I figured Kai had you filling in and you might need to get home. I can stay with Lani."

"You sure?"

"Yeah."

Jaleesa tossed the towel in the kitchen and grabbed her purse. "I'll make it home in time for bedtime stories. Matt always makes a mess by telling them ghost stories. Thank you."

"No problem." She settled on the couch next to Lani. "So what's on TV tonight?"

"What's going on with you?"

"Nothing. If you don't pick a show, I will."

Lani snatched the remote off the couch. Norah smiled. Coming back here leveled her out, righted her brain.

* * *

When Kai got home that night, he hadn't expected to see Norah's car parked in front of his house. She was supposed to be with Avery. Jaleesa hadn't called to tell him she was back. Unless Jaleesa didn't know. His mom would be asleep. A disgusting thought hit him and he hurried from the car. Norah wouldn't do that, would she? Bring her ex-boyfriend to his house?

He unlocked the door and rushed through as if he half expected to catch Norah in the act. What he found was her sound asleep on the couch just like the first night she'd worked for him. He sat on the table and smoothed her hair from her face. Her eyes popped open. "You're home."

"You're not supposed to be here."

She sat up, her eyes wary. "I was done early and figured Jaleesa would want to go home."

"And?"

"And nothing."

Her eyes said there damn well was something. "What happened?"

She bit her bottom lip and looked over his shoulder at the TV. "It was awful."

Kai's muscles tensed. He'd told her to take the time because he thought she needed to be with Avery. He knew she should've stayed here. "What was?"

"Seeing Ella. I walked into this perfect house and Kim was there and asked if I wanted to hold her and feed her. But I didn't. I just wanted to run away. I wasn't ready to face her."

"Do you regret it?"

"No. I *know* it was the best decision. I know she'll grow up happy and loved. But right now, holding her and then giving her back, it would be like being crushed under an avalanche of rocks." She breathed deeply. "Avery fed her and Kim took a picture of us together. I almost lost it. So I left."

Kai turned and sat next to her, but didn't touch her. He wanted to offer comfort, but she was so tense, he was afraid to make a move. "Can I see it?"

"What?"

"The picture of your daughter." He knew it would be a mistake but he needed to see. She pulled out her phone and opened a photo.

Kai's gut clenched at the sight of her curled close to another man. A young guy wearing a suit. A fucking suit. He wore glasses and a hat making him look like a hipster wannabe. It was affirmation of everything Kai already knew. Norah would never be his.

She didn't belong with a guy like him. He wasn't convinced she belonged with a tool like this Avery guy either. But someone more like him—sleek, polished, educated, accomplished.

She eased back on the couch and reached for his hand. "When Avery came to the car, I was ready to fall apart. He hugged me."

Kai flinched. He knew he shouldn't have, but he couldn't control it. If she noticed, she didn't comment.

"But it was like nothing. I didn't feel better in his arms. There was nothing there. All I could think about was . . ."

She drifted off and all Kai thought about was the fact that she felt nothing for her ex. Maybe he should've felt bad for her, or him, but he didn't. Satisfaction swelled in him. Then he realized she'd stopped. "What did you think about?"

"You." She turned her body and straddled him. "I kept wishing you were holding me, making me feel better. I tried to ignore that impulse. I dropped Avery off and then drove around going nowhere, until I was back here. I know we're just having fun and this is over when you're mom is better, but today all I wanted was you. And I don't regret that."

Kai ran his hands up her back and into her hair, pulling

her down for a kiss. It was only a matter of time until she realized she didn't belong with him. Avery might not have been the right guy, and Kai was pretty sure he wasn't either. But she'd chosen him. He'd take that for as long as he could.

Chapter Fourteen

Friday night, Kai had texted Norah telling her he'd be late after the game. She tried not to be miffed that he chose to go out for drinks while she waited for him at home. When midnight rolled around, she started to get worried. She sat on the couch, watching *Friends* with her phone in her hand, trying to decide if she should call.

She heard his key in the door and she tossed her phone on the table. Kai came around the corner looking like shit. She jumped from the couch. "Oh my God. What happened? Are you okay?"

Dried blood stuck to his cheek, his hair matted down, and a bruise darkened the left side of his face around a bandage. He dropped his hockey gear and held up a hand. "I'm fine. A fight during the game got a little wild."

"A little wild? You're covered in blood. Did you need stitches?"

"Yeah. Just a couple."

"That's why you're so late?" Now she was mad. "Why the hell didn't you say something?"

"I didn't want you and my mom to get worked up. I'm fine. I need a shower."

"You can't get your stitches wet."

He grimaced. "I'm not going to walk around looking like this."

"Didn't you listen to the instructions they gave you in the ER?"

"No. I just wanted to get out of there. I wouldn't have even gone if the coach didn't make me."

"Men are such babies. Come here." She grabbed his hand and pulled him to the kitchen. Pointing to a chair, she said, "Sit."

She went to the bathroom and grabbed some soap, shampoo, and towels. When she got back to the kitchen, he'd shed his jacket and his shoes. "Drag the chair to the sink."

He did as she said and when she had him situated, she pressed his shoulder for him to lean back. "I'll get your hair washed, but then you need to leave it alone for a couple of days. When do you get the stitches out?"

"Monday or Tuesday."

She turned the water on and let it fall over his head, keeping it from spraying on his wound and wetting the gauze. "Brings back memories of working at the salon."

"You worked at a salon?"

She looked down at him. His eyes were closed. "For a little while in high school. I was considering cosmetology school."

When she reached the back of his head, he winced and she felt the lump. "What the hell happened here?"

"Hit the ice during the fight."

"Did they check you for a concussion?"

"I'm fine."

She noticed the lack of a real answer, but she didn't comment. She washed the blood from his hair and then wrapped him in a towel. When he sat up, she went to work cleaning the rest of his face. His cheek was swollen and bruised. With a washcloth, she wiped the area.

His hand traveled up the inside of her thigh.

"What are you doing?"

"Distracting myself from the pain."

"Are you in pain? Did they give you anything?"

He grinned and she knew he was feeling fine. She tilted his head and looked at his pupils. They looked normal and equal. "Did you lose consciousness?"

"No."

"Do you remember everything that happened?"

"I went over all this at the hospital," he snapped.

She bit back her sigh. She wasn't a doctor and he wasn't her patient. Climbing on his lap, she straddled him and held his jaw. "A concussion is serious. Not something to blow off."

"I'm fine. I'm beat up and tired with a killer headache."

"I'll get you some ibuprofen. Did the doctor say someone should wake you every few hours?"

"How do you know this shit?"

"I was studying to be a nurse." She climbed off him and tugged his hand to get him to stand.

When he did, he suddenly seemed wobbly. Before she could say anything he said, "I'm tired. Let me go to bed."

He skirted around her and yanked off his T-shirt as he left the room. A large purple bruise was forming on his shoulder blade, but she knew better than to comment. She was torn about what to do. They'd planned on spending the night together. Regardless of his flirtation, he was in no shape to be doing anything. But she didn't want to leave him. What if he slipped into a coma?

He got to the hallway and asked, "You coming?"

That made the decision for her. She followed and when he headed to the bathroom, he said, "I'm taking a shower. I won't get my head wet."

She nodded and lingered by his bedroom door. "I'll change the bandage when you're done."

He took two steps and crowded her. His hand went to her jaw, his thumb stroking her cheek. "You're sexy when you're bossy."

She laughed. "That's a new one. Usually guys just tell me how annoying I am when I'm bossy."

"Doesn't count if those guys are your brothers."

He had a point, but it slipped from her mind when his lips touched hers. The kiss was gentle and intoxicating, but not driven. It was one of those kisses that when he pulled away, she wondered what they were to each other.

Kai took a fast shower and allowed her to change the dressing on his forehead with little complaint. He looked exhausted. In his bedroom, he dropped his towel and crawled into bed naked. Norah's stomach fluttered and she reminded herself that sex was *not* on the table.

"Stop staring at me and get your ass in bed."

She climbed in from the foot of the bed since Kai had lain on the edge closest to the door. When her head hit the pillow beside his, he kissed her temple and wrapped an arm around her. It felt possessive and comfy and Norah knew—just knew—she was reading more into his actions than she should. Just because he actually wanted her to spend the night without pouncing on her didn't mean they were more than friends, that this was a lasting relationship, that she should be falling in love with him.

Oh crap. The panic hit her hard. She hadn't even really had sex with him and she was falling for him. How the hell did she do this to herself? Kai's breath fluttered her hair and his arm flinched on her waist as his sleep deepened.

Two hours later, she was still awake. Torturing herself over her emotional fuckups was something she was good at. She'd done this with Avery and look how that turned out. She didn't know how to be objective when she was with a guy. Her brain turned everything into fucking rainbows and unicorns. She'd thought for sure it would be different with Kai. He wasn't the kind of guy to inspire thoughts of rainbows.

She shook Kai's shoulder to check on him. "Kai."

"Ugh."

"Kai, wake up."

One eye glared at her.

"What's your name?"

"Kai Ellis."

"Where do you live?"

"Chicago."

"Who's your mom?"

"Lani. And if you don't stop asking me stupid questions, I'm going to duct tape you to the bed."

His threat flashed some enticing images in her head. "Just making sure you're okay."

"Mmm-hmm." Then he was snoring again.

Norah tried to sleep, but her own nagging thoughts wouldn't allow it.

Kai got home late Saturday night and wished Norah had been there. He'd gotten used to her being part of his routine. Then he reminded himself she wasn't supposed to be part of his life. He'd hired her to be with his mom. Being with him was nothing more than a bout of fun. But no matter how many times he'd said it to himself, he didn't believe it. Waking Sunday morning without her hadn't been any better.

It didn't help that his mom talked about her all damn day on Sunday. It was as if she was going through the same Norah withdrawal he was. He'd gotten ready for the poker game and planned on cleaning the house, but Norah had everything done. He'd been taking all of that for granted. Food in the refrigerator, meals left over for fast lunch, a clean freaking toilet. She'd been doing way more than keeping his mom company.

Norah had taken over running their household and he hadn't even noticed. The tight grip he'd held on his life had slipped. The problem was, it wasn't bothering him nearly as much as it should. He found himself watching the clock after dinner.

The guys started showing up in the basement and Kai joined them. When Rooster walked in he took one look at Kai's bandage and said, "Thought you didn't fight anymore."

"Anything goes on the ice."

"Damn. That's a good one. Bet the other guy looks worse."

"You know it." He popped the top on a beer and sat at the table.

As they were dealing the first hand, footsteps on the stairs drew his attention. Norah paused on the last step, clearly intimidated to intrude. Weird, since she'd intruded in most areas of his life.

"Uh, just wanted to let you know I'm here."

He spun in his chair to get a good look at her. Something was off in her voice and he figured if he saw her, he'd know. But he didn't get a chance because she rushed at him. "Oh my God. Is that the same bandage I put on Friday night?"

How the hell could she know? "Yeah. You said keep it dry."

"I also said you needed to clean it out and take the bandage off. Ugh. You're such a guy. Come here." She yanked on his shirt.

Rooster started hooting and Kai recoiled from her touch. Her eyes widened and she released him. Her fingers flinched. "Sorry. Take the bandage off and let the wound breathe."

She turned and hustled up the steps. Kai tossed his cards on the table. "I'll be right back."

He caught her in the kitchen, pouring a glass of water. Without saying anything, he dragged a chair to the sink and sat. "Have at it."

"What?"

"Do whatever you planned to do before I scared you off."

"You didn't scare me."

She looked skittish and he hated he'd done that to her, but he still wasn't prepared for her to be around those guys. Not as his . . . girlfriend? Is that what she was?

Setting her glass on the counter, she edged closer. She picked at the tape holding the gauze. His hands landed on her hips and he moved a leg between hers. As she worked, her body brushed against him, but he could tell it was unintentional. She was distancing herself.

She cleaned the cut and eased back. "All set."

He gripped her hips tighter and moved to make her straddle him like she had the other night. When she was on his lap, tight to his body, his hands skimmed up her back. He stared into her light blue eyes and tried to figure out what she was thinking.

"I'm sorry I embarrassed you in front of your friends," she said.

"What?"

"Downstairs. Sometimes I forget—"

He didn't know what she'd planned to say, but he cut her off with a kiss. The taste of her settled the restlessness he'd been feeling all day. When they separated, he said, "You didn't embarrass me. I don't like you being around them."

"Why? They're your friends."

"You don't belong there."

She angled her head, waiting for more.

"I don't like the way Rooster looks at you."

This brought a smile and she threaded her fingers into his hair, pulling it from his ponytail. "Guess that means I'm not invited to play."

"Nope." He nipped at her bottom lip. "I missed you yesterday."

"You sent Jaleesa over for your mom. I went home." No emotion, no accusation, just facts.

"You were exhausted from waking me up all night."

"Someone had to make sure you didn't fall into a coma." A slight smile tugged at her lips. Her humor returned.

"Will you stay tonight?"

"What about your game?"

"They'll only be here a few hours. Then I'm all yours." The truth of the statement hit him hard. For however long she'd have him, he was hers.

A harsh whistle came from the basement as a reminder that his night wasn't supposed to be about Norah. She climbed off his lap and he missed her welcome weight.

"You better go before Rooster comes looking."

"Yeah." He heard the regret in his voice and felt stupid for it. "Will you be here when I'm done?"

"We'll see." She gave him one of her teasing looks, but there was something different in her eyes. Something bothered her.

He moved to the basement door before he totally lost his mind and took her to his bed. As soon as his foot hit the bottom step, Rooster started in with, "Bow-chicka-bow-wow," doing his best bad porn imitation.

"Shut the fuck up."

"Done playing doctor?" Dean asked, pointing at Kai's hair.

Kai quickly scooped it back into a ponytail.

"Nurse," Kai clarified. "She's studying to be a nurse." He didn't know why it was important for them to know that, but he didn't want them to think she was some random chick bossing him around.

Carlos tossed a quarter into the pot. "She looks good on you."

Kai checked his cards and added his own quarter. "What the hell does that mean?"

"It means she makes you happy. We can see it on your face, man. It's about damn time. We were ready to do an intervention and shit."

"You make no fucking sense."

Carlos leaned over while the other guys put in their bets. "You haven't had a woman around since what? Cindy? Eric, what the hell was that last chick's name Kai was into?"

"My memory ain't *that* good."

They all laughed and Kai knew it was at him and not with him. Carlos smacked his arm. "Thing is, man, we're all settled with our lives—except Rooster and he ain't about to change."

"You know it. Gotta spread the love around. One woman won't ever be enough for the Rooster." Then he crowed, drawing laughs around the table.

Carlos shook his head and refocused on Kai. "You've been lettin' life slip by. Norah is making you live."

"She's not making me do anything. My life is the same now as it was two months ago."

"Damn shame if it is," Dean added.

"He thinks he's fooling us. Maybe even himself. You're taking care of your mom. You started a relationship with a woman. It's not the same. Maybe you'll even come to my kid's birthday party this year."

Kai didn't want to tell Carlos that wouldn't happen. The only time he exposed himself to his old life was here in the basement during their poker game, where he had control. But Carlos wasn't just part of his old life. That wasn't who Carlos was anymore. He'd grown up and left the life like Kai, Eric, and Dean had.

"Enough of the bullshit. Let's play." Kai turned his attention back to the cards. These guys were not conversationalists. They didn't talk about feelings. They joked and bullshitted their way through games. No way was he going to discuss what he did or didn't have going on with Norah.

He also wasn't about to let on that he couldn't wait to get back to her.

Kai cleaned up after the poker game with his pocket fifty bucks lighter. They'd had no mercy on him tonight, taking advantage of the fact that he was completely distracted. Everything they'd said in that opening hand hung over his head. They read him better than he thought they could.

When he came upstairs, silence greeted him. Norah wouldn't have left without saying anything, would she? The kitchen was empty, lights in the living room were off, and his mom snored in her bed. Then he noticed the glow of light from his bedroom. Pushing the door open, he saw Norah sitting in his bed, hair damp. She wore one of his T-shirts and he hoped nothing else. Her laptop was open, propped on her knees.

Her eyes were shiny when they met his.

"What's wrong?"

"Nothing." She smiled. She angled the screen. "Kim sent me one-month pictures of Ella. Isn't she beautiful?"

Kai sat on the edge of the bed, the computer dipping in her hands as he did. He looked at the infant, who was sleeping beside a book. "What's with the book?"

"Kim plans to take pictures of Ella every month with the book. It'll be an easy way to see how much she's grown. One day, she'll be big enough to hold it and read it."

Kai looked at Norah. "Isn't it hard?"

"Yes and no. She has a chance to be a happy kid. I couldn't give her that. But I like to be able to see her grow."

He saw truth on her face. "She'll know who you are?"

"Yeah. At some point, I'll be ready to see her and spend time with her. In the meantime, I look at pictures."

"Was that what was bothering you today?"

She closed the laptop and asked, "What do you mean?"

"You seemed upset before. From more than me being an asshole."

She shook her head a little, her hair waving and dripping water on his shirt. "I spent the day finishing my applications to a couple of schools who will take my credits. I'll have a year and a half to finish, but I wasn't ready to see the tuition prices. Jimmy always paid my bills when I was in school in Boston. I never gave it much thought."

Kai had never even considered college, so he had no clue what it would cost, but he imagined a lot. "Isn't there financial aid or whatever?"

"I don't qualify for much. I'm hoping to get some loans. I don't want to ask Jimmy for more."

Kai didn't understand the dynamics of her family. She constantly referred to Jimmy almost like a father. He knew her dad was still around, had met him once when Tommy brought him to the studio. It wasn't his place to ask.

"How was your game?"

"Crappy. Lost fifty bucks."

She smiled again. "Maybe I should give you a few pointers. Help you work on your game face."

He took the laptop from her and placed it on the nightstand. Then he leaned over her, covering her body with his. "I lost money because I was distracted by you."

"Nice try. I wasn't even there. Can't blame me." She reached up and pulled his hair loose, running her fingers through it as it fell.

"You were in my head. Couldn't stop thinking about this." He lowered his mouth and kissed her.

Their tongues met and tangled and Kai knew he could get lost. Norah pulled his T-shirt and he rose up to whip it off. Norah was already tugging at the button on his jeans. He moved from her reach and leaned back to yank the blanket from her body. Her legs were bare, but as she reached for his pants again, he caught a glimpse of pink panties. It was almost more tempting than finding her naked. Just a bit of a tease.

He slid down her body, taking the panties with him, as he kissed his way down her thighs. She sighed at his touch. He followed the same path up and took the edge of the shirt she wore and raised it. Her hands clamped down over his.

"Problem?"

"I have stretch marks and flab still."

As much as he wanted her naked, he wouldn't push her to do something she wasn't comfortable with. Her nipples were already hard and poking through the cotton. He pulled the shirt taut and sucked on them. A moan slipped past her lips and her hands flew back to his head to hold him in place. She gripped his hair right over the bump on his head and he did his best to ignore the slice of pain because this was worth it.

"Get naked, Kai."

He climbed off the bed and dropped his jeans and under-wear. She rose on her knees and crossed the bed. Wrapping her fingers around his cock, she said, "Please tell me you have a condom handy."

"For what?"

"I want you inside me." She said it as if he were slow.

"You haven't gone to the doctor yet."

"I'm fine. My appointment is in like three days. She'll say I'm good to go. Three days isn't going to make a difference." Her hand stroking him made an excellent argument.

He gripped her wrist to stop the movement. "No doctor approval, no penetration."

She pouted. Actually fucking pouted. "I never figured you to be a rule follower."

He pushed her back onto the bed, taking her wrists in one hand and pushing them over her head. Then he bit that damn pouty lower lip. "I need to practice my art of making out. You're the one who said I've been missing out."

"Me and my big mouth."

He chuckled against her skin and then used his mouth to make her forget everything.

Norah practically skipped out of her doctor's office. Of course, everything was fine and she was clear to resume a completely normal life, including sex. Her doctor didn't even bat an eye when Norah asked for it in writing.

The note was tucked safely in her pocket as she drove to Kai's house. She had a busy day planned. Lani had physical therapy, and after her nap, they were going to the mall. Lani insisted on getting out and meeting her friends for a movie. She still wasn't quite ready to drive herself, so Norah had agreed to drive her. While Lani and friends were in the theater, Norah planned on shopping for something special to wear for Kai.

It was a little silly since he'd seen her naked, but this would be the first time they'd go all the way, so she wanted to look nice. At least until he took it off her, which knowing him wouldn't take long. Norah hadn't shopped for anything in a while. She couldn't remember the last time she went to a mall to look for clothes.

She sighed. She had no room in her budget for a wardrobe overhaul. What she owned would have to do for a while yet. The upside was that once she was back in school, she'd be wearing scrubs often while she did clinics, so she didn't have to worry about her wardrobe. And Kai never cared what she wore. He even liked her in his clothes.

She had to remind herself that by the time she was back

in school, she wouldn't be seeing Kai anymore. His mom was almost well enough to go back to Jaleesa's. In fact, she'd mentioned earlier in the week how since Kai's front steps were manageable, she wanted to try something more difficult. What then?

Would she be out of a job and a boyfriend? Although this thing with Kai started as a means to have some fun, it developed into more. They cared about each other. If pressed, she'd admit she was falling for him, but they hadn't discussed where they were going with this. Or even if they were going somewhere.

She parked her car behind Kai's and shoved the thoughts aside. Today was for celebrating. With the note in her hand, she stepped from the car and walked to the house. She still knocked before unlocking the door and she called out before wandering through. The habit had become routine.

"Lani, I'm here."

"Just like you are every day. But later today."

Norah smiled. "I told you I had an appointment. I'm still here in plenty of time to get you to therapy."

"Oh, yes. We wouldn't want to be late for that."

"You might want a sweater today. It's windy," she said as she kept walking toward the kitchen. Lani rarely gave her grief about getting her morning sugar and Norah tried not to worry about what that meant.

In the kitchen, Kai stood at the counter drinking his coffee. Nice to know she wasn't the only one who followed a routine. Too bad he was wearing a shirt today. She much preferred him shirtless. "Hey," she said.

"Good morning."

She unfolded the note and said, "It sure is."

"What's that?"

"A note from my doctor clearing me for everything."

He glanced at the note and one eyebrow ticked up as he reached for her hips. "Everything?"

She nodded and rose on tiptoe to plant a kiss on his lips. No matter what she told herself, this didn't feel temporary anymore.

"Makes me wonder," he said against her lips.

"What?"

"My mom told me she was going to Jaleesa's house tonight. Said she might stay over to practice on her stairs. Did you tell her something?"

Heat rose in Norah's cheeks. "No. What kind of person do you think I am? You think I'd tell your mom to get lost so I can have sex with you?"

His laugh was quiet and vibrated against her hands on his chest. "I meant did you tell her about the doctor today?"

She thought back. Had she told Lani where she was going? "I don't think so. I mean, I told her I had an appointment, but I don't think I told her for what."

Norah stepped back. "This feels creepy now." She lowered her voice to a whisper. "I can't have sex with you tonight if your mom is going to come in tomorrow and know."

He burst out laughing. Loud. Norah smacked his shoulder. "This isn't funny."

"Sweetheart, do you think she believes you wake up in my bed untouched?"

"She doesn't know I've spent the night in your bed. I've been careful to be up and dressed before her every time."

"Sometimes I forget you grew up without a mom. They have a sense. They know things. She absolutely knows."

Norah dropped her forehead to his chest. "Oh my God. What she must think of me."

Kai's hand rubbed down her spine. "She likes you no matter what you do. Most days, I think she likes you more than me."

"Norah, it's getting late," Lani called from the living room.

"Coming," she yelled. She pushed away from the comfort of Kai's body. "I wish you hadn't told me. Now I'll never be able to look your mom in the eye again."

He smiled and wrapped an arm around her shoulder. He kissed the top of her head. "You're fine."

"Before I go, I looked online for some ideas for my tattoo."

"Uh-uh."

"What *uh-uh*?"

"I won't put some clip art or overused image on your body. I'll draw something custom."

Her insides turned to a puddle of goo. For a guy who liked to believe he was an asshole, he sure had a way of making her feel special. "Really?"

"Of course. Nothing but the best for you, babe."

She tried not to make a big deal over it. She really did. He was an artist and did unique artwork all the time.

As she pulled away to get Lani to her appointment, he said, "Come back here when you're done with my mom. I shouldn't be late tonight."

Although she'd planned on spending the night with him, Norah felt a thrill at his invitation. Well, it was more of a demand, but the thrill was still there.

Chapter Fifteen

Kai knew he was in trouble when Norah had sent a picture to his phone of what looked like her upper thigh with a hint of bright blue lace. The picture itself wasn't the sign of trouble. That was enough to get his blood flowing. What was troubling was that the interruption at work hadn't bothered him at all. In fact, they'd ended up engaging in a text conversation about why she should send better photos.

He didn't have personal conversations while at work. He definitely didn't flirt. Norah had taken over his entire brain. Finally, he gave up and instead of trying to think of other things, he worked on the art for her dragonfly tattoo. With every stroke of his pencil, he imagined where he'd put this on her body.

Again, images of her laid bare in front of him came to mind. He found himself watching the clock. At seven, Puck was still working, but Kai had no other clients scheduled. Normally, he'd sit around and wait for Puck to finish, but today, he wanted to get home to Norah.

"I'm heading out. Make sure you lock up when you're done."

Puck mumbled his assent. Kai drove home faster than ever, with the exception of the day Norah had gone into labor. That felt like it was a lifetime ago. Things had changed so rapidly between them since. He parked in front of his house and jumped from the car. Keys in hand, he took the steps two at a time.

Inside the house, he heard the murmur of the TV, but Norah wasn't in the living room. "Norah?"

She came from the kitchen carrying a couple bottles of beer. "Saw you pull up. Figured you might like a drink."

The bottles dangled between her fingers as she strode toward him. She was wearing the same clothes he saw her in earlier, but her attitude was different. He took the bottles and set them on the table. "Not thirsty."

"No? Can I get you something else? Dinner, maybe?" Her eyes did that wide, fake-innocence thing he was pretty sure she'd practiced for years.

He pulled her close and held the back of her head. "Something else." He captured her mouth and tasted her. Her tongue collided with his and she tugged at his shirt. Holding her hand, he started to back her out of the living room.

She eased away. "I thought you wanted hard and fast against the wall."

He growled low in his throat. "Not this time. Right now, slow. I'm taking my time with you. But I'll still have you screaming by the time I'm done."

Norah turned and walked to the bedroom, holding his hand the entire way. If she wanted to think she had control, he'd let her for a minute. But that would end the second their clothes came off.

"Take off your shirt," he said. "I want to see the full picture of what you teased with earlier."

She crossed her arms in front of her and gripped the edge of the shirt. She paused and said, "I'm still flabby. And I have stretch marks, so keep your eyes at my chest. My boobs look good."

Pulling the shirt up, her bare skin was revealed. If he looked, he saw the stretch marks, light, little squiggly lines, but the bright blue of her lace bra drew his attention. She was right—she had great tits. He moved forward and cupped them both, kneading the flesh and pinching her nipples. She sucked in a sharp breath, but arched forward into his touch.

Her hair slid down her back and he had easy access to her neck. He kissed and bit and sucked at her pulse. She gripped his shoulders, her fingers pressing him close.

His hands slid around and cupped her ass. He lifted her up to him. She wrapped her legs around his hips, her hot center rubbing against his hard cock. The denim between them was killing him. He carried her to his bed and laid her down, flicking the bra open. Sliding her bra off, he stared at her chest. Nipples stood upright, begging for more attention. He tossed the bra aside and took a nipple in his mouth. The other he pinched lightly.

Norah moaned and rocked her hips. A moan was good, but he wanted more. He wanted her to be as wild as she made him feel. He pushed his hips into her, letting her feel how hard he was for her. She grabbed at the back of his shirt and gathered the material, pulling it over the back of his head. He lifted his face for her to remove it completely.

While he was up, he unbuttoned her jeans and hooked his thumbs in the sides to take them off. He debated on taking the panties with them, but he kept them in place. Her hips wiggled in invitation for him to continue. With her jeans gone, she was quite the sight splayed out on his bed. Dark hair spread out. Soft, pale skin, flush with desire.

Nothing like a waiting woman's body. He let his hands roam—over her neck, her shoulders, across her ribs to the edge of her underwear—until she whimpered.

"Kai." Her voice was strangled. "I like slow, but this is crazy."

Her chest rose and fell rapidly. Bracing her heels on the edge of the bed, she shimmied out of her panties. He immediately thought of her legs around his head. He'd get to the fast part soon enough. He grabbed her wrists in one hand and pulled them over her head.

"I didn't want those off yet," he whispered gruffly in her ear.

She bucked under him. "Well, I did. I want more."

She wriggled again and he realized she was using his hip to get off. He used his legs to pin her down and slid a hand between them. "Looking for this?"

He stroked her clit. Swirled his finger over the nub knowing she liked that particular motion.

"God, yes."

Her arms relaxed under the pressure of his hands. Her knees widened to give him better access. She was wet, but he still wanted more. He lifted his torso and lowered his mouth to her nipples again.

She moved her hips. "Inside, Kai," she begged.

He could've used his hands, but he wanted the first thing inside her to be his cock. "Not yet."

He continued his manipulations until she was climbing him to seek release. Her hands yanked the band from his hair and she gripped him at the scalp. He held her tight as she rode the waves of her orgasm. As she started to come down, he kissed his way up her body, back to her mouth.

"That was good," she said against his lips.

"Not screaming good, though." He stood and took off his jeans and underwear. Grabbing a condom from the nightstand drawer, he slid it on. He ran his hands over her thighs and she opened in invitation. With a single finger, he stroked her. She felt plenty wet, but he asked, "Do you need lube?"

"No, I'm good." She pushed up on an elbow and looked at him suspiciously. "Why?"

"I read that after a baby you might."

"You—"

He felt stupid for saying it, so he cut her off with a kiss. Her fingers were gentle across his shoulders and up his neck. This girl was the master of making him stupid.

Norah could barely see straight much less think, but something pinged in her heart. She shifted and angled her body to line up with his dick. She desperately wanted him inside her; she had for weeks now. He rubbed against her, causing a jolt of pleasure from her clit spiraling through her every nerve.

Then he pulled away again. She tightened her grasp on his hair and pulled his face up. When he looked into her eyes, she said, "Stop playing games."

"I'm playing by your rules. Enjoying myself."

He lowered his head and nipped at her neck. The following swirl of his tongue almost made her forget. When he moved like that, she'd let him do whatever he wanted. He was obviously good at everything.

But when his lips pulled her nipple into his mouth again a steady throb of want reminded her how empty she was. She pulled his hair again. This time, when his eyes met hers, they weren't playful. He disentangled her fingers and yanked her arms over her head again. Nose to nose, he said, "I told you I'm going slow. Move again and I'll tie you like this."

She shivered partly because the idea thrilled her and partly because holy fuck Kai was hot when he got bossy. When he kissed her this time, he bit her lower lip, enough to leave a sting, and then went back to driving her crazy with his hands and mouth. He drove her to another orgasm with his tongue and still didn't enter her with his dick or his fingers, but she was so relaxed she no longer cared.

"Falling asleep?" His voice was gruff and hoarse and sexy.

"No." She licked her lips. "Let me use my hands and I'll show you how unsleepy I am."

He looked up to where her arms extended, in nearly the same place he'd pushed them. She'd moved them briefly while she came, but he couldn't hold her accountable. She wiggled her fingers at him. "It'll be fun."

"I'm having plenty of fun." He reared back and spread her knees. Then he sank between them, settling against her. With one hand, he guided himself into her.

The motion stole her breath. He slid in and waited. "Okay?"

She took a moment as her body adjusted to him. His heart raced in his chest against her and he had one hand possessively on her boob. She nodded and hooked her legs on his hips. He pulled back and eased in again, so fucking slow. The man was deliberate in every movement. She thrust up to meet his hips and he groaned.

He released her boob and braced his elbows on each side of her and started a movement so rhythmic it was almost hypnotic. Norah had thought there was no way she'd come again. In general, a dick was not the way to get her there, but something about the press of Kai's huge body on hers and the swivel of his hips had the tension coiling again.

Kai reared up taking his body heat with him, causing another shiver. He grabbed her hips and brought her body high so she was basically lying only on her shoulder blades. He growled and drove into her fast and hard.

He was a glorious sight above her. Dark, wild hair, dark skin with darker ink swirling everywhere. Muscles in his arms and shoulders bulged.

"Come now, Norah."

"What?" Her mind blurred. "I can't."

"Touch yourself."

When she didn't move, he barked, "Now."

She moved a hand and bumped a finger against her clit, which sent shock waves through her. Every muscle in her body contracted and pulsed. She was briefly aware of Kai going still, but then he was on top of her again.

They both gasped for breath. Her heart raced. She slid her hand out from between them and threaded her fingers through his sweaty hair. Holding him tight, she came back to the world, Kai's room, the weight of his body on hers.

He kissed her neck and pushed up. His arms seemed wobbly. "You okay?"

"Oh, yeah."

A buzzing caught their attention.

"Shit." Kai rested his forehead on her shoulder. "My phone."

With what appeared to be Herculean strength, he climbed off the bed and reached into his pants pocket. The phone had already stopped ringing, but he cursed again. Before she could ask who it was, he dialed. "What's up?"

"Uh, yeah." He slid a look to Norah. "I thought she was staying there." He wiped a hand across his forehead. "Yeah, okay." He disconnected.

"Problem?"

"Jaleesa's dropping my mom off. The kids wore her out."

Norah bolted up. "Jeez. How long till she gets here? Do I have time for a shower?"

Kai's fingers wrapped around her wrist. "Whoa. You're not going anywhere."

"I am not having sex with you when your mom is here." She swallowed and found her throat a little raw. With that recognition, she realized other parts of her were feeling pretty tender too.

He held her jaw and kissed her gently. "Take a shower. Relax. Spend the night. You've done it before."

"Yeah, but that was before . . ."

"Before what?" The smirk on his face told her he knew exactly what.

"Before you had me screaming." She patted his thigh as she stood on wobbly legs. "Besides, I don't think my body can handle any more of you tonight."

Oh yeah, the soreness was settling in as she moved across the room.

Suddenly Kai was in front of her. "Did I hurt you?"

"I'm fine."

He touched her jaw again and forced her to look up.

"A little sore. It's expected." Worry stole across his face. She patted his cheek. "It's a good kind of sore. Kind of like when you're lifting weights in the basement, and when you're done, you can totally feel it, but it was worth it."

He took her hand and led her to the bathroom. He started the water and when it was warm, he pulled her into the tub.

Norah looked at his serious face. "Your mom will be here soon. I'll be mortified if she catches us in the shower together."

"Shh. She won't be here for at least a half hour."

He said nothing else. He simply washed her body and his. His touch wasn't exactly clinical and his tenderness aroused a lazy lust in her. Tender was not a word she'd normally use to describe Kai, but it fit perfectly here. Something happened to her in the shower, with his hands on her, taking care of her. Her heart felt too big for her chest. She needed to get out because she knew that feeling.

When they stepped from the tub, she patted herself dry and twisted the towel around her hair. She avoided looking directly at him because she didn't want him to see that she was falling for him. He'd said she couldn't hide anything.

From the corner of her eye, she saw Kai squeeze his hair and wrap the towel around his hips. Even though she'd seen him exactly like that many mornings, her mouth watered.

"My mom will be here soon. You want to put clothes on or just stare at me like dessert?"

Norah felt her skin go hot, and not in a good way. "I'll get dressed and get out of here."

Kai blocked her path. "I told you to stay."

She stared at his chest. Specifically at the ornate compass tattoo inked over his heart. She didn't believe for a minute that Kai let his heart act as his compass. "I should go. It's late and your mom is going to want quiet."

"It's nine o'clock."

It felt so much later. She didn't have another argument.

"Regrets?"

She tipped her face up to meet his. "Not one." She looked him in the eye to make sure he knew that was real.

"Then stay." His hand touched her jaw, his thumb caressing the corner of her mouth. Quietly, he added, "I have art for you to see."

"My dragonfly?"

He nodded. Then he kissed her jaw and her ear. His breath sent a shiver through her.

"Are you holding my dragonfly hostage to make me stay?"

"If it works."

She stepped back and pulled the towel off her hair. "Fine."

That he wanted her to stay should've thrilled her. He could've easily had sex and then expected her to leave, but he wanted her here. She liked to think he enjoyed having her in his bed, waking next to her. But as usual, she was afraid of seeing what wasn't there.

Kai waited in the bathroom while Norah got dressed. He didn't trust himself not to want more. He didn't know what had gotten into him. He was fine spending the night with a woman he'd had sex with, but he'd never craved it like he did with Norah. She continued to pull things from him that he never trusted.

He wanted to take care of her.

And that was all kinds of fucked up. He barely managed to take care of himself.

When he got to the bedroom, Norah had a pair of stretchy pants and a baggy T-shirt on. It was as if she was trying to hide her body. She combed her hair, sending a fine spray of water over the shirt.

He dropped the towel and stepped into a pair of sweatpants. Then he reached for her comb and ran it quickly through his hair and handed it back. "I'm starving. You hungry?"

She bit her lower lip. "I shouldn't be."

"I'd say we both should be. That was a workout and a half."

"I'm good."

"I'm ordering pizza. What kind do you want?"

She sighed. "Get whatever you want to eat. Don't worry about me."

He sat on the edge of the bed. "Is that because you're leaving or because you don't want to eat?"

"I don't know."

"Well, figure it out. Pizza will be here in thirty." He picked up his phone and called in his order. He shouldn't pressure her into anything. Doing so would give her the idea that their arrangement might be more than it was supposed to be. It didn't matter he wanted it to be more. She'd be moving on as soon as his mom did.

The doorbell rang announcing Jaleesa and his mom. Norah looked up with wide eyes.

With a smile he said, "Might as well stay now. There's no sneaking out without her knowing."

She stood and crossed her arms. "Shows what you know. I could go out the back and no one would know."

"Except your car is in front. My sister probably parked behind you and already noticed." He put an arm around her shoulder and led her from the room. "We're both adults, remember? Adults fuck. And they sleep in the same bed."

"Easy for you to say. You're not the one she'll be grilling tomorrow." In the living room, she separated from him and sat on the couch. Before he got to the door, she turned the volume up on whatever TV show she'd decided on.

As soon as he opened the door, his mom said, "It's about time."

"Sorry. I was changing."

She shuffled past him leaning on her cane more than she had been. "Saw Norah's car."

Jaleesa followed her in and closed the door behind her. At their mom's remark, she looked at him. As they made their way into the living room, she touched his arm. "Can we talk in the kitchen?"

She didn't wait for an answer. She just kept moving. Walking by, she said, "Hi, Norah. Good to see you."

Norah didn't say anything. There was no reason to since she'd be saying it to Jaleesa's back. She stared at him in wide-eyed panic. He gave a slight shake of his head. His mom sat on the chair instead of her usual spot on the couch.

In the kitchen, Jaleesa stood leaning against the counter. "How could you?"

"What?"

"You're sleeping with our mother's caregiver? Really, Kai?"

"What's the big deal?"

"I like Norah. More importantly, Mom likes Norah."

"I like her too. Your point?"

"She's a sweet girl. She doesn't strike me as one of your"—she waved her hand around—"playthings. She's been through a lot. She doesn't need someone toying with her."

"You know nothing about it."

She shook her head. "Is that why you sent Mom to my house?"

"That was Mom's idea. Whatever happens between me and Norah is no one else's business."

"Don't fuck this up, Kai. Mom is healing, but she has *weeks* more before she'll be ready to move back in with me."

"So you're saying you don't think I can handle a relationship for even a few weeks."

"Is that what this is? A relationship?"

He crossed his arms instead of answering.

"That's what I thought. For all the changes you've made in your life, you're still not ready to let someone in." With another shake of her head, she left.

He heard her say good-bye to Norah and their mom. He thought about what Jaleesa said. She was right. He didn't want to let someone like Norah in. He shouldn't have let Norah push things to where they were, but there was no turning back now. He wanted her too much, so he'd get all he could from her until she realized she was better off without him.

He went back to the living room. "I ordered pizza if you're hungry, Mom."

She waved him off. "I ate at Jaleesa's."

"Did you have a good day?" Norah asked.

"The movie with my friends was good. We walked around the mall a bit before Jaleesa came to get me. I think that's where I made the mistake. By the time dinner ended and the kids wanted to read and watch TV, I was done for." She heaved off the chair. "In fact, I'm going to bed now."

Kai went to her side. "Need some help?"

She shook her head. "Keep it down and let me sleep in."

Norah clicked the volume lower on the TV.

His mom winked at Norah. "I wasn't talking about the TV."

Norah's eyes went wide and her skin flushed pink. He laughed.

"Good night," his mom said.

He sat on the couch next to Norah and laughed. She slapped his thigh.

"Not funny."

"Sure it is. My mom isn't stupid. I told you she knew everything."

"Can I ask what Jaleesa wanted?"

"Nothing important." He slipped an arm behind her head and curled it over her shoulder. He didn't have too much experience with relationships because they tended to escalate and get complicated. Norah started out complicated and he'd handled it. He liked having her here. More than he should for a temporary arrangement.

Suddenly the thought of coming home to an empty house didn't hold the same appeal it once had.

Yeah, Norah had definitely complicated his life.

The complications felt worth it as she snuggled against him on the couch eating pizza. Thoughts of making this more than temporary swamped him.

When they were done eating, she bounced with a burst of energy. "Let me see my tattoo."

"What's your hurry?" He moved in for a kiss.

She slapped a hand on his chest and leaned away. "Uh-uh. You want a kiss, I want art."

He sighed to cover his excitement. He'd wanted to wait until the right time to show her. "It's in my car."

"Why would you leave it there?"

He traced a finger across her collarbone. "If I brought it in with me, you would've wanted to see it. I had other plans involving your body."

She shivered but gave him another shove. "Go get it."

He ran out barefoot and bare-chested, immediately regretting the move. The concrete and grass froze his feet.

By the time he got back to the living room, his toes were numb.

Norah continued to bounce excitedly on the couch. Her anticipation rattled his nerves in no way a client ever did.

He slid the art on the table and stepped back to wait for her response.

She picked up the paper and studied it but said nothing. She was uncharacteristically quiet for so long, he assumed she was trying to figure out how to tell him she hated it.

"I can change whatever you don't like. This is just a draft," he lied. He'd spent hours drawing and erasing and choosing the right colors.

She looked up with teary eyes and a gorgeous smile. "I love it."

He released a long breath and joined her on the couch. He watched as she traced the cursive letters of her daughter's name.

Brushing her hair over her shoulder, he wrapped a hand on the back of her neck. "Give it some time before you decide not to make changes. This is forever."

"I know. You delivered everything I wanted. Her name is pretty. I've never known a guy with such perfect penmanship." She paused and narrowed her eyes. "Too perfect. You did the letters on the computer."

"Normally, I do, but I wrote this." To prove it, he grabbed a napkin and wrote the name again. "I told you it'd be custom."

Her gaze returned to the art.

"What about the colors?"

"Kai, stop worrying. It's perfect." She leaned over and planted a soft kiss on his lips.

With every move, every interaction, she drew him deeper. He was no longer sure he'd be able to let go.

Chapter Sixteen

Kai was nervous. He hadn't been nervous about a tattoo since his first one. Then again, he'd never done work on someone he cared about before. A simple business transaction didn't matter. But putting his mark on Norah was a different story. He'd had sex with women who later came to him for a tattoo, but he'd had another artist do the work. No one even knew the connection. Norah was different. He couldn't explain why she was different, this tattoo was different, but it was.

He'd waited at the studio all night. The artists and clients were gone for the day and he'd locked the shop. Norah had stayed at home until his mom was settled in bed and then came to the studio. He wanted complete privacy for this work. He definitely didn't want to get in the middle of Norah and Tommy.

While he readied his station in the back room, Norah wandered around the front, looking at the art on the walls. "Did you draw all of these?" she yelled.

He came to the door and leaned against the frame. "Most of them. Puck has some up there and so does Tommy."

"Does that mean you'll take a picture of mine and put me on your wall of fame?" She walked back toward him.

"No." He didn't want her to know how personal this was for him. He pointed behind him. "I'm ready."

She took a deep breath. "I hope I am." She slid past him, her body brushing his. "Does it hurt a lot?"

"At the beginning it will, but then your body gets used to it."

She plopped on the chair. "Sure."

"I can't imagine it hurts any more than having a baby."

She smirked. "But I had some good drugs to get me through that."

He grinned. "Do I need to get the pussyball?" He remembered her joking about the tennis ball on one of her first visits to the studio.

She grunted. "Now I am offended. As if those of us who actually have pussies can't handle a little pain." She lifted her hips and shimmied out of her jeans. Then she added, "I'd like to see a man give birth."

As he watched the jeans peel from her body, he tried to focus. She wore the bright blue panties again. The ones she'd worn the first time they'd had sex. Images of her bucking beneath him had his dick twitching.

This was probably why it wasn't a good idea for him to do work on someone he was involved with. She slid the panties off next and rolled to her side. "Like this?" she asked.

"Yeah." He got the thermal image she'd already squealed and gushed over and applied it to her skin. He started the machine. "Ready?"

"I think so."

With his hand on her thigh, he pushed away thoughts of all the ways he'd touched her over the last month. Right now, she needed to be nothing more than a canvas. She hissed with the first touch of the gun, but she didn't flinch.

He worked in silence for a few minutes and paused. "You okay?"

"Yeah. It's like you said, you kind of get used to it."

He resumed work, but she still said nothing.

"I never figured you to be a cadaver."

She turned her head to look at him. "Excuse me?"

"Someone who doesn't talk while getting a tattoo. It's like working on a corpse."

"I was trying not to distract you."

His gaze traveled from her naked thigh to her hip. "Trust me. Conversation is the right kind of distraction."

"Why do you hang out with Rooster?"

"What do you mean?" Not quite the conversation he'd hoped for, but better than silence.

"I feel like you don't really like him."

"We're friends."

"But he's a friend you only see when you have a poker game at your house. A friendship shouldn't have parameters like that."

He knew what she was getting at, but he didn't know if he could explain. "Rooster and I have history. You know that. I can't live in his world anymore. I can't get caught up again. But I can't tell him to fuck off either."

"Do you want to?"

"What?"

"Tell him to fuck off."

"Sometimes. He showed me the ropes in jail. Kept me safe. I owe him."

"From almost ten years ago? If he's not doing anything to change his life and you don't want what he's doing, maybe it's time to cut him loose."

Her thigh tensed and he took a moment to rub it to relax. "Still okay?"

She licked her lips. "Yeah."

"When I told you to talk, I didn't mean discuss my life. Most people talk about themselves."

"I lead a boring life. I don't have any friends."

"What about school?"

She released a soft sigh. "I have one. I'm applying for a loan to pay for it. I'll be starting again in January."

It was another reminder that she had a life far removed from him. They dropped back into silence and he worked quickly and efficiently.

As he finished up filling in the dragonfly, she looked over her shoulder at him. "Is it wrong that I'm getting really turned on by this?"

Christ. He'd thought her silence was bad. Could she make this any more difficult? He paused in his work and glanced up at her. "What part is turning you on?"

"All of it. Sitting here half naked, you running your hands on me, marking me permanently." She wiggled a little and he wondered if she was getting wet.

"Hold still and let me finish." His voice was more gruff than usual, mostly because she could turn him on with a look. And that look was bearing down on him right now.

A little while later, satisfied with the color, he said, "Done."

She jumped up on her knees and twisted and bent to get a good look at the tattoo. He smiled and handed her a mirror.

"The skin is irritated, but that'll clear up." He waited for a reaction.

She swallowed hard and looked down at him with tears in her eyes. "It's amazing. Even better than I thought it would be."

Leaning over, she kissed him, long and deep. "Have you ever had sex in here?"

The thought had never occurred to him. "No."

"Good. I like to do new things." She climbed off the chair and pulled him to stand. She quickly undid his pants and pushed them to his knees. He was already semihard from watching her. "Sit down."

He took her spot on the chair. She leaned over and took him in her mouth, making him go from half-hard to let's-fuck in thirty seconds. She fished into her pants pocket for a condom and rolled it on.

Without another word, she climbed on him and took his cock in one motion. She pulled her shirt over her head. He tugged the cup of her bra down and rose to take a nipple in his mouth. Her sigh was nearly a moan. Careful of her tattoo, he gripped her sides and forced her up and back down. Where she seemed content to wiggle and slide, he wanted to thrust. She gripped his hair and tugged as she rode him.

"I'm close," he growled into her ear.

Her hand slipped between them. "Not yet. I want it together."

Kai held on to the last bit of control he could as Norah stroked herself, her fingers colliding with the base of his cock. Her muscles started pulsing and when she went rigid in his arms, he fell with her.

He held her close as they both came back. She surrounded every inch of his being. In that moment, Kai knew that when she walked away, he'd be the one left in the ashes.

Norah felt happier than she had in a really long time. The routine of going to work and spending time with Kai gave her purpose. She was looking forward to going back to school in a few months, and the experience of caring for Lani gave her the idea to work as a home healthcare worker while she earned her degree.

For the first time in forever, her life was on track. She flew down the steps to get ready for work and came to a sudden halt when she saw Jimmy sitting in the kitchen. It was ten in the morning. "Shouldn't you be at work?"

"Going in late. Wanted to talk to you."

"Okay." Anytime Jimmy wanted to talk, it wasn't good. She eased into a chair at the table.

"What's going on with you and this guy Kai?"

Tommy and his big mouth. "We're seeing each other."

"But he's your boss."

"Technically."

"There's no 'technically.' Is he paying you?"

Damn, that made it sound like she was a hooker. "He pays me to take care of his mom. When I'm off the clock, we hang out. We enjoy each other's company." She tried to lighten the tone. "This isn't a case of sexual harassment. Just two people who are attracted to each other."

It was almost weird talking to Jimmy like this. She was comfortable in a way she never thought she would be. Like they were equals.

Jimmy ran a hand over the top of his head. "He's not a good guy, Norah. He's a felon."

"You ran a background check on him?"

"Don't look at me like I've done something wrong. I find out you're involved with someone—and not from you, I might add—I want to know who he is."

Norah took a long, slow breath to control the snap of anger she wanted to release. "I get that you feel protective of me, Jimmy. But I'm an adult. Kai told me about his past. And it is his *past*. We all make mistakes. It doesn't have to define who we are."

"It's nice to think, but in some ways, our past does define us. Something like being a felon follows him everywhere. It limits his prospects."

"He seems to be doing fine running a successful tattoo studio in spite of those limitations." She pushed away from the table and threw her arms around her big brother. "Thanks for looking out for me."

"I guess that means you're still going to date him."

"Yeah. We like each other and while it started out as an escape from life, I think we have a chance at something more."

"Isn't this a little soon after Ella and what's-his-name?"

Norah had no doubt Jimmy remembered Avery's name. "What's soon? I haven't had a boyfriend since Avery, which was months ago. Kai and I are taking it slow." Kind of. Maybe.

Jimmy sighed the way she imagined a worried father would. "Be careful."

Norah smiled. "I try."

"This whole letting-you-be-an-adult thing sucks."

She laughed. "Just think—it'll be worse when you have your own kids. And if there is a God, those kids will be just like Moira."

"Better watch what you wish for. Karma's a bitch."

She liked this new relationship with Jimmy. She was finally feeling like she belonged here as an O'Malley; she was one of them.

Norah drove to Kai's feeling light. This was a feeling she could get used to. When she unlocked the door to Kai's house, she was met with a surprise. Lani stood in the middle of the living room alone, with no cane.

"The therapist told me to go without."

Norah rushed forward. "Oh my gosh. Congratulations!" She hugged Lani, which might not have been exactly professional, but the woman was more a friend than a patient.

Lani returned the hug and said, "Still not ready for dancing, but she wants me to try our walk without the cane."

"Wow."

"I should be ready to move back to Jaleesa's soon."

As much as she liked seeing Lani make progress, it was

a sad reminder Norah wouldn't be needed much longer. She'd soon be out of a job. And she didn't know what that meant for her and Kai. They'd originally agreed that when Lani was better, they were over, but things were different between them. At least they were for her.

Kai came from the kitchen and kissed his mom on the head. "She's pretty proud of herself."

"She should be."

"I have to get to the studio. Should be home by ten." Then he bent and planted a quick kiss on Norah's lips.

The movement startled her. For everything they'd done together and for all his talk about his mom knowing everything, he'd yet to do anything in front of Lani. "Have a good day," he murmured against her lips.

A smile broke across her face. This day got better and better.

Norah and Lani went for a walk, which was shorter and a little slower than their usual walks but Lani succeeded without the cane. The improvement was amazing. It was hard to believe that barely two months ago she'd gotten out of the hospital with her knee replacement.

That meant Norah and Kai had been a couple for much less time, but it felt longer. She kept reminding herself not to build things up in her head, but then Kai did things like kiss her good-bye in front of Lani and she began to think she wasn't alone. Her afternoon was quiet and while Lani napped, Norah started a new job search.

Regardless of what happened between her and Kai, once Lani moved back in with Jaleesa, she'd have to find a new job. Her goal was to bank as much money as she could before school started so she would need less in loans. Great in theory, not so easy in reality.

After dinner, Norah helped Lani plan another book club meeting. She insisted Norah join them this time. Norah agreed and immediately downloaded the book onto her phone. Lani was amazed and wanted Norah to teach her how e-books worked. Norah made a mental note to tell Kai that an e-reader would make a great Christmas gift for his mom.

By the time Lani went to bed, Norah was exhausted. She curled up on the couch and relaxed with some old *Friends* reruns. She couldn't help but be jealous of the friendships those fictional characters had. She'd make friends once school started. Or if she got a job in an office or something, she'd have coworkers. She'd been isolated for so long.

A thump at the front door startled her. She sat up and listened. Kai wouldn't have forgotten his key; he kept everything on one ring. A moment later a soft knock followed. Norah eased off the couch and went to the door. She peeked through the peephole. Rooster. What was he doing here?

She opened the door. "Hey."

His eyes popped wide when he saw her. "Shit. If you're here, that means Kai's not home, right?"

"He's still at work." She checked her phone. "But he should be home soon."

Rooster leaned heavily against the door frame, one arm wrapped around his middle. Norah knew Kai only had Rooster over for poker night, so something was off. He pushed off the wall with a wince.

"You're hurt."

He wavered. "I'll be fine."

Norah looked over her shoulder to make sure Lani hadn't woken. She was torn. This was Kai's friend, even if Norah wasn't particularly fond of him. She sighed. "Come around back. You can wait for Kai in the kitchen."

She closed the door and locked up. On her way through the house, she checked on Lani and closed her bedroom door. In the kitchen, she waited at the door for Rooster. It took him forever to walk around the house. When he walked in, she realized why. He was bleeding.

"Oh my God. What happened?"

"A fight." He was slightly out of breath.

She couldn't let him sit here bleeding all over the place. "Take your jacket and shirt off."

She went to the bathroom to grab the first-aid kit and when she came back, Rooster was still struggling with his jacket. She yanked at the sleeves and pulled the bloody shirt off him. The gash on his side wasn't too deep. She didn't think it would need stitches, but she was no doctor. Tugging on a pair of gloves, she got to work.

He hissed like a baby when she cleaned the wound and she had to remind him to be quiet so he wouldn't wake Lani. By the time she had the bandage in place, Rooster was feeling more like himself because he started flirting again.

As Norah cleaned up the mess, he asked, "So you and Kai are a real thing?"

"We're something." The last thing she would do was label her relationship with Kai for someone who would surely bring it up to Kai.

She sat near him at the table. "You've known Kai a long time, right?"

"Since we were boys. Came up together."

Norah wanted to ask questions, learn everything she could about Kai from this man who'd known him for so long. Before she could formulate a question, Kai came in from the living room. He took one look at the situation and anger blazed in his eyes. Norah tried to see what he saw and realized she was sitting with Rooster, who was shirtless, in Kai's kitchen, talking quietly.

She shot up. "It's not what you're thinking."

* * *

Kai saw red. Worry and fear filled Norah's face. He saw the bandage on Rooster's side. Rooster had brought shit to Kai's house. Involved Norah. This was exactly what he'd wanted to keep her from. "Get out," he said to Norah, and then pinned Rooster with a look.

"What? Kai, it's not—"

He spun to face her. "Leave."

Her face crumpled. "But—"

Kai stalked toward her. Her jaw snapped shut, cutting off whatever plea she was about to make. He grabbed her elbow and pulled her through the house. Pressing her bag into her arms, he pointed at the front door and said as calmly as possible, "Go home. Don't come back."

It killed him to say it, but he knew what she hadn't considered. Rooster only brought trouble.

"But your mom—"

"She'll be fine."

"I was trying to help. That's all."

He glared at her, willing her to leave before he caved. She needed to get out of his life. Tears filled her eyes and she walked out the door. When she was gone, he turned to Rooster, who stood in front of the sink, taking in the scene with Norah. "What the fuck are you thinking?"

"I got hurt. I needed help. Somewhere I wouldn't get heat."

Before Kai could think, his hands were on Rooster's throat. "You dumb shit. How dare you bring that here? To her? She's not one of us. She's clean and—"

He stopped talking. Rooster would never get it. He shook with anger. Rooster held up his hands in defeat.

"I came looking for you. Didn't know she was here. I told her it was a fight. She don't know nothing," Rooster gasped out.

Kai let go and stepped back, his hands clenched in tight fists.

"Look, man, I didn't have anywhere else to go. I needed someone I could trust."

As pissed as Kai was, Rooster could still trust him. "Do I want details?"

"No. I just need to hang for a while till shit cools down."

Kai had learned long ago that shit never cooled down around Rooster. Staring at his childhood friend, all he could think of was Norah asking him if he wanted to tell Rooster to fuck off. Right now, more than anything, he did. But he wouldn't. His loyalty ran deeper than that.

He got Rooster a fresh shirt and sat with him in the kitchen. Within the hour, the doorbell sounded, affirming what Kai had suspected. Whenever Rooster was in trouble, the cops would surely follow.

Kai wrote a note to his mom so she wouldn't worry when she woke and found him gone. Then he answered the door, ready to go to jail for being friends with Rooster.

"Kai Ellis?" the cop at the door asked.

"Yes."

"We're looking for Ricardo Garcia, goes by the street name Rooster."

"Why?"

"He's a person of interest in a robbery."

"I haven't—" Before he finished the sentence, a commotion on the side of the house drew their attention. A second cop had Rooster wrestled to the ground. Stupid fucker. All he had to do was sit and be quiet.

"He don't know nothin'," Rooster was yelling. "You leave him alone."

Even now, when Kai had been thinking about telling Rooster to get the fuck out of his life, Rooster was trying to protect him. The cop eyed Kai as if debating if it would be worth the paperwork to haul him in as well.

From his spot of being shoved in the back of a cop car, Rooster winked at him. Kai knew he wouldn't tell the cops Norah had helped him. The cop in front of him turned to where Kai looked at Rooster. Then he said, "You might want to get a new class of friends. At least get some smarter ones. This one parked his getaway car in front of your house."

Sure enough, Rooster's car sat at the curb. Kai hadn't even noticed because he'd been looking forward to coming home to Norah. Kai nodded to the cop. "Anything else?"

"Not right now. Detectives might want to talk to you about this."

"You know where to find me." Kai closed and locked his door. That had been the most benign conversation he'd had with a cop. He should feel good they didn't haul him in. But he didn't. Rooster shit all over his life again.

The blue and red lights flashed as the cars drove down the block.

"Kai," his mom called from her room. "What's going on?"

"Nothing, Mom. Go back to sleep." He couldn't face her tonight. He was too raw and angry.

His muscles ached with the tension they held. More than anything right now, he wanted to hit something. He stomped to the basement to work out the frustration.

Chapter Seventeen

The following morning, Kai woke feeling beat up and groggy. He'd had a hard time falling asleep and when he finally had, he'd been plagued with nightmares of jail. When he climbed out of bed, he noticed how late it was. He texted Puck and told him to open the studio and that he'd be there soon.

Getting up this late meant his mom was surely awake and he still wasn't ready to face her. He needed coffee and lots of it. He got as far as the kitchen with the hope that she was reading in bed. Instead, she sat at the table drinking coffee.

"'Bout time you got up. Where's Norah? She's usually here by now and if she's got an appointment, she almost always tells me ahead of time."

"Norah's not coming. You don't need her help anymore. You're not ready to go back to Jaleesa's, but you can fend for yourself." He poured a cup of coffee and prayed she'd leave him alone. The first gulp burned through his system.

"What did you do?"

"Nothing."

"Don't treat me like I'm stupid. I saw the squad car outside last night."

He grit his teeth. "It's nothing."

A knock at the door offered him an easy escape—at least for now. He set his cup down and went through the house to answer the door. Norah stood on the porch. Crap. Facing her was harder than looking his mom in the eye.

"What are you doing here?"

She dipped her head. "You were angry last night. I didn't think you meant what you said."

"I did."

Her chest rose slowly with a deep breath. "For the record, I'd never do anything with Rooster or any of your friends. I'm not like that."

Fuck. She thought he thought she'd cheated on him. Cheated? Like they were some exclusive couple? He stepped out the door, pulling it closed behind him, forcing her to step back. He sighed. "I didn't tell you to leave because I thought you were fucking Rooster."

"Then why?"

He leaned against the brick wall. She still didn't get it. "Rooster did something yesterday. As soon as I saw him, I knew. Within an hour, the cops were knocking on my door."

"What does that have to do with me? Or you?"

"Rooster's not your concern." He crossed his arms to brace himself.

"He's not yours either."

"You don't belong here, mixed up in this."

Her forehead wrinkled. "Cops at your door isn't your life. Rooster's fuckups aren't your life. How can you not see that? You aren't Rooster. You let him cling to you. I get it. He's your friend, but to let him ruin everything for you? For us? That's just dumb."

"You don't understand."

"You're right. I don't understand. You said you were done with that shit." She took a step back. "If I leave here now, I won't be back."

His fingers flinched and he held them tighter to his body. He wanted to reach out, to hold her, to keep her with him. But he stayed rooted to his spot.

Then she turned with her head held high and walked away. Kai watched her leave. He had to force every muscle in his body to tense to stop himself from going after her.

At the sidewalk, she paused, turned, and stomped back toward him. Her eyes glittered and she threw something at him. His key bounced off his chest.

"Give that to Rooster since he's more important to you than I am."

By the time he bent to pick it up, she was gone. As her car pulled away, it felt like a mountain had collapsed on his chest. He forced air into his lungs.

In the living room, his mom stood there, waiting.

"Leave me alone."

"I absolutely will not." She jabbed a finger in the air at him. "Why are you protecting that thug? He's never been anything but trouble."

"I'm not protecting Rooster. The police have him."

"But you would have. You'd've chosen him over Norah, which is plain stupid."

"I'm not."

"Yes, you are. I was starting to think you were better than your father."

He glared at her. He so did not need this bullshit right now.

Her eyes were glistening. "You're not protecting her. You think pushing her away is better than leaving her? You're wrong. Either way, she's still left broken."

Kai opened his mouth but no words came. His mom shook her head and walked from the room. He wasn't anything like his father. He'd never leave a wife and kids because he didn't want to deal with the hassles of a family. He made sure no one depended on him for that reason. He couldn't let them down.

And he was protecting Norah. His mother had no idea how wrong she was. Norah was unbreakable. He, on the other hand, felt like his heart had been ripped out and shredded.

Norah was numb. Almost like she wasn't in her own body. She drove away from Kai's house still in a daze. Just like that, everything they had was over because of some asshole from his past. Knowing she couldn't, and more importantly didn't want to, go back home, she drove to Moira's apartment in the hope that she'd be there.

She knocked on the door and was surprised when Jimmy answered.

"What's wrong?" he asked, just as she said, "What are you doing here?"

Moira jumped out from behind Jimmy and said, "Hey. Come on in."

Jimmy stepped back from the door and stared at Norah. "I came to see Moira."

"What's wrong?" he asked again.

"You're a great big brother, Jimmy, but right now, I need a girlfriend."

Jimmy's gaze bounced between Norah and Moira. Moira waved her arms shooing him off. He backed away and as he grabbed his jacket, Moira asked, "What is it?"

Softly, Norah answered, "He dumped me."

She wrapped her arms around Norah, pulling her into a hug. "Ah, shit. This calls for chocolate."

In the warmth of Moira's arms, Norah allowed the emotions to hit her. Moira maneuvered them to the couch and they sat, with Moira not letting go. Norah wanted to cry but for a change, she had no tears. Maybe she'd cried them all out over Ella and Avery.

"What happened?" Moira asked.

"I don't even really know. It's so stupid. I'm stupid."

"No, you're not."

Norah pushed away and pulled her legs up on the couch. "Yeah, I am. When it comes to guys. Every. Time. I fall fast and hard and I always think it's more than it is. I know I do this, and try to stop, but every time, I end up right here."

"Back up a little. This is about Kai, right? Jimmy told me about you and him."

"Yeah. And if you'd asked me yesterday morning, I'd have told you we were falling for each other. Things were going great, better than I could've imagined." She laid her head back and stared at the ceiling. "We were supposed to be temporary, anyway. Just an escape for as long as I took care of his mom."

The front door opened and Jimmy came back in carrying a grocery bag. Norah crossed her arms. "Don't you have a job?"

"Be nice. I came bearing gifts." He crossed the room, kissed Moira, and handed her the bag.

Moira opened it and pulled out two pints of chocolate fudge brownie ice cream. "You're the best."

He kissed her again. "I know how you are with chocolate." He turned to Norah. "Do I need to go kick some ass?"

Tempting, especially as she remembered Kai offering to beat up Tommy for making her cry, but she shook her head. It also wasn't what she'd expected from Jimmy after their last conversation about Kai. She'd figured he'd be giving her a giant *I told you so*. "No."

"Okay. I'll be around if you need me."

Moira patted her leg. "I got this."

Jimmy left again. Moira went to the kitchen and returned with two spoons. She handed Norah a pint of ice cream. "Chocolate might not cure a broken heart, but it definitely soothes it."

Norah pried the lid off and dug in.

"Now tell me what happened."

Norah explained what happened last night. "It all happened so fast. And I thought it was anger, you know? Like he chased me out because he thought I was messing around with his friend. So I went to see him this morning, and it wasn't just him being mad. He doesn't want me in his life because he has crappy taste in friends. Rooster committed some crime and the cops showed up at Kai's house. That's why he chased me out of there."

"I'm sure Jimmy will be glad to hear that. He might have a heart attack to get word that the cops questioned you."

Norah shot her a look and Moira answered with a smile.

"While that's understandable, why did he end things?"

Norah jabbed her spoon into the chocolate, getting irritated all over again. "Fuck if I know. He said something about me not belonging in his life because of shit like that." She set her pint on the table. "I told him that if I left, I wouldn't come back. Then I threw his key at him."

Moira nudged her. "Good for you. If he can't see what a catch you are, he doesn't deserve you."

Norah sighed. "Now you sound like Jimmy."

"You might not want to hear this, and if you ever repeat it, I'll vehemently deny it, but your big brother is a smart guy."

"I know. But I also know Kai is a good guy. *He* just doesn't believe it. He still sees himself as the criminal he was ten years ago." Norah stretched out her legs and then slumped over to lean on Moira. Having a girlfriend felt good.

"Men are stupid when it comes to love and women. Even the smart ones. He might get his head out of his ass. Your brother did."

Norah laughed. "I remember. I didn't know what Jimmy had done, but he moped around for days. He needed a nudge to make him wake up. I'm glad he did."

"So am I." Moira put her arm around Norah's shoulder. "Want me to go give Kai a nudge? Or a shove?"

Norah laughed again. "No. He needs to figure this out on his own. Love sucks."

"Except when it doesn't."

"Yeah." Norah reached for her ice cream again. "You know, if I had known having a sister would mean a shoulder to cry on and ice cream for breakfast, I might've looked for one a whole lot earlier."

Two days later, Kai was still a mess. His mom barely spoke to him. Then this morning Jaleesa called to yell at him because Norah had asked if she could use Jaleesa as a job reference. He couldn't even explain to Jaleesa why he'd fired Norah, but she must've sensed something because she let it go.

He sat in his office, feeling like the walls were closing in. This was what he'd feared from the beginning—his entire life and all its pieces imploding. Then, as if his day couldn't get worse, he heard a voice from the front of the studio.

"Where is he?"

He knew that tone in Norah's voice. She was pissed about something. He shoved away from his desk and met her at the doorway to his office.

"What the hell is this?" she asked, waving the envelope he'd sent home with Tommy.

He immediately knew it had been a mistake to leave the safe confines of his desk. He shouldn't be this close to her. "Your pay."

"This is way more than my pay. I don't need your guilt money."

"That's not guilt money." At least that's what he told

himself. "You were around a lot of extra hours the last couple of weeks."

"Most of which were spent fucking you. So now I'm a whore?" Her voice was loud enough to draw the attention of Puck and Tommy who froze, wide-eyed.

He grabbed Norah's elbow and hauled her out the back. As soon as the door slammed behind them in the alley, he had the overwhelming urge to press against her body and kiss her. Instead, he released her elbow. "Don't talk stupid. Of course I don't think you're a whore." He stepped farther away and ran his hands through his hair. "I fired you without warning. I figured you'd need the money, especially with school. Think of it as severance. We appreciate everything you did for my mom."

She shook her head. When she spoke, her voice was steady and cold. "Okay, Kai, treat everything we had like a business transaction. I'm sure that'll help you sleep better at night."

Fuck. He didn't know what he was doing. He hated that she was hurting. He hated that she knew he wasn't sleeping because of her. He hated not being able to touch her.

"Nothing between us was business," he whispered. He watched the fight leave her. Her eyes glistened and it tore at him. He took a half step closer, wanting more than anything to hold her and fix this fucked-up mess. "I—"

Before he could finish the asinine statement—what was he going to do, tell her not to go? That he loved her?—the back door flew open and Tommy came out. He looked between Kai and Norah and then said, "Client's here."

With a sharp nod and a last glance over his shoulder at Norah, he went back inside. Admitting to her how he felt couldn't change anything. It would only hurt her more. He swallowed his own pain and went back to work.

* * *

Tommy stepped close. "You okay?"

Norah nodded, unsure of her ability to speak. She wanted to follow Kai and fight, make him see. But if he wasn't willing to fight for them, why should she?

"You want to explain what happened?"

"Kai was being a good guy. It just wasn't enough to fix this, I guess." She tucked the envelope in her back pocket. "Part of me hoped that if I confronted him, he'd admit we had something great together."

"Guessing that didn't work as planned."

She licked her lips. "Nope." She stared at the door to the studio. "I sure can pick 'em, can't I?"

"You're an O'Malley. We screw up a whole lot before we get it right."

She bumped his shoulder. "Screw up? Or just screw? 'Cause I saw another new chick sneaking out the back this morning."

Tommy chuckled. "Maybe a little of both. Want to grab some lunch?"

"Yeah."

She looked back at the door again and then pointed down the alley. "I think I'll walk around and meet you at my car."

Tommy took her to some small hole-in-the-wall burger place she'd never heard of, but they had the best chocolate shakes. She made a mental note to tell Moira about it. While she slurped on her shake, Tommy doodled on a napkin.

"So what are your plans now?" he asked without looking up.

"I'm set to start school next semester. I'm going to start applying for jobs. I'd like to find something like I was doing for Kai."

Tommy glanced up with an arched brow. She threw a fry at him. "Not like that, you pig. I mean taking care of his mom. I'm good at it."

"You mean you're good at bossing people around."

"We all have our talents."

She looked at the napkin and snatched it up to see the doodle. "What is this?" She turned the paper and realized it was a cupcake.

"What? I saw one at a bakery yesterday. It was like a work of art. It was beautiful, but it made me want to take a bite."

Norah suspected there was more to it. "What were you doing at a bakery?"

"Blackstone's. Jimmy wanted me to order a cake for Sean's birthday."

"You guys still get birthday cakes from Blackstone's?" She had great memories of her childhood birthday cakes. One year, she had a princess cake with a doll in it and the cake was her gown. Tommy had teased her endlessly about it, but Jimmy got it for her because she'd asked for it.

"Of course. You think we're gonna bake something?"

"I didn't think about it. I guess I assumed you didn't do cake anymore. We're not kids." She couldn't remember the last birthday cake she had. Fourteen? Fifteen? Aunt Bridget thought it was frivolous, especially since Uncle Hank was always on a diet.

"Jimmy always makes sure we have cake on our birthdays and eat dinner together." He stopped suddenly. "Sometimes I forget you didn't have that."

She lifted a shoulder. "Jimmy always sent a gift and called. And you came to visit on a few of my birthdays. Who else would've taken me out and gotten me drunk when I turned twenty-one?"

"As crappy as it was, you know Jimmy only sent you there because he worried."

"It would've been better if he sent you, too."

Tommy barked out a laugh. "Aunt Bridget would've keeled over if she had to deal with me."

"True." She sighed. Even with the hurt she was feeling because of Kai, she was okay. "It's good to be home."

"We're glad you're back too, squirt."

"When are you guys gonna stop calling me that?"

"Never." He checked his phone. "I gotta get back to work."

Norah dropped him off at Ink Envy and swore to herself that she wasn't trying to see inside to get a glimpse of Kai.

A week had passed since he'd seen Norah, and Kai still wasn't sleeping right. Every time he closed his eyes, he saw her face. Every time he rolled over, he reached for her body. Every time the phone rang, he longed to hear her voice. But she was gone. He'd told himself over and over that it was best. It was what he wanted. Now he could get back to his life. Exactly the way it had been.

He also discovered he sucked at lying to himself.

The studio's line rang and a moment later, Puck called, "Hey, Kai, there's a collect call. What do you want me to do?"

A collect call meant Rooster was reaching out. "I got it," he yelled back.

Kai picked up the line in his office and accepted the charges for the call.

"Hey," Rooster said.

"Why are you calling?"

"I need some help."

Kai groaned. He should've expected this. "What?"

"I need some money for a lawyer."

Money for a lawyer, not his kids. Kai paced a circuit through his small office. "Use a public defender. You're not getting out of this one, and you know it. It would be throwing money away."

"Come on, man."

"No, Rooster." And as the words came out, the weight on Kai's chest shifted. It was time to let go. Everyone had been right. This was no longer his life. "I'm not getting caught up again."

"So it's gonna be like that."

"Yeah, it has to be. I'm trying to build a life here and you keep fucking up. You want to live like that, where you think nothing of getting picked up. I haven't worn cuffs in a decade. That's how I want to live."

"So you're not gonna help."

"No. Not anymore. You brought that shit to my house. To—" He'd almost said Norah's name, but caught himself. He needed to keep her out of it. But the thought alone brought her back to the forefront of his mind. The hurt he'd caused by sending her away and letting Rooster stay.

Damn it. He'd done exactly as her family had. Sent her away, leaving her alone.

"I had no place else to go. You're my boy." Rooster's voice brought him back to the conversation.

"Not anymore." He disconnected before Rooster could ask again because he feared he'd lose the bit of strength he had. Strength he'd gotten from Norah. With the exception of his mom, no one called him on his shit like Norah had. She deserved better than what he'd done.

His mom had been right. He'd chosen Rooster over Norah. The image of her standing in the alley, her eyes begging for him to give her what she needed, crashed into his head. He'd almost told her he loved her. He sank into the chair behind his desk. How the fuck had that happened? He loved Norah? A temporary escape. That's what she'd called them.

He couldn't breathe. The momentary relief he'd felt from breaking away from Rooster disappeared. He jumped up and stepped out the back door. Images of a tearful Norah assaulted him. He sucked in a lungful of air and closed his eyes. For the first time in a long time, he didn't know what to do, what he wanted.

Fuck that. He knew he wanted Norah.

The problem was, he wasn't sure how to get her.

He left Ink Envy, telling Puck he'd be back later, and he went home to see his mom. When he parked his car, he caught sight of her down the block, walking slowly back toward the house. From the curb, he called out, "Good to see you're still doing your walks."

"The only way to get better and away from you is to exercise."

That stung. He walked to meet her. "I'm not my father."

She tilted her head and arched a brow. "Could've fooled me."

"I'm here. I've always been here. I moved you into my house so you wouldn't feel abandoned."

She continued to stare up at him.

"He left without looking back."

"And you pushed Norah away."

"I know. And you're right. I shouldn't have."

She stopped and held a hand to her ear. "What was that? Did you just admit your mother was right?"

"Yes."

"Good. What are you going to do about it?"

"That's why I'm here. I have no idea."

"Did you talk to her?"

Remembering their last conversation over the money he gave her, he said, "I fucked that up."

"Talking has never been your strong suit."

He hung his head. Like he didn't know that.

"Actions, now, that's where you're good."

"What do you mean?"

She nudged him to continue the walk back to the house. "I've never seen a man go after anything with such single-minded determination as you. You're a doer. Whether it was getting into trouble or getting your tattoo parlor. You make things happen."

He hadn't thought about it that way. For him, it was just doing what needed to be done. Hearing his mom talk about him, though . . . She sounded proud.

She continued, "All you need to do is show her you want her back. That you're ready for her now even though days ago you weren't. She's a smart girl. She'll need more than words anyway."

He held out his elbow for his mom to take. She didn't really need the help or support, but he wanted to. Jaleesa had been right too. He'd kept too much separate for too long. Norah bled into all parts of his life and he'd survived. His heart was a little worse for the wear, but he'd been happy with her crashing all over his life. He liked coming home to her, seeing her in the stands while he played hockey, knowing she wore his tattoo on her hip.

As he helped his mom back into the house, he started to think about what needed to change in order for him to prove to Norah that he wanted them back. When he needed to prove to Jaleesa and Matt that he was ready to own his own shop, he'd changed almost everything in his life.

This should be easy. There was only one part of his life standing in the way of him having Norah and he'd already told Rooster no more. Now he just had to figure out how to show her he was serious.

Chapter Eighteen

Norah was more excited for Sean's birthday than was natural. It wasn't like a cake and presents were coming her way, but something about being home with her family for a special occasion made her ridiculously happy. Maybe it was the idea of a celebration to cover her pain. She woke today and swore she wouldn't cry over Kai anymore. Moira was right. If he didn't see what a catch she was . . . Who was she kidding? She wanted him no matter what.

Stupid heart.

She returned her thoughts to party planning. She'd offered to pick up the cake, but Tommy insisted on getting it. Something weird was going on there, but she'd pressure him later to find out.

For now, she hung streamers and balloons in the living room. Her dad came in. "What's all this shite?"

"Stop being cranky. You know it's Sean's birthday."

"His birthday was last week."

"I know when my brother's birthday is. This is when we could all be together. So we're celebrating."

"We do cake. Even that's silly for a grown man."

She climbed off the step stool. "So what if it's silly?

I haven't been around for too many celebrations. I want this to be fun."

"He's twenty-six years old. A bottle of whiskey and a woman would be the fun he's looking for."

"And he can go out and get that after dinner. But family time comes first." She put the stool away in the kitchen. "Are we going out for dinner?"

"Nah. Jimmy's picking up pizza."

"Pizza? And you have the nerve to talk about being grown." She shook her head, but pictured all of her brothers gathered around the dining room table fighting over pizza and laughing.

Kevin was the first to arrive and, right behind him, Tommy rushed in. He saw Kevin and said, "Good, you're here. I need some help."

"With what?"

"I got a present for Sean, but I need your help carrying it in."

"I thought we didn't do presents," Norah said.

"We don't, but I couldn't pass this up. It's something we'll both use."

"What?"

"Kai sold me his poker table. It'll fit perfectly in the basement by the washer."

At the mention of Kai's name, her heart gave a little lurch. Why the hell would he get rid of the table?

Tommy tapped Kevin's chest. "Come on."

They were still in the middle of setting it up when Sean walked through the door with Jimmy and Moira. Jimmy yelled for Kevin and Tommy.

Norah grabbed plates and napkins from the kitchen and Kevin snorted. "Since when do we use plates?"

"Would it kill you to eat like a human?" Moira asked. She set a pan near the end of the table.

"What's that?" Kevin asked.

"Brownies for the birthday boy." She hugged Sean and kissed his cheek.

"What do I get on my birthday?"

"Hmm . . . Sorry, I think I'm busy that day."

"You don't even know when my birthday is, do you?"

"Does it matter?"

Norah watched the exchange. "What's up with you two?"

"We're just playing. Ain't that right, Moira?"

"Oh sure, all fun and games."

Jimmy came to the table balancing bottles of beer for everyone, except Norah. "Where's mine?"

The total look of shock on Jimmy's face made her smile. "Did you actually forget I'm old enough to drink?"

"Uh . . ."

Moira touched his arm. "Now's a good time to close your mouth. There's not really a good way to answer."

Norah snatched Jimmy's bottle. "Thanks."

The pizza lids were thrown open and slices were passed around. Everyone started talking at once and the noise was overwhelming and welcome. She'd forgotten what it was like to have all the O'Malley men together in one spot. They were loud and physical and took up so much space.

She was glad she had Moira to help balance things a little. All she needed now was for her other brothers to find girlfriends and things could be even.

The doorbell rang and Kevin got up to answer, taking his beer with him as if he thought Norah might steal his, too. The voices at the door were low, but pulled Norah's attention. Kevin stepped into the living room and pinned her with a look. "There's a guy at the door for you."

Norah shoved away from the table and went to the door. Kai stood there clutching a bouquet of roses. Kevin crowded her at her back. She shoved at Kevin's chest. "I got this."

Kevin eased back a step but didn't go inside.

She sighed. "Do I have to get Jimmy to make you leave?"

"Who's he?"

She took a deep breath, unsure how to answer. "My ex-boss and . . . ex-boyfriend?"

"Are you asking me?" Kevin said.

"It's complicated."

"Wait—Ella's dad?" He scowled and his hands fisted.

Kai said, "I'm not Ella's dad. I didn't even meet Norah until this summer."

Kevin eased back and took a long pull on his beer. He waved at her to go ahead and talk.

"Go away, Kevin."

"It's almost time for cake." Over her head, he looked at Kai. "We're in the middle of a family party."

"I'm sorry. I didn't know. I won't take much time."

Kevin stared at them.

"Christ," she mumbled. Then she yelled, "Jimmy."

She heard movement from inside. Then Jimmy stood behind Kevin.

"Can you tell Kevin to go away? Kai is here to see me. I deserve to have some privacy."

Jimmy looked at Norah, then at Kai. She didn't know what he saw, but it was enough for him to tap Kevin's shoulder. "Leave them alone."

Before Kevin could respond, Kai shifted the flowers to his left hand and stepped closer with his right hand extended. "Good to see you again."

Kevin scowled. Jimmy didn't shake Kai's hand, so he dropped it. But he kept his eyes on Jimmy's. "I know I fucked up with her. But if she gives me the chance, I'm going to make it right."

Kevin opened his mouth, but Jimmy grabbed him by the back of the neck and hauled him in.

Norah turned back to Kai. And waited. As much as she wanted to rush to him, she held back. She'd been telling herself for over a week that she deserved better. It always sounded good in her head when she was alone.

"These are for you." He handed her the bouquet.

She hesitated, but took them. Her mind raced with possibilities. Her heart thumped at the sight of him. He'd told Jimmy he wanted to make things right. Yet he stood in front of her saying nothing.

He stepped closer, right up in her space. Looking down at her, he studied her eyes, her lips, then took a giant step back. He ran his fingers through his hair. "I'm sorry. I shouldn't have pushed you away."

"Why?"

His mouth opened and he stopped as if the question made no sense. "I told you from the beginning I didn't want you around Rooster. He has a way of pulling people down and you're better than that."

"So are you."

"I'm not. But I'm trying to be. I'm trying to fix my life so it's the right place for you."

She wanted to jump on him and hold him and kiss him. "I was happy where I was."

"I wasn't." As if he knew where her mind had gone, he took another step away from her. "You have too much faith in me, and I need to make sure it isn't misplaced. I need to do this right."

He lost her again. Do what right? If he wanted to be with her why did he keep backing away? She licked her lips and stepped forward searching for the right question. He backed up again and hit the rail. His arms shot out and grabbed her arms just above the elbow.

"Do me a favor and stay right there. This is hard enough without you being close and showing me your tongue and . . ."

She giggled. This was silly. So she made a show of licking her lips nice and slow. He closed his eyes.

"I came here tonight to apologize and ask you out."

"Huh?"

He opened his eyes, but still didn't release her. "Tommy pointed out a long time ago that I hadn't even taken you on a date, but we were sleeping together."

"Tommy should mind his own business. We did what worked for us and our schedules. It wasn't like it was all sex all the time. We hung out and talked and got to know each other. I don't need some sappy candlelight dinner for it to be real."

"You deserve the sappy candlelight dinner. Just now you didn't even know what to call me. Boyfriend?" he mimicked, but it didn't escape her that he'd dropped the ex. "You deserve better than questions. I'd like to take you to a party tomorrow."

"Okay." As soon as she agreed, she thought maybe she should've made him work harder for it. If she made things easy, it would be easy for him to push her away again. She stepped away from his grasp.

"It still won't be candlelight. Unless you count candles on a kid's birthday cake."

"Kid?"

"Carlos's kid. They're having a birthday party, but instead of dodging it like I usually do, I want to bring you as my date. As my girlfriend."

"I'd like that."

"Okay. I'll pick you up at three tomorrow. Go back to your family and tell them I'm sorry for the interruption."

Then he turned and walked away without touching her or kissing her, but leaving her wanting it all. Norah went back inside and was greeted with silence. Everyone sat and stared at her.

"Well?" Moira asked.

"He asked me out on a date. To a kid's birthday party."

The guys all looked confused, but Moira jumped out of her chair and gave her a hug.

When no one spoke, Moira said, "That means Kai is getting his head out of his ass."

Kevin tossed a bottle cap against the table. "I was really hoping he'd be a dick so I had someone to beat up."

Norah rolled her eyes at him. "Shouldn't you be happier he's not?"

Kevin shrugged. Then he pointed at her. "Why haven't I heard about this guy before now?"

"You're living your life and I've been living mine?"

"And why does he know the great Jimmy, but not me?"

"Because you're only around when you want a free meal or to stir up trouble."

He smiled. "I guess you got a point."

"Is it time for cake yet?" Sean asked. "I got a date to get to."

Tommy went to the kitchen and came back with the cake and what looked like way more than twenty-six candles.

"Dude, how old do you think I am?"

Tommy laughed. "I figured if one extra candle was good luck, a box would set you straight."

They all laughed together and sang and ate cake. Life was about as perfect as it could get, except for her nerves attacking.

She was starting to question if agreeing to a date with Kai was smart. She didn't know what to expect. He said he wanted to do things right, but things had felt pretty freaking right for a long time, even without dates. Somehow that hadn't been enough for him. He pushed her away even though she would've stood by him regardless of what happened with Rooster.

What was supposed to be different this time? What if she let herself love him and he pushed her away again? She couldn't handle that.

* * *

Kai was nervous about the date. The whole thing was awkward. He didn't know how to act. Was he supposed to pretend he and Norah had never split? That they were a couple? Even though she hadn't fully agreed to give him another chance?

Fuck. All these questions were killing him. He needed to just do. He'd pick Norah up and show her his life was different, that he not only had room for her, but that he wanted her there.

At 2:55, he stood on her porch and rang the bell. Norah opened the door and his mouth dried. She wore a bright blue dress that matched her eyes and skimmed the middle of her thighs. Her sandals had small heels and straps that crossed over her feet and ankles. Her dark hair swept over her bare shoulders. She carried a sweater. He was torn over whether he wanted her to have to use it.

"Is this okay?" she asked and he realized he was staring.

"You look amazing." He held out a hand for hers.

For the first time ever, she hesitated. Norah had never once shied from his touch. Unease crawled back over him. "Problem?"

"No," she answered with a smile, and took his hand.

He led her to his car and once they were situated, he said, "You met Carlos at my house. You won't know anyone else there. I probably won't know many people, so we don't have to stay long. We can say hi and drop off the present and then leave. We can go have dinner or something."

"You don't need to cut your plans short because I'm with you."

"I'm not. I don't want you to feel uncomfortable."

"It would be nice to meet your friends. You know, and *not* be shooed off."

"Ouch. I only did that because of Rooster."

He drove for a few minutes in uncomfortable silence. He usually liked quiet, but not from Norah. "Any luck finding a job?"

As soon as the question left, he knew it was stupid. He was the one who fired her and left her unemployed.

"I've filled out some applications but nothing yet."

They dropped back into silence.

This date might kill him. Luckily, there was no traffic and they made it to Carlos's house quickly. After he parked, he reached behind her seat and grabbed the present. Norah looked at the package.

"Did you wrap that yourself?"

"Yes. I bought it myself too."

"What is it? Wait. Don't tell me." She grabbed the present and shook and squeezed it. "Boy or girl?"

"Girl."

She smirked. "Too easy. It's a Barbie doll."

"Bad choice?"

"I don't know. Does she like Barbies?"

"Hell if I know. I haven't seen her in a long time."

Norah rolled her eyes. "That's why you ask before you go shopping. At least it looks pretty."

"I'm sure that'll make a difference to Ruby."

"You'd be surprised."

He got out of the car and met her on the curb. He took her hand again. "I'm really glad you're here with me."

She nodded. Even without the physical distance, she was holding back.

"Do you regret saying yes?" he asked.

"I'm not sure."

Well, hell. That wasn't what he'd hoped to hear.

She took a deep breath and stared at the ground.

"Say the word and I'll take you back home. I'll hate it, but I'll do it."

She shook her head, focus still on her feet.

"What is it?"

"I said yes like it was automatic, and then I started to think." She looked up to face him. "I want this. Almost too much. If I jump into your arms, what's to say you won't push me away again? What's so different?"

Her voice was quiet with her questions, but her eyes, as always, held strength and determination. And a bit of fire.

"I didn't come to you just because I missed you." He turned and leaned against the car beside her. "I talked to Rooster. He asked for money and I told him no. It was the first time I've ever turned him away, but it felt right. For the first time a weight was lifted off me. Like I was finally free."

"I wasn't looking for you to dump your friend for me."

"I did it for me. Even if you walk away from me right now, I won't be looking for Rooster. He was the one part of my life I hadn't moved on from. I wasn't ready. Or I didn't have a reason to." He bit his lip and looked down the street at all the SUVs and minivans lining the street. Flowers on the doorsteps, kids yelling and playing tag. Suddenly he had so much he wanted to say to Norah, but the old frustrations boiled up.

"You okay?"

He turned back to her. "You make me feel like a stuttering first grader."

A hint of a smile lifted the corner of her mouth. "I don't know if I should be flattered."

He caressed her cheek. "You should. I have so much I want to say, but the words won't come out right."

"I can be patient."

He took a deep breath, inhaling her scent, which balanced him. "Jaleesa told me I compartmentalize too much. I had work, hockey, and home. Nothing overlapped. Until you. It bothered me at first, but then . . ."

"Then what?"

"I started to look forward to seeing you all over. I was afraid Rooster would screw up your life like he had mine." He shook his head. "No. I made my own choices and I've lived with the consequences, but Rooster was a constant reminder. I didn't want that around you."

"I'm not sure I understand. You cut Rooster out of your life and that's supposed to give me comfort that you won't run away or push me away again?"

He could admit maybe it didn't sound logical, but to him, it made sense. "That's part of it. The other part is taking down the walls of the compartments. Coming to this party is the first step. The only time I saw Carlos was at our poker games. Now I'm going to a family party."

"With me."

"With you because you're part of my life. At least I hope so."

His explanation seemed to work because a smile eased across her face. "Why did you sell Tommy your poker table?"

"I won't need it anymore." He pushed off the car. "You ready to go in?"

"Yeah."

Norah held Kai's hand and absorbed everything he'd said. She couldn't imagine anyone making life changes for her. She hadn't expected that. She sure as hell hadn't expected him to talk that much, to really open up. "I like it when you talk to me," she said as they climbed the steps to Carlos's house.

"It ain't easy."

His honesty made her laugh. "For the record, I like the quiet and brooding too. It's hot."

Carlos answered the door and greeted them. "It's good to see you again, Norah. Glad you made it, Kai. You guys are just in time for the piñata." He held up a princess castle piñata.

Norah and Kai followed him through the house and to the backyard. He swung the rope over a tree branch and then looked at Kai. "Will you do the honors?"

"What?" Kai looked worried.

"Hold the rope so the kids can swing at the piñata."

Kai took the rope from Carlos. Carlos called a bunch of kids over. Judging by their size Norah guessed they were six or so. Carlos blindfolded the first girl and handed her a bat. As he began to spin her, Kai called out, "Hey, they're coming at me blindfolded and swinging a bat. How is that an honor?"

Carlos laughed. "You're a big boy. You can handle it."

Norah laughed along with him as Kai lowered the piñata and tried to keep a safe distance. A woman walked up next to Norah and said, "Hi, I'm Maria, Carlos's wife. I don't think we've met."

"Hi, I'm Norah. I came with Kai." She pointed to him in case Maria was unaware who he was, which seemed silly.

"It's so good to meet you." She embraced Norah as if they were long-lost friends. "Carlos told me about you. How good you are for Kai."

Norah didn't know how to respond. She'd only met Carlos a couple of times. What could he know about her?

"Don't look so shocked. Carlos tells me everything. And if you're the reason Kai finally came over, I know you're special."

"I don't know about that. I think he planned to come even if I didn't."

"Well, I'm glad you're here. Can I get you a drink?"

Norah looked at the cup in Maria's hand. "I'll have whatever you're having."

"Spiked punch it is." She tilted her head and Norah followed her back into the kitchen.

Spiked was a bit of an understatement. It tasted like more alcohol than juice, but it was good. The piñata didn't last long, but the contents kept the kids occupied for a while. Norah enjoyed the buzz of noise in the house from the party. Kai had come back in from the yard and came straight to her.

"Having fun?"

"Yeah."

He stood beside her without touching her. They walked through the buffet line to load up plates of food and Norah ate until she thought she might burst. She saw a different side to Kai during the course of the party. He was a little more relaxed. That was probably because he knew more people than he said he would. In addition to Carlos, both Dean and Eric came with their wives.

In some ways, Norah felt left out. These people had known each other forever and she had none of the experiences or memories they had. But it wasn't bad. Everyone shared stories and made her laugh. As the party wound down, the drinks were flowing, and the kids settled in the living room to watch a movie.

Carlos walked the room and called the adults out to the yard to sit around a small fire pit. Norah stopped at the bathroom and by the time she made it to the yard, no chairs were left. Kai moved to stand to give her the one he was in, but instead, she pressed on his shoulders and sat on his lap. "It's okay, right?"

"Yeah."

She didn't think it was her imagination that his voice was gravelly as her butt connected with his thighs. She shifted so she could see the others in the group. There were a few people she hadn't met yet, but Kai's poker friends were familiar.

"Gonna miss those poker games," Dean said. He pointed at Kai. "You've been on a hell of a losing streak."

Norah listened and realized Kai had sold the poker table because he canceled the game with his friends. She swiveled to look at him, and he hissed before sliding her closer to his knees. "You're not going to play poker anymore?"

"No."

Like that was some kind of explanation. "Why not?"

"Making changes."

She lowered her mouth to his ear. "I don't expect you to give up your friends and time with them. That's not how this works. Look around. All of these guys are married or have girlfriends and still made it to poker."

"I know."

A grunt of frustration bubbled up in her throat. "This doesn't qualify as talking."

He closed his eyes slowly, like he needed to concentrate. He wasn't drunk. She'd only seen him have a single beer before dinner. When he reopened them, he simply said, "It's time to go."

She stood, a little shocked that he'd gotten pissed off because she wanted to talk, but she said nothing as they said good-bye to everyone and thanked Carlos and Maria for having them. Kai was suddenly in a rush, tugging her down the gangway toward the front of the house.

Norah yanked her hand back. "What the hell is going on?" Her voice was quiet but sharp. She didn't want to draw attention from the yard.

"What?" He turned back to where she stood waiting for answers.

"I thought we were having a good time. But you barely touched me all night and when I point out all you're offering are one-word answers, you bolt." As she spoke, her anger crept up. "I guess things aren't all that different after all." She stepped forward to move past him. "Take me home."

Kai didn't let her get far. He grabbed her arms and

spun her until her back was against the side of the house. His nostrils flared with his breath. "I'm trying to change. For you."

She clenched her jaw. He could go ahead and be mad.

He braced one hand against the brick near her head. "I barely touched you tonight because I want you to know that this is about more than sex for me. Not touching you is hard." His other hand landed on her hip. His fingers flexed. "I couldn't offer you more than one-word answers because you were sitting on my lap making my dick hard."

That made Norah smile and her anger eased a little. She tilted her head up and kissed his jaw. "Then why run out?"

"Because I want you."

His words were strangled and his fingers dug into her hip giving her a thrill. She pushed her hips into him. "So take me."

He growled and lowered his mouth to hers. It was fast and hard and hot. Barely restrained. And Norah wanted this with him. They kissed and stroked and breathed together in the gangway between the houses until loud laughter from the yard reminded them of their location. Kai pulled back.

He ran a thumb over her lips, her jaw, and down her throat until his palm rested against her rapid pulse. Her hands were fisted in his T-shirt. They stared at each other in the dark, breathing heavily.

"I really like doing that with you."

He grinned. "Feeling's mutual."

"But sometimes, I need the words, too."

"Understood."

She arched an eyebrow at his answer.

He chuckled and stepped back, taking her hand. As he led them to his car, he said, "I canceled the poker game and sold Tommy the table because it was a way to move on. Carlos and Dean and Eric? They're not like Rooster any more than I am, but I kept them all in the same box. I avoided things like this party because I didn't want to extend any part of my old life into my new one. A poker game at my house was contained. Limited."

Norah listened to everything he said. It made sense, even if a bit extreme. "But you're not cutting out all your friends?"

"No. I invited the guys to come to the hockey game next weekend."

"Really?" She loved the idea that for a change, he'd have people in the stands cheering for him.

"I told you I was going to prove I want you in my life." He opened the door and waited for her to climb in. When he got behind the wheel, he said, "You need a lot of people in your life. You don't belong hiding out in my living room or in my bed."

He started the engine. Norah twisted in her seat. "But you don't."

"Don't what?"

"Need a lot of people."

"I've always had these people in my life. A lot of them when I really sat to think about it. But they never knew each other. Now they will."

One thing Norah realized about Kai was that although he wasn't naturally much of a talker, he definitely knew what to say when he did. "I never considered it hiding out, Kai. I waited in your living room or in your bed because I want to be with you."

He gripped the wheel tightly. "The only way for me to make this work, to make change happen, is to go all the way. If I give myself an out, I might take it. It's how I got out of the gang. Everything has to change at once or it might not happen."

The pieces fell into place for her. He'd changed as much

about his past life as he could. Except Rooster. "The poker game was your out."

He nodded. "When I went to jail, I felt like I lost everything. When I got out, I kept all the parts of my life separate, so if I screwed up in one area, I could still hold on to the rest." He reached over and stroked her cheek. "I want you to be part of all of it."

Between the touch and the words, all she could do was smile.

He pulled out and started driving. She reached out and put a hand on his thigh. "You know, I normally don't put out on the first date, but given the circumstances, I think an exception is in order."

He grabbed her hand, brought it to his mouth, and kissed it. His lips were warm and sent a shiver through her. "What makes you think I put out on a first date?"

His joke caught her so off guard she burst out laughing. Then he joined her. She knew they had possibilities. They'd figure out how to be together and make it work. His words and actions told her that he believed in them. She didn't have to have enough faith for the both of them. Plus, he'd given her one hell of a first date.

Turn the page for a special sneak peek at the next
For Your Love novel,

In Your Arms,

coming in January 2017 . . .

And don't miss Shannyn Schroeder's
O'Learys series, now available!

More Than This
A Good Time
Something to Prove
Catch Your Breath
Just a Taste
Hold Me Close

"Damn it." Emma stared at the plume of steam snaking up through her hood and popped the lever before slamming her car door. She'd been doing so well today. Not one curse word, not even under her breath. Not even after her heart-to-heart with her boss to talk about the importance of making sure kids showed up on the first day of school. Not after waiting for a roomful of parents to show for back-to-school open house only to be greeted with three. Out of twenty-six.

Hard to convince parents their kids shouldn't miss school when the parents aren't interested. They didn't care if funding got cut or if she lost her job.

She'd managed to keep her frustration in check through all of that. But this, her car, might drive her over the edge, especially since Nicky assured her he'd fixed the hose. As she levered the hood up to assess the problem, she prayed she wouldn't have to kill her brother for taking her money and lying to her. She paced and waited for the engine compartment to cool so she could test her theory. The sight didn't make her day any better.

"Goddamn fudge monkey." The halfway-improvised curse did nothing for her. No, this was definitely one of those situations where she shouldn't feel guilty about using all five of her allotted swear words at once. "Fucking lying piece of shit asshole." Then she kicked the bumper but almost lost her balance because of the stupid heels she wore to look professional.

Stomping back to the driver's seat, she reached in for her phone and called Nicky only to get his voice mail. She inhaled deeply and forced a softer tone. "Hey, Nicky. Guess what? I'm sitting on the side of the highway right now with steam *pouring* from my radiator. You know anything about that? 'Cause you should. I paid you to replace the hose. Yet I'm looking at the same damn hole."

So she'd exaggerated the trickle of steam, but she needed Nicky to understand how pissed she was. She should've just taken care of it herself. She knew how to fix it. High school shop class taught her a few things. Her boyfriends had taught her more. But Nicky needed cash and she hated fixing anything on her car, so she'd paid him to do the work. She hadn't considered that he wouldn't do it. Tossing her phone back on the seat, she stood and thought about her options. Calling the auto club would mean waiting at least an hour. They never rushed anywhere. Glancing down at the clothes she wore, her only good suit, she knew if she attempted a temporary fix to get off the expressway, she ran the risk of ruining it.

She took her keys from the ignition and opened the trunk to look for duct tape. Once the engine cooled she could seal the hole and get to a shop. She dug through the junk that had mysteriously accumulated in the trunk. An old blanket, an empty box of animal crackers, and her emergency kit. She unzipped the pouch to find two bandages and antibiotic ointment. No flares, no cables, and of course, no duct tape.

Her first boyfriend, who had taught her to drive, gave her an emergency kit. Her second boyfriend had taught her the value of carrying duct tape. Knowing Nicky, he probably

swiped it one of the many times he'd borrowed her car. The
least he could've done was tape the hole. She slammed
the trunk shut and couldn't resist calling her brother an
asshole one more time. By her count, she was now two
over her allotment for cursing.

As she moved back to grab her phone to call the auto
club, a motorcycle rumbled close to her location and pulled
off the road. Great. Just what she needed: another guy to
add to the mess that was her day.

He cut the engine and swung a leg over the bike to dis-
mount. The tight jeans over black boots and topped with a
stretched white T-shirt weren't lost on her. He took off his
helmet and Emma braced herself for what would surely
follow. He'd come over and hit on her and she'd get more
pissed off. Just as she thought about reaching in her bag for
her pepper spray, he turned around and smiled at her while
running a hand through his short hair.

With the setting sun off to the side, his face was lit with
a glow and amazingly blue eyes stared at her. His smile
wasn't a bit lecherous. Just friendly.

"Hey. Need some help?" He took only one small step
closer. He looked her up and down and waited for a response.

"No. It's a hole in my radiator hose."

One eyebrow lifted. As if she shouldn't be able to diagnose the problem. Men.

"Can I take a look?"

She waved her arms out. "Go ahead." At least while he
was under the hood, she'd have time to get her pepper spray
and her phone.

Sitting on the edge of the driver's seat with her feet tapping, she waited on hold with the auto club. Blue Eyes
came closer to the door and cleared his throat. She glanced
at him.

"You're right. It's the hose. Only a small hole, but it needs to be replaced."

No duh. "Thanks. I'm calling the auto club now for a tow."

"Do you have a shop you want to get it to?"

"Wherever they tow me is where I'll go."

"If you want, I can do a temporary fix and take you to the shop I work at. It's only about a mile off the highway. It'll save you towing fees and you can get out of here now."

She sighed as the easy listening music played in her ear. Climbing from the car, she said, "I already thought of that. My duct tape is missing from my trunk."

He laughed. "Something tells me I should be worried about a chick who carries duct tape in her trunk."

She suddenly realized how bad that sounded and laughed too. Nothing about this day was going right. "I have it for emergencies, not to tie up my captives."

He crossed his arms, causing his shirt to tighten on his biceps and drawing her eye to a tattoo peeking out. He smiled and added, "Maybe I should take your picture to let my friends know who I'm with in case I disappear."

Oh, man. He was cute. She really didn't want him to be cute.

"How do you propose to fix it?" she asked.

He flicked a thumb over his shoulder. "With the duct tape I have in my saddlebag."

"Now who should be worried?" The words slipped without her thinking about the fact that she was flirting. She knew better. She really did.

His smile slipped and his face became serious. "Feel free to keep your distance. I'm just doing what I hope someone would do for my sister if she was stuck on the side of the road. Besides, a body won't fit in a saddlebag."

He turned to his bike and opened the side compartment. Emma waited until he returned with a roll of tape. Leaning on her front fender, she smiled. "Hey, I was kidding. I appreciate this. My brother was supposed to fix this. I thought it was done. I wouldn't have kept driving if I'd known he'd flaked." Which shouldn't have surprised her at all. Nicky always flaked.

"No problem." He unrolled a section of tape and tore it with his teeth.

Emma had no idea why she found that sexy, but she did. No, she knew exactly why. This guy was ticking off all the things she loved but avoided because they were bad for her: a motorcycle-riding, tattooed mechanic with a sense of humor and a killer smile.

After wrapping the hose, he pulled a dark blue bandanna from his pocket and wiped his hands. Then he extended his right hand. Another tattoo on the inside of his forearm. A pair of crossed hockey sticks. "Sean."

She shook his hand, which still bore the grease marks of his work. "Emma."

"Nice to meet you, Emma. Why don't you start it up and we'll make sure this'll hold?"

She went to the open door and bent to turn the key. The engine roared but no steam puffed out.

He closed the hood. "If you want to take it to another place or have your brother fix it, this'll work for a little while. Don't push it though."

"If you give me directions to the place you work, I'll take it there now. It only seems fair that you get the job." She paused, thinking about the time. "Unless you're closed and won't be able to take me."

"The boss is always there late."

"I don't want to put you out. You were already nice enough to stop. You can get on with your weekend." It was late on a Friday night of a holiday weekend. The unofficial end of her summer and she was looking at having work done on her car.

"Not a problem. Follow me."

She nodded and got back behind the wheel. She watched as he put his helmet back on, covering his slightly messy hair. As she put her car in drive and eased back into the lane, she followed Sean and tried to ease her tight muscles. Even after laughing with him, her tension hadn't dissipated.

The heat in her car was stifling and her clothes clung and pinched at her. She knew it was all in her head, her frustration poking her, but she rolled the window down anyway. They pulled off at the next exit and Emma tried to think how she'd get home. Her mom would be working and couldn't afford to leave. Nicky would never answer his phone now that she'd called him on his garbage. He'd probably dodge her for a week hoping she'd cool off.

Looked like she'd be calling a cab.

True to his word, Sean turned into a lot for a garage a few minutes later. He waved his arm to point where she could park. After turning the car off, Emma grabbed her keys and stuffed her phone and charger in her bag and got out. Sean stood at the back of her car waiting. She handed him the keys.

From the door of the garage, a guy in his forties wearing a blue jumpsuit called, "O'Malley? Thought you were done for the weekend."

Sean turned to the man. "I am. Brought you a customer." He turned back to Emma. "That's Dominick. He'll take care of you."

She followed Sean over and listened as he filled Dominick in on the problem. Dominick wiped his hands on his thighs and pointed to the office. "Let's get your paperwork done. I should be able to get this done by tomorrow afternoon."

Finally. Something went her way. She turned to Sean before following Dominick. "Thanks again."

He nodded and turned away.

As she followed Dominick, she considered her options. Mom lived only about a mile away, but the thought of walking in these heels didn't appeal to her. Plus, she'd be stuck at her mom's house all night, which didn't sound any better.

It would take two buses to get to her apartment. In rush hour. The buses would be packed. That left her standing in her heels while surrounded by sweaty bodies. A cab was the way to go, but she hated wasting more money for cab fare.

She authorized Dominick to do the work and walked back out into the warm air. She looked to the street and thought again about walking to her mom's.

"Need a ride?"

Sean's question startled her. She'd figured he'd be long gone by now. "Don't you have something better to do than take care of a woman you don't know?"

He shrugged. "Thought maybe you'd want to get a drink. You look like you could use one."

"That's an understatement." The fear of losing her job weighed on her all day. Without teaching, she'd go back to being like her mom. She wanted more than that. She'd worked too hard to go back to that kind of life. She took a deep breath. "Do you really have a sister or did you just say that to put me at ease?"

"I have a sister. Her name is Norah." He pulled out his phone and scrolled across the screen. He gave her the phone.

A picture of Sean standing next to a girl who could've definitely passed for his sister. They had the same eyes. When she handed the phone back, he added, "I don't lie."

Emma knew better than to believe him. Guys like him lied. But they were also a ton of fun. And right now, she could use some fun. She needed to forget everything about this day.

* * *

Sean waited for Emma to decide. She shifted from one foot to another. Those heels were fucking sexy but didn't go with the rest of the package. The suit said business, but the shoes said party. Not that he was some shoe aficionado. He'd just spent enough time picking up women in clubs to know that they wore shoes like that to draw attention.

Emma definitely grabbed his attention on the side of the road. Her fury had radiated off her as she beat on her car, slamming doors and yelling at no one. In the ride to the garage, she seemed to have lost some steam.

She looked at the phone still in his hand and then at his bike.

If he wasn't mistaken, he caught the telltale glimpse of longing. He knew that look. Someone who really wanted to be on a bike, like maybe she missed it. The look was familiar because he felt it every time he saw his bike in the middle of winter.

"I'm not really dressed for going for drinks."

"I'm not complaining." A chick wearing a suit wasn't his type, but those shoes . . . As a bonus, her short skirt would definitely ride high as she straddled the bike. And him. His blood rushed south with the thought.

"Can we make a quick stop so I can change?"

"You live close?" Not that it mattered. He'd drive her wherever as long as it led to drinks and hanging out.

"No, but my mom does. I can borrow something there. She's only about a mile from here." She edged closer to the bike.

Sean handed her his helmet. She took it without bitching about messing up her hair. Good thing to know about her. She accepted safety and didn't mind messy hair. He easily thought of similar situations.

She tied her hair into a ponytail at her nape and slid the

helmet on. As she adjusted the helmet to fit as best it could, he climbed on and held out a hand to her.

"Have you ridden before?"

She nodded. "It's been a while though."

"I'll take it slow. Where are we going?"

"Take Fullerton east. I'll let you know when to turn." She hiked her skirt up to an almost indecent spot and swung a leg over. "I'll tap you when we're close."

He almost asked if she'd tap when she was close to coming during sex, but thought it might end their date too quickly. He wasn't sure what to make of Emma. The girl wearing the buttoned-up suit didn't match the one who wanted to ride and hiked that skirt like it was nothing. Getting her to relax was going to be interesting.

When he started the engine, she scooted closer and wrapped her arms around his waist. Yeah, that felt good.

The sun dipped low in the sky, but was still strong enough to warm his skin. He was so used to wearing a helmet that he almost forgot how good it felt to ride without. If his brother Jimmy ever found out, Sean would be in for another lecture, but at the moment, he didn't care. What Jimmy didn't know wouldn't hurt anyone.

Sean eased onto the street and followed the directions Emma had given him. The neighborhood was alive for a Friday night. Kids ran across lawns and into the street. Smells of food cooking on grills reminded him that he hadn't eaten dinner. A couple of houses had cars up on blocks in the driveway, for those few houses lucky enough to have a driveway. Some people sat on front steps hoping to catch a cool breeze to break the heat of the day. Cars lined the street and he was glad he drove a motorcycle. Parking would be a bitch around here.

Emma tapped his chest and he pulled over at the corner in front of a fire hydrant. He held out a hand to help her off and couldn't help but look as she tugged her skirt while climbing off. She removed the helmet. Her ponytail loosened and locks flew around her face.

"It's a few houses back."

"I'll wait here." He took the helmet from her and watched as she pulled her bag from across her body.

A little more than ten minutes later, she was on her way back. The sight of her knocked the wind from him. Snug jeans and fitted tank top covered her and a sweatshirt was tied at her waist. She'd traded the heels for a pair of sneakers. Her hair was now completely down and waves flew around in the breeze. For a moment he considered that she'd lied about it being her mom's place because he didn't know any moms who dressed like that. But her bag was overstuffed, he assumed with her clothes.

He pushed off the bike. "That was fast."

She offered a crooked smile. "I really need a drink. The radiator hose was the last in a line of things ruining my day."

"Hop on and you can tell me all about it over a beer. Or wine. Or whatever."

"Tonight's a whiskey night."

Sean liked the sound of that. They mounted the bike and she put the helmet on. Before he started the engine, he asked, "Any place in mind?"

"No. You pick."

Since he normally didn't drink in the area, he drove closer to his neighborhood and parked beside his favorite dive bar. It was dark and relatively quiet. They could shoot pool or play darts or just listen to music. He helped Emma off the bike and locked his helmet down. Then he led her into the bar and directly to a corner table.

"This okay?" he asked before sitting.

She glanced around. "Fine."

She swung her bag over her head and plopped it on the

free chair between them. A waitress came by. "What can I get you?"

"A shot of Jack and lite beer."

"Miller."

"Bottle or tap?"

"Bottle," both he and Emma said. Emma's mouth eased into a small smile.

After the waitress left, Sean asked, "So what makes this a whiskey night other than your brother screwing up your car?"

"Work stuff."

"What do you do?"

Before she could answer, the waitress returned with their drinks. Emma grabbed the shot and slammed it back. When she set the glass back down, he noticed a butterfly tattoo peeking out from the tank top on the back of her shoulder. She looked at him. "I'm a teacher."

He froze. He hadn't expected that. One look at the suit she wore and he'd assumed some kind of office job, secretary or something. She was a teacher. He laughed as she took a gulp of beer.

"What's so funny?"

"I can't imagine any teacher I ever had doing a shot of Jack in a bar like this."

A dark look passed over her face, but then she covered it with a smile. "I guess we all have some surprises."

He reached over and brushed her hair off her shoulder. "I can guarantee I never had a teacher as hot as you. I never would've gotten out of school otherwise."

Emma snorted at him and then took another drink of beer. "You already got me to the bar, buddy, no need for compliments."

Sean's hand slid away. He didn't know how to read that. Women usually liked some sweet talk. "Being honest. If you were my teacher I'd spend all my time imagining you naked."

"Show me a good time and you might not have to imagine it." Her voice was low and a little husky.

"You mean rigging your car to get you to safety, giving you a ride on my bike, and buying you a drink wasn't enough?"

She laughed. That too was a low, sexy sound. "I might be easy, but not that easy."

"I can guarantee a good time once you're naked." She didn't look convinced. "In the meantime, we can shoot some darts in back. Or play pool."

"Okay, let's go." She grabbed her bag and her beer and slid from the chair.

Sean hadn't expected her to want to play, but if that showed her the good time she wanted, he'd play. She bee-lined for the dartboard. As she yanked darts from the cork, he asked, "Is your brother older or younger?"

She paused and glanced over her shoulder. "Older. Why?"

He watched her mark 301 on each side of the board. She'd obviously played before. "Making conversation. Any other siblings?"

"Nope. How about you?" She pointed at the board.

He nodded. "Three brothers and one sister."

"Holy cow. Five kids? Who does that?"

He accepted the darts she handed him. "Irish Catholics. I live in a neighborhood full of 'em."

"Where do you come in?"

"Dead middle. Two older brothers, one younger, and the baby is my sister."

"Uh-oh."

"What?"

"Middle-child syndrome. Always being forgotten, struggling to get a piece of attention." She pointed a finger in his general direction. "Explains the whole rebel thing you have going on."

Rebel? He didn't think of himself as a rebel. He just did what he wanted. "You're off base."

"I bet your oldest brother is super responsible."

She had him there. Jimmy was the most responsible guy he knew. Sean had always attributed it to Jimmy taking care of them after their mom had been killed. "There are extenuating circumstances."

One of her eyebrows arched up. "You and the older brother next in line are middle children. If you're the rebel, my guess is that he's the clown."

Sean froze as he lined up his first shot with a dart. "It's a little eerie that you did that. I'm not much of a rebel, but Kevin has always been the clown."

She bumped him out of the way. "Ladies first." She let a dart sail across the room. Triple-point eighteen. "And the two youngest are coddled by everyone in the family because they're the babies."

She threw her other two darts for a double twenty and a nineteen.

"How did you do that?"

She pointed at the board again. "Good aim."

"No. The things about my siblings." Sean paused and remembered Leena who had picked him up at a bar last summer. It wasn't until after he'd gotten her home that he'd discovered that not only was she one of Jimmy's exes, but she was weird. "Did you ever go out with Jimmy O'Malley?"

"No. Who's Jimmy?"

"My oldest brother." He took his mark and threw the dart. Fifteen. First shot and she was already kicking his ass. He halfheartedly finished his turn.

"As far as I know, I've never met an O'Malley. Pretty sure I'd remember." She took a swig of beer. "As far as understanding birth order, I did a paper on it a few years ago. Fascinating stuff. I bet I could do a whole thesis on the dynamics of a family like yours."

He laughed. "My family isn't that interesting."

She stood to take her turn as he yanked his darts from the cork. "Hey, by your explanation, your brother would be super responsible like mine. He'd never say he'd fix your car and not do it."

She smiled. "Extenuating circumstances."